BOOKS BY STEPHEN BIRMINGHAM

Young Mr. Keefe
Barbara Greer
The Towers of Love
Those Harper Women
Fast Start, Fast Finish
"Our Crowd"
The Right People
Heart Troubles
The Grandees
The Late John Marquand
The Right Places
Real Lace
Certain People
The Golden Dream
Jacqueline Bouvier Kennedy Onassis
Life at the Dakota
California Rich
Duchess
The Grandes Dames
The Auerbach Will
"The Rest of Us"
The LeBaron Secret

The
LeBaron
Secret

LITTLE, BROWN AND COMPANY
BOSTON   TORONTO

STEPHEN
BIRMINGHAM

The LeBaron Secret

A NOVEL

FIRST EDITION

The characters and events portrayed in this book are
fictitious. Any similarities to real persons, living or dead,
are purely coincidental and not intended by the author.
For purposes of the story, some geographical details
have been changed.

Library of Congress Cataloging-in-Publication Data

Birmingham, Stephen.
  The LeBaron secret.

  I. Title.
PS3552.I7555L4   1986   813'.54   85-18208
ISBN 0-316-09649-0

BP

*Published simultaneously in Canada
by Little, Brown & Company (Canada) Limited*

PRINTED IN THE UNITED STATES OF AMERICA

This book is for Melissa

The
LeBaron
Secret

From the will of Peter Powell LeBaron (1905–1955):

Clause 6(a). I hereby direct that all outstanding shares held by me in Baronet Vineyards, Inc., hereinafter referred to as the Company, shall be divided and distributed at the time of my death as follows:

Thirty-five percent (35%) to my beloved wife, Assaria Latham LeBaron;

Five percent (5%) to my beloved daughter, Melissa Margaret LeBaron;

Five percent (5%) each to my two beloved sons, Eric O'Brien LeBaron and Peter Powell LeBaron, Jr.;

Thirty-five percent (35%) to my beloved sister, Joanna LeBaron Kiley, also known professionally as Joanna LeBaron;

The remaining fifteen percent (15%) of said shares in said Company shall be divided, equally, among any and all living issue of my aforesaid sister, Joanna LeBaron.

PART ONE

Morning,
Noon,
and Night

One

THIS WAS THE WAY those who were in the audience that night
remembered it:

The young lead singer, who always performed bare to the waist,
his hairless chest slung with gold chains, suddenly screamed in the
middle of his song, flung his guitar across the stage, and shrieked,
"Pythons can be replaced!" And with that he seized the snake that
had been coiled around his shoulders, grasped the animal by its
tail, and, brandishing it like a charioteer's whip, proceeded to flail
it — thrash it — furiously against the stage floor. Fluid, which was
not blood, spurted from the snake's mouth. This, the audience
realized, must be the animal's brains, or something even more
horrible from its insides. Then, still clutching his bleeding arm, the
singer, who called himself Luscious Lucius, stamped down hard,
again and again, on the snake's head with the sequined high heel
of his cowboy boot until the creature lay limp and lifeless at his
feet.

At first, there had been a burst of giggles — nervous and uncertain ones — and an excited squeal or two, as the audience asked
themselves if this was a part of the act, if that was real blood flowing
down Luscious Lucius's bare arm. Or catsup. The scream, the
smashing of the guitar onstage — those had been part of The Who's
act, hadn't they? But then, with a collective gasp that was more
like a moan of disbelief, the audience of nearly two thousand,
mostly teenagers, realized that the bloodshed they were seeing on
the stage was very real indeed. For just as Lucius was building up
the sound and tempo of his last song, prancing about the stage
and humping his guitar, the python, with which he always performed his famous finale, had suddenly drawn its head back and
then struck, plunging its fangs hard into his biceps. The music had
stopped, there had been the scream, the guitar had been hurled,
and, for a beat, the singer, looking skinny and frightened and alone,
stared dazedly at his bleeding arm. There were screams from the
audience. They had all come for cheap thrills, for something vis-
cerally salacious (there were rumors that Luscious Lucius sometimes exposed himself on stage), and for phony, raunchy horror.
But they had not come for this brand of realism, and the shrieks
now were like those from a roller coaster when a car has become
derailed. Half the audience were on their feet by the time Luscious
Lucius began unwinding the snake from around his body, where
he had draped it, and beating the creature to death before their
eyes. There was pandemonium in the auditorium as a crush of
young people filled the aisles and pushed toward the exit doors.

"Look," the singer shouted into his microphone over the noise,
one hand cupping his bleeding arm, "stay loose! It's cool. Shit,
man, I'm okay! The show's not over. Pythons get old. Like they
get mean, man. Like she'll be replaced. Don't go yet . . ." And to
try to hold his audience, he tossed a handful of glitter into the air.

But no one was listening, and, in the middle of the singer's plea
from the scene of the carnage, the stage manager, realizing that
the evening was beyond rescue — the glitter was the curtain cue,
anyway — had the good sense to ring down the curtain fast and
bring up the houselights.

The *Peninsula Gazette* reported the incident the following morning:

PYTHON BITE DISRUPTS ROCK CONCERT;
SINGER BEATS SNAKE TO DEATH ONSTAGE BEFORE 1800

A seven-foot-long Indian rock python, a feature of the act of the punk rock group that calls itself The Dildos, suddenly turned vicious last night in the middle of a performance at the newly restored Odeon Theatre downtown and bit the group's lead singer, Maurice Littlefield, 23. Littlefield then proceeded to beat the giant serpent to death onstage while a capacity crowd of 1800 screaming fans looked on in horror. Littlefield, who bills himself as Luscious Lucius, was bleeding copiously from the left arm.

The python, called Sylvia by the group, had performed with the group for about three years without incident, and was considered tame and harmless. Littlefield was taken to Mercy Hospital and treated for snakebite and lacerations. He was released about one hour later, and doctors said his wound from the bite is not considered serious. The rock python is not a poisonous reptile.

The audience, meanwhile, reacted to the onstage episode with revulsion. Most were young people, and the reaction of Tracie Hodgman, 17, of 345 Morris St., Menlo Park, was typical. "It was gross enough that the snake bit him," she said. "There was like blood everywhere. But then when he started to beat it to death it was like *really* gross. I threw up after. I used to think The Dildos were a really neat group, and I was a real fan of Lucius. But now I'm not so sure."

While the curtain descended on the performance, the audience rushed to the exits, where a few scuffles ensued, but no serious injuries were reported.

The Odeon Theatre, beneficiary of a $3 million restoration last year as part of a long-term plan to renovate the Market Street area, had drawn a capacity crowd for last night's Dildos performance. Other cultural events are scheduled throughout the coming year.

Gabe Pollack parks his old Dodge Omni in front of the big White Wedding-Cake House at 2040 Washington Street and, as San Franciscans do automatically, turns his right front wheel hard into the curbstone before setting the brake and turning off the ignition, even though Assaria LeBaron's house is not set on a particularly steep section of Pacific Heights. It is an automatic reaction. Bite your right front wheel hard into the curb when parking. Prevent runaway vehicles. That duty performed, Gabe Pollack, a little stiffly — his back has been giving him some trouble lately — lets himself out of the car and starts up the short drive to the porte cochere of the White Wedding-Cake House.

It is the rainy weather that is doing it, causing the back to act up. It is not his eighty-one years, he tells himself. It is another damp, chilly February morning in the city, and yesterday's rain has turned into foggy drizzle, and the city — even the White Wedding-Cake House — has a gray, swirly-smoky look. It is what the English call a silver day, though the moisture has given a crisp, shiny look to the green leaves of the lemon-tree hedge that lines Assaria LeBaron's entrance drive. Gabe Pollack's breath comes out in little silver puffs, and just before stepping under the porte cochere Gabe Pollack looks up to the second-floor windows of Assaria LeBaron's sitting room to see whether, perhaps, his arrival is being watched. And sees — or thinks he has seen — the white panel of a glass curtain fall into place, as though someone's small hand has just let it drop. But he cannot be sure he has seen this. He moves, now, under the porte cochere, up the three white marble steps to the front door, and rings the bell.

There is a little wait, and then the door is opened by Thomas, Mrs. LeBaron's majordomo, in his gray morning coat.

"Good morning, Mr. Pollack."

"Good morning, Thomas."

Inside, Thomas assists Gabe out of his raincoat. "Rather chilly this morning, sir."

"San Francisco weather," Gabe says. "Sun was actually shining when I left Palo Alto. Rain started at Daly City."

Thomas says something that sounds like "Chuck-chuck," and bows Gabe toward the waiting elevator.

Stepping inside, Gabe says, "Chilly morning, and I suppose I am to expect a chilly reception from your mistress."

"I couldn't say, sir," Thomas murmurs. He closes the elevator door. With Thomas's gray-gloved hand at the controls, the elevator, an ancient Otis hydraulic, begins its slow ascent to the floor above. Its wrought-iron cage is a wild tracery of latticework, slung with wheat-sheaves and vines, grape leaves and poppy blossoms, and it performs its assigned tasks so slowly that, as Sari herself has said, two people could consummate a love affair in the time it takes for this apparatus to make its journey from one floor to the next; there would certainly be time enough for them to become very good friends. It irritates Gabe, slightly, that Thomas makes him take the elevator whenever he comes to visit Sari. He could easily handle the stairs. All reminders that he is getting old irritate Gabe Pollack. Such as the young boy — Boy Scout? — who offered to take his elbow the other day to help him across Post Street. The other day. It was a good five years ago. I don't look old, he tells himself. In my shaving mirror I still see a young and, yes, randy fellow in his, maybe, twenties, thirties? Forties, maybe. To make conversation during their upward trek, Gabe says, "I suppose it's about the story in today's paper."

"I wouldn't know, sir."

"Well, I'm in the newspaper business, and my job is to print the news."

"Oh, I'm sure of that, sir."

"Sometimes your mistress doesn't quite understand that."

"I wouldn't know about that, sir."

"I'm sure she's got a bee in her bonnet."

"I just couldn't say, sir."

At last the elevator reaches the second floor, and Thomas opens the door and steps aside. "You're a few minutes early, sir," he says. "Madam isn't quite ready. She asks that you wait for her in the south sitting room."

Gabe Pollack says nothing. He does not mention that his message from Thomas's mistress has been "Come and see me as soon as possible," and he does not ask Thomas how, when one has been asked to come as soon as possible, it can be possible to be a few minutes early. And the south sitting room is a bad sign, a sign of ill omen. It means that he is in for a session with Sari, not a visit. The south sitting room is a room Sari uses to conduct business, the closest thing to an office-away-from-the-office in her White Wedding-Cake House. The south sitting room, as its designation implies, faces south, faces the street, and has no view to provide any sort of distraction. The large, formal drawing room, with its fine French furniture, faces north, offering a view of the Golden Gate, the Bay, and everything else beyond. In the formal drawing room, he would be served coffee and one of Cookie's splendid sweet rolls. In the south sitting room, there will be none of that. Rebelliously, for a moment, Gabe thinks that he will make his way into the drawing room anyway, ignoring Thomas's instructions, but on second thought he decides he had better not. No point in irritating the old girl any more than he has already. If the south sitting room it is to be, so be it, and he crosses the hall into the designated room and takes a seat in the most comfortable chair the room provides, a stiff-backed Victorian affair by Belter deco-rated, like the elevator, with a great deal of carved scrollwork and fruited vines. This chair faces the long library table that Sari uses as a sort of desk, and in this position Gabe feels exactly like an errant schoolboy who has been summoned before the principal.

Now the house is strangely silent, no sound of footfalls any-where, only the sound of the ticking of the gold and black-marble ormolu clock on the mantel. *Ping, ping* goes the clock on the mantel, above the fireplace with its fan-shaped ornamental screen of heavy, polished brass, a fireplace that Gabe Pollack has never known to contain a lighted fire. Outside, dimly, on the street, the day continues drizzly, with blowing fog. Across the street, in their sentry boxes, the two policemen who guard the Russian Consulate have put on waterproof slickers. The guards stamp their wet boots. Sari LeBaron likes to say that she is pro-Communist. The Soviets provide her house with free security.

Except for the ticking of the clock, the house is silent. The White Wedding-Cake House. It has always been called that, locally, since the beginning, and it is appropriate because the house was indeed a wedding present to Assaria LeBaron and her late husband, Peter Powell LeBaron. Architecturally, too, it resembles a wedding cake, all white marble, rising tier upon tier — three tiers in all before the crowning balustrade — Palladian in concept, if not in pure design, its facade embossed with carved stone garlands, swags, and fur-belows, to make its ultimate romantic statement. No guilty con-science here, the house has always seemed to say. Nothing to be ashamed of here, despite the ugly rumors. We belong to a joyous house, the carved wreaths seem to say, the wreaths that form arched eyebrows over the windows facing Washington Street, the eyes of Capitalism gazing serenely down at the Soviets across the way. "I was born in Russia, you know," Sari LeBaron enjoys telling her friends. "But I got out just in time, with wolves snapping at the wheels of my troika!" Sari likes to embellish tales.

The house has also been called unpleasant names. "Sixty rooms!" crowed the morning *Chronicle* when the house was completed in 1927. "Ninety rooms!" corrected the afternoon *Examiner*, the same day. Of course, both papers were lying like hell, or were just having fun indulging in hyperbole, unless they were counting all the clos-ets and the basement storage caves. There are no more than twenty principal rooms in this house, plus servants' rooms, of course, and in its heyday this house took a full-time staff of eleven to maintain it — a butler and a footman, Peter LeBaron's valet and Sari's per-sonal maid, a cook and a scullery maid, two housemaids, a sewing woman and a laundress, and a chauffeur-handyman. Now Sari makes do with three, plus a couple of dailies, and the laundry is sent out. Still, it is an imposing house, and there is no question but that Papa LeBaron spent a pretty penny having it built — a prettier penny, in fact, than he could quite afford. By 1931, there were liens against it, liens that had to be paid off. Where did so many liens come from? Out of the walls, like mice, the liens came, and bred and multiplied.

If these walls could talk, Gabe thinks, what secrets they could tell. "Is love important?" she had asked him here. "I mean, is it important to be *in love?*" And, "I want to go to China. I want to see the Orient. I want to walk the Great Wall, visit the Forbidden City, see the palace of the Great Mogul. Peter loved San Francisco so, he never wanted to go abroad. At best it was New York . . . or Bitterroot. Do you know I've never been to Los Angeles? 'There's nothing to California south of Tehachapi,' Peter used to say. But now I want to go to China. Take me to China, Gabe."

But today the talk would not be of love, or of distant Far Eastern voyages. Today would be all business in this room, and there would be no coffee, and none of Cookie's famous sweet rolls — coffee served with chunky crystals of brown Demerara sugar, sweet rolls filled with apple, cherry, blueberry, and peach preserves, and dusted with cinnamon. Gabe has not yet had breakfast, and his stomach is grumbling. There have been a series of Cookies, all with their own names, of course, but all called Cookie, since Sari LeBaron sees no reason to learn the names of employees with whom she has no direct contact. She and Thomas plan the menus, and these in turn are presented to whichever Cookie happens to be in the kitchen that year. If a woman can cook, and doesn't mind being known as Cookie, she can work for Sari LeBaron. There is only one qualification demanded of a Cookie. "Can she do a galantine?" Sari will ask. If the answer is yes, she will get the job, though in Gabe Pollack's memory not one of Sari's Cookies has ever been asked to prepare anything remotely resembling a galantine.

The clock ticks away, and still Gabe Pollack waits. Having been asked to come at once, he has jumped in his car and driven to the city, breaking the speed limit on the freeway, and now he has managed to arrive a little early. It is often this way, when she feels she must give him a dressing-down. She makes him wait. It is as though she is gathering her strength for the dressing-down, and there is no doubt in Gabe's mind but that today she is going to give him the sharp side of her tongue. Don't forget, he could tell her, that I can remember when you weren't so effing rich and powerful, when in fact it was I who told you what to do. Well? she would say to him. What good does remembering that do you? Looking straight at him with those extraordinary black eyes, she would say to him: Does your ability to remember when I was not so effing rich and powerful provide you with any special weaponry? If so, I'd like to have you effing demonstrate that now. Show me, Gabe, what all your effing memories will do. Make memories turn back that clock. Make memories remove the Bay Bridge and bring the ferries back. Make memories blow out a single candle on your eighty-first birthday cake.

Do you know, he replies, getting nastier, that some of the things that are said about this house are not all that pleasant? Have you heard it referred to as the Doge's Palace? Worse yet, have you heard it called the Dago's Palace? I have. Do you know that you — and your husband — are not universally loved in this city?

I am beloved, she answers him, *because I am rich.*

Gabe shifts in the Belter chair, crosses his legs, and with one hand reaches around and rubs at the achy spot in his back. And now there is a new sound. It is the whirring sound of Assaria LeBaron's motorized wheelchair as it makes its way down the long gallery, across the carpet, toward the south sitting room.

"Is that you, Gabriel?" he hears her call. And that is another ominous sign, when she calls him by his full name. Batten down the hatches, he thinks. All the storm warnings are up from Point Reyes Station to Point Lobos.

"I'm here."

And she swings herself through the door and into the room. "You were talking to yourself!" she says.

Rising, he says, "I wasn't."

"Of course you were. I heard you. But don't worry, we all do it. Sit down, Gabe," and she extends her hand to him, to be kissed.

Taking the hand, he thinks: I will now kiss the Pope's ring. "How are you, Sari?" he says, and kisses Her Holiness's hand.

"Very well," she says brightly. "And you? I was so pleased when Thomas told me you were here. Now tell me, Gabe. What can I do for you?"

He hesitates. She may, or she may not, be playing games with him. One can never be entirely sure with Sari. Studying her, looking for a clear clue, he is struck, as always, with her smallness, her daintiness. It is hard to believe that so much strength and energy can have been encapsulated in such a single, small woman. The hands are tiny and delicate. The figure — and the wheelchair emphasizes this, of course — seems so fragile as to be almost frail. It has been said that, as we get older, we acquire the looks we deserve, and if that is the case, Assaria LeBaron must be among the most deserving of women. Though her hair is white now, and though her former Titian-haired beauty is apparent more as a shadow seen through layers of gauze, there is still that smooth, almost olive-colored skin, and those extraordinary dark eyes that can either be fierce or playful, depending on her mood, and that look quite merry now. "What can I do for you?" she repeats.

"I had a message waiting on my desk this morning that you wanted to see me."

"Oh," she says. "Well, I guess I did suggest that it would be nice if you stopped by."

"There was nothing — important — on your mind?"

"Oh, I guess it seemed important at the time. It doesn't seem all that important now. What it was is all water over the dam."

"Was it that story — about the snake?"

"Well, yes, actually. I was a little upset by that. But then I realized, after all, you run a newspaper, and your job is to print the news."

"Yes!" He tries not to say it too defensively.

"And I sometimes tend to forget that, don't I?"

"Yes." It is all an echo, of course, of his conversation with Thomas in the elevator. What Gabe Pollack himself sometimes tends to forget is how close in collusion Sari LeBaron and her manservant are. He is more than her legs and an extra pair of hands. Thomas is by now, after all these years, an adjunct to her personality, answering for any shortcomings that may have developed in any of her senses — an extra pair of eyes, of ears, even an extra nose and set of taste buds. "I'm afraid Cookie has over-sweetened your sorbet, Madam. Shall I speak to her about it?" "Yes, do." Together, these two comprise a kind of fully functioning super-being, an unbeatable combination.

Sari pushes the button that activates her motorized chair, and wheels herself deftly behind the long library table that serves as her desk — moving herself with the same ease with which she famously navigates the crowded aisles of Saks and Magnin's. She fixes her eyes on him, and there is a bit of a crackle in them. "You look tired, Gabe," she says. "You work so hard. You must be looking forward to retiring."

Here it comes, he thinks, and says carefully, "No, as a matter of fact, I'm not."

"You must be. And I'm sure you have your successor all picked out."

"No, I don't have that done, either." And then, "Sari, I wonder if Josie could bring us some coffee?"

She waves her hand impatiently. "Josie's busy. I've had my breakfast, and I'd rather talk. I suppose it is to be that young one with the shoes."

"Who?"

"Your successor."

Shoes, he thinks. He knows the man she is talking about, and tries to think if there is anything remarkable, unusual, about Archie McPherson's shoes. "You mean Archie?" he says.

"Yes."

"Well, I suppose he's a possibility, but I really haven't given that much thought to it."

"I'm wondering. Will I have any say in the matter?"

"What matter?"

"The matter of who succeeds you at the newspaper. Well, I suppose that doesn't matter. You don't tell me how to run my business, and I don't tell you how to run yours."

Oh, no, he thinks. Hardly at all.

"It's just that I very much hope that you don't choose him. He seems to me to be quite unworthy of you, Gabe. He's the one who wrote that story about me flying my plane. The *Chronicle* and the *Examiner* were tasteful enough to bury that as a small item in the back pages. In *your* paper, he made it front-page news. And he's the one who wrote this snake story — am I correct? Also on the front page."

"Yes, that's true."

She sighs. "I was sure of it. I've learned to recognize his — style, if one can call it that. The kind of yellow journalism — sensationalism — that our late friend Mr. Hearst was so fond of. It seems — beneath you, Gabe."

"As you said, my job is —"

Her expression is sad, now, pained and weary. "It's just that I've tried," she says in a faraway voice, "I've tried so hard — Lord knows I've tried — to make my Odeon Theatre a place this city could be proud of, a proud showcase for the performing arts on the highest level. My dream, my little dream — my Odeon — was to make it one of the city's shining crown jewels. Three million dollars — oh, it isn't the money, Gabe. The money meant nothing to me, as I'm sure you know. But I can't help thinking — three million dollars later, and what do we have? A snake act. What will it be next, I wonder. A dog-and-pony act? How about midgets? My beautiful dream. Everyone in San Francisco must be laughing at me this morning! Do you know that the head of the California SPCA was on the phone to me this morning at eight — accusing me of killing innocent animals? *Me!* 'Don't you have any *say* about what goes on in your theatre?' he asked me. I said —"

"Now, wait just a —"

"And all because of your reporter's story! Don't *you* have any say about what goes into your paper, Gabe?"

"Now just let me —"

She waves her hand. "The *Dildos!*" she says. "Do you know what a dildo is? I do, because I looked it up!"

"It can also mean a refrain syllable in music," he says. "Or a West Indian cactus plant." Thank goodness he had looked up the word this morning, too.

"Nonsense! Don't give me that. It's an artificial pee-pee, and you know it!"

"Now, Sari. Just simmer down for a minute, and —"

"What I want to know is who *chooses* these acts at the Odeon. I don't — though the SPCA man seems to think I do. As you very well know, Gabe, I deliberately — *deliberately* — declined a position on the Odeon's board of directors, because I felt I'd done enough already, and I didn't want to have any sort of veto power. But you — *you*, Gabriel J. Pollack, *you* are on that board! You must have *some* sort of say about the caliber of acts that get booked in there! That's what I'd like to hear from *you*. How did this whole thing come about in the first place? And then, on top of *that*, how did you let that nasty little reporter put that story on the front page of your very own paper? Just to make me look ridiculous? Was that it?"

"Of course not, Sari. Frankly, it was to sell newspapers. Our early edition sold out at the stands in half an hour."

"Is that all you care about — *money?* What's happened to your *standards*, Gabe? You used to have them!"

"I run a business, a business with stockholders, just the way you do, Sari."

"And what about that last line?" she demands, her voice rising. " '*Other* cultural events are scheduled throughout the coming year.' *Cultural* events. If that wasn't snide — if that wasn't sarcastic — if that wasn't someone trying to take a sly poke at me — then I — then I don't know my ass from a hole in the wall, if you'll pardon my French!"

He is silent for a moment. Then he says, "I believe the correct French is 'not knowing your ass from a hole in the *ground.*' You never were attractive when you were angry, Sari."

"Oh, dear." She closes her eyes now, makes two tiny balls of her fists, and bows her head in an attitude of sudden contrition. "Oh, dear. I'm sorry. It's just that I try — I try so hard. I know I make mistakes, but I try not to. It was that SPCA man calling, out of the blue, reading me the story — I hadn't even seen the paper — that did it. Don't forget I'm on *their* board, Gabe. And my first thought was, how will this look? And I thought — sometimes I think here am I, an old woman alone — handicapped — trying to run a business in a man's world, all alone. So many responsibilities. So many demands. Trying to do — too much. Sometimes it all just seems — too much for one — one lonely old woman." Gabe watches as, incredibly, two identical tears squeeze out from her closed eyelids and course down her cheeks. It is a performance worthy of a Bernhardt, and he almost laughs, but to do that would be unwise. "All, all alone," she repeats, and he watches as she extracts the lacy white handkerchief she keeps tucked in the wristband of her dress, places it against her face, and blows her nose noisily. "Forgive me, Gabe. I didn't mean to quarrel with you."

"Now, now," he says. "We're not going to start feeling sorry for ourself, are we?"

"Dear Gabe." She opens her tear-filled eyes and looks at him. "How long have you and I known each other? Fifty years?"

"Longer," he says. "Longer than that."

"Sometimes I think — sometimes I think you're my only friend. Sometimes I think you're the only person I can trust. Not my family, not even my children. At the office it's — Eric. I can feel Eric trying to usurp me. But you — you I've always felt I could trust. And that's why, when I feel that trust betrayed — it hurts me so." She wrings the handkerchief between her clenched fists.

He covers both her hands with one of his. "You can trust me, Sari," he says.

"We've been through a lot together, haven't we?" she says. "It hasn't all been a bed of roses. But — we're still here."

"Still here."

"Do you still love me a little bit? Are you still my Polly? Are you still my darling little Pollywog?"

He chuckles. "Still your darling, aging little Pollywog."

"Good." She sniffles some more and dabs at her cheeks and nose again. The worst of the storm, it seems, is over. But there may be more to come. She has tried invective, then tears, but there is still no indication that their session is over. Ah, Sari LeBaron, Gabe Pollack thinks, your aging Pollywog knows you much too well. This moment may just be the calm eye in the center of the hurricane. "Now," she says, seeming to regain her composure, "just tell me how this — snake act — got booked into my beautiful new Odeon."

"The answer isn't going to make you happy, Sari."

"How can I be any more upset than I am already?"

"It was your daughter's idea."

"Melissa's? You're not serious!"

"I'm afraid I am. She made a very convincing presentation to the board. She felt that the Odeon should, from time to time, offer something for young people. That it shouldn't all be symphony or opera or ballet, or Shakespeare. She felt that an occasional concert should be scheduled that would draw young people to the theatre. Last night's group was her choice."

"*Melissa!*"

"And, as it turned out, she was quite right. Last night was a sellout."

"And a bloody scandal!"

"It wasn't Melissa's fault that the snake decided to — misbehave. The act went very well — without any incidents — in, I think, Omaha."

"*Omaha*. This is supposed to be sophisticated San Francisco. Not some prairie cowpatch. Melissa! I might have known Melissa was to blame. Sometimes I think that wretched child is to blame for everything."

Gabe Pollack refrains from pointing out that the wretched child is now — what? — fifty-seven years old. Instead, he says, "In terms of box office, it was a very shrewd suggestion."

"You see what I mean about not even being able to trust my own children? Of course, she said nothing to me about it!"

"*Should* she have, Sari? As you point out, you've deliberately distanced yourself from the theatre's board."

"Did it to spite me, probably — the way everybody does. To embarrass me. Typical. Well, I'll deal with her."

He spreads his hands. "She's your daughter, not mine," he says.

" '*Other* cultural events,' " she snaps.

"I admit that last sentence was — unfortunate. I should have caught that when the copy came across my desk."

"You can say that again!"

"Tell you what I'll do for you," he says, leaning forward. "I'll run a nice follow-up story on the Odeon. Listing all the *really* cultural events coming up on this year's calendar. The Baltimore Symphony, the San Diego Ballet, the Houston Orchestra, Pavarotti. Today's story didn't mention you by name. But I'll see that the follow-up does — gives you full credit for what you've done with the Odeon, and what you're still doing in the south-of-Market area. Would that make you happier?"

She considers this. "Well, perhaps," she says at last, a little sulkily. "Perhaps. A little."

"Making it quite clear that last night's program was hardly typical."

"A freak occurrence. Conceived by a freak."

"Well, I wouldn't put it quite that way."

They sit in silence now, but Gabe Pollack knows that their meeting is not over. He knows it, and she knows it. When it is over, she will give the signal. It is always that way, and Gabe knows her so well, has known her for so long that he knows the almost Byzantine way her mind works, the little games she plays with people, pitting one set of circumstances against another to get, in the end, the result she wants. However oblique and illogical her approach may seem, there is always method in her madness, which is why, in her business dealings, she is considered such a difficult woman to bargain with. It has been said that Assaria LeBaron thinks like a man, but Gabe Pollack disagrees. Men approach problems, for the most part, directly, through the front door. But Assaria LeBaron creeps up on them stealthily, through a back entrance, and then through a maze of alleys and secret passageways. This has been the secret of her extraordinary success in, as she puts it, a man's world — that, and her quite theatrical sense of timing. The American stage, Gabe sometimes thinks, lost a great actress when Sari LeBaron became a businesswoman. Men think in terms of objects, things. Sari LeBaron, like women since the beginning of time, thinks in terms of techniques.

She sits in front of him, frowning slightly, spreading the fingers of her small hands, studying the perfectly lacquered nails and the huge square-cut diamond solitaire on her ring finger. Finally she says, ''Fire that damned reporter! That what's-his-name. With the shoes.''

''Archie McPherson? Well, now, Archie's a good —''

''He seems to be conducting a personal vendetta against the whole LeBaron family. And he's doing it on your payroll — a circumstance that is not without a certain irony, if you see what I mean.''

He studies her face for a moment or two, then smiles and says, ''I can read you like a book, Sari. The reason why you want me to get rid of Archie has nothing to do with the stories he writes, does it?''

She flashes him a dark look. ''What are you talking about?''

''It's because Archie and Melissa have been seeing a bit of each other. Isn't that it?''

''Oh,'' she says. ''So you know about that.''

"I know they've had dinner a couple of times, yes."

"But what does he *want* with her, Gabe? Besides her money, of course — they all want that. But what's he sniffing around her for?"

"Sniffing around? I imagine he simply finds Melissa a fascinating woman. Lots of people do." But this is dangerous territory because Sari has been known to display signs of being jealous of her daughter and the certain special attentions Melissa receives, so Gabe decides not to pursue this line of reasoning.

"What does he see in her? She's years older than he is."

"Archie is thirty-nine, forty."

"Of course, it's easy to see what she sees in him. She's always liked younger men. Are they having an affair, do you think?"

"I don't know. I doubt it." Gabe decides not to tell Sari that Archie's interest in Melissa could not be sexual — could not possibly be, unless — but never mind, he thinks, and decides to tell her what he believes is the truth. "I think Archie's interest in Melissa is purely as a journalist. I think he'd like to do a story on the LeBaron family."

Sari claps one hand to her breast, and her look is one of horror. "But you wouldn't *allow* him to do that, would you — with some of the things you know?"

"No, I assure you I would not."

"Thank God. There's some loyalty left in the world, at least."

"No, rest assured I wouldn't. Not while he's working for me, anyway. So perhaps it's in our best interest that I do my best to keep him on the payroll."

"Has he mentioned this to you — a story about us?"

"In passing, yes."

"You see? That's exactly what I'm afraid of. And with him seeing Melissa — Melissa is so terribly unreliable. She can't be trusted, never could be. Melissa is the loose cannon in this family, Gabe."

"I know."

"And if she's drinking — who knows what she might try to tell him."

"I understand."

"You see," she says, "I'm quite sure that there's something very

funny going on. I've told you that I've been having trouble with
Eric at the office — little things, things I don't need to go into here.
But trouble. And I'm beginning to suspect that there may be a
connection between this, and Melissa seeing this Archie person,
and these — these unfavorable stories that have been appearing. I
think there is a connection."

"Some sort of conspiracy, Sari? Aren't you being a little para-
noid?"

"I'm not so sure, Gabe. I'm not at all sure. There's something
fishy going on. I may be a lot of things, but one thing I'm not is
stupid. And I have good hunches. I've been able to build this
business into what it is by playing my hunches. I have *damned*
good hunches, and I have a hunch right now that something very
funny is going on, and that it involves Eric, Melissa — the loose
cannon — and your Mr. What's-his-name. He's good-looking, isn't
he?"

"Yes, I guess you'd say so."

"But common-looking."

"Common?" He laughs. "I keep forgetting that you've joined
the aristocracy, Sari. Have you met the man?"

"No, thank goodness. But Thomas has seen him — seen him
coming to call on our Miss Cannon. Thomas says he's very
common-looking. Thomas has very good hunches, too."

"Well, Archie's a good reporter. Came to me from the *Seattle
Tribune*. I'm lucky to have him."

She throws him a sly look. "Your new little pet, Polly?"

"I'm a businessman. Businessmen don't have pets."

"With his shoes."

"What's all this about his shoes?"

"Thomas tells me he wears yellow shoes. Yellow — like the
brand of journalism he practices!"

"Well, tell you what. I'll tell him to stop sniffing around Melissa.
I'll call him off the scent."

"I still wish he were thousands of miles away from San Francisco. You see, I'm concerned, Gabe. *Deeply* concerned."

"Of course," he says easily, "if you'd buy out the *Gazette* — as

I've often suggested you do — you could fire whomever you pleased."

"I don't want to buy your silly old *Gazette,*" she says. "I own enough of this town already."

This is true. Mrs. Assaria LeBaron, widow of Peter, has fallen heir to more than she needs, more than she really wants, more than she could possibly give away if she restored a hundred Odeon Theatres to their resplendent, turn-of-the-century, gilt and red-plush glory. The carved cupids embracing above the proscenium, the great chandelier, the gold curtain, every detail. She owns too much, and it's a cliché, but it is an embarrassment of riches. One seventy-four-year-old woman should not own so much. The houses, the downtown office buildings — "Lease, don't sell," Papa Le-Baron, her father-in-law, used to say — the apartment houses in neighborhoods that even she would be afraid to visit, the baseball team that keeps losing games but offers handsome tax write-offs in lieu of victories, the two shopping malls in San Mateo County, and a large percentage — thirty-five percent, to be exact — of the shares of Baronet Vineyards, Inc., one of the last family-owned wine companies in California, and producers of America's largest-selling, popular-priced table wines, under the Baronet label. In the big White Wedding-Cake House at 2040 Washington Street — in a place of honor under Grandpa's portrait at the west end of the long central gallery that runs the length of the second floor — sits, on a crude wooden platform made of a pair of stubby-legged up-turned sawhorses, the very first barrel of wine (or so it is said — who knows the truth of these things?) ever to roll out of Grandpa's little backyard winery — wine distilled from muscat grapes grown in Grandpa's backyard vineyard in Sonoma. It is said that Grandpa brought the seeds for his vines with him from Italy. Grandpa, they say, started out selling wine to his neighbors, but he kept the first barrel for himself. It is a big and blackened and ugly old thing, coopered — again, so they say — by Grandpa himself, and at first glance an old wine barrel does not seem an appropriate decorative touch in the portrait gallery of a large and otherwise formal house. But it has always been prominently displayed in one LeBaron

house or another. And still legible are the words, etched into the
oaken staves with a wood-burning tool:

> Back of this Wine is the Vintner
> And back thrugh the Years his Skil
> And back of it all are the Vines in the Sun
> And the Rain
> And the Masters Will
>
> *M. Barone*
> *Au. 1857*

M. Barone was Grandpa, Mario Barone. It was Papa, Julius
(born Giulio), who changed the names, fancified and Frenchified
things. It was Julius who prepared the elaborate family tree prov-
ing, or so he claimed, that even though, by the nineteenth century,
the Barones were poor Ligurian peasants, the family had originally
come from France, where the name had indeed been LeBaron,
and where Julius had unearthed fifteenth- and sixteenth-century
ancestors who were contes and contesses, ducs and duchesses, even
a roi and a reine or two. The preposterousness of all this amuses
Sari, and it also amuses her to show the old wine cask to visitors,
pointing out the misspelled words that betray an unlettered immigrant. Of course, Sari never knew Grandpa, who died before
she was born, but she has a special fondness for the old cask, and
so here it sits, a brooding presence, weighing nearly three hundred
pounds, thirty-one and a half gallons of Lord knows what after all
these years, for its bung has never been removed.

Only one thing is certain: It is filled with something, for wine
casks, like hearts, must be kept filled to stay alive and, once emp-
tied, they quickly shrink and crack. Oh, there have been times —
at long-ago wildish parties and the like — when someone has
boisterously suggested that the old wooden bung be pulled and
Grandpa's wine be sampled, but this has never been permitted,
thank goodness. If it had, what came out might be enough to poison
them all, Sari sometimes thinks. Sari has also been warned that
the cask might someday explode. Well, if it did, that would be
poetic justice, wouldn't it? For everything to end in an explosion
of putrefied muscatel gone green with age? But Sari doubts that

this would ever happen. Sari knows a great deal about wine and the ancient, almost lost art of cooperage (Baronet wines are now aged in glass-lined metal tanks). That particular, gentle arch of a hardwood barrel stave, and the way it is bound with its fellows in hoops to form a perfect, solid cylinder, the concave ends of the staves then fitted together tightly — this was how the craftsman could guarantee that his sturdy cask would withstand the most furious internal pressures for all eternity. Get Sari LeBaron started on the history of wine making and she can go on for hours. For instance: In the ruins of Pompeii, buried for centuries under layers of lava, Vesuvian cinders, and volcanic ash, were found intact wine casks. Intact, after nearly two thousand years.

The wine cask as a decorative feature of Sari LeBaron's house is often noted by writers who come to interview her about her civic pursuits: a wine cask in the portrait gallery. How quaint! "A reminder of the family's humble beginnings," they write. And "Clearly the LeBarons have a sense of humor." Rubbish! Julius LeBaron had no sense of humor whatsoever. "Baronet — An Honest Wine for the Working Man" — this is one of the advertising slogans still used. And, on the sides of the big red tank trucks with their scrolly white lettering, hauling their loads to the bottling plant, a newer one: "Baronet — Simply Put: Simply Priced and Simply Delicious," which was thought up by Sari herself, thank you very much, even though her son Eric sometimes tries to hog the credit for it. But it is true that from this humble old barrel sprang everything — the summer place at Tahoe, the winter place at Santa Barbara that belongs to Joanna LeBaron now, the ranch in Montana for anytime in between. Et cetera. Et cetera. It is an irony that Peter LeBaron's widow is not unmindful of — that the blue-collar popularity of their inexpensive wines should have bought them all these costly palaces and possessions. And all this is what is at stake. This, Sari LeBaron often thinks, is why I worked so hard. It must have been. If not, then why?

As though he is reading her thoughts — as, indeed, he often can do — Gabe Pollack says to her, "It's what you wanted, isn't it?"

"What? I was wool-gathering. What do you mean?"

"This." He gestures around him. "All this."

"Oh, perhaps. Perhaps. I suppose so."

"You could have had a quite different life, you know, once upon a time."

"Oh, I know," she says a little crossly. "Ancient history. I could also have been a housewife in the Bronx, I suppose, if I'd wanted that."

"You had your choices. You chose this."

"I know."

"Of course, I've always felt that whatever you chose to do you'd be successful at it."

"Ha!"

He studies her face. "There's more to this, isn't there — more that you're not telling me. It's more than just Melissa, isn't it? What is it? You're frightened of something, aren't you? Can you tell me what it is? What's frightening you, Sari?"

"Nonsense!" she says. "Me — frightened? That's bull-do!" And she drums her lacquered fingernails sharply on the library tabletop.

This is a signal and Thomas, as though on cue, steps quietly into the room. It would not surprise Gabe the slightest little bit if Thomas has been standing, all the time, just outside the sitting-room door, listening to their conversation, every word. "Excuse me, Madam," Thomas says. "Just to remind you of your ten-o'clock appointment at the office."

"Yes, Thomas. Thank you."

Gabe rises as Thomas withdraws. "I'll see that a follow-up story is written right away, on the Odeon," he says. "And this one I'll write myself. An editorial, I think. And I'll speak to Archie on the other little matter we discussed."

"Dear old Gabe," she says, now all smiles and dark, twinkly eyes, as though she has forgotten everything they have just been talking about. "It was so good of you to come by, such a nice surprise. Just the boost I needed on a rainy day. Dear old Pollywog. Why are you always so good to me?" And she offers her hand to be kissed again.

Because, he thinks, if I weren't so good to you you'd feed me to the lions. And first you'd cancel all your ad pages in my paper. But he says nothing, and kisses the upraised hand.

*   *   *

If you have spent any time in the Bay Area — and certainly if, like us, you live here — you will have heard stories about Assaria LeBaron. She is something of a local legend, a character, as they say. Some of the stories are true, some not. Many of these tales are fictions. You may have heard, for example, that she was once an artist's model, and also that she was once a dancer. You may have been told that she was the bosomy young woman who posed, loosely draped, for the statue that stands atop the Dewey Monument in the center of Union Square, and you may have heard that she posed for this sculpture in the nude, and that when the statue was delivered the prudish city fathers insisted that the draperies be added. But how can any of this be true? Sari did not come to San Francisco until the 1920s, long after the Dewey Monument was completed and in place. You may also have heard that she was the model for some of the female figures that appeared, undraped, on the friezes of the old Post Office building. But put two and two together. The friezes and the Post Office went in the Great Fire of 1906. Assaria LeBaron was born in 1909. All these stories are untrue. Untrue, untrue, all of it, and remember that you read it here.

In San Francisco, Sari LeBaron has long been known as "the Tiny Terror," and she earned that sobriquet long before it was applied to the late Truman Capote. Some of that reputation is deserved, some is not. It is true that her name is occasionally uttered in tones of dread within the boardrooms of certain banks and in certain law offices along Montgomery Street. When she is hammering out a contract for a new distributorship, for instance, she can be an absolute demon with her demands until the lawyers throw up their hands in despair and give her every article and subclause that she wants. "We are arguing, now, over pennies, Mrs. LeBaron — *pennies!*" the lawyers will cry. "Well, if it only amounts to pennies, then why not let me have them?" she will answer. Watch her, late at night, with her old-fashioned adding machine, going over the company's books, checking monthly sales figures, finding tiny discrepancies that even Messrs. Price and Waterhouse have overlooked somehow. Still, no one in this town will deny that Sari, almost single-handedly, rescued Baronet Vineyards, pulled it out of the shambles that Julius LeBaron left it in, and made Baronet what it is today. It was even she who first proposed the name Baronet Vineyards for the company's label, who suggested that the company's former designation — M. & J. LeBaron, Vintners — was unmemorable and hard to pronounce. "Vintners," she said, "with a *t* between the two *n*'s, is hard to say. 'Vineyards' has a nice romantic sound, and 'Baronet' gives a high-class name to what, let's face it, is a middle-class wine." Who knows how much that small change, alone, may have had to do with the company's surge in sales during the fifties and sixties?

Still, though she is — always has been — a definite stickler when it comes to such matters as balance sheets and profit-and-loss statements and fractions of percentage points, her reputation for tight-fistedness is undeserved. On the contrary, she is loved in many circles for her generosity — generosity of the strictly personal kind. For example, she is one of the few women in San Francisco who regularly tips her favorite salespeople at Gump's and Saks and Magnin's and all the rest, and the checks that go out from her at Christmastime to employees and others who she feels have given her good service add up to thousands of dollars. Take the case, too, of Miss Sophie, who sells lingerie at Magnin's. Miss Sophie mentioned to Sari LeBaron one day that the motor on her Deepfreeze had burned out, and she had had to throw out all its contents. The next morning, on Miss Sophie's doorstep, there arrived a new Deepfreeze, packed with fillets of beef, turkeys, Columbia River salmon, and other fancy comestibles. Are these the actions of a penurious or hard-hearted woman?

At times, she can display an almost total personal disregard for money. One example will suffice. Sari LeBaron has an estimable collection of jade pieces, which are displayed in various vitrines and on tables around her house. One night in — I think the year was 1971 or 1972 — at one of her dinner parties, a male guest who had indulged in a bit too much John Barleycorn decided, as a joke, to slip a jade piece off one of the tables and drop it into the pocket of his dinner jacket. It was a pink jade jackal with emerald eyes. The next morning, regretting his action, he sent the piece back to her in the center of a flower arrangement. Sari, who had not noticed that the piece was missing, merely glanced at the arrangement and ordered that it be sent to Children's Hospital. Two days later she received this letter from the hospital:

> My dear Mrs. LeBaron:
> I want personally to thank you for your generous gift to Children's.
> The flowers are beautiful, and the jade tiger [*sic*] is exquisite. We have had our art appraisers examine it, and are assured that it will bring in excess of $25,000.
> We thought you would be pleased to learn that we are adding your name to the bronze plaque in the entrance foyer.
>
> Sincerely yours,
>
> Richard J. Walters
> Director

Of course, she could have asked for the piece back, explained that it was a mistake. But she laughed the whole thing off, took it as a great joke.

George Hessler, who pilots her 727, calls her "Nugget" because she periodically gives him nuggets of unrefined gold, knowing he collects them, from her own collection of souvenirs of the Gold Rush days. She gave him a particularly large one after that episode which she and Gabe Pollack spoke of on the very February morning we have been talking about. Well, you might argue, he deserved it, since what happened was Sari's fault entirely. Still, if she hadn't interceded, George could have lost his license.

You will hear a lot of idle gossip and speculation about the LeBarons in this town, and you will hear much malicious fun made of the way the LeBarons seem to have worked so hard to erase, and renounce, their national origins and have tried to invent new ones for themselves. Well, this was mostly Papa Julius. You will also hear that, for all their airs, the LeBarons somehow always manage to "marry down." It is true that, for all his airs, Papa Julius LeBaron married down. Mama LeBaron was the former Constance O'Brien, and Julius always tried to pretend that his wife was some sort of kin to the legendary William S. O'Brien, one of the "Irish

Big Four Silver Kings" of the 1850s and 1860s. Not so. Constance's O'Briens were the Irish chambermaid O'Briens, and her mother scrubbed toilets at the Palace Hotel — though that is an unkind thing to say, for Constance was a good and pious woman, and her parents were honest and hardworking people. It is also said that Peter LeBaron married down when he married Sari, and it is pointed out that Sari LeBaron's own origins are shrouded in a certain amount of mystery. This is simply because there are some areas of her past that Sari LeBaron does not wish to discuss. And, given hindsight, in light of everything Sari has done, would you say that Peter married down? He married a woman of far greater intelligence and spirit and courage than he — for all his famous charm. Have you heard about the time, in the late summer of 1946 during the Teamsters' strike, when Sari herself drove truckloads of freshly harvested grapes from the Sonoma vineyards to the crushing sheds — where the grapes must go as fast as possible after harvesting — and, warned of trouble from the Teamsters, drove with her husband's loaded pistol beside her in the cab of the truck? On the road one morning, a striking Teamster saw her, recognized her, and tried to force her off the highway with his rig. She grabbed the pistol, aimed, and shot out two of his tires. For that, Peter married "*down*"?

Much of the idle gossip and speculation you may have heard about the family is untrue, if not downright absurd. Someone just the other day said, "Where did Peter Powell LeBaron get his middle name *from,* anyway?" (Powell is an old and respected San Francisco name.) To which someone else at the party, fancying himself a wit, said, "I think it's from the Powell Street cable car — I gather that's where he was conceived, somewhere between Post and California." Gossip. Actually, he was named in honor of Archbishop Terence Powell — as I've mentioned, Constance was very pious. And you will hear speculation about how Peter P. and Sari met, and there is a story that they met under scandalous circumstances in one of the notorious private rooms over the Old Poodle Dog. Nonsense. Sari was introduced to the LeBarons in a very ordinary way by Peter's sister, Joanna, who was her best friend. You will also hear that Sari "had" to marry Peter because he had put her in a family way. This is also untrue. In fact, when the whole proposition of marriage was made to her, she was quite startled, even though she was — or let us say she thought she was — in love with him. At the time, yes. At the time, another man she thought she really loved had turned *her* down. Was her marriage, then, on the rebound from this other love? Not really. Remember that Peter was a very handsome man, a very glamorous figure.

She loved him. She told me so. And he loved her. Or said he did.

Much of the gossip is fueled by jealousy. One area of the city that admires Sari is the gay community, not that she gives a fig for them. No, that's not quite true. She simply can't quite understand the gay community, can't quite comprehend what it's all about, and prefers not to think about it all that much. But the reason why the gays admire her is because of her interest in renovating that still rather sleazy area south of Market Street — "south of the Slot," as they say here — Howard Street, the Fillmore District. Her restoration of the Odeon Theatre was a part of that ongoing project. The Fillmore District is still pretty run-down, and there are plenty of winos there — "Sometimes I think I'm responsible for the winos," Sari has said — but there are some architecturally fine old buildings there, Victorian-style houses and the like. Sari has bought some of these properties, and offered them at low-cost, low-interest loans to buyers who will agree to spend a certain amount to fix them up. These houses have appealed especially to homosexual couples. For some reason, they're clever at that sort of thing. Quite a few shabby old houses have been turned into showplaces, thanks to Sari. The winos and the homosexuals don't seem to mind each other. The homosexuals call Sari "the Queen Bee."

You may have heard that Sari and Peter's eldest child, Melissa, is peculiar. It is true that she is unmarried, and shares the White Wedding-Cake House at 2040 Washington Street with her mother. Years ago, Sari turned the whole first floor of the house into a spacious apartment for Melissa, with her own entrance, so she can come and go as she pleases, which she does, though Thomas tends to keep tabs on these comings and these goings. Thomas! If Thomas should depart this earth before his mistress does, Lord knows what

Sari would do. But there is absolutely nothing wrong with Melissa's mind, no matter what they say. Melissa has been given all the tests — the Stanford-Binet, the Minnesota Multiphasic Personality Inventory, et cetera — and her mother has been given the results. Sari could show them to you if you like. They show Melissa to be perfectly normal in every way. In most ways, at least. You may have heard that Melissa is a nymphomaniac, and an alcoholic. Melissa's problem, if it is a problem, is more that she seems to get involved with a somewhat seamy, somewhat sordid element. This rock group, for instance. She seems to be attracted to what her mother calls "lowlifes." Naturally, this worries and upsets her mother. It would worry any mother. The doctors used to say she would outgrow this. She hasn't.

Melissa's problem, if it is a problem, is — to Sari's way of thinking, at least — that she is basically a shy and insecure and introspective sort of person. This is why she excites so easily and why, when she is upset or disappointed, her reactions become . . . unpredictable. This is also why, at times, she drinks too much. The doctors have also suggested a chemical imbalance, but part of it all — and Sari herself will admit this — may be Sari's own fault because of an error that was made . . . an error, a misplacement of trust . . . long ago, before Melissa was born, before Switzerland and all that . . . but that is getting way ahead of the story.

Of course, many people think that the trouble is that Sari fussed over Melissa too much, always did, still does. Being fussed over became a habit with Melissa, a bad habit she couldn't break. As a child, she liked it, you see. Now she demands it. And of course Peter — poor Peter — was no help, no help at all.

Then there are the twin sons, Eric and Peter, Jr., identical twins. They are both handsome devils — take after their father — with fuller, darker, curlier heads of hair than any two young men nearing forty have any right to have. To this day, when they are in a room together, most people cannot tell them apart. Sari always could, of course; a mother always can. But it was easier for her because Eric — born three and a half minutes after Peter — was nicked in the left temple by the doctor's forceps, and bore a small scar from this from the very beginning. Though the scar is very faint now, it has never gone away, and you can see it if you know where to look.

Though identical in appearance, the two boys are quite unlike in temperament. For years, Eric was Sari's little workhorse, clever and industrious, good with figures, and in 1980 Sari rewarded him for all his hard work by naming him vice-president and director of marketing for Baronet. All well and good. But lately — is it the mid-life crisis we hear about? — Eric has been kicking up his heels a bit, straining in the harness, feeling his oats, as they say. This displeases Sari, who, after all, is still his boss. If there is any problem with Eric, it might seem, it is that Sari has tried too hard to carve Eric in her own image. Perhaps it is a mistake for any parent to try to carve a child — for any human to try to carve another human — in his or her own image. Perhaps. Long ago, Sari would have liked to have carved Melissa in her own image. That didn't work, either.

Meanwhile, Peter, Jr., soars through life like a bubble rising from the stem of a glass of champagne. He takes nothing seriously, unless it is having a good time. Peter loves fast cars, beautiful women, staying up all night in nightclubs — in an earlier generation, he would have been called a playboy. He works for Baronet, too, where his title is superintendent of the Sonoma vineyard, but he doesn't work very hard, and once arrived for work — his Jaguar weaving uncertainly down the road — still in black tie, fresh from an all-night party on Russian Hill. When Sari heard about this caper, there was hell to pay, believe me. Peter's nickname is "Peeper" or "Peep." This is because, when he was a baby, his Aunt Joanna used to say that he made sounds "just like a little peeping frog" when he cried. The nickname stuck, and today Peter's friends all call him "Peeper" or "Peep." This is, you can see, a family fond of nicknames.

Peeper has never married, and shows no indication that he ever will. His relations with women don't last very long, and once he has bedded them down a few times he seems to lose interest. But since 1968, Eric has been married to Alix, and you cannot say that Eric LeBaron "married down." Alix is the daughter of Harry Tillinghast, the president of Kern-McKittrick Oil, and was considered quite a belle when she married Eric. "The debutante catch of the year," said the *Chronicle* when Alix came out at the 1965 Cotillion. "Oil and wine don't mix," said Sari, when Eric told his mother of his intentions, but the marriage has worked out happily enough. Happily enough. They have two teenage daughters, Kimberly and Sloane, also twins. Two sets of twins in two LeBaron generations. But in the case of the girls, they are fraternal twins — the two-egg kind, rather than the one-egg. Both girls attend the Sarah Dix Hamlin School, which their mother attended. Alix is a bit of a snob. She has enrolled the girls as boarders, for example, though they could easily commute from the Peninsula, because she feels that the boarding students — who of course pay a higher tuition — are higher in the school's pecking order, socially, than the day students. Of course, she is right. The two groups hardly know each other's names. Alix pronounces her name "A-*leeks*," though her given name was Alice, which she found too common-sounding.

Despite their different sorts of lives, Eric and Peeper are close, very close.

And so there you have the LeBarons. There was one other child, who died. But we must not forget Joanna. Joanna is very important. Joanna is Peter Powell LeBaron's sister, the same age as Sari, and if you live in New York you have no doubt heard of her. She has had a spectacular career in advertising, and now heads her own Madison Avenue agency, LeBaron & Murdock. She lives in great style in Manhattan — a duplex at 1040 Fifth Avenue, overlooking the park, the same building where Jackie Onassis lives. She spends most of her time there, although, as we mentioned, she also has a house in Santa Barbara. Joanna has no connection with Baronet Vineyards, Inc., except indirectly. It should come as no surprise that her agency has the Baronet advertising account — $20,000,000 worth of business, for which she takes a commission at a "family rate" that is supposed to be a secret. It isn't, really. It is ten percent instead of the usual fifteen. Joanna married once, briefly, long ago, and then resumed the name LeBaron. From this union there was one son, Lance, who also eschews his father's name and styles himself Lance LeBaron. He is a perfectly nice fellow. He works far from the wine business, as a stockbroker with

Merrill Lynch, though his Uncle Peter left him some Baronet stock. He is two years younger than Melissa. Married. No children.

And so you see that in the fifth generation there are only Eric's two daughters. That is why Eric's actions and behavior are important to his mother, why nothing must go wrong at this point. Of the two girls, Kimmie is her grandmother's favorite. Why? Probably just because Kimmie is the prettier, livelier, more popular of the two.

Sari would like to carve Kimmie in her own image.

As for everything else, pay no heed to the stories you will hear, hereabouts, about the family. They have been called "rich as Croesus." Well, how rich *was* Croesus, anyway? Did anyone ever count his wealth? Hundreds of years before the birth of Christ, did the ancient, ignorant, downtrodden Lydians even know their king that well? Baloney, says Sari LeBaron. Baloney and bull-do. They also like to talk here of the LeBaron "family curse." Do we still believe in curses and witchcraft and spells? More baloney and more bull-do. Pay no heed, either, to various versions you will hear of the circumstances surrounding Sari's crippling accident, or of the circumstances of Peter LeBaron's death, et cetera, or that there is "something funny" about Melissa, based on Switzerland, and all that gossip that still goes on.

There is only one truth about the way things happened, and only Sari LeBaron knows it all.

She, and perhaps two other people.

One of them is me.

Two

*T*ODAY IS THE DAY for the boys from Madison Avenue to come out to San Francisco, as they do twice a year, to present their advertising campaigns, the television commercials and so on, for Baronet wines. Sari has heard along the grapevine that the Madison Avenue boys live in terror of these semiannual trips, that they spend weeks beforehand not only pulling together their layouts and storyboards, but also planning what they all will wear, in order to make the best impression on the old lady. She has heard that the entire trip between La Guardia and San Francisco International is spent not only in going over notes and market-research reports, but also on straightening trouser creases, hitching up socks, and checking neckties for spots. She can imagine them, getting on the airplane, carefully turning their jackets inside out and folding them, flatly and neatly, in the overhead storage bins so that they will arrive unwrinkled.

The boys always manage to dress much the same — in dark gray or dark blue three-button suits that bear the unmistakable stamp of Brooks Brothers, with white or pale blue button-down shirts, ties with tiny paisley patterns on them, and slip-on shoes with gold-colored bits clamped across their tops. It is the way they suppose San Francisco businessmen dress (which it really isn't quite), and Sari is certain that they don't dress that way back home in New York. San Francisco, they have been told, is a quiet, elegant city (which it really isn't), where the women wear mink jackets and hats and short white gloves, even in summer (which they haven't done for years), and where anything that would smack of Hollywood must be painstakingly eschewed. But this is all right. And it is all right, too, that they dread these San Francisco meetings. After all, there is that $20,000,000 in annual billings to take into consideration, a sum that, in Sari's opinion, is not to be sneezed at. And even though LeBaron & Murdock might be considered something of a family agency, there would be nothing to prevent Assaria LeBaron from — if she took a notion to — firing the lot of them and taking her business to Benton & Bowles. Benton & Bowles would be only too happy to take on Baronet. Only too happy.

There are three Madison Avenue boys — Sari knows them well — and they have names. One is Mike Geraghty, thirty-fivish, a red-headed and freckled Irishman with a pleasantly open face. He is the account executive and, as such, he is the highest in their pecking order. It is Mike who assumes the privilege of standing closest to Sari's desk — not over her shoulder, mind you, for that would be too presumptuous, too intimate; no one in the organization would have the temerity to do that. Mike stands, instead, just a little to the front, and a little to the side, of where Sari sits, with the newspaper-advertising proofs spread out in front of him for Sari's inspection.

The other two young men are from the agency's Creative Department. One is Bob Petrocelli, the art director who designs the ads. The other is Howard Friedman, the copywriter who writes the words. These two sit, a little apart from each other, in straight chairs in front of Sari's desk. An Irishman, an Italian, and a Jew, the three are a carefully calculated ethnic mix. Also at the meeting, seated on the big leather sofa at a short remove from the others, is Sari's son Eric.

The five are gathered in Sari's office now, and the meeting has begun.

The corporate headquarters of Baronet Vineyards are located in one of the older buildings on Montgomery Street, and the office that Sari LeBaron now occupies was originally designed to reflect Papa Julius LeBaron's notion of what a winery executive's office should be — grand and appropriately baronial, with decorative touches borrowed from both California and medieval Europe. The walls and high ceilings are paneled in lustrous dark walnut, embossed with heraldic shields and escutcheons, and the polished marble floor is laid out in an egg-and-dart design of white and gold. Sari's desk is framed by immense windows of stained glass that depict, in their various panels, sword-bearing conquistadores in tight-fitting cuisses and kneepieces, golden breastplates and épaulières, and ostrich-plumed helmets, as well as tonsured monks in cassocks and surplices bearing jugs and pitchers of wine. The chairs and sofa are all large and vaguely Spanish in design, covered in a rich black leather that gives the room its own smoky, waxy, male smell; and tall brass column lamps support heavy, fluted parchment shades that are painted with more heraldry — shields and crests and other armorial trappings.

The room is also boldly self-congratulatory. Set into a wall above the sofa, in an illuminated glass case, are displayed examples of Baronet products over the years in their various forms, shapes, and sizes — half-pints, pints, fifths, quarts, liters, half-gallons, and gallons — and varieties: the whites, the reds, the rosés, the golden Angelicas, and so on. On the opposite wall, in an identical case, there is a collection of wineglasses of various origins and vintages. And the wall that faces Sari's desk is what Papa liked to call his Trophy Wall. Here, in frames, are all the awards, medals, tributes, and citations — both civic and industrial — along with the signed photographs from United States Presidents, every one from Calvin Coolidge through Ronald Reagan (with Franklin Roosevelt excepted), that the LeBarons and their company have amassed over the years. These are grouped around a gold-framed portrait of black-mustachioed Grandpa Mario Barone, painted from an early photograph. But even here the hand of the crafty revisionist of history has been at work. The plaque below the portrait of the man responsible for all this gives him a name he would never have answered to: "Marc LeBaron," and, below this, the words "Founder: 1830–1905."

Since Julius LeBaron's day, only one decorative detail of the office has been changed: the removal of the two brass cuspidors that used to flank the desk. Sari saw to that.

Now, in Papa's big swivel chair, she sits behind the walnut partners' desk. Her wheelchair has been put away in a closet, since none of the Madison Avenue boys is supposed to be reminded of her handicap. Mike Geraghty lays out the proposed ads, one by one, for her to consider, contemplate, study. He places each new glossy page on top of the last in the order in which — if Sari approves — they are to make their appearance to the wine-drinking public. The backs of his well-manicured fingers are downed with a light peach-fuzz of pink hairs.

"Now, let's go through the whole lot again, Mike," Sari says at last.

"Certainly, Mrs. LeBaron."

The other two young men say nothing, merely sit stiffly in their chairs in attitudes of attention and profound respect. Months of work are at stake here, and everything hangs on Sari's approval or disapproval. Thus far, she has registered neither emotion, and the brow of Howard Friedman, the copywriter, has begun to glisten slightly. The proposed new slogan is his.

"Well, I see what you're trying to say here," she says at last. " 'Baronet — The Wine You Can Trust.' You can trust the Leaning Tower of Pisa not to fall down. You can trust the Statue of Liberty not to drop her torch. But —"

Anxiously: "Yes, Mrs. LeBaron?"

"But what are we doing with all these pictures of *banks?* What does a bank have to do with wine?"

"You see, Mrs. LeBaron," Howard Friedman interjects quickly, "the idea is that you can trust Baronet wines just the way you can trust your bank to take care of your money. You notice, in the copy, we've used the phrase 'The wine you can bank on.' "

"I see that. But what I can't see is why anyone would want to bank on a wine. Am I missing some subtle point?"

"Banks," says Mike Geraghty, "are trusted American financial institutions. The very bedrock, you might say, of our American capitalist system."

"Don't forget — I'm pro-Communist!" She says it with a wink.

"Ha-ha, yes. Well, Americans feel very strongly about their banks. The dream of every young American man or woman is to be able to walk into a bank and cash a check, his or her own check. That couldn't happen in Russia or your other Iron Curtain countries. We've done some very deep-level psychological research stuff on this, Mrs. LeBaron, on Americans' deep-seated feelings about their banks, and —"

"I'm sure you're right, Mike," Sari says, waving her hand impatiently, "but I still don't see the connection between people's feelings about their *banks* and the *wine* they drink. That's what I don't get about all of this."

"Banks," says Mike Geraghty, "are solid. They can be trusted. They're like an old friend. Who is more trusted in any town or city in this country than the local banker?"

"The local doctor, perhaps?" Sari suggests.

"But that raises health issues, doctors," says Mike Geraghty, "and of course we don't want to go into anything like that, we really can't get into an area like that, Mrs. LeBaron, saying that wine is good for you, good for your health, nine out of ten doctors, that sort of thing. Why, the government would —"

"I'm not suggesting that," Sari says. "All I'm saying, Mike, is — why banks?"

"We're trying to give Baronet a more upscale image, Mrs. LeBaron," Howard Friedman says. "The bank, the banker — conservative, trustworthy, the person in town everyone loves —"

"Well, I certainly don't love my banker," Sari says. "He happens to be a horse's ass. But what do you mean by this upscale business?"

"The banker. The town's most upright citizen, the pillar of the community."

"Are you trying to say that bankers drink Baronet wines?"

"That's implicit, yes, in the copy. A subliminal message. Up-scale."

"But that's bull-do, Mike. Bankers *don't* drink Baronet wines — not in this town or any other. They drink a Beefeater martini with a twist, or Johnnie Walker Scotch. Or something equally respectable."

"Of course, that's only a very minor copy point, Mrs. LeBaron. That's the subliminal, the upscale part. The main point is —"

"Yes, let's get back to the main point," Sari says. "The main point of all this is 'Baronet — The Wine You Can Trust,' as I see it. So let me ask you this: Is there any reason why anyone should *not* trust Baronet wines? Is there any reason why anyone should trust Baronet more than any other wine? Trust Baronet to do what? Not get you tipsy? Not make you upchuck, or give you cirrhosis of the liver if you drink too much? Not give you a hangover? Face it, Mike, our wine is cheap jug wine, always has been. It's not champagne, and it's not Scotch or bonded bourbon. Baronet is blue-collar stuff. Kids drink it in fern bars that can't afford a liquor license. They drink it at fraternity-house parties. They buy it by the gallon to spike the punch. We're not trying to be Beaulieu or Paul Masson or even Almaden. We're just a plain old honest wine with a low sticker, and people drink it because they get a pleasant buzz. We're the house wine, seventy-five cents a glass in some of your not-so-better restaurants. That's what *we* are, and always have been."

"But with the taste emphasis changing these days, Mrs. LeBaron, and the —"

"Bull-do! If the public were turning away from our wine, we'd see it in the bottom line, wouldn't we? If we're doing something wrong, we'd see it in the sales figures, wouldn't we? But we don't. So why are we changing our ad approach, with this upscale business? Next thing you know, you'll be suggesting I buy ad space in *Town & Country,* or *Architectural Digest,* or la-di-da books like that! If you want to give me something new, give me something lighthearted — something that's about good, inexpensive *fun.* Are *banks* lighthearted? Banks are about interest rates." She spreads the palms of her hands flat on the desktop and looks at each of the three young men in turn. "If you ask me, gentlemen, if there's one thing Baronet wines are not about, *it's banks.*"

There is silence now, and all around the room the Madison Avenue boys' faces are crestfallen and disconsolate, and all at once Sari feels almost sorry for them. They are so very young, and their young hopes look so very dashed. "Tell me," she says in a gentler tone, "has my sister-in-law approved any of this stuff?"

Their expressions grow even more morose. It is difficult for them, after all, to hear all their hard work dismissed as "this stuff."

"Miss LeBaron reviews every agency presentation very carefully before it is presented to the client," Mike Geraghty says rather stiffly.

"Well, Joanna must be losing her marbles," Sari says.

With that, Eric LeBaron clears his throat softly, leans forward on the sofa, and makes a steeple of his fingers. "Excuse me, Mother," he says. It is the first time he has spoken.

Sari throws him a quick look. "Yes, Eric?"

"Excuse me, Mother, but I think I see what these fellows are trying to do."

Now there is a collective, if inaudible, sigh of relief in the room. All is not yet utterly lost for the boys. Another opinion is at least being offered, and there is a fleeting chance — a fleeting one — that the day may be saved, even though the boys know from long experience that it is Sari who tells her son what to do, and not the other way around.

"I'm not saying I'm one hundred percent in favor of this particular campaign," he says carefully, and the briefly hopeful looks on the other men's faces fade quickly. "But I see what they're trying to say, and I think I should tell you that what they are showing us today is based on a suggestion of my own a while back."

"Of *yours?*"

"Yes," he says. "You see — the idea of an upscale campaign for

Baronet is based on a very definite national trend that has been going on for the last ten, twenty years.''

"What trend is that?''

"Wine has become a fashionable drink. It has become the drink of choice for upwardly mobile people, particularly young people — young urban professionals, the people who —''

Sari waves her hand impatiently. "I know all that,'' she says. "Are you trying to tell me something I don't already know? That trend started in the late nineteen sixties. Are you trying to tell me I'm behind the times?''

"Of course not, but the point is —''

"The point is that those people, those yuppies you're talking about, don't drink *our* wine. Why, they wouldn't touch a bottle of Baronet with a ten-foot pole! You won't see *our* wine being served at any Park Avenue parties, Eric. On the Bowery, sure. Why, every wino they pick up on skid row is lugging a pint of Baronet Thunder Mountain Red in a paper bag!''

"But what I am trying to say,'' he begins slowly, and Sari can see the small forceps scar on his left temple beginning to redden, as it often does when he is angry or upset. No one else notices this, but she does. Good, she thinks, let him squirm a bit. "What I am trying to say,'' he continues, "is that we don't have to direct our entire marketing effort toward skid-row winos and Bowery bums.''

"You want to turn a sow's ear into a silk purse — is that it?''

"There is another market, Mrs. LeBaron,'' Mike Geraghty interjects.

"I know there is! But it's not *our* market.''

"But is there any reason, Mother, why we shouldn't also try to tap this other market, with an advertising campaign designed to make the Baronet name just a little bit respectable?''

"And turn our backs on the market we've got already? Kill the goose that lays the golden eggs? I tell you, our market doesn't read *Town & Country*. It reads the *National Enquirer* and the girlie magazines. It doesn't watch the 'MacNeil-Lehrer Report,' it watches ball games and prizefights. Our research shows us that. We're sold in *supermarkets,* Eric, to men and women who drive home in pickup trucks."

"But do we have to concentrate on that market *exclusively?* While this other market is —"

"Don't change horses in midstream — did you ever hear that piece of advice? Don't take your money off a winning horse — that's another."

"And, while we're exchanging clichés," Eric says, "there's another about putting all your eggs in one basket."

"Bull-do!"

The three other men in the room are now all extremely uneasy. It is painful for them to have to witness a member of their own sex being taken to task by a member of the opposite one, particularly when that member of the opposite sex happens to be the man's own mother. Eric, they know, is talking marketing. That is supposed to be his bailiwick, and to talk marketing is supposed to be his right. A marketing vice-president is supposed, at least from time to time, to offer marketing suggestions and advice, and that is all he is doing.

There is a silence, and then Mike Geraghty says, "You see, Mrs. LeBaron, what we have been proposing is some sort of advertising campaign that would begin to add some respectability, some dignity, to the popular image that the Baronet label now has, in preparation —"

"In preparation for what?"

"In preparation for the possibility of introducing a new line of higher-priced wines. Of château quality. With new packaging, with a new label — retaining the Baronet signature, of course. 'Château Baronet,' in fact, is one of the labels we've been tossing about."

"Who's 'we'? Is this some new idea of Joanna's?"

"No, actually it was mine," Eric says.

"Only a suggestion, of course," Mike Geraghty says, "in an effort to capture a share, at least, of this upscale market."

"Belatedly," Eric adds.

"What do you think of the name Château Baronet, Mrs. Le-Baron?" Mike Geraghty says. "We rather like it."

Sari makes a face. "*Château* Baronet," she says. "Sounds kind of pansy to me. Well, I'll tell you what I think. I think this is all a terrible idea. I think it's worse than terrible. I think it's a lousy idea, I think it stinks."

Now the sighs are audible.

"Let me tell you something about wine," she continues, folding her hands across her desk and adopting the attitude of an all-wise mother superior in a convent addressing a group of unschooled novices. "Wine is crushed from grapes, and grapes grow on vines, and vines grow in soil, in earth. In the earth, they depend on rain and on sun — on nature — on sunny days and cool, dry nights. In some of our northern vineyards, like Napa, we let wild mustard grow between the vines in spring. Why wild mustard? No one knows exactly, but wild mustard seems to nourish grapevines in certain areas. Up in the foothills, weeds like clover and vetch seem to work better — no one knows why, but they do. Nature again. Later, closer to harvest time, these weeds are all plowed under, and this also seems to help the vines. Provides soil texture. You see, that's what I think all you boys sometimes seem to forget — you, in your Madison Avenue offices, Joanna in her duplex on Fifth Avenue, even Eric here in his office in the city. You've forgotten the wild mustard, and the clover, and the purple vetch. How many of you have ever watched the bees, the way a hive of bees will attack a vineyard? A single bee can suck a grape until it's as dry and empty and wrinkled as a dead balloon. I've watched this, watched with tears in my eyes, and watched as those bees fell, one by one to the ground, drunk from their drinking on our vines.

"And the larks! 'Hark! hark! the lark at heaven's gate sings,' you think, but larks can be some of our worst predators. Those pretty songbirds can be some of our most voracious scavengers — insatiable! — and a summer of larks for us is a summer of disaster. As a girl, I used to watch the Chinese field hands chanting, shouting, flapping their arms, beating gongs, trying to frighten off a flock of larks from the vines. Did no good at all! Forces of nature, you see." She pauses for effect. "That's what I think you've all forgotten, sitting there in your ivory towers. We're not Park Avenue aristocrats. Hell, we're *farmers*. We work the land. We study the sky and sniff the air for signs of rain. We battle nature every day. We're real people, and we're ordinary people, and those are the people who drink our wine, and that's how we've made our reputation." And she brings down her fist, hard, on the top of the walnut partners' desk. "And that's how we got rich."

After a moment, Eric says dryly, "Well, thanks for the lecture, Mother."

"That wasn't a lecture," Sari says. "That was a sermon!" She pauses, and then smiles. "Well," she says, "how about some lunch? I don't know about any of you, but I'm starving." She presses the button on her desktop and rings for her secretary, Miss Martino.

Eric rises. "Sorry," he says, "but I can't join you. I have an engagement."

He can do this. He can escape, with an excuse, but the others cannot. As long as the Madison Avenue boys remain in San Francisco, they belong to Assaria LeBaron. Sari nods a curt farewell to Eric, and Gloria Martino appears at the doorway, notepad and pencil in hand.

"Something to drink before lunch, boys?" Sari asks.

Mike Geraghty speaks first. "I'll have a nice chilled glass of Baronet Chablis," he says.

"Good!" says Sari. "I'll have a touch of Baronet vermouth" — she winks at them — "mixed with a couple of jiggers of Beefeater gin."

Eric LeBaron strides into his office on the other side of the building and flings himself into the chair behind his desk. Marylou Chin, his willowy Eurasian secretary, has followed him into the room. "Well," he says, "she did it again. Let me have it, in front of the whole Madison Avenue gang. *Shit!*"

Ordinarily, Marylou would have simply made clucking noises with her tongue, murmured something noncommittally sympathetic, and then asked him if it was all right if she took her lunch hour. But just in the last few weeks the nature of their relationship has changed, and so, instead, she closes the office door behind them, takes a seat in the small chair opposite him, crosses her legs, and carefully lights a long filtered cigarette, studying his face. "How much longer are you going to let her treat you like this, Eric?" she asks at last.

"Shit, I don't know," he says. "Until they carry me out of here with a ruptured, bleeding ulcer, I suppose."

"It's — it's intolerable, is what it is."

"I know."

"You work so hard, you give her so much, and she rewards you by treating you like some sort of galley slave. Like shit, as you say."

"I know."

"You're the one who should be running this company. Not her."

"I know I could run it a damn sight better," he says.

"Of course you could." She shapes the ash on her cigarette against the rim of his ashtray. "Was it — was it the same sort of thing today?"

"Of course. She simply refuses — refuses to consider anything that even remotely smacks of a new idea. Refuses."

"You've offered her so many good ideas."

"The Madison Avenue guys had come up with a new campaign that was, frankly, shit. But they were on the right track. But she, of course, derailed them before they could even get the train out of the station. Refused to listen to anything anybody else had to say."

"Poor Eric."

"You should have heard her little speech today. All about larks and honeybees and wild mustard and purple vetch — whatever the hell that is."

Once more she shapes the ash on her cigarette. "You know," she says, "I've been thinking."

"Thinking what?"

"There was an article a couple of weeks ago in *Newsweek*. In fact it was the cover story. It was on Alzheimer's disease, that thing old people get. It's like senility. They can remember something that happened fifty years ago, but they can't remember whether they opened the refrigerator door to put something in or to take something out. She's what now — seventy-four? Do you think that might be what she has, Eric?"

"Ha! I wish it were."

"I mean — well, that thing she did with the plane. That was really pretty crazy. I know how embarrassed you were by that. We were *all* embarrassed. 'Is that the woman you *work* for?' friends said to me."

"No, she was just acting up. Just being cute. Just seeing how much she could get away with — she and George Hessler. And I'm sure as hell George had something to do with it. Must have. She let him do it because she thinks he's cute."

Marylou Chin laughs softly. "Well, he is pretty good-looking," she says. "But after all."

"No," he says, "she's always been like this, I'm afraid, M'lou. As long as I've known her. Which of course is all my life."

"What about when your father was alive? Was she the same way with him?"

He frowns. "That was a little different. They were more like a working partnership. In business together. Dad was a smoothie, Mother was the toughie. When heads needed to get banged together, that was Mother's job. They came to Dad to apply the Band-Aids. That was what he did best, smoothing over the hurt feelings Mother left in her wake."

"Poor Eric," she says again. "It just hurts me so to see what she's doing to you!"

"A working partnership, that's what that marriage was. You know, sometimes I've tried to imagine my mother and my father fucking, and I just can't. I just can't picture the two of them — you know, making love. Fucking. And yet they must have, two or three times at least."

They sit in silence for a while, and very slowly Marylou Chin stubs out her cigarette. "Well, I know what I think you ought to do," she says finally.

"What's that?"

"Confront her. Tell her exactly what you think. It's wrong for you to keep your thoughts and feelings bottled up like this. I think you should go to her and tell her that you don't intend to take this kind of treatment anymore. Give her an ultimatum."

"Ha," he says. "What good would that do? She'd just say, 'Fine, get out.' And then where'd I be? Out on the street, without a job.''

"But she'd be a fool — an absolute fool — to let you go!''

"But don't forget, I know her, M'lou. I know her much better than you do, and I've known her much longer. I *know* her, I tell you.''

"Well, even if she were foolish enough to let you go — why, there are dozens of companies that would be just dying to snap you up, all over town!''

"You don't understand,'' he says. "This is my career. I'm nearly forty years old, and I've worked for this company for half my life. I've made this company my career. Even summers, home from college, I was out there with the braceros, picking grapes, getting paid by the box lot, working for Baronet. It's the only job I've ever had.''

"But there are plenty of other —''

"If she were mad enough, and she might well be, she could see to it that no other winery in California would hire me — ever. She has that kind of power, M'lou. I've seen her use it.''

"It's — inhuman, is what it is!''

"That's my mother. No, I'm afraid that isn't the solution.''

"But even without a job, you'd have —''

"Money, you mean?''

She hesitates, biting her lower lip. She is skating on thin ice here. As his secretary, she manages his personal checkbook, makes periodic deposits and withdrawals for him. But of his overall financial picture she knows little, and she is, after all, only his secretary. She decides to make light of things. "Well,'' she says easily, "the newspapers always include you in the list of San Francisco's wealthiest men.''

"A regular Gordon Getty, eh?''

"No, I simply mean that — considering who you are, with your talent and brains — you could do anything you wanted in this city.''

"Yeah.'' He is frowning now, looking not at her, but hard at the surface of his desk. "Yeah, well, one of the things I'd like to do right now is my alleged job as marketing director of Baronet.''

"But she won't let —''

"She does happen to be the president of the company, M'lou."

"It's just that I can't stand seeing her use you as her — whipping boy!"

"Are you calling me a pantywaist?"

"No! You're one of the brightest, most talented men I've ever known. But that woman —"

"That woman also happens to be my mother."

"Of course! And of course you love her. But any mother who loved her son wouldn't treat him this way." The ice beneath her feet grows ever thinner, but she plunges on. "It's just — it's just that I wish you'd let me take you to my Assertiveness class, Eric. We're into some consciousness-raising stuff now. We meet every —"

"Yeah, well, I don't think I need your Assertiveness class, M'lou. Thanks, anyway."

"I've made you angry, haven't I? Oh, Eric, I'm sorry! But it's just — it's just that I thought you were asking for my opinion."

"Yeah, well, I'll handle things. Don't worry about me, M'lou."

She laughs unhappily. "It's my Assertiveness class, I guess. It's made me too assertive. I'm sorry."

"I just don't want you getting any gray hairs over this. Leave things to me, okay?"

"Of course, Eric."

They sit in silence for a while. Miserably, she thinks: I have made him even more upset.

He thinks: This is all my fault for bellyaching to her in the first place.

"Well —" she says, and with the fingers of her right hand she flicks an imaginary ash from the skirt of her blue silk suit. Then she uncrosses her long legs and stands up. "Well, I'm skipping lunch today, so I'll be right outside if you need me for anything."

"Thanks, M'lou."

"Can I order a sandwich for you?"

"Uh — no, thanks."

She hesitates. "Will I — be seeing you tonight?" she asks him. Still frowning, he shakes his head. "I think — not," he says.

"I've been getting some grief on the home front, too. So I think I'd better say not."

"Poor Eric."

He looks up at her.

"Tomorrow, maybe?"

"We'll see," he says.

"I'm sorry if I made you angry. Really sorry."

"No, not angry." He smiles at her faintly. "Skip to M'lou," he says. "Skip to M'lou, my darling. Skip to M'lou, my dear."

She tries to return the smile. Then, slowly, she turns away from him and moves across the room on her slender high heels. At the door she hesitates again. "Shall I leave your door open or closed?"

"Closed, I think."

She opens the door, lets herself out, and then very quietly closes the door behind her.

Alone in the office, Eric thinks: Skip to M'lou. And then thinks: In this direction lie only frustration, confusion, and despair. He has just decided to give her up. For the third time this week.

He sits for a long time in the empty office, staring at the hunting prints (pink-coated hunters pursuing the fox) without seeing them, avoiding with his eyes the low table against one wall, where, in three matching silver frames inscribed with his initials, the photographs of a blonde wife and two pretty daughters smile at him with expressions of remarkable self-assurance and confidence, none of them in need of an Assertiveness class.

Finally, he reaches for the telephone on his desk, lifts the receiver, and presses a short series of musical numbers. When a woman's voice answers, he says, "Gloria, may I speak to my mother, please?"

"I'm sorry, Mr. LeBaron, but Mrs. LeBaron has left for the day. May I help you?"

"Then connect me with the house, please."

"I'm sorry, Mr. LeBaron, but Mrs. LeBaron left instructions that she would be receiving no calls."

"Thank you, Gloria." He replaces the receiver in its cradle. Then he looks at his watch. What time will it be in New York? He mentally adds the three hours. Not quite four. He picks up the phone again and taps out a longer series of numbers. *Very well,* he thinks, *I am now ready to play exactly the kind of game, Mother, that you will understand.*

"Aunt Joanna?" he says when she answers. "I think I need to come to New York to see you."

Assaria LeBaron has ordered her driver to take her directly from lunch with the Madison Avenue boys to Candlestick Park, where her ball club, the San Francisco Condors, is in spring training. There is a great deal of fuss and to-do and general consternation when her motorized chair materializes through the entrance of the temporary field house and makes its way across the linoleum of the foyer. Harry Olsen, the team's manager, rushes up to her, and says, "Mrs. LeBaron, the boys have just come in from the field — they're in the showers right now!"

"That's all right, I just want to have a few words with them, Harry."

"They're looking just great, Mrs. LeBaron," he says as he hurries behind her chair. "But we had no idea you were coming, Mrs. LeBaron, and right now, right at the moment, the boys would love to see you, I know — but right now — if you could give them a few minutes, Mrs. LeBaron, I'll tell them you're here — but right at the moment, *the boys are in the showers, Mrs. LeBaron!* Mrs. LeBaron!" Hurrying behind her, as she propels herself down the long corridor, around the corner, past the massage tables and the piles of exercise mats, past the weight machines and the row of urinals, where the air smells of a mixture of camphor and wintergreen oil and rubbing alcohol, toward the locker room and the sound of showers running.

"Don't worry, this won't take a minute," she says.

"*Boys!*" Harry Olsen shouts ahead into the sound of running water. "*Mrs. LeBaron is here!*"

Around one last corner, and into the big room full of steam.

There is a series of sudden yelps as the players recognize their visitor, and there is a collective grab for towels, and jockstraps that have been lowered to below the knees are hastily hoisted into position as the showers are, one by one, turned off.

"Boys, I know you're busy," Sari says cheerfully, "and I know you've got plenty to do this afternoon. But I wanted to drop by while I was in the neighborhood and have a few very brief words with you. There's a little matter I'd like to clear up, and I thought you ought to get it from me, personally — straight from the horse's mouth, as the fellow says. Now I know there've been published reports in the press — you've read them, I've read them — to the effect that I bought this club as a tax shelter. That, of course, is what reporters always do: speculate. Nobody knows what I do with my taxes besides myself, my accountant, and the IRS. So much for that. But that sort of speculation leaves the impression that I don't give a tinker's damn whether this team wins or loses. Boys, I'm here to tell you personally that that's not the truth. Not only do I care, but I care deeply. I bought this club because I thought it was a club that had it in it *to win ball games!* That's what I have faith you can do, and that's what I want you to do, and that's what I expect you to do. I want you all to give this club your best, and I want you to know that I'm behind you *all the way.* I want a team that will go into the World Series — if not this year, the next, and if not the next, then the year after that. Boys, I want a pennant, and I think you've got what it takes to give me that. You've got the *right stuff,* and that's why I bought this club. I want you to know that while you're out there, sweating and fighting and playing great ball on the field, I'll be up there in the stands sweating and rooting and praying — yes, praying — for you. I want you to know that I'm not going to be some kind of absentee landlord. I'm going to do my best for you, and I know you're going to do your damnedest for me, and someday we're going to be going to the Series together — and when we get there, *we're going to win!* Meanwhile, Harry here tells me you're training great, and you're looking great. Good! That's what I want to hear. Keep it up! We're in this together, all for one and one for all, and I'm behind you all the way and I know that you're behind me. That's all I wanted to say — good luck, good work, and God bless you all. You've got what it takes, and I love you for it. So now get out there — and *play ball!*"

Just as quickly as she arrived, she is gone.

In room 315 at the Marriott, the one out by the airport, the five members — four male, one female — of the group that calls itself The Dildos are snorting cocaine. At this very moment.

"So what the fuck are we going to do?" says Maurice Littlefield, who calls himself Luscious Lucius; who, without his makeup, is badly acne-scarred; and who, though he may be its lead singer, is not the group's brainiest member.

"Zip-dee-doo-dah," says one.

"Hey, man, listen to this," says another. He strikes a chord on his guitar. "Man, is that fuckin' cool?" He lies back on one of the two queen-size, unmade beds, his legs spread apart, his eyes staring at the ceiling, the guitar across his chest. He is the tallest of the group. Their respective names don't matter here.

"But what the fuck are we going to *do?*" Littlefield says again.

"Fuckin' board of directors won't pay us for the gig," says the tall one to the ceiling. "They're saying we 'presented material that was offensive to the public taste.' They had that in the contract."

"So what the fuck do we do? Fuckers owe us five thousand dollars."

"What the fuck did you have to kill Sylvia for? That was what did it."

"*The fucker bit me!*" Littlefield cries. "What the fuck do you think this is?" And he points to his bandaged upper arm.

"But did you have to do it right on the fuckin' stage? That was what did it. Fuckin' snake."

"I told you we should've took our money up front," says the female member. "Remember I said that?"

"Maybe we should hire a lawyer."

"Yeah, and pay him with what? Lawyers cost fuckin' money, man, and they want their money up front."

"What I want to know is how do we pay for this fuckin' motel room? How do we do that?"

"That's easy. We wait for dark, load our shit into the RV, skip town, and try to line up another gig."

"Yeah. Like we did in Topeka, and look where that fuckin' got us. Now we can't work anywhere in the whole state of Kansas."

"Is that where Topeka is — Kansas?"

"Fuckin' city."

"What we need is a hit single. That's what we really need. A hit single. A gold record."

"Yeah, and meanwhile how do we eat? What do we do?"

"Like, maybe, rob a bank?"

"You mean it — rob a fuckin' bank?"

"Only kidding, asshole."

"So what do we do?"

Still gazing at the ceiling, the tall one says, "What about that broad? Someone told me she was loaded."

"Loaded with what?"

"Money, asshole. Loaded with money. C-A-S-H — cash money."

"Which broad?"

"The one that came to hear us in Modesto. Shit, man, she was the one who got us last night's gig."

"Where was Modesto?"

"Shit, man, Modesto, California. A few months ago, remember? Came to hear us, and came backstage after. She got us this gig. She lives here."

"Oh, yeah. But wasn't she kind of *old*, man?"

"What the hell? She said she liked our sound. She said could we do this gig, remember?"

"Lucius'd have to fuck her to get the money out of her."

"I'm not fuckin' some old broad!"

The tall one sits straight up on the bed. "What the fuck difference does it make, asshole, how old she is, if she's got money? If she's got money, she can roll us out of here, and keep us rolling for a few more weeks till we get another gig."

"Yeah, Lucius should fuck her. Lucius got us into this fuck-up to begin with."

"Right! You get to fuck her, Lucius!"

"Fuck her, Lucius!"

"Shit, man, I don't even remember her name."

A silence.

"She was real thin. Brownish-colored hair."

"Oh, wow," says the tall one. "That's going to make her real easy to find. There can't be more than one thin broad with brownish-colored hair in San Francisco. We'll find her easy. You're an asshole, Lucius."

"She told me her name. McLaren?"

"No!" the tall one says.

"McCarran?"

"No, asshole! Her name is LeBaron — Melissa LeBaron. They make wine. You are a *total* asshole, Lucius."

"I'll fuck her! I'll fuck her!" Lucius says.

It is night now, and the big White Wedding-Cake House at 2040 Washington Street is quiet, its curtains drawn and closed against the night. We are a contented house, the curtained windows seem to say from under their carved marble eyebrows, the windows that address the quiet street. We are the sleeping eyes of a house at peace. There are no bad dreams, no scandals, to disturb our sleep, no unquiet memories to jar us from our slumber. This, at least, is what the south facade seems to be saying, but the north facade, invisible from the street, tells a different story. Here the house is wide awake, the curtains on the big windows of the north-facing drawing room kept fully open at her behest, because Assaria LeBaron never tires of her view, and wants it spread out for her inspection instantly, at whatever moment she might choose to admire it. The fog has lifted now — almost lifted — and only the very tops of the twin towers of the Golden Gate Bridge are obscured in clouds, and the orange lights that adorn the bridge's cables glitter like chains of stars. One can also see a few faint lights from Alcatraz, as well as from Tiburon and Belvedere, and the hills of Marin beyond.

From here, the waters of the Bay seem calm, but this is deceptive. The Bay is filled with tricky tides and dangerous crosscurrents, as prisoners who used to try to escape by swimming from Alcatraz soon discovered, and these tides and crosscurrents never sleep, and only drowned bodies ever made it to the shore.

The south facade of the house is dark, but from the north bright lights shine from all the windows, and at times like this the house seems all eyes and ears, and there are whispers that only Sari hears. *Is love important? I mean, is it important to be in love?*

In the drawing room, Thomas has filled the silver ice bucket and the Baccarat decanters, and everything is in readiness for Assaria LeBaron's cocktail hour — the monogrammed linen napkins (*ALLeB*), the silver jigger, the silver martini pitcher, the long-handled silver spoon, the ice tongs. But Sari has not entered the drawing room yet, and there is no one there to admire the expanding view as the fog continues to lift, and she has not yet mixed her first cocktail. Instead, for some reason, she is still in the long central portrait gallery, where the old wine cask sits. She touches this.

At times, though not tonight, the wine cask is warm to the touch, indicating that some sort of chemical activity, some form of fermentation, is still going on inside. The wine has not turned to vinegar but is still living, growing, changing. Also, there are times, under certain atmospheric conditions, when the wine cask will weep. Tiny beads of moisture will gather along the tight seams of the staves — more proof that Grandpa LeBaron's wine is still very much a living, breathing thing. Sari looks for these little beads — they sometimes appear on chilly nights like this one — but finds none.

There is another feature of the portrait gallery that some people never notice, but that others find peculiar. All the portraits on the walls, except for Grandpa's, which is an exact duplicate of the one hanging in Sari's office, are of children. This was Julius LeBaron's whim. "It will make the house stay young," he said. And so all the members of the family were painted at around age fourteen or fifteen, which Julius considered the perfect years between childhood and adulthood. It has become a family tradition, and it has been carried on. Though the clothes they wear vary according to the period, all the portraits contain certain details in common. All the boys are painted with hoops and dogs, the girls with birds and musical instruments.

There is Sari's husband, Peter, dressed for his first year at Thacher.

And there is Sari herself, painted as the artist imagined her at that age — for she did not meet Peter until she was some years older — seated at a piano. (Sari LeBaron cannot play a note.) And there, a certain distance away from these two, is the extraordinary Joanna, in her Miss Burke's School uniform.

There is Melissa. "When did she get to be a beauty?" Peter once asked. She's always been a beauty, you silly man. And there are the twins, Eric and Peeper, dressed by Robert Kirk, about to set off for Choate together. They were inseparable then, and even though Sari refused to dress them alike, they somehow always managed to do so. Athalie should be here too, but of course she isn't. Where is Athalie?

"Forget Athalie, Sari. Forget she ever existed."

But she did exist. She lived in my body for nine months. She had a name.

A girlish portrait of Alix, Eric's wife, is not there, for she has no business being there. She is not family. But Eric and Alix's twin daughters are there — Kim and Sloane — twins, but so unlike. One, Kimmie, is so pretty, while the other, Sloanie, is so . . . not unpretty, really, but plain. The phenomenon of twinning — no one really understands it fully. It is commoner in certain countries and cultures than in others, quite a rarity among black people. At the time her own twins were born, Sari was told that her age might have had something to do with it.

There is young Lance, Joanna's son.

The voices crowd in now, filling the long gallery.

"Pick a card, any card." This is Melissa.

Her mother picks a card. It is the jack of spades.

"Look at it, but don't show it to me. Now slip it back into the deck. Now we shuffle them." Melissa shuffles the cards, then fans them out, face up. "Your card," she cries triumphantly, "was the three of hearts!"

"No, Melissa, it was the jack of spades." Why hadn't she lied and let the trick succeed? Why, in a game of checkers with Melissa, had she never let Melissa win? At best, the game would end up as a draw — a black king and a red king, endlessly pursuing each other across the board, the story of their lives.

And now, in front of Joanna's portrait, Sari is listening to herself and Joanna, giggling, giggling and whispering together in the Japanese Tea Garden in Golden Gate Park as girls. "You've seen a man's *thing*, haven't you?" Joanna asks.

"Oh, of course," Sari half-lies. "But how does it *start?*"

"It starts with" — more giggling, more whispering — "it starts with — tickling."

"Tickling?"

And then she hears, imagines she hears, Joanna's throaty-husky voice, slurry from champagne: "Oh, my sweet . . . oh, my sweet . . . tickle me there . . . and there . . . and *there* . . . oh, yes . . . oh, my sweet. . . . Oh, oh, oh. . . . Oh, yes . . ."

But this erotic fantasy is interrupted by a voice from a long-ago maid who says, "Mrs. LeBaron, it's Mr. LeBaron senior on the telephone. He says it's urgent." And there is, in a secret compartment of a Regency games table in the drawing room, still a piece of green blotting paper on which, if held up to a mirror, can faintly be read the words, "I can no longer face this life . . ."

All these voices and messages inhabit the picture gallery tonight. Mama LeBaron, drunk in church, cursing the Host.

"Agnus Dei, qui tollis peccata mundi, miserere nobis . . ."

Mama, staggering toward the altar, pushing aside the hands that reach out to try to restrain her, screaming, "Where is the mercy for *me?*"

And then, an outside voice, from one of her many admirers: "Isn't Sari remarkable? What she's had to put up with from that family! Isn't she simply wonderful? She can manage *anything!*"

Except human beings. Who said that? Where did that disloyal voice come from? How dare such a statement be made in this house tonight!

"Pick a card, any card."

The trick fails again. "No, Melissa . . ."

They switch to a game of tic-tac-toe. No one wins it. The way Assaria LeBaron plays it, no one ever succeeds in drawing a straight line through their *X*'s or their *O*'s.

Would it have been different, Sari asks herself, if I had not made the decision that I did long ago and once upon a time? There is no point in asking. Sari makes her way out of the portrait gallery and into the lighted drawing room with its wide view of the lighted bridge, of Alcatraz and the other islands and, beyond these, the lights of Marin; away from the voices. In the drawing room are the makings of her customary martini. This is her evening ritual.

This house is my Alcatraz, she thinks, this house I never asked for, never said I wanted. I have been made a prisoner here, surrounded by objects I never chose. You will have eleven servants at your beck and call. But I'm not sure, Peter, how good I'll be at becking and calling!

Sari moves toward the drinks cart and the martini preparations. But no, first there is a small matter of business to attend to. She goes to a small French writing table, finds a sheet of her crested stationery and a pen, and writes:

> *My dear Archie:*
> *Thank you so much for the story in this morning's paper.*
> *And — ho-ho-ho! — weren't we lucky that the snake ''misbehaved''? We hadn't expected that, but that made it ''frontpage stuff!'' Anyway, I think this will help produce the precise results I'm after.*
> *Call me when you receive this note. I have another small favor to ask of you.*
> *Fondly, and, as always, in strictest confidence,*
> *A.L.LeB.*

She folds the letter, tucks it into an envelope, addresses it and seals it, then places it in a drawer for Thomas to hand-deliver in the morning.

Then she picks up the telephone and dials. "Melissa, dear," she says when there is an answer. "I'm about to have a cocktail. Would you like to come upstairs to join me?"

Outside, on the dark street, the guards at the Russian Consulate are changing. Facing them, the curtained windows of the house across the street say: We are a contented house. There are no secrets here, no uneasy ghosts to rattle our sleep. We are at peace.

Three

IN THE VILLAGE of Hillsborough, California, there is a curious social code, which only the initiated fully understand. Hillsborough is a very fashionable place to live, but those who understand the code know that, even if one lives there, it is not fashionable to say so. Hillsboroughites who are of the right sort always say that they live in Burlingame, which is just down the road. If you hear someone say that he or she lives in Hillsborough, you know immediately that that person is an upstart or a show-off or a climber, or all three. No one understands this code better than Alix Tillinghast LeBaron, who, though she lives in Hillsborough, is always careful to say that she lives in Burlingame. Alix LeBaron is a keen observer of all of San Francisco society's arcane rites and rituals.

She is also a woman who, for a ringing telephone, will drop absolutely nothing. At the moment, she is in the process of applying lacquer to her fingernails, and she has just reached the difficult part — applying the paint to the undersides of the nails, a procedure that requires great concentration and steadiness of hand, and many Kleenexes that her maid, standing beside her at her dressing table, dispenses to her, one by one, from a mirrored container. The telephone on her bedside table has rung five times now, and Alix has paid it no heed, preferring to direct her attention to the little bottle and the brush, and to the problem of the underside coating, which must go on just so, and must not be allowed to bleed over onto the flesh of the fingertips. "Damn!" she says, because that has just happened, and she reaches for a Q-Tip and the bottle of remover, for now she must start all over on that nail. The telephone rings a sixth time and a seventh.

Finally, Alix says, "Better get that, Katie, since nobody else seems to be going to."

Katie goes to the telephone. "Mrs. LeBaron's residence." And then, "One moment, ma'am." Covering the mouthpiece with one hand, she says, "It's Mrs. Tobin, ma'am."

"Damn!" says Alix again. Katie brings the telephone to her, and Alix LeBaron takes the receiver very carefully between the thumb and forefinger of her right hand, wiggling the other fingers in the air to speed the drying process. "Sweetie," she says into the phone. "Are you coming?" And then, "Oh, divine, darling! Oh, I'm so happy . . . no, of course that's no problem, darling. Bring him along. An extra man is always nice. See you in a bit, darling." She hangs up the phone without saying good-bye. To her maid, she says, "They're coming. Don't you hate it when people RSVP at the last minute? And they're bringing a friend. I'm sure he'll be ghastly — all their friends are. I hate the Tobins. Has Mr. LeBaron come in yet?"

"Not yet, ma'am."

Sitting there at her dressing table, wiggling her fingertips in the air to dry, checking the details of her makeup in the mirror, she thinks: *He is, I'm certain that he is, I know he is.* How do I know? I don't know how I know, perhaps it's woman's intuition, but I know that I know. He is. It is not the commonplace things — the vaguely explained late evenings at the office, though there have been a few of those — not things like that. It hasn't been any of the cliché things — the filament of long blonde hair on the shoulder of his blue suit jacket (a filament of long blonde hair could be her own), or the sudden whiff of an unfamiliar, exotic perfume, or the discovery of a stash of billets-doux. It has been nothing as precise or as incriminating as that. It is more a subtle change in his manner and attitude toward her, the occasional furtive look at her across the dinner table, a preoccupied air about him that she has noticed, and a forgetfulness. The other morning, spooning sugar into his coffee, he had for no apparent reason added a second spoonful to the cup, something she had never seen him do before. And the other night, as they were having drinks, she had noticed that he had two lighted cigarettes burning in his ashtray. It was little things like this — nothing definite to go on, to be sure — that had convinced her that her husband was getting it on with someone else. *Who is it?* she had almost asked him.

And then — Wednesday, it was, of last week — she had asked him as he left for work, "Do you think the Jap would have time to address the last of these invitations for me?" It had always been their little joke, calling his Oriental secretary "the Jap." He had referred to her as "the Jap" often, many times before. Their joke.

"Do you mean Miss Chin?" he had said.

"Yes — the Jap." But he had always known who the Jap was before.

Was it the Jap? But that would seem too much of a cliché, the obvious suspect, the secretary at the office. That was who it always was in soap operas and in comic strips, and short stories in *McCall's*. Surely Eric would have better judgment, better . . . taste. Of course, one heard a lot about male menopause, male mid-life crisis.

And now . . . tonight. He knows they are having a lot of people in for cocktails, important people — Herb Caen, the columnist, the William Crockers, the Jimmy Floods, the Tobins, and so on. And yet — where is he? It is now ten after six, and guests are invited for six-thirty.

Her nails are dry now, inside and out, and with a soft badger brush Alix applies a touch more blush to her cheeks, blends it in, and studies her reflection in the cool glass as Katie places the choker of twisted pearls at her throat and adjusts the emerald clasp. Alix reaches for the rheostat switch and dims, just slightly, the makeup lights that frame the mirror, thereby increasing her self-allure. I haven't held up badly, she tells herself. I've held up better than a lot of people I can think of. At thirty-six, I can still fit easily into the Jacques Fath I wore at my coming-out party. I've held up better than, for instance, Ann Getty, for all her money — Ann Getty, whom I happen to hate. I could have an affair, too, if I wanted to. If I wanted to, I could have an affair with . . . Peeper.

Why not? He'd probably do it, and so would I.

This is not a new notion of Alix's.

Having an affair with her husband's twin brother is an idea that is not without a certain . . . piquancy. She has always wondered just how identical the twin brothers *really* are. Are they identical in — *that* way, too? Often, seeing Peeper in his swim trunks, lounging by the pool, or bouncing on the diving board, or doing a handstand on the grass — showing off — she has thought: If only he would drop his trunks for me, then I could see if they are identical in *every* way. Of course, it would take more than just dropping his trunks to tell. There would have to be quite a bit more than that — *a lot more.* His swim trunks, even those skimpy bikini kind he sometimes wears, tell her nothing at all. It would be interesting to find out. She is pretty sure she could find out, and pretty sure he wouldn't mind.

That would show Eric.

Maybe tonight, she thinks, I'll make a little move in that direction.

"If you don't need me for anything else, ma'am, I think I'll see if I can help out downstairs."

"Thank you, Katie. You don't think the shoulder straps of this are too narrow?"

"You look just lovely."

Yes, she says to her lonely, lovely reflection in the glass, I will seduce Peeper, and I will begin tonight, and he will cooperate, and it will be only, simply fair. In her private rationale, she is entitled to an affair with Peeper. With Eric, she has always felt that she possesses only half of a matched pair, like owning a single earring, or inheriting only half of Aunt Sarah's Spode. And instantly in the mirror the scene is transformed from her suburban dressing room to the summer moonlit terrace by the pool, where the two of them are alone. Smiling, he lets her slide the bikini briefs down the length of his body with its smooth swimmer's muscles, and she finds him, as she knew she would, in a state of violent, stallion arousal. She sits on the moonlit chaise beside him, and kisses it. "You are so lovely!" he whispers, and cups one of her breasts in his hand, brushes his lips against the nipple as she studies his swollen member in her hand, so like Eric's, and yet somehow wildly *different*. Alix leans forward toward the mirror, and the ivory-handled hairbrush falls into her lap, and she presses the handle against herself, just as Peeper is pressing himself against her now. In the mirror now her face is flushed with sexual excitement, which makes her beauty seem only more luminous. Between her legs, the handle of the brush presses more persistently.

Now the second part of her fantasy begins, for Eric has joined them, and one of them has entered her from the front and the other from behind, and now she is complete, filled up with both of them. But of course this would never happen. Eric would never participate in such an outrageous, orgiastic tripling — sober, hardworking Eric and merry, carefree Peeper, the two opposing halves of that same split cell — but Alix can imagine it, anyway. In her imagination, there are no limits to the distances the three might go.

No, she will have to settle for Eric and Peeper separately.

And of course Eric will find out about it. She will have to confess it to him, and he will react to the news with a murderous frenzy of jealous rage — rage! But she will blame Peeper. In a torrent of tears, she will say, "But, darling, he forced me to! I must have been out of my mind to let him, but he looks so much like you I couldn't seem to resist him — it was all so sudden, I felt so helpless! Oh, darling, forgive me — it will never happen again, I promise you!"

(But it might happen again. That would show Eric again.)

But Eric will not forgive her, ever, and in his rage he will kill

Peeper, and now that familiar feeling of disorientation and anomie settles upon her, as the rest of the dreary scenario plays itself out, a feeling of cockroaches crawling around her heart.

Now Peeper is dead, and Eric has divorced her. She has gotten to keep the house, an arrangement that is almost standard in these cases. Eric has given her custody of the girls, and a large financial settlement. But what future does a thirty-six-year-old divorced woman with two teenage daughters have in a place like Burlingame — while Eric has gone off and married whoever she is?

But wait. Eric will be in prison. But perhaps not. A sympathetic judge — male, of course — will acquit him of the murder of his brother, or recommend leniency. Eric was the wronged party, it was a crime of passion. Temporary insanity. *Gentlemen of the jury, I charge you that the defendant is an upstanding member of this community, a pillar of his church, with no previous record of criminality. Standing before you is a decent, God-fearing citizen, driven to a murderous rage by the lustful, willful actions of his former wife. I therefore recommend . . .*

And so Eric will go off and marry whoever it is, and she will be left all alone in a big house in Burlingame, a divorced woman with two grown daughters, invited nowhere, a social pariah whom no man except a common gold digger will want to marry. She will lose her membership in the Burlingame Country Club. This is also standard in these cases. The club wants no single or divorced women. The widows of deceased members are bad enough. The club is obligated to keep those women on. But to single women and divorcées there is no such obligation. The Francisca Club will drop her, too, for during the ·divorce and murder trial the scandal of her adulterous behavior will have made headlines in all the papers. EX-DEB BEDDED DOWN BROTHER-IN-LAW! SOCIALITE SEDUCED HUBBY'S TWIN! And so she will end up all alone, hovering somewhere at the brink of middle age, friendless and clubless in an affluent country-club suburb of married couples, while he . . .

She will consider moving to the city, as others in her situation have done, and where they find the situation exactly the same. And where they find each other. And so they travel together, take cruises together, these lonely, untethered, aging women, looking in vain for husbands. They have their faces lifted, they color their hair. In the end, they may marry their hairdresser, and let his boyfriend move in with them.

But still. But still. Perhaps she will have an affair with Peeper, and *not* let Eric find out. But where would be the fun — where would be the sweet taste of revenge — in that?

"Hi, honey." His voice from the next bedroom interrupts her lubricious reverie and its dispiriting aftermath, and the ivory-handled hairbrush slides from her lap and lands on the white carpet with a soft plop.

"Darling, you're late! People are due here any minute."

"Sorry — got tied up on the phone."

"Well, hurry and get yourself *guapo*. I'll see you downstairs."

His head appears in her dressing-room door. He is tying his tie. "I forget," he says. "Did we invite Melissa tonight?"

"Darling, you know we agreed not to. We agreed that even if she is your sister, an extra single woman is a drag" — telling him exactly what she has been telling herself.

"Oh, yeah."

"Herb Caen wants to write this party up. We don't want it to be a drag." Privately, she is thinking that she cannot stand Melissa. She is also thinking: He didn't use to forget who we invited to our parties.

She rises now, in front of her mirror, adjusts the thin shoulder straps of her new Dior, and smooths the front of the dress. There is a slight feeling of wetness between her legs, but there is no time to change now, and besides, this is the dress she told Herb she would be wearing. She mists her hair and earlobes with a few more dashes of L'Air du Temps, and prepares to go downstairs and be the delightful, gracious, beautiful, and always popular Peninsula hostess that Herb Caen will tell his thousands of *Chronicle* readers that she is.

Half an hour later, the Eric LeBarons' cocktail party is in full swing.

"Darling, you look gorgeous!"

"Darling, so do you!"

"... And then we go to Acapulco for two weeks, and from there we fly directly to Cancun ..."

"How old *is* Ann, anyway? Thirty-eight? Thirty-nine?"

"I love your hair."

"There's a new little man at Magnin's, who ..."

"And so I said to her, 'If you're going to do this in a tent ...' "

"Who's that man standing by the piano, talking to Molly Tobin?"

"My dear, I've no idea!"

"He looks slightly — windblown, don't you think?"

"Yes, a little too blow-dried."

"... The minute you get to Las Brisas, you should call ... "

"Alix, darling, how *cute* of you to have your two little girls helping to pass things!"

"Seriously, I think it's important for them to learn how to run a cocktail party."

"Is that her own hair, or a wig?"

"Her! Why, that little tramp has been down on everything except the *Titanic!*"

"I *love* it!"

"And so I said to my product manager, 'You can't just put that red horse up there on the roof and have it sitting there, flapping its wings. It doesn't *mean* anything. It doesn't *say* anything.' "

"This is what Alix calls her 'A Group.' "

"Hmm."

"I sold mine at thirty-three and five-eighths, but now —"

"Her doctor told her that whenever she had a craving for a cigarette she should have a drink, and *now* look at her!"

"It's a wig. Her hair was short when I saw her last week at the club."

"Just how rich *are* the LeBarons, anyway?"

"You've heard the story of how Peter Powell LeBaron got his middle name —"

"They call the Washington Street house the Dago's Palace."

"... a barrel of wine in the portrait gallery ... "

"Wasn't that a riot about Assaria LeBaron in her jet?"

"Just took the controls, and — *whoosh,* under the bridge!"

"She must be quite bonkers."

"They say that if you cross her she'll chew you up and spit out the pieces."

"Where did she *come from* — does anyone know?"

"Well, her maiden name was Latham, which means nothing to anyone. Anywhere."

"I've heard that she was some sort of dancer, or show girl, and that Peter Powell LeBaron had to marry her."

"Oh, I've heard that too, for years. They went off to Europe on their honeymoon, and came home with —"

"Melissa. Five months later."

"Oh, I think it was longer than that — a year, maybe, but still. At the time, everybody thought it was awfully peculiar. I mean, getting pregnant on your honeymoon is one thing, but then doesn't one usually come *home* to have the baby? I mean, to make it an American citizen and all that."

"Poor Melissa."

"Actually, I like Melissa, but . . ."

"Yes, I know what you mean."

"They say that for years Assaria LeBaron has been having an affair with Gabe Pollack. Who owns the *Gazette.*"

"But isn't he a little — *minty,* as they say?"

"Minty?"

"Hush, darling — Alix is coming toward us. Alix, darling, how lovely you look!"

And so on. And so on.

The young man with the windblown-looking hair has approached Eric with his hand outstretched. "My host," he says. "Hi, I'm Archie McPherson."

"Eric LeBaron," Eric says. "Good to meet you, Archie."

"Nice of you and your wife to let me tag along," he says. "You have a beautiful home, and this is a swell party." A pause, and then, "Actually, I knew you and your brother at Yale."

Eric studies the young man's face, trying to connect it with some face from the past. "We knew each other at New Haven? I'm sorry, but . . ."

"Oh, you didn't know me," Archie says. "But I knew you. Everybody knew the LeBaron twins. You both ran with the Choate and Hotchkiss set. You were both Zeta Psi and Skull and Bones. I was just a scholarship kid from a public high school in Willimantic, Connecticut, so I didn't run with the right crowd. You and your friends used to look right through guys like me when we passed each other on the Quad."

"I see," Eric says, put off and annoyed. "You came with the Tobins tonight, right?"

"That's right."

"Well, you're running with the right crowd now." He tries to keep his tone pleasant, and yet somehow the remark comes out sounding nasty, snotty. But it is too late to retract it now, and so, smiling slightly, he moves away from Archie McPherson.

"Peeper, darling," Alix is saying. "You look a little sad tonight. Withdrawn."

"Sad? Withdrawn? On the contrary, Allie, I feel just great. Good party."

"Did you come alone, or bring a date?"

"Alone tonight," he says. "Right now, I'm between dancing partners."

"Ah, that's sad. You know, I sometimes worry about you, Peeper. With girls, you seem to go from pillar to post."

"Maybe that's sort of the way I like it, Allie."

"But wouldn't you like, someday, to have a really lasting, loving relationship with some special someone?"

"Get married, you mean?"

"Well, either that, or . . ."

He winks at her. "I say, why buy a cow when milk is so cheap?"

"Peeper, don't be common!"

"Is my Italian-immigrant background beginning to show, Allie?"

"No, but I just mean — aren't there times when you're all alone at night, in your apartment on Telegraph Hill, that you feel a little . . . well, a little lonely and neglected, and would like —"

"Got someone special in mind, Allie?"

"No, of course not, but —"

But a departing guest has cut into their conversation.

"Alix, it was a perfectly lovely party," the guest says. "You always do things in such a super way . . ."

And when Alix has turned away from this leave-taking, Peeper has disappeared.

Finding his brother, Peeper nudges Eric into a quiet corner of the living room. "Had a little chat with Mother today," he says.

"Really, Peep? What about?"

"Well, I was really pleased," he says. "It looks as though she's finally going to give me some real clout in the company — not just managing the goddamned Sonoma ranch."

"Really? What's she offering you?"

"She's talking of making me co–marketing director, along with you. Won't that be neat? We'll handle marketing together — as a team. Isn't that a neat idea, Facsi?" Sometimes, in playful moods, the brothers call each other "Facsi," which is short for "Fac-simile."

But Eric is not in a playful mood now. He is appalled at this news, and he takes a short step backward. He is appalled, and aghast, and stunned, and more hurt than he has ever imagined he could feel, hurt and betrayed. What she is talking about is nothing short of cutting his own job in half. Worse is the fact that she has made not one single mention, not given a single hint, of this pro-posed change in the directorship of marketing to him. She has gone behind his back, and offered her proposition to his twin without so much as consulting the man whose sole bailiwick marketing of Baronet supposedly is. Eric's head is suddenly so hot with anger and insult and resentment that he cannot speak, and making it even worse is having to look at his twin brother's happy, excited, expectant face. This horse's ass is standing here waiting for me to *congratulate* him, he thinks. *This horse's ass!*

"Won't that be neat, Facsi?" Peeper says. "Best thing is, I won't have that goddamned commute to Sonoma every day. I'll be work-ing right downtown with you!"

Still Eric cannot speak. How is it possible that his twin cannot be sensitive enough, intelligent enough, to understand how Eric feels?

From across the room, Alix sees the stunned and stricken look on her husband's face and, touching her father's sleeve, she says, "Daddy, do you think Eric's cheating on me?"

"Why, Buttercup, whatever makes you think a thing like that?" Harry Tillinghast asks.

"I don't know. Just a feeling. Call it woman's intuition, or whatever."

"Hasn't he been — treating you well, honey?"

"It's not that. It's just — just the way he's been acting lately."

"Well, honey," her father says, "I don't think he's cheating on you. If he ever did, he'd need to have his head examined." Then he says, "But I do know there's another woman in his life."

"Oh? Who?"

"His mother," Harry Tillinghast says.

"Oh," she says, disappointed. "Oh, that."

"What Eric needs now, more than anything, at this particular point in time, is to be given his head. He needs to take over that company — run it himself." He squeezes his daughter's arm. "And, Buttercup, your old daddy's gonna help him do it. Wait and see."

More guests are departing now, and there are more thank-yous and farewells and see-you-at-the-clubs. Standing beside Alix, sharing the hostly duties of accepting thanks for their hospitality, Eric says to her, almost absently, "By the way, I have to go to New York tomorrow."

"Really? Why?"

"Business."

"May I go with you?"

He shrugs. "Sure, if you'd like. It'll only be a couple of days. I'll be in meetings most of the time, but you can shop, I guess, or —"

"Well," she says, almost petulantly, "as a matter of fact I *can't* go with you. Sally Carrington is having a bridge luncheon at the club, and I accepted a month ago."

"Well, then —"

"Not that you care a bit whether I go with you or not!"

Looking sadly, not at her, but at some point in the distance over her left shoulder, Eric says, "Aw, honey . . ."

By nine o'clock, all the guests have gone, or nearly all. Alix LeBaron has stalked upstairs without saying good night, the help is in the kitchen cleaning up, and the girls are in the den watching television. Harry Tillinghast, who lives just down the road — actually *in* Burlingame, in fact — has stayed on, and he finds his son-in-law in the library, alone, hunched in one of the big leather chairs, nursing a brandy.

"Mind if I join you for a nightcap, Eric?"

"Sure, Pop." He gestures toward the bar.

Harry Tillinghast goes to the bar, fills a glass with ice, splashes in a healthy dollop of Scotch, and fills the glass with soda from the silver siphon. Then he takes a seat in a chair opposite his son-in-law. "Well, son," he says, "that was a real nice party."

"Thank you, Pop. Glad you could be here."

"I thought my little Buttercup looked beautiful, and your two little angels are turning into regular little ladies."

"Yes."

"My. How time goes by. I can remember bouncing those two little angels on my knee."

"Yes."

"You've been a good father, Eric, and a good husband to my little girl. It's been a good marriage, hasn't it? Everything is — good between you, isn't it?"

"I hope so," Eric says.

"Good," Harry Tillinghast says. "Good. Glad to hear it." The two men sit in silence for a few moments. Then, "How are things at Baronet?" Harry asks.

"Business is — okay," Eric says.

"Good," Harry says. "I hear by the grapevine — no pun intended — that Pepsi-Cola is after Baronet again."

Eric shrugs. "They've been after us for years."

"So I understand," he says, and chuckles. "Now that I'm one of your stockholders, they've even sent out some feelers in my direction. I told them I was just small potatoes in Baronet, very small potatoes." He pauses, and then, "I don't suppose you'd ever think of selling."

"No way."

Harry Tillinghast extracts a long cigar from his jacket pocket, and carefully trims it with a gold cigar clipper, then places the cigar in his mouth and lights it with a matching gold lighter. The flash of gold is everywhere about Harry's person — his cuff links, his big signet ring, even a gold belt buckle. "Assaria wouldn't stand for it, I suppose," he says around the cigar.

"That's right."

"How are you and your mother getting along these days, son?"

"Oh, about the same as usual," Eric says. "We have our ups and downs." She is now trying to strip me of half my job responsibilities, he thinks. But he cannot bring himself to tell his father-in-law this. The insult is too fresh, the humiliation too new.

"Mustn't let her shove you around, boy," Harry says. "I know your mother, and I know she has a tendency to shove people around."

Eric says nothing.

Puffing on his cigar, Harry says, "You know, I've been thinking quite a bit lately about Baronet — about the future of Baronet. It's not just because I've recently become a stockholder. I've been thinking about *your* future. What's going to happen to the company, Eric, when you mother goes? She's not young, Eric, and none of us are getting any younger."

"Mother is immortal." He is feeling a little drunk.

"Well, nobody is immortal, boy," Harry says. "And when your mother goes, with all that stock she owns, her estate could be in for some very heavy taxes. *Very* heavy. Which her heirs would have to pay. Why, you could lose the company just like *that*," and he snaps his fingers.

"Mother says if she ever sells, it'll only be for cash. And she says there's not enough cash in the world to make her sell."

"Very foolish of her, isn't it," Harry says. "Very foolish. All the cash she gets will just be gobbled up by taxes — you know that."

"Try explaining that to Mother."

"Any woman in her position would — if she were well advised — sell Baronet for stock. Either to Pepsi, or to someone else. If she were well advised."

"No one gives advice to my mother."

"Or, if she were forced to sell, by a majority of other stockholders."

"Ha!" Eric says. "No way!"

"Now, don't be so defeatist, Eric. There's always a way — that's my motto. Where there's a will, there's a way."

"Not with Mother."

"Don't be too sure, Eric," Harry says. He takes a deep puff on his cigar and exhales a series of perfectly formed smoke rings. Staring at the ceiling and the dissolving rings, he says, "What would you say, Eric, if I told you that I was interested in taking over Baronet?"

"I'd say you were crazy."

"Maybe so, maybe no. It's a damned good company, and what I'm saying is that I — and by I, I mean Kern-McKittrick — am interested in taking over Baronet. And by I, I also mean you and I. I'll need your help."

"Pop, there's just no way to do it."

"Because my object in doing this would be to put you in the driver's seat. Completely. Baronet would become a division of Kern-McKittrick, and you'd be head of it. Completely. You'd be at the helm, and she'd be out. What would you say to that?"

Eric shakes his head. "I dunno, Pop. I just dunno."

"She's not the majority stockholder, you know. There's yourself, your brother, your sister, your aunt Joanna, your cousin Lance — and me. With enough votes on our side, we could get her out. And you in."

He shakes his head again. "Pop, I just don't think we could ever pull it off."

"Look at it this way, son. Your mother owns thirty-five percent of the outstanding shares, correct?"

"Correct."

"And your aunt Joanna owns another thirty-five percent — correct?"

"That's right."

"And, together, you and I own five percent. Melissa owns another five, and Peeper another five. Would Peeper and Melissa go along with us?"

"I wouldn't count on Peeper for too much at this point," Eric says.

"Then there's your cousin Lance. Somehow, he got fifteen percent under your daddy's will."

"The will was meant to be fair — fifteen percent for his kids, and fifteen percent for his sister's kids. What happened was that Joanna only had one child."

"I understand that. My question to you is this: If it came to a vote, would Lance vote with his mother, or against her?"

"With her, I guess."

"Yes, that would be my guess, too. He's never shown any interest in Baronet beyond collecting dividends, has he?"

"It's been at least five years since he's even come to California."

"So you see, Joanna is our key. With her votes and Lance's plus yours and mine, we have a clear majority — fifty-five percent."

Eric considers this for a moment. "Yeah," he says at last, "but Joanna, besides being my aunt, is also my mother's oldest and dearest friend."

"Somehow, son, when big money is involved, friendship turns out not to count for much — even the oldest, dearest kind. Sounds cynical to say so, but that's what I've found in business. Money talks, and the bigger it is the louder."

"But suppose Mother threatened to take our ad account away from Joanna's agency unless Joanna agreed to go along with her? How would that look in the press? 'LeBaron and Murdock lose family account.' Pretty humiliating."

"If Joanna's worried about that, she must know your mother isn't such an old and dear friend," Harry says.

"No, but that's just the sort of thing Mother might —"

"So all we do is make that part of the deal. If Joanna will go along with us, we agree to keep the business with her agency — hell, for twenty, twenty-five years, whatever she wants. *And* we sweeten the deal by agreeing to pay her full commission, which she isn't getting now."

Eric studies his father-in-law's face. "You know," he says. "I'm beginning to think it might work."

"Plus, I understand that this morning your mother turned down a new ad campaign that Joanna's people had worked up. And turned it down in not a very ladylike way, or a very friendly way. Joanna won't be too happy about that, will she?"

"How," Eric asks slowly, "did you hear about that?"

"Peeper mentioned it tonight at the party. He and your mother had some sort of meeting this afternoon."

Peeper! That stupid horse's ass! How much else did Peeper tell him? Probably everything, Eric thinks. But he says, "That ad campaign happened to be shit!"

Harry spreads his hands. "That's neither here nor there," he says. "The point is that Joanna's not going to be very happy when she hears about this morning's meeting, is she? Not all that happy about the way her old, dear friend is treating her. Peeper told me that Assaria said that Joanna must be losing her marbles — right in front of Joanna's own account exec and creative team!"

Peeper!

"Golly, if that goes into her people's conference report — and it might, because I gather those boys were sore as hell — how's that going to make Joanna feel about her old, dear friend?" Harry leans toward him. "Joanna's our key, and this may be just the moment, boy, to make Joanna a nice fat offer of Kern-McKittrick stock if she'll help us vote your mother out. You see, the trouble with your mother is that she doesn't keep her promises. I think you've had some evidence yourself of that."

Suddenly Eric laughs. He has just remembered Fairy Ferris, and the call-back list. "Her call-back list," he says.

"What's that?"

"After Dad died, and Peeper and I were still pretty young, Mother told us that she was going to have to be both a mother and a father to us now. And then we were sent away to school, and we hardly ever heard from her. Once a month there was our allowance check, with a typed note from her secretary. Oh, she'd telephone us a couple of times a week, and Peeper and I'd get a message that our mother had called. But half the time she called it was either during study hall, or after lights-out, or in the middle of a soccer game, or some damn thing like that, so we didn't get to talk to her. We'd call back, and be told that she was in conference and we'd be put on her call-back list. She never wrote us letters.

"Hey, we used to ask ourselves, where's this mother-and-a-father bit? And then, in the middle of our first year at Choate, Peeper and I got into big trouble — when you're thirteen, any trouble seems like big trouble. We were scared we were going to be expelled, and so I tried to call my mother — it was about this guy we all called Fairy Ferris, who was trying to sort of blackmail us — and —" Eric sees his father-in-law stifling a yawn, and Eric stares down at his empty glass. "Anyway," he says, "it's a long story, and pretty boring. But when I tried to get Mother on the phone to tell her, her secretary wouldn't put me through, even though I said it was an emergency. Her secretary said all she could do was put my name on Mother's call-back list. There were about a hundred names on the list ahead of mine, so it was about eight hours before she returned my call, and by then — well, never mind."

"Well, I've never understood your mother," Harry says. "She'll say one thing and then do another. She likes to keep things stirred up. Maybe she thinks that by keeping things stirred up she gets everybody to work harder. Maybe she thinks that if people don't know what they're supposed to be doing from one day to the next, it'll keep them on their toes and they won't settle into a routine. This new plan to make Peeper co–marketing director, for instance."

"So Peeper told you about that, too."

"What's that going to accomplish besides stirring things up between you and your brother? I say that's no way to run a business. All that does is create divisiveness and a bunch of unhappy executives on your team."

"Yes," Eric says with a sigh. "It does that."

"So what you're trying to tell me, with that story about her whatchamacallit list, is that you're sick and tired of being treated like a thirteen-year-old, right?"

"I guess so," he says. But it wasn't that, not really.

"Well, I agree. We've got to let you achieve your full potential. And, like I say, Joanna is our key. And I'm not saying that it's not going to be tricky. It may be *very* tricky. We've got some rough road to cover, there's no denying that. There's no free lunch, as the fellow says, and it would be a good idea to get Peeper and Melissa on our side, too —"

"Forget Peeper!"

"Well, at least Melissa, then. And with Kern-McKittrick behind you, boy, I'm telling you *it can be done!*" With his free hand, he reaches out and clamps his palm firmly across Eric's knee. "Son," he says, "I've built a life, built a career, built a business worth more than eight hundred million dollars, watched myself become a rich man, done it all with just one basic philosophy — nothing is impossible. Everything is *possible.* If you want a thing hard enough, bad enough, big enough, the impossible is *always* possible. Everything I've done in life, I've done believing that. So — are you with me, son?"

Eric looks across at him, and their eyes meet and lock. "As it happens, I'm having dinner with Joanna in New York tomorrow night," he says.

"Strike — while the iron is hot. Don't tell her her campaign was shit, even if it was. Tell her that it was brilliant, and how your mother gunned it down." Harry's tone, now, grows sentimental, and his eyes grow moist. "I want it for my baby girl," Harry Tillinghast says. "And I want it for my beautiful grandkids, and for *your* grandkids, and *their* grandkids, and I also want it for you, son. For *you.*"

Four

IN THE WHITE WEDDING-CAKE HOUSE at 2040 Washington Street, atop Pacific Heights, it is ten o'clock, and Assaria LeBaron and her daughter, Melissa — who has stayed on for dinner at her mother's suggestion — are also having a nightcap, in the north drawing room overlooking the Bay and the Golden Gate. The fog has lifted completely now, and the tops of the bridge's towers are fully visible, and tomorrow may be crystal clear, though one cannot be sure. Often, in the hours just before dawn, the fog will come sweeping in from the ocean again, and by daybreak the city will again be enshrouded.

On the whole, the evening has gone well to Sari's way of thinking — giggly and intimate, the way the two so often used to be together. The evening has been a sentimental tour down memory lane, with Sari as its guide, concentrating, of course, only on the happy memories. Do you remember . . . ? they have been asking themselves. Do you remember when you were a little girl, Melissa, five or six, and we were spending the summer at Bitterroot, and you came running into the house and said, "Mother, there's a whole celebration of dandelions on the front lawn!" Did I say that? You did, you did, and I thought, what a wonderful expression — a celebration of dandelions! And I thought, what a wonderful imagination Melissa has! No, I don't remember that, Mother, but I do remember the day, at Bitterroot, when the bees swarmed in your hair. Oh, yes, yes, I remember that vividly. I'd been swimming in the lake, and I was letting my hair dry in the sun. First one bee came, and I started to brush it away, and then more came, and then I saw the whole swarm coming, and I saw that the swarm intended to settle there, hanging down my back from my hair. And we were all so terrified, Mother — I remember that I screamed. We all thought you were going to be stung to death! Yes, I remember that you screamed, and I remember telling you to hush, that there wasn't any danger. You see, even then I knew my bees. Bees in a swarm will almost never sting. I knew that all I had to do was sit very still, no sudden movements, and wait until the bees had decided where to locate their new hive. After about twenty minutes, they began to fly away, and soon they were all gone, and I wasn't stung, not once. I was so terrified, Mother! Not I — it was a very peaceful feeling, really, almost like a religious experience — at least the closest thing I've ever had to one.

The lake. Do you remember the time Father threw me off the pier, into the deep water of the lake, thinking that this would make me teach myself to swim? No! I remember no such thing! I guess I was afraid to tell you, Mother, afraid you'd think it was just another one of my crazy fantasies. But it happened. I was sitting on the edge of the pier, splashing my feet in the water, and he suddenly reached down, lifted me by the armpits, and tossed me out into the deep water. I remember myself slowly sinking, and thinking to myself, Well, so this is what it is like to drown. I am drowning now, and this is what it is like. As the water got darker around me, I made no effort to save myself, and simply let myself sink like a stone. You mean you didn't kick your legs, move your arms . . . ? No, and I remember my first mouthful of water. *Melissa!* Because, you see, I used to think Father wanted to kill me. I thought at the time: Well, my father wants me to drown, and now he is drowning me, so I will drown.

Melissa — what a foolish, foolish thought!

He never loved me, you know. I remember being quite surprised when I felt someone's arms around me, pulling me to the surface, and realized he had jumped in the lake to save me.

(Or, in your perverse way, you wanted to terrify your father, punish him by making him think he had almost drowned you, Sari thought, but she has not said this.)

Change the subject. Do you remember the wonderful picnics we used to have, Melissa? Do you remember the day your father shot the spider? Bees I understand, but spiders have always terrified me. Suddenly, while we were having our picnic, this huge spider came crawling toward me across the grass, and this time it was *I* who was screaming. And your father simply reached into his belt, where he always carried his pistol, pulled the pistol out, and shot the spider! Why did he always carry a pistol, Mother? Well, remember that we are talking about the nineteen thirties, Melissa. There were lots of labor troubles in those days, trouble with the field hands. He thought it was a good idea to carry a pistol in his belt, just to let them know that he had it. To my knowledge, he never used it except that one time, to kill my spider . . .

(Except — except one other time. But change the subject.)

Do you remember . . . ?

Oh, oh, oh. What fun we had.

Now, over their nightcaps, Melissa is showing her mother the snapshots from her trip to Paris, where she went for Christmas to visit galleries and museums, and Sari is paying only half-attention to the photographs. It has been a long day, and though she has accomplished much, there is still much more that remains to be accomplished. In the soft lamplight, with her hair framing her face, Melissa's years seem to fade away, at least many of them, and her youthful beauty becomes visible. The same fine facial bones are there, and Melissa still wears her hair in a youthful style. *When did she get to be a beauty? She's always been a beauty, you silly man. It's just —*

To Sari's way of thinking, Melissa is too thin. But that is the way she's always been, proud of her size-six figure, proud of her size-four shoes, which, with high heels, enhance her slender legs. Melissa is always weighing herself and measuring herself, the better to rid herself of any errant pound, any errant inch, the minute it appears on her Fairbanks scale or tape measure. Accepting the snapshots as Melissa hands them to her, one by one, Sari makes the appropriate pro forma comments. "Ah, the Palais du Louvre . . . I haven't been to Paris for years, I must go back . . . ah, the Eiffel Tower . . . and Versailles . . . lovely . . . oh, look, the Christmas lights on the chestnut trees along the Champs-Elysées . . . the fountain at Concorde . . . lovely . . . the Place de l'Opéra . . . oh, I remember these places all so well, Melissa. But now where's this?"

"Vincennes."

"Oh, of course, of course."

"And this is me, in front of the Plaza Athenée. I had the doorman take it for me."

"Very pretty. . . . And now who's this?" Another unfamiliar view.

"My ski instructor."

"Very good-looking. But — ski instructor? Where did you ski in Paris?"

"This wasn't Paris. This was in Saint Moritz."

Sari hesitates. "Saint Moritz? You didn't tell me you were going to Saint Moritz, Melissa."

Melissa glances at her mother. "Didn't I?"

"You most certainly didn't."

"Well," Melissa says, "I did. It was so close, and so I thought, why not?" She hands her mother another picture.

"Another of the handsome ski instructor. Do I detect a romance here, Missy?"

Melissa laughs. "No, but he helped me work on my parallel turns."

Taking another picture, Sari says, "And who is this gentleman?"

"Andrea Badrutt. He owns the Palace Hotel."

Sari stares at the picture. "Andrea Badrutt. He was just a little boy when I first knew him. He's an old man now."

"Yes, and quite lame, I'm sorry to say."

"Andrea Badrutt," she repeats. "So you stayed at the Palace."

"Yes."

"And never mentioned a word of this to me. I find that quite extraordinary."

"I guess I just forgot," Melissa says. "I wanted to go back and see the place where I was born."

"How very — odd. Whatever for?"

"I don't see anything odd about a person's wanting to see the place where she was born," Melissa says.

"I still find it odd. I would never want to go back to see the place where *I* was born."

"Well," Melissa says carefully, "I guess I'm a person who's always done odd things, aren't I, Mother?"

"Oh, no," Sari says quickly. "Not odd. Unconventional, perhaps. And imaginative. 'A celebration of dandelions' — I'll never forget that. But I do think it's odd that you never mentioned this part of your travel plans to me. And — but never mind." Change the subject. "Speaking of attractive young men, have you seen any more of that nice Archie McPherson lately?"

"Not recently, no."

"He's so attractive. And I think he likes you. Have you been to bed with him yet?"

"Mother! What a thing to ask!"

"Well, you know me," Sari says. "I believe in calling a spade a spade. I'm a Thoroughly Modern Millie, as they say. I wouldn't give a hoot — not one hoot — if you'd been to bed with an attractive man, as long as he's not a gold digger after your money, or that sort of thing. And Archie's not that sort, I can tell."

"He's Eric and Peeper's age, for heaven's sake."

"Well, I always thought you were attracted to younger men. Nothing wrong with that. Nothing wrong with being attracted to younger men, though I myself was always attracted to somewhat older men. Difference in tastes, that's all."

"Well, I *haven't* been to bed with him!"

Change the subject. "By the way, I was so sad to read about what happened at your rock concert."

"*My* rock concert?"

"Weren't you the one who arranged it?"

"Yes, but how did you know that, Mother?"

"Someone — I forget who — said that you were the one who wanted to book them into the Odeon. Anyway, it was too bad about what happened."

"I'm sick about it," Melissa says. She rises and moves to the bar, and splashes more whiskey in her glass. This is a bad sign — another drink, when Sari knows that Melissa has been trying to control her drinking — but there is nothing to be done about it. "I'm just sick about it," she says, her head lowered. "And now the stupid board has voted not to pay them for the evening. For presenting offensive material. It wasn't *their* fault that the snake bit someone!"

"Very embarrassing for you, of course."

"Not embarrassing for me — but terrible for them! To come all this way to put on a performance, and not get paid."

"Oh, but I expect they have pots and pots of money. All those rock stars do. They have million-dollar mansions in Beverly Hills."

"Not *this* group. They're young, they're just starting out. They've been playing little dink-donk cities like Stockton and Modesto. This was to be their first big chance, their first important engagement. And now — no money."

"Well, after all, a snake act —"

"The audience loved them up until that point! What happened was just an accident. The audience was cheering them up to that point, Mother! It was wonderful, up until then!"

"Well, I wouldn't fret about it if I were you, Missy." Change the subject. "Have we seen all the pictures from your trip?"

"The little lead singer — he's just a boy — the one who was bitten — called me up this afternoon. Practically in tears. My heart ached for him. I've arranged to meet with them tomorrow, to see what can be worked out. They've had expenses to come here, and now no money to pay for anything. I may end up deciding to pay them out of my own pocket."

"Now, Missy, I hardly think that would be necessary."

"But don't you understand? I feel responsible. Morally responsible. It was all my idea — don't you see?"

"Well, I think that's awfully nice of you," Sari says gently. "Even though, if it were me — but never mind."

"It's only five thousand dollars. But it means everything in the world to those poor kids right now."

"Well, your money is yours to do with as you wish," Sari says. "But perhaps there's a moral to be learned from all of this."

"Moral? What moral?"

"Well," she begins carefully, "sometimes I wish you'd consult me before undertaking some of these projects of yours, Missy, before getting so — involved. If you did, I might be able to —"

She is still standing by the bar, alternately sipping from her drink and staring into the glass. "Consult?" she says slowly. "Why should I consult you, Mother? I'm fifty-seven years old. Why should I consult you on anything?"

"Oh, just because . . . because . . . because I've had a few more years' experience in community service, Missy, and — ha-ha — a few more years' experience at living. And because I care — deeply — about you, Melissa, and hate seeing you getting into these pickles."

"Pickles? I'm not in any pickle!"

In the distance, there is the sound of a telephone ringing. "Who could be calling at this hour, I wonder," Sari says. And then, "Well, I've said all I intend to say, Missy. I just want you to know that I'm always here when you need me, and if you ever think you'd like my opinion or advice, you might just find that the old lady's opinions and advice aren't all that bad. That's all. Don't look so angry! Remember what your father used to say when you were little? 'Be careful, or your face might freeze with that expression.' "

"My father never said that to me."

"Anyway, I think it's time we both went to bed."

But Thomas has appeared at the door in Pullman slippers. "It's Mr. Eric," he says, "for Miss Melissa."

"Eric!" Sari cries. "How did he know you were here?"

"Probably," Melissa says, "because he called downstairs first, and my housekeeper told him that *here* was where I was."

"I thought I left instructions that there were to be no calls!"

"I'm sorry, Madam," Thomas says. "But you did not say no calls for Miss Melissa."

Melissa throws Sari a challenging look. "I'll take it here," she says to Thomas, and walks to the other end of the room, where the telephone sits on a stand.

And Sari turns her wheelchair in the opposite direction, pretending to shuffle through the stack of snapshots in her lap, elaborately pretending not to be listening to the conversation.

"Eric," she hears Melissa say. "Well, I'm busy tomorrow afternoon. . . . Oh, I see. . . . Well, that would be fine. I'll see you then. 'Night, Eric."

After a moment, in a disinterested-sounding voice, Sari says, "Well, what did Eric want at this ungodly hour?"

"He wants to have breakfast with me tomorrow before he leaves for New York."

She spins her chair around sharply to face her. "New York! I know of no trip to New York! I've authorized no trip to New York for Eric! What's he going to New York for?"

"He didn't say, Mother. Business, I suppose."

"He's up to something — I knew it! I knew it all along. He's up to something, and he's going to see Joanna. My hunch was right! And I know who's behind this, too!"

"Who, Mother?"

"Harry Tillinghast! I've known that ever since Eric sold him that Baronet stock of his. That, too, was unauthorized."

"I always thought that each of us was free to sell our stock to whomever we chose, Mother."

"I should have been consulted! Eric had no right to sell that stock without consulting me! Do you realize that that's the first time in the history of the company that a single share of Baronet has ever passed outside this family?"

"But Harry is Alix's father."

"He's not a LeBaron! He's an oil man, and he's a slippery, wheeling-dealing conniver, and now that he's got his toe in the door he's trying to pull off some sort of deal behind my back!"

"You don't know that, Mother."

"I know that oil and wine don't mix — they're the most poisonous combination there is — and I know I've never trusted Harry Tillinghast. He is a scoundrel and a scum!" She pauses to catch her breath. "Very well, Missy," she says. "Here's what I want you to do. I want you to have breakfast with your brother tomorrow, and find out just as much as you can. Find out why he's suddenly going to New York, find out what he's going to do there, who he's going to see — *everything*. And then I want you to report straight back here to me. Do you understand?"

Melissa is moving slowly across the room now toward her mother's chair, and she pauses in front of the fireplace with its high carved marble mantel. "Stop," she says finally. "Just stop. Stop giving orders. Stop giving orders to me, and to everybody else. Stop trying to control everybody. Stop trying to control where I go on my holidays, stop trying to control whom I see and what I do, and whom I sleep with, and how I spend my money. *Stop trying to control me. Just stop.*"

"I try to control you because you can't control yourself!"

"Then tell me who my mother is!"

"Oh, Melissa, please — not again."

"Tell me who my mother is! It isn't you, I know that."

"Now *you* stop. We've —"

"It couldn't be you. No mother who cared about her daughter would have done what you've done to me — turned me into a lonely, neutered, neurotic spinster!"

"You've had too much to drink!"

"A lonely, neutered, neurotic, alcoholic spinster!" There is a Baccarat millefiori paperweight on a low table just beside the fireplace, and Melissa seizes this and, all in the same motion, hurls it hard against the marble hearth, where it explodes with a flash of fire. "Tell me who my mother is!"

There is a long silence, and the thousands of tiny shards of colored glass glitter on the marble hearth in the lamplight like the lights from the bridge, and from Marin County in the distance behind them, tiny lights of pale green, gold, and bright red.

Finally, Assaria LeBaron says in a dead voice, "I loved that little piece, but of course you knew that. It was quite old, nearly as old as you are. Your father bought it for me in Paris. I'm sorry you did that, Melissa."

"Then tell me who my mother is."

*   *   *

Alone in his bedroom in Burlingame, Eric LeBaron cannot sleep. The brandies after dinner should have done the trick, but they have not. He has a full day of work and travel ahead of him in the morning, and he knows he must sleep, but still he cannot. His mind is racing, racing full of thoughts. "You are talking about driving a wedge between the members of my family," he had said to Alix's father. Harry had replied, "The wedge is already driven. Assaria is the wedge."

Alix has gone off to bed in her own room in some sort of snit. What it is about, Eric cannot imagine. He had thought the evening went reasonably well. All the people whom Alix had wanted to be there were there. But on the doorknob of her bedroom door she has hung her little needlepoint pillow by its pink velvet loop. On the pillow, in needlepoint, are depicted a snoozing bunny and the words PWEASE DO NOT DISTURB. I'M WESTING. So that was where she was, in whatever sort of snit she was in. Sooner or later he will find out what it is all about. He is really in no great hurry to know.

In the darkness now he is trying to think what it was that first made him fall in love with Alix, where the turning point came between Alix as a pleasant dinner partner, companion, and date, and Alix as the woman he would ask to marry. There was her beauty, of course. The *Chronicle* had crowned her "Deb of the Year," or something like that, that year, her debutante year, sixty-five or sixty-six, whatever it was. But then, he remembers, he had also found her funny and cute — fey. I'M WESTING. The baby-talk bit. *Do you like butter? Does-ums?*

Yes, he remembers them sitting in the grass on a hilltop over-looking Half Moon Bay, and she had reached down and picked a buttercup and held the blossom under his chin. "Do you like butter?" she had said. And then, "Oooh — you don't like butter!"

"What in God's name are you talking about?"

"Look — hold it under my chin. Now, do you see the yellow reflection on my skin? That's how you tell whether a person likes butter. If a person *likes* butter, you'll see the yellow reflection from the buttercup. If they don't like butter, there's no reflection. You don't give off any reflection, Eric. So."

"That's about the silliest damn thing I ever heard of. I do happen to like butter."

"My daddy taught me that little trick. He calls me his little Buttercup."

No, the best way to deal with Mother, he has decided, is absolutely straight from the hip, absolutely straight on, absolutely open and above board. Mother expects deviousness, tricks, secrets, plots, conspiracies, whispered conferences behind closed doors, tapped telephones, that sort of thing. She is the Richard Nixon of the business world. Her logic is often Byzantine in its complexity. She is unaccustomed to — indeed, often completely thrown by — total candor and honesty. I have nothing to hide from you, Mother, and so I'm laying my cards on the table, face up. I am trying to put together enough stockholder votes from the other members of this family to take over this company and, yes, Harry Tillinghast is behind me all the way. It's as simple as that. If you want to call it a battle, then call it one, but it's going to be a battle that's fought right out in the open, no secret deals, no double-crosses, just a good, old-fashioned fight for control, with everyone deciding just where he or she wishes to side in the matter. The matter will be decided in the only fair way, in the only democratic way, at the ballot box, one vote per share. If I lose, I lose, but I'm going to do my damnedest to win, and I'm going to fight a clean fight. No behind-the-door or under-the-table deals, no blackmail or bribes or secret payoffs. At least, that's how *I'm* going to fight for this thing, Mother. Of course, how *you* choose to fight it is up to you, and may the best man win. Yes.

If she won't see me, or come to the phone for me, I'll put it to her as straightforwardly as possible in a letter. A registered letter. Return receipt requested. And the same registered letter to all the others. And one to myself, which I will leave unopened, as proof of my good faith and fair intent and whatever and whatever, for we are dealing with Eric, the good little Boy Scout, here. I'll get the lawyers to draft the letter. Yes. Make a mental note of that, he tells his racing mind.

At some point, the press may have to be brought in on it, and here Gabe Pollack might be of some use, but maybe not. Make a mental note of that also.

Fairy Ferris. Fairy Ferris must have had some other, ordinary name — John, George, Howard, whatever — but what it may have been has long ago been forgotten. He will always be remembered as Fairy Ferris.

At Choate, where they were sent at age thirteen, the twins were placed in separate classes whenever it was possible. This was supposed to encourage competitiveness and individuality, and their mother approved of this arrangement. By the time they arrived in Wallingford, Fairy Ferris had already achieved a certain reputation. He was an older boy, a fourth-former, and though nobody at Choate would admit to liking him, there were rumors that certain boys didn't mind doing certain things that Fairy Ferris liked to do with them.

In school, for some reason, Eric was excellent at math but terrible in English, while Peter was good in English but poor at math. For this reason, Eric would always do Peter's math homework for him, and Peter would write Eric's English compositions. Since their handwriting was virtually identical also, none of their teachers suspected the deception. For tests and exams, if it was to be a math test, Eric would slip into Peter's classroom and take his seat at Peter's desk. For English tests, Peter would do the same for Eric. In a vague sort of way, the boys knew that this was cheating, but it seemed to them like cheating of the mildest, most harmless sort.

One late autumn day in Wallingford, that first year away at school, Eric had just taken a math test for Peter, and was approached in the corridor by Fairy Ferris.

"You're Eric, aren't you," Fairy Ferris said.

"No, I'm Peter," Eric said.

"I know you're Eric," Fairy Ferris said. "You have that little scar on your temple. Your twin brother doesn't have one."

Eric had reddened. "So what!" he had said.

"I know what you've both been doing," Fairy Ferris said. "What would you do if I said I'm going to tell Headmaster?" Eric will always remember the way he pronounced the word, "Head-*mah*ster."

Then Fairy Ferris had said, "If you'll both give me a blow job, I won't tell."

That was when the twins had tried to call their mother in California.

Eric remembers Miss Curtin, who was their mother's secretary then, as an even worse dragon than Gloria Martino. "Your mother is in conference," Miss Curtin had said. "I'll put you on her call-back list."

"But Miss Curtin, this is *important*."

"I'm sorry, Eric, but all I can do is put you on your mother's call-back list. She will return each call in the order that it was received."

"How many calls has she got to return before she returns mine?" Eric had asked, feeling desperate.

"Well, I don't know *exactly*," Miss Curtin had said in a peevish-sounding voice. "Do you expect me to *count* them for you? But there are quite a few."

"Miss Curtin — *please!*"

"This is an office, and this is office routine, Eric," she had said. "My instructions are to make no exceptions."

"Miss Curtin, this is an emergency!"

A pause. Then Miss Curtin had said, "Well, perhaps if you will state the nature of the emergency to me, I will see what I can do to help you."

"Miss Curtin, I *can't!* I've got to talk to my *mother!*"

"I will put you on her call-back list."

That night their mother had called them back, but by then Fairy Ferris had had his blow job.

"You said this was an emergency, Eric," Assaria LeBaron had said. "What's the emergency?"

"Well, it isn't anymore," he said glumly.

"I was sure the school could handle it, whatever it was," she had said. "And don't ever say something is an emergency when it isn't. Don't forget the story of the little boy who was always crying 'Wolf.' He cried 'Wolf' so often that when the real wolf came, nobody paid any attention to him. Don't be the kind of boy who cries 'Wolf,' Eric."

Years later, the twins would try to make a joke of it, just between themselves. "Remember the time we had to blow old Fairy Ferris?" one of them would say.

"*Yuk!*"

But at the time it had been no joke. He had made them take turns, and they had both been in tears throughout the whole thing.

"Remember old Fairy Ferris?" one of them would say, throwing soft punches at the other.

"And we got put on her call-back list."

"One of the things we were going to ask her was what a blow job was."

"Wonder what she would have said?"

"Well, we found out."

"*Yuk!*"

"But don't be too hard on her, Peep. Dad hadn't been dead very long. She was trying to run the company all by herself. And that damned Miss Curtin —"

"And it wasn't *that* much of an emergency. And we handled it."

"*Yuk!*"

"Wonder whatever happened to old Fairy Ferris . . ."

"Probably in prison for child molestation."

"No. Justice being what it is, that shithead is probably the president of the richest bank in Texas!"

Laughing, making a joke of it, exchanging soft punches, back and forth at each other's shoulders. At least it had been a shared experience.

But that had been before, when they were still friends.

"You are talking about driving a wedge between the members of my family."

"The wedge is already driven. Assaria is the wedge."

"My daddy calls me his little Buttercup."

Was that all it was?

Buttercup . . .

And stripping the blossom of its petals, one by one. She loves me, she loves me not . . .

                              *   *   *

In her bedroom on the third floor of the house on Washington
Street, Assaria LeBaron is also wide awake, though it is past eleven.
The curtains have been drawn against the night, but both the
bedside lamps are lighted, and Sari, in a marabou bed jacket, is
sitting straight up in the center of the oversize bed, propped by
many pillows of assorted sizes. All around her, on the satin bedspread, are scattered many objects — scraps of mail, newspaper
clippings, a ledger book spread open, face down, pencils, ballpoint
pens, an address and telephone book marked "Carnet d'Adresses,"
a copy of the *Social Register,* many sheets of lined notepaper covered
with scribbled notes, sheets of yellow legal foolscap, covered with
figures, and sheets of graph paper on which she has been making
pie charts. Other pieces of paper appear to be legal documents of
one form or another — certificates with scrolly headings, contracts
stapled between heavy covers — and at the edge of all this paperwork lie two sleeping Yorkshire terriers who live on this floor,
except when Thomas walks them. The clutter on the bed also seems
to consist of much, much more. On one of the bedside tables sit
a glass of hot milk, untouched, and a banana, something Thomas
brings her every night before retiring. With a pencil in one hand
and another tucked behind her ear, Sari sits figuring and figuring,
working on the pie charts.

Control, she thinks. I try to control you because you can't control
yourself. This company is the family, and this family is the company, and that is all there is to it. If I am going to control the
company, it follows that I must also control the family. I cannot
control one thing without controlling the other, and so I control
what I control. But, she thinks, I cannot seem to control what the
pie charts inevitably reveal, no matter how I construct them. There,
damnably, appears the name of Harry Tillinghast on every one of
them as a minority, but unwanted, shareholder — the foot in the
door with a thin slice of the pie.

"Why," she had demanded, "would you have sold some of your
shares to that man?"

"Quite simply, Mother," he had said, "because I needed the
money."

"*Why?* Can't you get along on your salary and your dividends? Peeper seems to manage!"

"Peeper," he had said, "doesn't have a wife. He doesn't have two children to educate and clothe and feed and send to the orthodontist. Peeper doesn't have a big house to keep up, with a pool and a tennis court, and a gardener to pay, and servants. Peeper doesn't have country-club dues to pay, or riding lessons and tennis lessons to pay for, and I could go on and on. I haven't even mentioned taxes."

"You're supposed to have a rich wife!"

"Alix and I keep our financial affairs entirely separate. We agreed to that from the beginning."

"You mean Alix doesn't pay for *anything?*"

"Alix believes that it's a man's responsibility to take care of his family, the way her father did."

"Well, what does she *do* with her money, for heaven's sake?"

"She invests it. Someday, of course, it will go to the twins. Sometimes she'll buy something for herself — a piece of jewelry, that sort of thing."

"Look at Melissa! Melissa manages very nicely on nothing but her dividends. She doesn't even have your nice fat salary."

"*Melissa!* She has none of the responsibilities that I have. She doesn't even have any rent to pay — she lives in your house!"

"Oh, but I charge Melissa rent. Melissa pays me rent."

"Yes — I know what Melissa pays in rent. A token hundred dollars a month for an apartment that's as big as a city block. She pays the lowest rent of anyone in San Francisco, Mother."

"But if you needed money, Eric, why didn't you come to me?"

"Frankly, I didn't want to."

"Why not?"

"Male pride, I suppose. Not wanting to ask for money from a woman."

"Bull-do! I'm your mother, as well as chief executive officer of this company."

"I've already given you my answer, Mother."

"But why would you sell to *him*, of all people? A man who hasn't the slightest interest in —"

"He approached me, said he was interested in owning some

Baronet stock. He made me a good offer, and that was that."

"I suppose I'm not entitled to ask what that offer was."

"I'll tell you — it was seven hundred dollars a share."

"*Seven hundred!* You sold him two thousand shares for seven hundred a share? You *gave* it away, you silly fool! Why, the book value alone is —"

"I know it's difficult to put a price on the stock. But we both did some figuring, and seven hundred was a price that seemed fair to us both."

"So you let him look at our books."

"As a stockholder, he's entitled —"

"You let him look at our books *before* he became a stockholder."

"Well —"

"That stock was left to you by your father for *you.* Not for Harry Tillinghast. Harry is not family."

"He's Alix's father."

"But he's not family. Let me ask you just one more question. Why did you do this without consulting me? No — don't answer that. I know why, and you know why. You did it without consulting me because you knew I'd disapprove. And so you did it the sneaky way. You went behind my back."

And so, for what Eric did he must be punished. That is all there is to it. He must be punished, and brought under control. Divide and conquer is her theory, and so she is going to cut up his job and give part of it to Peeper.

And yet, tonight, she is not at all sure that her strategy is working. Is her plan about to backfire? Does she have a tiger by the tail? Why else would he be going to New York, unless it was to try to get Joanna on his side?

Nor does her strategy seem to be working well with Melissa — at least on the evidence of tonight's performance.

She goes back to the pie charts, and is confronted once again with what she has come to think of as the Lance Problem. The Lance Problem has always existed. She knows the terms of her husband's will by heart, and she knows Peter intended to be fair: Fifteen percent to be divided, equally, among his living offspring . . . and fifteen percent "shall be divided, equally, among any and all living issue of my aforesaid sister, Joanna LeBaron." This was Clause 6(a) of the Last Will and Testament of Peter Powell LeBaron. But the Lance Problem created an imbalance in share ownership among the four members of that generation, and gave Lance LeBaron what could be the swing vote in any sort of . . . confrontation.

Sari is on perfectly good terms with Lance LeBaron, although, in fact, she has not spoken to or laid eyes on him in several years. She is not even sure of his current address, though she could look it up right there, in the *Social Register*. Princeton, she thinks, is where he is living now. But the fact is that she has never really trusted Lance since that time, years ago, when she had caught him . . . but that is ancient history, water over the dam. That belongs to the irretrievable past, and has nothing at all to do with what seems to be threatening her now.

Of course . . . of course, she thinks, there is one solution to the Lance Problem. A very difficult and painful one, but it exists. Very painful, very hard, very sensitive, but it could be used. If it came down to the wire, in the end, in the final analysis, would she have the strength to use it and create all that pain, open up all those scars, cut into the scar tissue that has hardened into a thick cicatrix over all these years? She closes her eyes and considers this.

"Sari, darling, remember that you owe me a rather large debt."

"And, Jo, you also owe a rather large debt to me."

"Remember, Sari — we made a pact, a pact in blood."

Her eyes fly open again. She tries now to make some sort of organization out of the piles of papers on her bedspread, and finally gathers them all together in one thick stack and places the stack down near the foot of the bed below the place where the two little dogs are sleeping, sleeping without a care in the world. Then, with a reach, she switches off both bedside lamps, lies back against the pile of pillows, and closes her eyes again.

Control, she thinks. Am I finally losing control?

"You know, Nugget, flying a plane can get kind of boring after a while." This is George Hessler, her pilot, speaking.

"Boring?"

"Flying from point A to point B, and then back to point A again. There's a certain monotony. Want to take the controls now, Nugget?"

"Fine."

Secretly, he has been giving her flying lessons in the company jet, and he is an expert teacher.

They are flying north, now, over the Golden Gate, and the hills of San Rafael are in the distance.

She executes a wide left-hand turn now, out over the ocean and then over the Farallons, and then another left-hand turn. "Boring?" she says. "Well, let's have some excitement. How wide is the bridge?"

"I have no idea. Why?"

"Never mind. Wide enough. Here we go." And she begins her steep descent, heading for the bridge.

"Nugget, what the hell are you doing?" he cries. But from the blaze of excitement in his eyes, she knows that he knows what she is going to do, and is not going to stop her.

"Four-oh-five, we have lost you from our screen, sir," says the voice from the tower at San Francisco International. "Four-oh-five, please radio your position, sir. Four-oh-five —"

"Turn that damned thing off!" she shouts.

Down they go — six hundred feet, five hundred feet.

On the bridge, there is chaos as afternoon motorists see the big jet heading for them. Some cars pull up along the walkway, while others try to speed on to safety on the other side — all, no doubt, thinking of Air Florida and the crash into the Fourteenth Street Bridge in Washington.

Three hundred feet, and the wash from the jet engines churns the water beneath them into a furious foam of whitecaps.

Two hundred feet, and they are under the bridge, through, between the two towers, and out again. "Bull's-eye!" Sari shouts, and they are both laughing and cheering and weeping and slapping each other on the back so hard that Sari can barely see. But she knows her plane, and begins her ascent.

"Bull's-eye! Bull's-eye, Nugget!"

On the bridge, there is panic. There is hysteria. Some motorists have stopped and got out of their automobiles on the insane theory that if the plane were going to strike the bridge, it would be better to go down bodily than encased in a car.

But all their problems are far behind Sari now, who is heading toward Alameda.

In control.

The United Airlines red-eye flight from San Francisco to New York is never spoken of in the warmest terms. It leaves San Francisco at midnight, and almost immediately after takeoff, it seems, it is heading into the eastern sunrise for a seven-thirty arrival at La Guardia, and therefore sleep on the red-eye is difficult. The Madison Avenue boys, sitting three abreast in the crowded coach section, should at least have been trying to sleep. But instead, in the wake of their defeated advertising campaign, they have elected to drown their sorrows and to drink theirway across the continental United States. By now they are drunk as lords, and not on Baronet wine, either. A large collection of miniature Scotch, bourbon, and vodka bottles decorates their tray-tables.

"Solution. Dilution. Pollution." This is Bob Petrocelli speaking. "Dilute her — her Geritol with cyanide! A cyanide solution! A cyanide dilution!"

"I *like* it! I *like* it!" roars Mike Geraghty, who has been ordering doubles while the others have stuck to singles. "Mix it up and bring it around!"

Howard Friedman says nothing. For the last fifteen minutes he has been struggling in vain to control a violent case of hiccups.

"Bull-do!" There are more roars of laughter.

"Bull-do!" And still more laughter.

"Hey, who am I?" says Bob Petrocelli all at once. He is the liveliest of the threesome, and is sitting in the aisle seat. "Gotta guess who I am. Ready-set-go, here I go!" He stands up, a little unsteadily, and steps into the aisle. Then he kneels on the carpeted floor of the plane and starts lumbering up the aisle on his knees. "Guess who I am! Guess who I am! Can anybody guess?"

The others are laughing so hard now that their heads fall down into their open tray-tables, and at least a dozen little empty bottles go scattering and clattering to the floor.

Up the aisle continues Petrocelli on his knees, crying, "Guess who! Guess who! Bull-do! Bull-do!"

The pretty young female flight attendant, wearing an expression of great forbearance, moves down the aisle toward him from the forward section of the cabin. "Sir, I'm going to have to ask you to return to your seat," she says. "We have begun our initial approach into the New York area, and the fasten-seat-belt sign has been illuminated by the captain."

"Bull-do!"

In the northwest corner of the Sonoma vineyard — where more than four thousand rolling Baronet acres are under cultivation, given over to Semillons, Palominos, and Alicantes — Constance and Julius LeBaron lie sleeping in their quiet graves. They were buried here because, for obvious reasons, their bodies could not be received in consecrated earth. Also, it was Julius LeBaron's firm wish that he and his wife be buried where they died. Just before their simplest of wooden coffins, which they had also requested, were closed and lowered into the ground in 1930, a ripe walnut was placed in each of their mouths. This is an Old World custom. It struck many people as peculiar, since Julius LeBaron was a man who, all his life, had seemed determined to rid himself of every trace of the Old World, including his name. But this was his request. And the two trees that have grown up, side by side, at the gravesite are regarded by others with varying degrees of ambivalence. Some thought that Julius and Constance's funerary requirements were merely bizarre. Others considered them downright barbaric.

Peter Powell LeBaron could never bear to visit the two walnut trees, the sight disturbed him so. To him, the trees seemed accusatory, admonishing. Sari's twin sons, on the other hand, who never knew their grandparents, think little or nothing about these presences, nor does Melissa. To her, these grandparents exist only in the dimmest of early childhood memories.

To Sari, the trees symbolize a certain grandeur and high mystery — the cycle of nature, new life springing up out of death. The pair of walnut trees bear their own fruit now, and more trees will grow, and continue to grow, generation after generation. There is even further symbolism here. In the old days, vineyardists often planted walnut trees in alternating rows between the vines. The theory was that, if one crop failed, the planter would always have another crop to harvest, and it was also supposed that the trees would provide needed shade and wind protection for the vines. The old-timers were dead wrong, of course. What happened was that, in a poor year, both crops failed. And in a good year, both crops were no more than mediocre. The practice was abandoned, and the growers went back to the only system they could really rely on, which was luck.

Sari visits the two walnut trees often. For her, there is a sense of awe and wonder engendered by this little grove, a sense of continuity and peace. The trees are set off and protected by a sturdy grape-stake fence. Inside the gate, set into the ground between the trees, is a plaque announcing that this is where her in-laws lie. The plaque gives Julius's and Constance's dates, and the strange, stern imprecation he chose for their epitaph:

> Haste and escape for your lives,
> Look not behind you,
> Awake and fly from the wrath to come,
> Escape to the mountain,
> Lest ye be consumed.

It is Sari who sees to it that the bronze plaque is always kept brightly polished.

PART TWO

Beginnings

Five

THERE IS NOTHING particularly mysterious or strange or se- cret about Assaria LeBaron's origins, despite the stories and the gossip you will hear. Her old friends know the real story — or as much of it as she herself remembers. Because, you see, the only fairly uncommon thing about her story is that both her parents died when she was eight years old, and she was an only child, and so grew up with no one to do her remembering for her. How much can you remember, unaided, of what you did and who you were when you were only eight? Very little, I expect. But most of us grow up with parents, or perhaps an older brother or a sister, who will help nudge the earliest memories for us, poke them, stir them up like embers in a fire, reminding us of things we did and said when we were little, who will remember the name of our first-grade teacher, whose face now is only a shadow in our mind. But Sari, orphaned at eight, had none of these, and grew up with strangers. *Not* in an orphanage, by the way. That's just another of the stories. In some ways, she was uniquely suited for marriage to Peter Powell LeBaron, for the LeBarons always seemed to be trying to reconstruct their history, rewrite their past. ("A distant cousin of William S. O'Brien, the legendary Silver King," reported the *Chronicle* when Constance O'Brien married Julius — baloney, as you already know.) In a sense, it was fitting that when Assaria Latham married their son she had almost no past at all — though they didn't think so, but that's getting ahead of the story.

She remembers a few things.

All the mirrors in the little house were covered with sheets or women's shawls, she remembers that. *Vanity of vanities, saith the Preacher, all is vanity.* And all the people in the house removed their shoes and moved about barefoot or in soft cloth slippers, and when not walking they sat on low stools or benches. *One generation passeth away, and another generation cometh, but the earth abideth forever.* A bowl of fresh water, for the ritual of washing of hands, is placed at the feet of the twin coffins. She remembers all of that, and the mirrors covered with sheets and shawls.

Several reasons are given for this today, though they were not given to Sari at the time, nor did she ask. Some say that if you look into a mirror during this time of mourning, you will see the ghosts of the departed in it. Others say that the mourner must not be distracted from the solemn presence of the dead by a glimpse of his own reflection in the glass, and that this is why no housework, no work of any sort, must be done in this period, not even study of the Torah, and why women do not fix their hair or powder their faces, and why the men do not shave their beards, during these seven days. But still others say that the Angel of Death himself, whose name is *Malchemuvis,* is vain and puffed up with his vanity, and when he has visited a house, and if he should see his image in a mirror, he will primp and preen himself in front of it. Then he will be tempted to come back to that same house soon for another visit with its occupants, and another look at his reflection in the glass. *Malchemuvis* must not be angered or threatened or challenged. Instead, he must be quietly thwarted, frustrated, and confused as to where he is. When he cannot see his handsome reflection in a glass, he will leave, uncertain about where he has been, and will forget his way back for a long time. *All the rivers run into the sea; yet the sea is not full; unto the place from whence the rivers come, thither they return again.*

The coffins were taken away.

The next day they were simply gone. But every day, at morning and at evening, a group of men came to the house to recite the Kaddish. "May the Almighty comfort you among the mourners for Zion and Jerusalem." The lapels of their shirts bore short rips. There was no other conversation.

Then, Sari remembers, when that time had passed, there was talk among the others in the house, frightened talk. These would have been friends and neighbors. What is going to become of the little girl? She is all alone. Who will take her in? Who can afford to feed her, clothe her, bring her up? She has no close family, no aunts, no uncles, no grandparents, even? No. She is all alone. War is everywhere, mutinies, strikes, riots. You can smell it in the streets, the smell of death. Soon it will not be safe anywhere, anywhere in Europe. And for a child alone. Something must be decided. Something must be done, and soon.

Then Sari remembers the beginning of her own fear. How does one remember fear? She remembers fear gripping at her stomach, clutching at her with knotted fingers, fear filling her mouth with the taste of dust, fear — white fear — seeming to freeze that part of her head behind her eyeballs, fear pounding in her eardrums. Fear seemed to paralyze her, and of the next few months all she can really remember was that fear.

Later, she would be given an explanation of what had happened. She would be told that it must have been typhus, or what was called "Spanish influenza," and she would read the statistics. This epidemic, the worst to afflict mankind since the Black Death of the fourteenth century, would kill nearly twenty-two million people, three million people in Russia alone, more than one percent of the world's entire population, while the war was killing nearly ten million more. But at the time all she knew was that one day she had had two people, a mother and a father, looking after her, and that the next day she had no one at all, except these frightened strangers who wandered in and out of the house, whispering, making incomprehensible plans. The year was 1917.

"Where are my mother and my father?"

The strangers would shake their heads sadly, but would not tell her.

Her mother's red scarf with a golden fringe — she remembered that scarf more vividly than she remembered her mother's face, because that scarf had been her mother's favorite — was taken out into the street, doused with paraffin, and burned, along with all the rest of her parents' clothing. "Why are you burning everything?" Again, they would simply shake their heads and tell her nothing. Later, she would suppose that it was assumed that her parents' clothes were infected with the typhus, and therefore must be burned, but at the time all she could remember was the horror of seeing her mother's beautiful scarf being consumed by orange flames, its golden fringe twisting into a mass of tiny, blackened worms, then unraveling into ashes.

Who were these people? Friends, neighbors, she supposed, but they had no names. They came and went, one at a time, on some sort of prearranged schedule, to stay with her, to feed her, to put her to bed at night, to bathe her once a week. Why could none of them take her into one of their own houses? She could only later guess that there was no one who was willing or able to take on the responsibility of another mouth to feed. She must go to America, she had heard that. Only in America could a child be safe. But where in America, and to whom? And how? These discussions, as the friends and neighbors came and went, seemed to occupy days, weeks, months, but perhaps the dilemma had been solved sooner than that, for memory plays tricks.

Then, at last, after many more days and many more discussions, a plan was worked out, and now the voices were excited, joyous. And yet, somehow, this enthusiasm for her imminent departure only increased the little girl's fear, drew all the fears and confusions together into one tight knot of terror in her chest. "I don't want to go away!" she remembers sobbing. "I don't want to go!"

"Yes, you do," they said.

A purse was collected among the others in the village for her passage. Over and over they repeated to her the name and address of the person in America whom she was going to stay with, until she had memorized it: "Mr. Gabriel Pollack, Wabash one hundred and seventeen. Terre Haute, Indiana. United States of America, U.S.A. He is your father's first wife's sister's son." The rabbi and his wife, she was told, would take her to Hamburg. They would put her on the boat and find some good person to take care of her during the trip. Once she was in America, any remaining problems would solve themselves because — it was one of the wonders of America — America was a land of foreigners and strangers who were always helpful to other strangers and newcomers. Everyone knew that. But, just in case, a carefully written-out set of instructions, with Mr. Gabriel Pollack's name and address, which she already knew by heart, was sewn into the hem of her long black skirt. Another was placed in the lining of her undershirt, and, for good measure, one each was placed in the yellow wicker hamper and the small brown cardboard valise that she would carry with her. The lid of the wicker hamper was tied down with knotted ropes, one length of which was left looped to form a handle. The cardboard valise was secured with twine. Thus weighted down, and rustling from the pieces of paper sewn and tucked within her garments, she was instructed how to carry her two pieces of luggage, one article in each hand, and never to lose sight of either of them. Last of all, a huge and heavy black mohair shawl smelling of camphor was produced, folded into a triangle, and fastened about her head and shoulders with pins. This shawl, she was told, would be her blanket on the boat, since the boat to America would have no beds but only shelves on which people could sleep. Behind her, the tip of the shawl's triangle fell nearly to her ankles, but this was a good thing because it would be as cold as winter once the boat got out to sea.

By now, the sheets and scarves had been removed from the mirrors, and the mood in the house was buoyant as the friends and neighbors saw the prospect of being unburdened of their duties to the orphaned child. All the furniture was gone from the house now, too. And why, being driven away from the house in the horse cart by the rabbi and his wife, does she remember looking back and seeing the house itself go up in flames? That may not have happened, but she remembers it.

She does not remember much of the trip to Hamburg on the train, nor even what the rabbi and his wife looked like, only the mounting terror. The rabbi and his wife were two large, dark figures seated on either side of her, nothing more, but she remembers sensing that they, too, were frightened of this journey. There were many stops along the way when soldiers in uniform, carrying rifles with long, sharp bayonets attached to them, moved through the train, swinging their rifles from side to side, asking stern questions, demanding to see documents and papers. The rabbi and his wife held her hands tightly each time another line of soldiers came toward them. And she does remember that, when the train arrived at last in Hamburg, the rabbi's wife gave her a small sack of coins, suspended from a leather shoelace, which she was told to hang about her neck, under her dress, and keep out of sight at all times. This was to be opened only for emergencies.

And she remembers her first sight of the ship — that great dark hull, tall, black, and forbidding — that was to take her away. Her terror reached a kind of climax then, and she was for a moment unable to breathe, and then she remembers flinging herself on the ground in a terrible, screaming tantrum, and hands reaching out to control her and voices telling her that she had nothing to be frightened of, that she was going to love America and her new home. And then she remembers strong arms — a woman's arms, she thinks they were — lifting her, still kicking and screaming, and carrying her aboard the ship. She remembers no good-byes at all.

Of the journey itself she remembers only a seemingly endless period of darkness, a rolling, pitching darkness that seemed to last for weeks — since periods of sleep were never interrupted by any daybreak — on a hard, narrow bed. But hands reached out to touch her from time to time, to place cool cloths on her forehead and to brush her lips with water, for she was running a fever. Then suddenly she was lifted out of bed, and there was daylight, and she was told that she was in New York.

All at once there was blinding sunlight. The place must have been Ellis Island, though at the time it had no name. All she remembers is being inside a room larger and loftier than any she had ever seen. Bright sunlight was streaming down in long, dusty shafts from tall, barred windows, and crowded into this vast room were more people than could possibly have been on her boat, but then she could not be sure. They stood in long lines, men, women, and children like herself, all carrying baskets, bundles, and valises like her own. But the first impression of America that she remembered longest was its smell — the pungent, gamy, garlicky smell of unwashed humanity. It was a smell of old, soiled, and damp clothing that had been piled on a closet floor for days, and suddenly pulled out into the room to air. Once, years later, one of her Cookies had prepared an unsuccessful vegetable soup. Putting down her spoon, Assaria LeBaron had said to Thomas, "This soup smells exactly like Ellis Island!"

Mixed with this stale-grocery smell was the faintly acrid smell of ink, the smell one experiences when one presses one's nose into the spine of an open book. It was a smell of bureaucracy. For all around, it seemed, were officers with pens and inkwells, filling out long sheets of paper, making cryptic notations on them, asking unintelligible questions, shouting instructions, as the people were herded from one long line into another. And over everything else was the ammoniacal smell of disinfectant soaps, a smell that burned the nostrils and brought tears to the eyes, that seemed to emanate upward from the wooden floorboards. And yet the tired faces of the people looked happy and excited.

But all at once, in the confusion of sights and smells and noises, there arose, like a thunderstorm coming, a great sound of sobbing and moaning. Something very wrong was happening, and there was a huge surge of people forward. From the cries, it was clear that some people were being turned away. There were some people whom America did not want. Old people were being separated from their sons and daughters, children from their mothers and fathers, husbands from their wives. There were shrieks and cries and the futile flailing of arms as people reached out to clutch and cling to one another, but were forced apart. It was the fear of typhus again, and she watched as a small baby was snatched out of its mother's arms. In panic, the people rushed together against a line of policemen with sticks, but they were forced backward, and linked hands were forcibly unjoined. She remembers herself being tightly pressed, terrified, between bodies, between the skirts and buttocks of women and the coats of men, and even the sunlight was blocked out, and once more she felt she could not breathe. She was too frightened by then to cry out, and the person who had brushed her lips with water was nowhere to be seen. But at least her fever was gone, and she could think more clearly, and she remembers a man lifting her and placing her high on his shoulders, carrying her forward through that sea of weeping, angry people, away from it, then setting her down in a quieter place. Then he too was gone.

Now there was a young man in a policeman's or soldier's uniform who seemed very tired, and his nose was rubbed red as though he had a bad cold, and he spoke to her in a language she couldn't understand.

Though she had no idea what this runny-nosed young man was saying to her, she sensed that he was asking her a series of questions. And so she answered him in the words she had memorized: "Mr. Gabriel Pollack, Wabash one hundred and seventeen. Terre Haute, Indiana. United States of America, U.S.A. He is your father's first wife's sister's son." But, to her dismay, she realized he had no idea what she was trying to say to him in her labored English, and he only looked more tired and discouraged and asked her more unintelligible questions. She recited her words once more, but again to no avail, and all at once she was certain that America was turning her away. The young soldier sneezed loudly, and gave her a despairing look.

Somehow, on her way across the Atlantic, or in that confused scene at the pier, she and her wicker basket had been parted from each other, where or how she would never know — even now. But she still had her brown cardboard valise, and remembering the piece of paper that had been placed inside it, she knelt on the floor, untied the valise, found the piece of paper, and showed it to the young officer.

How is it possible to forget whole weeks of time, and yet be able to remember vividly one gesture? The young man yawned noisily, took her piece of paper in one hand, and drew the back of his other hand wetly across his streaming nose. He read the words the neighbors had carefully printed:

> Mr. Pollack, Gabriel
> Wabash # 117
> Terre Haute, Indiana
> United States of America, U.S.A.

He asked her another short question, in a kinder voice now.

Once more, she didn't understand him, but, since he seemed to expect a positive reply, she eagerly nodded yes. With that, he scribbled something on the entry card she had been given, stamped it with his stamp, and motioned her into a long line of people. Later, she would like to say that she might never have been admitted to America at all if the immigration officer hadn't been very tired, and hadn't had a bad cold. "I'm probably an illegal alien," she would like to say.

Somehow again, from that point onward, she was able to remember another piece of advice that one of the neighbors from home had given her: "If you ever think you're lost, just sit down on your suitcases and wait for someone to help you. In America, everyone helps everyone else."

Outside the immigration depot at last, she sat on her remaining suitcase, and an elderly gentleman carrying a bouquet of white flowers spoke to her.

She didn't answer him, but showed him the magic piece of paper.

Picking up the cardboard valise with his free hand, and steering her by the elbow, he escorted her to what turned out to be a railroad station.

The railroad stations of the remainder of the journey — New York, Cleveland, Indianapolis — blurred into one. The stations themselves were huge, vaulted, noisy, and confusing places, each one more elaborate and ornamented than any visions she had had of the palaces of the Czars.

As the trains made their slow way westward across America,

the little girl was so exhausted from her fear and confusion that nearly all she could do was sleep. She slept for over a thousand miles, through the two days and a night that the journey took. Only from brief waking moments did little things stand out in her mind. On one train, a kind woman sitting next to her offered her a strange-looking fruit whose skin had to be peeled back, in long strips, in order for one to eat it. The woman showed her how. It was a banana. On another train, a man who had at first frightened her — he had a purple-black face and large black hands — gave her a small pillow to prop behind her head as she slept.

Finally — this must have been in the Indianapolis railroad station, where she sat again on her suitcase — there was a tall woman with an anxious, distracted air, who was carrying a suitcase much larger than Sari's own, and who asked her a great many, always unintelligible, questions. When she looked at the much-folded piece of paper, she indicated that Sari should stay where she was, and then disappeared. When the woman returned, she was smiling, and she then escorted Sari to the proper gate for the train to Terre Haute.

Somehow, the little girl sensed that a transaction involving money had taken place, and carefully she lifted the little sack of coins from under the bosom of her dress, loosened the leather lace, and offered the tall woman one of the coins.

The woman studied the strange gold coin, looking puzzled, turning the coin this way and that. Finally, she smiled again and handed the coin back, pressing it into Sari's hand. Then she helped Sari carry her cardboard valise aboard this last train, and blew her a good-bye kiss. Later, Sari would learn that this woman had sent a telegram to Mr. Gabriel Pollack, telling him when to expect the child, but at the time there was only more confusion and uncertainty as to why this woman had refused to accept the good ten-kopek piece.

And then, at the very last, waiting for her at the Terre Haute station as if by some sort of miracle, there to collect her at this last granite and marble palace, was the tall young man who turned out to be Mr. Gabriel Pollack himself. His handsome-homely face was smiling shyly as he picked her out from the crowd, which could not have been hard to do, in retrospect, considering the bulky, foreign-looking dress she was wearing, her head in that big camphor-smelling shawl, her cardboard suitcase beginning to fall apart at the corners. And she realized that here, at last, was someone — a living and breathing human being — who actually expected her, was waiting for her, and was ready to take her to an actual house at a specified destination. At that precise moment she made a promise to herself that never again in her life would she let herself be frightened of anything. Ever.

But who knows whether she actually made such a promise to herself at the age of eight? Sari LeBaron, as we know, has a tendency to exaggerate things, dramatize things.

In the beginning, she thought of him as her new father, because he seemed about her father's height and age. Only later did she discover that, at the time, Gabe Pollack was only fourteen. And the woman at whose house Gabe Pollack lived, Mrs. Bonkowski, she decided was her new mother. Like her real father, Gabriel Pollack was gone from early in the morning until late at night. He worked, he explained, as a messenger and delivery boy for a newspaper called the *Republican*. A small cot had been set up in Gabriel Pollack's room for her, and in her old home she had also slept in the same bedroom as her parents. In the house, Mrs. Bonkowski performed the same tasks her real mother had done — cooking, mending, washing clothes. As had been the case in the old home, there were certain chores that the little girl was expected to do — help hang out the wash, help dry the supper dishes, and at Mrs. Bonkowski's house there were many dishes to do because there were four other boarders, in addition to Gabriel Pollack and herself, all of them men. Mrs. Bonkowski was teaching her English.

"This is called a 'coffeepot,' " Mrs. Bonkowski said. "Say it. Coffeepot. Before Bonkowski died, rest his soul, I had a grand life. We had a cabin at Lake Wawasee. That's upstate. I never thought I'd come to this, taking in p.g.'s — that's what I call them, p.g.'s — paying guests is a better class than boarders, but that's the life and what's to do since Bonkowski passed away? Died of consumption. He was a skinny little man, but he was a good provider, Bonkowski was. Up on Lake Wawasee there's Indians, red Indians, and we even had one to fetch us stuff from the store. This is called a — what? An 'apple-corer,' I guess you call it, to core apples with. Say it. Apple-corer. Red Indian used to catch rabbits for us, even deer, possum sometimes, but I didn't care for that. We lived off the fat of the land. I never thought I'd be taking in p.g.'s, Jews even, like your friend, and me a Disciple of Christ. Never trust a Jew, my mother used to say, a Jew is either at your feet or at your throat. Bonkowski was a Polack, but he was no Jew. Catholic, mackerel-snapper, cat-licker, my mother used to say. Bonkowski played pinochle, but never for money. He was a good provider, worked at Samson's Lumber Yard, and thank the dear Lord for his insurance. Without that, the dear Lord knows where I'd be. This is called a 'ladle.' Say it. Ladle. It's like a big spoon. I have a set of silver spoons, you know, sterling silver, Bonkowski bought them for me. They're put away in a safe place, believe you me. Who can you trust these days? We're getting niggers here lately. Railroad brings 'em. You can trust a red Indian, but you can't trust a nigger. They're shiftless. We've got to think up a new name for you. *Anzia* — that just doesn't sound like a white-person American name, Anzia. Sounds Dutchy. In America, everybody is the same, you know, and that's the beauty of it. The dear Lord knows how I've suffered with a name like Bonkowski, a Polack name. Nobody can pronounce it, nobody can spell it, and sometimes even I forget how to spell it, that's how long it's been since Bonkowski passed away, but that's the way the name comes on the insurance check, so I suppose I'm stuck with it. I'll think of a good white-person American name for you, just give me time. You can't go off to school with a name like Anzia. You'll be laughed off the face of the map with a name like that. This is called a 'bread knife.' Say it . . .''

Mrs. Bonkowski, she explained, had been raised in a small town in central Kansas, "in the heart of Saline County, near Salina, everyone knows where that is," and her two sons, Tescott and Culver, had been named after two nearby towns. She had never had a daughter, but if she had she would have named it Rosalia — another Kansas town. "Isn't that a beautiful name, Rosalia? But you can't have that. Rosalia was saved for my daughter, if I'd had a daughter, so that name's already spoken for. I'll think of something. Just can't have you going off to school named Anzia and be laughed off the face of the map. Which it sounds like a Jew name, you see, not that I mind your friend Gabe, even if he's a Jew, he's a good boy. How about Assaria? Assaria was just down the Smoky Hill River from Bridgeport, first big town between Bridgeport and Salina, not far from Tescott, and not far from Culver, either. Sort of the middle, Assaria. I think I like that. What do you think of that? I think I like it. And now we've got to give you a good white-person American last name. That last name of yours *I* can't pronounce, and I've had two years high school. Let's see. Let me think. I'll think of something. How about Latham? That was a little-bitty place down in the southeast corner of the state, real pretty. Yes, I think I like that. What do you think? I like it — Assaria Latham."

And that was how, out of a dream of lost prairie villages, Assaria Latham got her name. "Say it. Assaria Latham."

It was summer, and soon, she was told, it would be time for her to go to school.

And that is really all there is to know about her early childhood, which is always the least interesting part of a person's life to tell about. Except, perhaps, one or two things.

A year or so later, when she was nine or ten, she suddenly said to Gabe, "You know, I can't remember my parents' names!"

He remembered them, of course, and told her. But by then they were the foreign names of strangers.

That, and the fact that by the time she was fourteen she had fallen in love with him. But he didn't know that then.

"You know, it's almost like thought transference," Joanna LeBaron is saying. "I was just about to telephone you and say I wanted to see you, when you telephoned and said you wanted to see *me*. My brother and I — your father and I — often used to have experiences like that, thinking the same thing at the same time. Have you ever had that, with your twin?"

"Sometimes," Eric says. "We used to."

They are sitting in the living room of Joanna's New York apartment at 1040 Fifth Avenue, overlooking the museum and Central Park, and the park has just received a dusting of light, fresh snow. And this isthe extraordinary Joanna LeBaron herself, in a long, pale green hostess gown by Adolfo, still tall and pencil-slender, her silver hair brushed with streaks of honey. This is the woman whose photograph you will still see in *W,* and *Vogue,* and *Town & Country* — photographed not only for her beauty and her sense of fashion, but for less frivolous things, such as her business acuity, and her extraordinary success in what is usually considered the man's world of advertising. The secret of her success, she has often told interviewers, is her sense of organization. Everything in her house, like everything in her office, is organized, and she will often show interviewers her closets — the racks of dresses in clear plastic bags, each arranged according to color and season and time of day; the drawers of sweaters and blouses and gloves and stockings, also arranged according to hue; the tall racks of shoes, one rack for daytime, one for evening, and so on. "Organization is the key," she often says, and then, with her husky laugh, "I often think that if I were marooned on a desert island, the first thing I'd do would be to organize the grains of sand on the beach according to size, shape, and color." Because the colors of her living room are varying shades of yellow, she always keeps this room filled with bowls of yellow flowers — roses, yellow calla lilies, or, tonight, with the first yellow tulips of the season her florist has found for her.

Joanna stands by a window now, holding a glass of sherry, looking out at the nightscape of the park and the snow. Eric is sitting in a lemon-colored, satin-covered loveseat, legs crossed, sipping a Scotch and soda.

Turning from the window, Joanna says, "Anyway, I'm glad you came, darling boy. Now who'll state his business first?"

"You," he says. "You, Aunt Joanna."

She laughs. "Age before beauty, is that it? Well, I'm afraid what I have to say to you may strike you as unpleasant, darling."

"Go ahead. I'm a big boy now."

"I've decided," she says, "to resign the Baronet account. You look surprised. Well, it wasn't an easy decision. I never thought this account would present a problem, but now — from what Mike Geraghty has reported to me of yesterday's meeting in San Francisco — there is one. You — and I was behind you — have been wanting to turn Baronet wines in a new and exciting direction. While your mother —"

"Wants to stay exactly where she's been since nineteen fifty-five."

"Exactly. Or so it seems. Tastes in wines have changed dramatically in the last twenty years, as you and I know. There is a whole new market now for light, elegant table wines. Wines served in bottles with graceful shapes, snappy-looking labels — chardonnays, Chablis, merlots, cabernet sauvignons. Look at what Almaden has been doing, look at Bob Mondavi. The young-urban-professional market. We thought we were ready for Baronet to tackle that market. But your mother —"

"Wants to stick with the skid-row winos. The market she knows."

"So it seems. And I can't, in good conscience, go along with that any longer, Eric. LeBaron and Murdock can't go along with that. I run a service business, but I can't serve a client who's going at cross-purposes with what I believe ought to be done. I can't work with a product I don't believe in any longer. I can't work like that. If I've stopped believing in a product, I can't help sell it. It's as simple as that. I'd be betraying my employees if I did that. I'd be betraying my whole industry. Worst of all, I'd be betraying myself. And I've tried bloody hard never to do that. So there's my decision, darling boy. I hope you understand."

"I do. Completely."

"I never thought it would come to this, but it has. Now the campaign Mike presented to you and your mother may not have been —"

"I thought it was —"

She holds up her hand. "Never mind. It doesn't matter what you thought of it. That campaign is quite, quite dead, darling. It's been flushed down the agency loo, and we won't be offering another. The relationship between my agency and Baronet has come to its quiet, dignified end with that quiet, dignified campaign we tried to do for her."

He nods.

"Of course, it wasn't easy for me to decide this," she says, and now there is an audible catch in that throaty voice. "There's the sentimental attachment to the account, and the family attachment. Baronet was my very first account when your father first asked me to try my hand at it. It was right after you and Peeper were born, and it represented a whole new life for me at a time when — well, at a time when my life seemed particularly empty. Baronet was the account that got me started — as a person. It was the account that was responsible for my first success. It was the foundation of this agency, and I've never been able to thank your sweet, divine father for doing all that for me. Your darling father had the key to my salvation."

Eric says nothing. At this delicate, emotional moment, it would not serve any purpose to remind Aunt Jo that his mother has always taken the credit for giving Joanna her agency, and that Eric has seen — in the files — old interoffice correspondence from 1945 that bears this out.

Now Joanna laughs her husky laugh. "But I can't take sentiment into consideration, can I? And — and this is no secret, darling — Baronet has never exactly been a super money-maker for us, since we've always drawn our commission at family prices. In that sense, resigning the account will not result in any great financial loss to us."

"I can understand that."

"And meanwhile, because I happen to be bloody good at what I do, and because the merchandising of wines happens to be something on which I've made my reputation, I wouldn't be honest with you if I didn't tell you that there are at least three other major vintners who are eager to give me their business — which I haven't been able to accept up to now because of conflict of interest."

"And who would pay you the full freight."

She laughs again. "Well, there's that. But money's only money. Still, it's bloody nicer to have it than to bloody not, isn't it, darling?"

"Yes. Which brings me to —"

"Of course, from the public-relations standpoint, there may be some unfortunate aftereffects of this decision of mine. The trade press, for example, will probably try to treat it as some sort of family feud."

"Which, in a sense, it is."

"Well, I intend to do everything I can to avoid creating that impression. I plan to prepare a very mildly worded release, saying that after nearly forty years of a pleasant and profitable relationship, Baronet and my agency have come to a friendly parting of the ways due to differences in advertising and marketing philosophies. Something like that. Of course, what your mother says to the press may be another matter."

"She'll probably be furious, call her own press conference, and call you a dirty double-crosser."

"Or say that I'm getting soft in the head. I gather she said something to that effect at yesterday's meeting. Well, I'm afraid I have no control over what darling Sari might decide to say."

"And the two of you used to be the best of friends."

"Darling boy, we still *could* be. I've always wanted to be her friend. We've been friends since we were both sixteen. People used to call us Mutt and Jeff, because she was tiny and dark, and I was tall and blonde. But somewhere along the line the friendship began to change, and she began to see me as some sort of competitor. Mind you, I don't mind being seen as her competitor, because I've always been a very competitive sort of person. What I *do* mind, however, is when she treats me as one of her bloody employees. That started to happen after your father died. I am *not* one of her employees. I hold the exact same position in Baronet Vineyards that she does, and in terms of the company I expect to be treated as a peer. That's been the basis of some of our recent — differences." Moving toward him, she says, "You know, Eric, sitting there in that soft light, you could be your father thirty years ago. It was so tragic that he died when you and Peeper were so young, and you couldn't have grown up to know my brother as a man. That's the real tragedy."

"Yes."

"And so," she says, "that's my sorry decision. I regret having to make it, but I have."

"But maybe not," he says.

"What do you mean, darling?"

Leaning forward in his chair, Eric says, "Now let me get to the business I want to discuss with you, Aunt Jo."

"Of course. I'm simply bursting with curiosity to find out what's going on in that handsome head of yours."

"As you know, we're one of the very last family-owned wineries in California of any size. One by one, the others have all been taken over by larger corporations, as a result of mergers and acquisitions, and they've profited enormously from this trend, which has placed large amounts of working and expansion capital within their reach."

"I realize this."

"Over the years, we've been approached by various outsiders — Uniroyal, Gulf and Western, Pepsi — but we've always been the holdouts. We've refused to sell."

"Yes. Darling Sari has refused to sell."

"And, as you also know, I sold some of my shares in Baronet to Harry Tillinghast a while back. It pissed Mother off, but it was a purely private transaction between Harry and me."

"Pissed her off! She bloody well hit the ceiling, if I know Sari!"

"Now Harry has come up with an acquisition offer for the company that I think we ought to seriously consider. For each Baronet share we own, Harry offers twelve point five shares of Kern-McKittrick. Kern-McKittrick is currently trading at about fifty-three, so I think you'll agree that's not a bad offer, and Kern-McKittrick is as good as gold. I wouldn't be surprised if, when we get into actual negotiations, we can't get Harry to sweeten his offer a bit. But for an opening bid, it isn't bad."

"Very interesting," Joanna says. "Of course, Harry Tillinghast isn't exactly my favorite man."

"Nor mine," says Eric. "But we're not talking about marrying the man. We're talking about marrying his company. And, as you know, in the marketplace Kern-McKittrick is nothing but blue chip. And Harry himself may not be likable, but he's honest, and he's strong, and he keeps his word."

"That's true."

"If we become a subsidiary of Kern-McKittrick, Harry offers to put me in the top spot, with complete autonomy. Of course, he may feel he has a certain amount of control over me, but I'll also have a certain amount of control over him."

"Oh? How's that?"

"Harry is particularly anxious to keep my somewhat shaky marriage from falling apart."

"I see," she says. With a perfectly lacquered fingertip, Joanna touches one of the yellow tulips in a tall vase full of blooms, and rearranges it until it is just so. "Of course, the only thing I really want is your happiness, darling boy," she says.

"Thank you, Aunt Jo."

"And," she says to the still wayward tulip, "for me — besides a lot of Kern-McKittrick stock, what would I get?"

"I'm coming to that. For you, Harry offers an exclusive contract to handle Baronet's advertising for as many years as you care to specify. And he offers to pay you full commission on your billings."

"Hmm," she says. "How very nice of Harry."

"The thing I like about the deal is that it's someone we know. It isn't some anonymous outsider like Pepsi-Cola. It's still like keeping it in the family. We all know Harry, and we know what we can expect from Harry, and we know his track record."

"Yes. You get to keep the company, and Alix gets to keep her dishy husband."

Eric clears his throat. "The thing I want to know from you, Aunt Jo, is — if you agree to go along with this, and I hope you will — will Lance go along as well?"

She hesitates, very briefly. The tulip now is posed to her satisfaction, and she steps away from the flower arrangement, giving it one last look of critical appraisal. "Yes," she says. "I think Lance will do whatever I suggest."

"Then," he says, steepling his fingers, "with you and Lance and Harry behind me, we'd have fifty-five percent of the voting shares. Enough to pass the acquisition."

"And Sari would be —"

"Out."

"Out," she repeats. "Poor, darling Sari. How's her health, Eric?"

"She's just fine. Oh, we could toss her some sort of bone — make her honorary board chairman, or something like that."

"She won't like it."

"No, probably not," he says quickly, "but think of what you and I could do together, Aunt Jo. We could take Baronet in the direction we both believe it ought to go. We could take it in any direction we chose. We'd be a real team, at last — think of that. I think we should do it, Aunt Jo."

She moves across the room and takes a seat on the loveseat beside him, and immediately the air between them is suffused with the wild and heady scent of her perfume, which he knows from many Christmas-stocking presents in the past is always My Sin by Lanvin. With one hand, Joanna lifts the lid of a large silver cigarette box. Inside the box, her almost obsessive fetish for organization continues to reveal itself. Organized, in separate sandalwood compartments of the box, are various kinds and brands of cigarettes — filtered, unfiltered, mentholated, non-mentholated, long and short and extra-length. Each in its own designated cubicle. She selects a long, slender, filtered cigarette with an ivory tip, and lights it carefully with a silver table lighter. This action in itself is significant. Joanna LeBaron rarely smokes, and when she does it is an indication that she is disturbed, or angry, or that she has something very important on her mind. The lighter snaps shut, and Joanna exhales a stream of smoke.

"You're ready for another drink, darling," she says. "You can't fly on one wing, you know. And while you're up, fix me one, too. I think I'm ready for something a little more serious than sherry. Make mine a neat Scotch this time." She hands him her empty glass.

Eric rises, and steps toward the bar, where all varieties of liquors are arrayed in matched Baccarat decanters, silver necklaces of labels slung about their necks, and the disembodied odor of My Sin follows him across her living room. Fixing their drinks, he cannot help but think how differently, in style, these two women — Joanna and his mother — go about getting what they want. In technique, Assaria LeBaron is all subtle plots and politics and under-the-counter payoffs — a bit of old-fashioned blackmail is never ruled out — a wily gambler with extra aces up her sleeve. Joanna, in contrast, is all softness and silkiness and sentimentality — breathy and feminine and flirtatious, and seductive, and . . . My Sin. Joanna is Irene Dunne, and his mother is . . . a three-card-monte player. And yet both these women are after the same thing, the name of which is: Power. He returns with their freshened drinks.

"Ah, that looks divine, darling," she says, accepting her glass. Then, plucking an invisible speck of lint from the skirt of her Adolfo gown, she says, "I'm thinking . . . thinking."

"A penny for your thoughts, then."

"It's very tempting, isn't it," she says at last. "Tempting for you, and also tempting, I must admit, for me. What about Peeper?"

"Mother's been doing a lot of sucking up to Peeper lately. I expect she's got him on her side."

"And . . . Melissa?"

"I had breakfast with Melissa this morning," he says, "and went over with her very roughly what I have in mind. Of course, sooner or later, I intend to bring everyone in on this."

"What did Melissa say?"

"She seemed — well, interested. But preoccupied a little. I got the impression this morning that Melissa's mind was miles and miles away. You know Melissa."

"Miles and miles away. In Switzerland, perhaps."

"Huh? But the point is, we don't need Peeper and we don't need Melissa. We have enough share votes without them."

"Darling, I wish it were as simple as that."

"Why isn't it?"

"It — isn't. Not quite. We need Melissa. Or at least we might, depending . . ."

"Why? With you, with Lance, with me, and —"

"No, Eric. Melissa could be very important. Melissa could be pivotal."

"But why, Aunt Jo? I don't see why."

Quickly, she stubs out her mostly unsmoked cigarette in an ashtray and, in the same deft motion, empties the ashtray into a silent butler. With Joanna, even her cigarette ends must be organized, each deposited in its proper place. She takes a quick swallow of her drink.

"Eric," she says, "there is something you should know about Melissa . . ."

In California, it is still daylight.

In Gabe Pollack's office at the *Peninsula Gazette* in Palo Alto, a piece of unedited copy has just come across his desk. It is rough-typed on yellow foolscap, and Gabe picks it up and reads:

HEIRESS TO PAY FOR
CONTROVERSIAL ROCK PERFORMANCE

San Francisco heiress Melissa LeBaron has let it be known that she will personally pay the full performance fees for The Dildos, the controversial rock group whose appearance at the Odeon Theatre last Thursday night was disrupted by a bizarre outbreak of violence.

Previously, the 11-member board of directors of the Odeon had voted 10 to one to withhold the group's concert fee on the grounds that the concert had included material that was offensive to the public taste, in breach of the group's contract with the board. Miss LeBaron's was the single dissenting vote, it was learned from a source close to the situation today.

At Thursday's concert, pandemonium erupted when, in a solo number, the group's lead singer, Maurice Littlefield, 23, was bitten in the arm by a seven-foot rock python which Littlefield was using as a part of his act. Littlefield, who bills himself as Luscious Lucius, then proceeded to beat the huge snake to death on the Odeon's stage in front of the horrified audience.

Today the Gazette learned that Miss LeBaron has decided to pay the group's fees out of personal funds. Their fees are said to amount to something in the neighborhood of $5000. "I feel responsible, morally responsible," Miss LeBaron is quoted as having said. "It was all my idea." It was Miss LeBaron who first proposed the group's concert to the Odeon's board last October.

Melissa LeBaron is the daughter of Mrs. Assaria Latham LeBaron and the late Peter Powell LeBaron of San Francisco. The LeBaron family owns and operates Baronet Vineyards, Inc., and other enterprises in the Bay Area. Miss LeBaron's mother was the principal benefactress of the Odeon Theatre's $3 million restoration last year, though Mrs. LeBaron is not a member of the theatre's board.

Gabe pushes a button on his desk, and speaks into the intercom. "Archie, would you step in here for a minute?"

Archie McPherson appears, and Gabe waves the sheets of yellow paper at him. "Yours, I presume?"

"Yes, sir."

"Very interesting. Now would you mind telling me just who this 'source close to the situation' might be?"

"Sorry, sir. But my source insisted on absolute confidentiality. I couldn't get the story without promising that."

"I see."

"But I assure you, sir, the source is excellent. Every word of the story is true."

"I see," Gabe says, looking back at the sheet of copy. "The way you've worded this — 'Melissa LeBaron has let it be known . . . Miss LeBaron is quoted as having said' — you don't quote her directly, and yet you quote her. So you are quoting what your source said she said — correct? So I am assuming that your source is not Miss LeBaron herself."

"Correct, sir."

"Let me just ask you one question, then," Gabe says. "All I want you to answer is yes or no. Was her mother your source?"

"Sir, I can't —"

"I said yes or no."

Archie looks at his feet and grins sheepishly. "Yes," he says.

"Fine. That's all," and Gabe waves him out of the office with a motion of his hand.

Now Gabe Pollack is mad as hell. This time he is not going to sit like a schoolboy, hat in hand, in an uncomfortable chair in her stuffy south sitting room, waiting for her to arrive and give him a dressing-down — waiting, not even offered coffee or a sweet roll, not offered anything at all while she treats him to the sharp side of her tongue. This time he will beard the lioness in her den himself, and tell her exactly what he thinks of her machinations. Quickly, he dials her private number at the house, and when Thomas answers and, at first, hesitates, Gabe says, "Tell her that this is extremely urgent."

Presently her voice comes on the phone. "What's up?" she says cheerfully.

"Sari," he says very slowly and carefully, "I would like to know what the hell you are trying to do, feeding stories to my reporters behind my back."

"Stories? What stories?"

"This story about Melissa paying for the rock concert, for one."

"Why, Gabe, I had nothing to do with —"

"Don't lie to me. You've been lying to me all along, haven't you? Pretending to be angry at a story we ran, when it was a story you yourself helped engineer. I should have known. I know how you operate only too well, Sari."

"Now, Gabe —"

"You," he says, "can create as much discord and dissension as you want within your own family, and as much discord and dissension as you want within your own company. But when you try to create discord and dissension on my newspaper, you're going too far, and I won't stand for it."

"Gabe, please let me —"

"Archie McPherson isn't conducting a personal vendetta against Melissa. *You're* conducting a personal vendetta against Melissa — don't ask me why — and Archie is just your little tool. Well, leave my paper out of your little family fights and power battles, Sari — understand? Leave my paper and my reporters out of whatever the hell is going on at Baronet."

"There may be something big, Gabe. Something's going on — I've got a hunch. When it happens, your paper will be the first to get the scoop."

"At this point, I don't want any more of your goddamned scoops," he says. "And may I ask why, when you want a story planted in my paper, you go around behind my back to Archie, and not directly to me? Let me take a quick guess at the answer to that one. For every story that Archie writes that shows Melissa, or one of her projects, in an embarrassing light, you can get *me* to write

one about Assaria LeBaron and all her wonderful work in the
city — restoring south of Market, or whatever it is you want that
shows *you* in a good light — right? It's always the same old story
with you, isn't it? Play one against the other. Why kill one bird
with the stone, when you can kill two or three? Well, that little
game is over, Sari."

"Dear Gabe," she says. "Dear old Gabe, dear old Polly. You're
upset. Come for dinner tonight. We'll have champagne, we'll talk."

"Fat chance of that!" he says, and, the minute the words are
out of his mouth, he realizes he is beginning to sound a little
childish. "What's up between you and Melissa, anyway? Not that
it's any of my business, and not that I really give a damn."

"I'm — just — trying — *to bring Melissa under control!*"

"You've been trying that for fifty-seven years without success.
What makes you think you can do it now?"

"She's a loose cannon, Gabe!"

"So — what else is new?"

"This is my last-ditch effort. I've never tried it this way before.
And if I succeed —"

"You're going to bring Melissa under control by getting people
to snicker about her latest escapade with a rock group and a snake?
You're full of bullshit, Sari."

"I'm trying to get her, for once in her life, to listen to me, Gabe.
I'm trying to get her to trust my judgment, to listen to my advice,
to follow my suggestions — to do what, in the long run, can only
be the best thing for her. That's all I want — what's best for her!
I can't tell you too much about what's going on at Baronet right
now because I don't know all the details myself. But I do know
that, if there's a showdown, I'm going to have to have Melissa on
my side, following my instructions, trusting my judgments, and
doing — for her own good — as I say. She's got to see, in this
business, that I'm wiser than she."

"Well, I still don't see why newspaper stories like these are going
to get her on your side."

There is a pause, and then she says, "Perhaps you will when I
tell you that — if things come to a showdown, and they may — I
may have to explain to Melissa that I am sitting on a story that, if

it were ever made public, would ruin her forever, everywhere. Not just in San Francisco, *everywhere*. And a story that would ruin a few other people in the bargain."

"Well, I don't intend to let you use my newspaper as an instrument for blackmailing your daughter."

"I'm not talking about the *Peninsula Gazette*. I'm talking about the networks, the *Wall Street Journal*, the *New York Times*."

He says nothing.

"Now," she says, "are you beginning to get an inkling of the scope of my concern? Dear old Gabe, you are my oldest friend in all the world. Please believe me, trust me that I know what I'm doing."

"I thought at least we could be honest with each other, level with one another," he says.

"I'm being as honest with you now as I can possibly be," she says. "Now come for dinner tonight. We'll have dinner, just the two of us."

"I can't tonight. Busy."

"Well, at least try to trust me," she says. "And remember that you owe me a lot. After all, where would you be if it weren't for me?"

"And where would *you* be if it weren't for *me?*"

"That's right. We owe each other. Tit for tat. More or less."

"Are you implying that I owe you more than you owe me?"

She laughs softly. "Don't worry. I'm not calling in any of my markers. Dear old Gabe, I'm glad you're not upset with me anymore. Good-bye, dear Gabe. And —" she adds quickly, "print the story, Gabe."

After he has hung up the phone, he stares for a moment or two at the typewritten sheet of yellow foolscap. Then, very quickly, he initials it in the upper left-hand corner, and places the copy in his "Out" box.

In room 315 of the airport Marriott, Melissa LeBaron and the young man named Maurice Littlefield are making love on one of the pair of queen-size beds. "Oh, fuck, baby . . . fuck . . . fuck . . . fuck . . . ," he is saying to her, clutching her roughly. "Oh, you fuck good, baby . . . like a fuckin' bunny . . . ball me, baby . . . ball me . . . ," in a hoarse, insistent voice.

But already Melissa is wondering, is wondering if this is what she wanted to have happen when she came out here this afternoon to discuss their compensation, if this is what she really planned, if she had secretly known, expected, that it could end up this way, making love with a young man less than half her age in a common motel room, in a motel full of transients and salesmen stranded by canceled flights. Had she expected this to happen, and somehow let him know that she expected it? And yet, when he had reached out and touched her, and whispered a coarse suggestion, she had been filled with such a yearning that she felt she must take him into her arms and into her body. He had seemed so sweet, so young and innocent, so lost and in need of comforting, that she had immediately complied with his request, and so it is happening whether she expected it to or not.

Now it is over, and he has pushed himself off her and lies on his side, with one elbow propped on a pillow, and Melissa turns herself slightly away from him, feeling disappointed and depressed. She had tried her best. But there had been no orgasm, no bursting rush of feeling, no charge or current through her body, nothing at all. Outside, the winter sun is going down, and there is again a light rain, which descends in drizzles across the windowpanes. In this light, the room itself looks grimy and unkempt, and even the bright chintz curtains, designer-chosen to make the room look cozy and inviting, now look dusty, faded. Outside, there is the slick hiss of tires on the wet pavement of the parking lot, and the sound of car doors slamming. I should be in Capri, she thinks, in Capri dancing with a Capriote. Behind her, she hears the sound of Littlefield lighting a cigarette, and a sharp exhale. His weight shifts slightly. His pale, skinny body and his narrow, bony, hairless chest are turned away from her, but they are still in her mind's eye. Beauty is in the eye of the beholder, of course, but what is in the eye that the beholder beholds? His arm is still bandaged, but the bandage is soiled now, and gray, and there is an odor — a stale, medicinal odor of this, and of his cigarette smoke, and the sick-sweet smell of sweat and spent semen — in the air. She should get up now, hop into the shower, towel herself dry, slip into her clothes again, make a little joke, and be on her way. But she does none of these things, and continues to lie there in the growing darkness, where even the sight of her own white, dieted body, the belly kept flat through exercise, her breasts tipped slightly to one side, and the inevitable stretch marks, manages only to fill her with despair. Behind her there is more motion, as Littlefield pulls on his discarded underpants, Jockey shorts, the kind that little boys wear. There is the snap of the elastic waistband against his stomach.

Melissa's almost visionary inspiration of barely an hour ago seems to have disappeared. On her way out to the motel, in a taxi, she had had this crazy idea. This group had talent, there was no question about that; their young audiences loved them; their sound was right, their sound was now, their beat was new, and their message was today. But they probably had no sense of organization, no sense of business whatsoever. Off the stage, no doubt, they squabbled and bickered with one another. She could become their manager. She could handle their publicity, book their dates, plan their tours, and teach them how to handle money. The name they had chosen for themselves was, of course, quite simply awful, but she could insist that they change that. She would change it to something upbeat, lively, provocative but on the sly side, something memorable like The Beatles, The Who, The Rolling Stones. In the taxi, she had thought of several such names, but they escape her now. She was certain that the group did drugs — didn't they all? — but when she became their manager she would change all that, too, for along that route did not lie the way to fortune and stardom, platinum record after platinum record. Oh, yes, that was one of the names she had thought of in the taxi. Call them The Platinums, and perhaps for a gimmick, have all their hair dyed platinum blond? Too much like David Bowie? Perhaps. Think young thoughts, she often told herself, keep up with what young people are talking about, doing, listening to — that is the way to stay young. The python was a tacky gimmick, as well as an unreliable one. Under her management of the group, there would be no more pythons. All this and more, she had thought of in the taxi, but all of it has lost its luster now.

Finally, she says, "I have something for you." She leans over the edge of the bed and reaches for her purse, which lies near the heap of her clothes beside the bed. From an inside pocket, she fishes out the folded check and hands it to him, without comment.

Lying on his back with his cigarette clenched between his teeth, he examines it farsightedly, at arm's length, turning it this way and that until he can catch it in the light that remains. He whistles softly and says, "Oh, Mama!" Then he leaps to his feet, standing on the mattress, and cries, "Oh, Sugar Mama! You are my Sugar Mama! You are this boy's Sugar Mama, yes indeed!"

Melissa rolls off the bed, picks up her lace-trimmed bikini panties, and steps into them. She reaches for her bra. "I'm not your Sugar Mama!" she says angrily. "I'm not anything to you at all. Don't think I'm giving you that check for letting you go to bed with me! I was going to give it to you anyway. That check was written before I left my house. That check is to compensate you for your engagement here, and nothing more. I'm giving it to you because I thought your group deserved it, and because I felt responsible. I don't have to pay men for making love to me!"

But he has already leaped off the bed and is in the bathroom now, urinating noisily into the bowl beyond the open door, and probably can't even hear her.

She snatches up her blouse and skirt. "Listen to me!" she cries. "Don't call me your Sugar Mama! I'm paying you for a concert date, not for your lousy lovemaking! And don't think you can come back to me for any more. I don't pay for sex, and I don't ask for sex! So don't think you can come back to me and offer more sex, and get more money, or think because I've let you have sex with me you can come back and blackmail me! I didn't ask for sex with you! And your sex stinks — do you hear that? Your sex stinks, and I hate you! Do you hear that? Stinks!" The only reply is the sound of the toilet flushing.

"*Stinks!* You're a rotten lover!"

Of course this is all a far, far cry from the proposition she had thought of offering him, on her way over here in the taxi. And the only thing she is sure of now is that she will probably never see or hear from him again.

*   *   *

In the house at 2040 Washington Street, Assaria LeBaron has decided that she is finished with Archie McPherson. He has betrayed her confidence, and so that will be the end of him. He has served whatever usefulness he had, and now he will be dispensed with. Probably, knowing that she and Archie have been in cahoots, Gabe will fire him anyway, and he will move on to some other part of the country, out of her life, good riddance. And yet — and yet — there is one more way in which he might prove useful, and perhaps that one avenue should be explored. But she will think about that later. Right now, there is something else to occupy her mind. Her granddaughter Kimmie has dropped by for tea. They are moving through the long picture gallery now, side by side, toward the drawing room where Thomas has set out the tea service, a tray of little sandwiches, and the fixings for Sari's martini, which she usually prefers to tea.

"Great-Grandpa's wine barrel," Kimberly LeBaron says, as they approach it.

"Your great-*great*-grandpa," Sari corrects. "In a family, it's important to keep the generations straight. Your great-grandpa was Julius. Mario was his father, so that's two greats to you. And look," she says suddenly, "it's weeping. See those tiny beads of moisture collecting between the staves? It happens in certain kinds of weather. And it means that something, some change, is going on inside. Wine, you see, never dies. It goes on growing, changing, for centuries — forever, if you let it. Someday I want to take you out to the vineyards, and give you a little wine history lesson. Count Haraszthy — everything. Would you like that?" Sari has always had a special place in her heart for this exquisite child.

What is it about little girls in their early teens that Assaria LeBaron has always found so beguiling? Papa LeBaron must have sensed it, too, wanting the children all to have their portraits painted at that age. With Kimmie, it is that little bunched business around her cheeks and eyes and chin — traces of baby fat that she still retains — a reminder that the face has not quite finished forming itself, has not quite made up its mind what it is going to be. It gives Kimmie a questioning, questing look — a look of puzzled, but pleasant, anticipation. The nose has not yet made up its mind, either, but already there is a hint of nostrils that will one day flare imperiously when the face takes command of a situation, and issues a polite but firm order. In Kimmie, sitting there in her fresh white blouse and neatly pressed green and white kiltie skirt with her carefully cut brown bangs across her forehead, it is possible for Sari to see herself at that age. Yes, Kimmie is destined to be a beauty, and Sari is pleased to see that Kimmie has inherited her own good looks. This may sound like vanity on Sari's part. So what? It is.

"Count Haraszthy?"

"Count Agoston Haraszthy — a Hungarian nobleman who came out to California with the forty-niners. He started everything. He brought with him a hundred thousand vines from Europe — hundreds of varieties — and planted them here. He had the vision. Later, he went to Nicaragua and tried the same thing, and got eaten by crocodiles for his trouble."

"Tell me the story, Grandma."

"Tell me a story," Sari says. "Do you remember when you were a little girl, and you'd ask me to tell you a story? And I'd say I had two stories, one about a good little girl, and one about a bad little girl, and which did you want to hear?"

"I don't remember that, Grandma."

"You always wanted to hear about the bad little girl, of course!" Or was that Melissa?

"I don't remember that, Grandma."

"Well, it could have been . . . someone else." Sari wheels her chair to the tea table. "Now, sit right there where I can see you, Lambchop," she says. "And I know how you like your tea. One lump with a slice of lemon. Help yourself to sandwiches."

"Grandma," Kimmie says. "Why are you and Daddy mad at each other?"

"Why, whatever gave you that idea, Kimmie?" Sari asks.

"I happened to hear him and Mummy talking about you the other day. And he called you a — well, it wasn't a very nice word."

"Well," Sari says easily, "your father and I are having a little business disagreement right now, that's all it is. It's nothing personal. I love your father very much, you know that. Business disagreements have nothing to do with family disagreements." Or do they? How can they not when the family is the business, and the business is the family? "And now," she says brightly, "would you like me to tell you all about Count Haraszthy? He was a very colorful figure."

Stirring the tea in her teacup, pressing the lemon slice against the side of the cup with the back of her spoon, Kimmie looks thoughtful. "Maybe some other time," she says. And then, "Tell me about Great-Grandpa."

"Great-great, you mean?"

"No, just plain great. Great-Grandpa and Great-Grandma, who are buried under the walnut trees out in Sonoma. Why were they buried there, and not in Saint Francis Cemetery, along with the rest of the family? You've always promised that someday you'd tell me that story, Grandma."

Sari studies her granddaughter's face. How old is Kimmie now? Fifteen. Old enough to hear it, probably. "Now, that was a very sad story," she begins.

"Tell it to me, Grandma!"

But where to begin? With Mama LeBaron interrupting the solemn raptness of the mass? *Misereatur tui omnipotens, Deus et dismissis peccatis tuis. . . . Misereatur vestri omnipotens Deus et dismissis peccatis vestris, perducat vos ad vitam aeternam. Induligentiam, absolutionem, et remissionem* . . . And Constance LeBaron rising drunkenly from her pew, and starting toward the altar, shouting, "Indulgence . . . absolution . . . *is there any eternal life for me?*" And the hands reaching out, trying to persuade the drunken woman to return to her seat, stop trying to disrupt — but no, Sari decides, she will not begin there. She will leave that part out. *De mortuis.* Even though that was the day it happened.

"Well, to understand what happened," she begins, "you have to put things in the context of the times. There were two very terrible periods in the history of this country, and one followed right on the heels of the other. This was long before you were born, but you may have read about them in your history books at school. The first was Prohibition, and the second was the Great Depression. Have you read about those two periods?"

"Oh, yes."

"The first, Prohibition, was the ruination of the wine makers. Most growers plowed their vineyards under and tried to turn them over to row crops — tomatoes, beans, almonds, walnuts, and apricots. But there is something about these valleys of ours — Sonoma, Napa, parts of the San Joaquin — a combination of soil and climate, the warm days, the cool, dry nights, that makes it seem as though God had designed them just for the growing of wine grapes, and nothing more. The new crops did poorly, nothing but wine grapes wanted to take to the soil.

"Meanwhile, the artisans — the coopers who made our barrels, the tasters, the blenders — went off into other trades and soon forgot their art. Most of our coopers were Italians, and many of them went back to Italy. In the space of little more than a decade, wine making became a lost art. And, meanwhile, your great-grandpa, Julius LeBaron — imprudently, as it turned out — continued to live very high off the hog. In the big house on Nob Hill — that Standard station on California Street is where his house was — and the servants, and the trips to Hawaii every winter on the *Lurline*. He was living on his investments, he said. And then the stock-market crash came in twenty-nine, and all the investments just . . . disappeared. Vanished. Gone with the wind. And so —"

"And then? Then what?"

"He was a ruined man. One day in nineteen-thirty, one Sunday after church, he wrote a letter outlining how he and his wife wished to be buried. And then he took her by the hand and led her out into the Sonoma vineyard, or what had once *been* the Sonoma vineyard. They knelt, all alone, side by side among the dead grapevines, and said a little prayer, asking the Almighty for forgiveness for what they were about to do. Then he placed the barrel of his pistol — all vineyard owners carried guns, it was part of the uniform — against his wife's temple, and fired, and then he put the gun to his own temple, and fired again. They found them there a few hours later."

Kimberly is silent for a moment. Then she says, "Then what did you do, Grandma?"

"Me? Do? Your grandfather was utterly devastated. His parents' deaths seemed like the end of the world to him. Immediately we discovered the huge debts. This house — this house he gave us as a wedding present — wasn't even paid for. But I said to my husband, 'Look — we still have the land. The land in Sonoma and Napa and so on.' I said, 'We have the land, and Prohibition's going to end. Let's go out there and start replanting vines. In five years, we'll have a harvest!' And so that's what we did, he and I, and his sister Joanna working beside us. All day long on our hands and knees, planting vines, and then at the end of the first year, chip-budding them. You should have seen my hands, thick with calluses, covered with cuts from the grafting knives. I used to think I would never see my fingernails clean again, the dirt was down so deep underneath them. We worked right along with the field hands — the Chinks, and the wetbacks, and the Okies from the Dust Bowl. I know those aren't nice names to call them, but that's what they were called in those days. We were field hands ourselves. And I remember standing out there in the vineyard with the Chinks and the wetbacks and the Okies from the Dust Bowl, shouting, beating gongs, trying to frighten away the larks — thousands of insatiable birds — that were about to devastate our first harvest. And did devastate it. But we were young then, and full of piss and vinegar, and we decided not to be discouraged. So we went right on, and when the next year's harvest succeeded, we were glad we did. And now, here we are. In this state of California, where agriculture is the number-one industry, ours is the third-largest segment of it — an eight-billion-dollar-a-year business, I read the other day in the *Wall Street Journal*."

Once more Kimberly's face is thoughtful. Finally, she says, "That's a wonderful story, Grandma. But there's only one part that I don't understand."

"What's that, Lambchop?"

"If Great-Grandpa and Great-Grandma were all alone in the vineyard that day they shot each other, how does anyone know that that's the way it happened — that he shot her first, and that they knelt and said a little prayer?"

"*Aha!*" Sari cries, sitting forward in her chair. "That's the sixty-four-thousand-dollar question! *Exactly! Who knows* how it happened? Maybe she shot him first! But do you know that you're the first person in three generations to have the wit or guts to ask that simple question? You're growing up, Kimmie! You're growing up when you begin to question the tales your elders tell you! Good girl! All I can say is that's the tale they like to tell, but why should you believe a word of it? But then that's the story of this whole family, isn't it? Tall tales . . . fictions . . . lies . . . deceptions." And why, all at once, is Sari weeping — weeping like the old wine barrel in the picture gallery? "Lies . . . deceptions . . . cheats!" She fumbles at the purse in her lap, extracts a handkerchief, and dabs at her streaming eyes.

"What's the matter, Grandma?"

"I don't know. Why am I crying? The story of this family — deceptions and tall tales. Oh, what's happening to me? What's happening to this family, Kimmie? I just don't know!"

"Please don't cry, Grandma. I love you, Grandma!"

Her weeping will not stop. "I loved your grandfather so," she sobs. "Why did he have to do this to me?"

Six

A VISIT FROM KIMMIE inevitably makes Sari remember her own school days. By comparison, she thinks, Kimmie has had it very easy.

To begin with, though Mrs. Bonkowski had succeeded in teaching her a number of English words during that first summer in Terre Haute, Sari had not learned to read the language at all. Therefore, though she was theoretically old enough to enter the third grade, she had been placed in a kindergarten class. She can remember sitting, painfully, in one of those undersize chairs, her knees crunched uncomfortably under a tiny desk in a roomful of five-year-olds, feeling awkward, foreign, and stupid while the five-year-olds recited the alphabet and spelled out simple words whose letters made no sense to her at all. Her teacher, a Miss Hazeltine, seemed a very rough and cross old lady, and when it came to Sari's turn to recite, and Sari could not, she simply passed her by and went impatiently on to the next child. At eleven o'clock each morning, each member of Miss Hazeltine's class was required to take a nap for half an hour. Small rugs were brought out and unrolled on the floor in rows, and each child curled up on his or her assigned rug for the nap period. But Sari was too old for these morning naps, and her rug was too small for any degree of comfort, and for her restless tossings and turnings and inability to sleep, she was scolded by Miss Hazeltine for trying to disrupt the class. "I see you're determined to be nothing but a troublemaker," Miss Hazeltine said to her. Meanwhile, when Sari tried to make friends with boys and girls closer to her own age in the classes above her, they treated her as though she were some sort of freak. Soon they had a jeering name for her — "Polack-Pants." When she tried to explain to them that she was Russian and not Polish and that there was an important difference, they just laughed at her and walked away. Of course, she was too ashamed to tell Gabe Pollack or Mrs. Bonkowski about any of this, and so when either of them asked her, "How was school today?" she would try to smile, and lie, and say, "Just fine!"

But secretly she had become convinced that she would never learn to read English. She had heard that American law required that every American boy or girl must go to school until age sixteen. The yawning, horrible eternity of eight long years of kindergarten — at her too-small desk and on her too-small nap rug — loomed miserably ahead of her, and Miss Hazeltine did nothing to dispel the accuracy of this vision.

Then — it must have been nearly halfway through that kindergarten year — a third-grade teacher, Miss Sharp, took notice of her. Miss Sharp, despite her name, was not sharp at all. She was round and smooth and young and pretty, with a face and body that seemed to contain no corners or angles at all. Everything about her was an unbroken series of curves and gentle ellipses. Miss Sharp began keeping Sari after school to coach her with her reading, patiently and calmly. Sari remembers particularly one of Miss Sharp's teaching techniques. She would get Sari to memorize the words of songs. She remembers:

> Come to the church in the wildwood,
> Come to the church in the vale —
> No-o spot is so dear to my chi-ildhood . . .

And so on. And then she would have Sari sing the songs while reading the words from the printed text in the songbook. As they sang and read, Sari would suddenly remember her own mother singing to her as a little girl in Yiddish, and the words to a song that meant, "Little rose red, little rose red . . . little rose red of the heath . . ." That was all she could remember of that song, just a fragment of it, but she was suddenly able to see her mother's face clearly again, and smell the coal fire in the stove, and the loaves of bread baking, and hear, from outside the little house, the knife-and-scissors-grinder calling, "Sharp knives, ladies!" as he made his way through the streets of the village. One day, Miss Sharp appeared wearing a bright red scarf that even had gold fringe on it, pinned to the bosom of her dress with a cameo brooch, and it was so like Sari's own mother's scarf that it was possible to believe that her real mother had been sent back to her.

> Ma-axwelton's braes are bonny,
> Where early fa-alls the dew . . .

And even songs in French:

> *Frère Jacques, Frère Jacques*
> *Dormez-vous . . . ?*

And then the miraculous moment came when, all at once, those indecipherable little squiggles of black ink on the printed page transformed themselves into letters, and the letters into words, and the words into sentences, and the sentences into a story that not only made sense but was exciting. Suddenly Sari was able to read a whole page of a book without making a mistake, and then two pages, and then a whole chapter. That was when Miss Sharp announced that she was ready to join the children her own age in the third grade.

On her first day in third grade, there was a spelling bee. Sari won it! She was the star!

And by the end of her first year in school, she was told that she could skip the fourth grade and go directly into the fifth.

In the fifth grade, of course, she was a year younger than the other boys and girls in her class. They refused to be her friends not only because she was younger, but because she was too smart.

But it was in the fifth grade that Sari Latham became aware of . . . the Van Dusen Sisters.

The Van Dusen Sisters were something.

The Sisters, Coralee and Roxanne Van Dusen, were twelve and thirteen, respectively, and yet they were both only in the fifth grade. Both should have been further along in school, of course, but instead of having been allowed to skip a grade, the Van Dusen Sisters had been Held Back. This troubled the Sisters not at all. They despised school, and hated their teachers, and, in turn, their teachers despised and hated them. Coralee and Roxanne Van Dusen were above all that. They strode about the hallways of the school like grand duchesses on a yacht, and paused, posing in their high-heeled shoes, hips and pelvic bones thrust forward in the manner of the fashion models of the day, tittering and whispering their little confidences and secrets to each other. The Van Dusen Sisters had no friends whatsoever, but didn't care. They were aristocrats, sufficient unto themselves, and looked down their noses with disdain at all who were not members of their private, chosen circle.

The Van Dusen Sisters were not rich. No child at Sari's school was rich. The rich children of Terre Haute lived in another part of the city altogether, and went to something called Country Day or else far away in a region of the universe that was known vaguely as "The East." The rich children were the sons and daughters of food and meat packers, brewery owners, the owners of a sanitary can plant, or the paint and varnish works, the box factories, and the paper and rolling mills. One never even saw these people. And yet the Van Dusen Sisters, who had never met any of these people either, affected all their supposed haughty and high-toned and roguish and impudent airs.

With their stylishly shingled hair-dos, the Sisters fairly pranced about. They wore not only wobbly French-heeled shoes, but also the daringly short-short skirts that were presaging the Flapper Era.

The Shocking Sisters were five years ahead of their time! The Sisters rouged their knees, painted their lips, and dusted their faces chalky white with Freeman's Face Powder, which cost twenty-five cents for a single tiny box. Furthermore, the Sisters both had *breasts* and, even more than that, wore tight brassieres to bind themselves down and achieve the fashionable flat-chested look. The Van Dusen Sisters were the talk of Terre Haute, even of the whole of Vigo County. It was said that at night Coralee and Roxanne Van Dusen went out and spooned with young men who drove Overland 4 automobiles, and it was even whispered that the Sisters didn't mind "going all the way," whatever that meant. Their circle of acquaintanceship was said to extend far beyond the city limits and county lines — to as far away as soldiers stationed at Camp Atterbury!

At school, the Van Dusen Sisters never said hello to anybody. They simply made their impertinent observations or asked their rude questions, and strutted off. But what impressed Sari about the Van Dusen Sisters the most was the fact that, somehow, they had managed to achieve grown-up status instantly, and had stepped from little girlhood into full adulthood without having to be bothered with any of the growing pains or insecurities or self-doubts of adolescence. They were *finished people.* They were not only *there,* in the wondrous world and landscape of grown-upness, but they seemed to *belong* there, to be *at home* there, and never to have lived anywhere else. They seemed *always* to have been at ease lighting up their Murad cigarettes and (it was said) tilting back their silver flasks of hard liquor. It was not that Sari envied or admired the Van Dusen Sisters exactly. It was more that she wondered if it would ever be possible for someone as shy and uncertain as herself to step, with such supreme self-confidence, into the world of grown-up men and women who talked in grown-up ways and did grown-up things.

When Sari entered the sixth grade, the Van Dusen Sisters were still in the fifth. Coralee and Roxanne had been held back again, a fact they seemed to regard as some delicious private joke. Indeed, the Sisters attended classes only sporadically — only when, it was said, the truant officer came after them. And when they did appear at school they spent most of their time with their bobbed heads together, whispering, and from their whispers you would occasionally hear words and phrases such as "hangover," and "getting my period," and "moonshine hooch." Sari was quite sure that the Sisters were unaware of her existence, was sure they had never even noticed her, since they had never once so much as glanced in her direction. And so she was startled one day to discover that her presence had at least made a passing impression on their gaudy, glamorous lives.

It had become a fact of Sari's life that the only real friends she had at school were the younger children she had gotten to know during those first months of kindergarten. Too young — and, again, too smart — to be tolerated by her present classmates, she was still treated fondly by the younger children. She joined them at lunchtime, and at recess times, played their games with them, and, because she was three years older, frequently was picked as captain of their teams. One day, during lunch hour, she saw the Van Dusen Sisters striding imperiously toward her in their thin high heels. She had expected to pass by them unnoticed, as usual, but today, for some reason, the Sisters suddenly stopped and planted themselves in front of her.

"We know all about you, Polack-Pants," Coralee Van Dusen said in her customary abrupt, confrontational way.

"We know," echoed Sister Roxanne, snapping her chewing gum loudly.

"We know why you only play with all the little kids."

"We know, Polack-Pants. It's not because they like you. Don't get that big idea."

"It's because the little kids are the only ones you can boss around!"

Then they were off, hips swinging, short skirts swishing. And Sari had stood there, all alone, in the corridor of her school, for several minutes, close to tears. With their worldly ways and knowledge, were they right?

Perhaps what the Van Dusen Sisters said was true.

Perhaps Sari belonged to no world at all.

Perhaps she never would.

The Van Dusen Sisters never spoke to her again. By the seventh grade, they had simply disappeared.

At home, it was somewhat different. But there it was Gabe Pollack's world, and Mrs. Bonkowski's world, and she did not really belong to either of them. At home, Gabe Pollack liked to talk, and clearly he enjoyed having Sari as his principal listener. At night, sitting up in bed, hugging her knees, in the room they shared on Wabash Avenue, she listened to him.

"Do you know what the most powerful weapon in the world is, Sari?" he asked her once. "More powerful than any weapon of war? More powerful than the bank account of the richest millionaire?"

"What's that, Gabe?"

He smiled at her, reached out to the low dresser that stood between their beds, and picked up a yellow pencil. "This," he said to her. "Mightier than the sword. With this little pencil, you can write words. Words can be put into sentences. Sentences can express ideas. Ideas can change men's minds. And men's minds can change the world." On looking back, Gabe's youthful notions do not seem terribly startling or original, but to Assaria, six years younger than he, they seemed both profound and fascinating.

It was at this dresser that he sat, many evenings after work, and wrote his stories. The stories had a double purpose. They were to help Gabe improve his command of English, and he also someday hoped to sell them to his editor, so that he could call himself "a real newspaperman," and not just be a delivery boy. Often, when he had finished writing a story, he would read it aloud to her. The stories were always based on some aspect of the city's life that he had observed during his working rounds, and a typical one would begin: "Today, on a bustling street in downtown Terre Haute, a poor Negro shoeshiner was offering his services to the city's businessmen as they passed by, crying, 'Shine, suh? Shine, suh?' All at once, as if from nowhere, and for no reason that was clearly perceptible to onlookers, a well-dressed young dandy with a sneer on his face and contempt in his eye, lunged toward the lad and, with the toe of his well-polished boot, kicked . . ." The stories often had a moral — the triumph or the vindication of the underdog or the little fellow — and Assaria found them beautiful and heart-breaking. And yet Gabe had not succeeded in selling any of them. But he remained cheerfully undiscouraged, and continued to place his stories in the editor's pigeonhole in the mornings when he arrived for work. "This is America," he would say to her. "This is the land of the little fellow, where if a fellow works hard enough and long enough, he gets his due." Once he said to her, "Someday, I'm going to run my own newspaper — a newspaper for the little fellow. I'll do it. Wait and see."

And sometimes he would read to her from other people's works. His favorite author was Herman Melville, and his next favorite was Joseph Conrad, because Conrad had been born with another language — Polish, in fact — and had taught himself to write in English. She could remember him reading to her from *Lord Jim:*

> She strode like a grenadier, was strong and upright like an obelisk, had a beautiful face, a candid brow, pure eyes —

And Assaria said, "I'd like to grow up to be just like that!" Then he finished the sentence:

> — and not a thought of her own in her head.

"But not like that," she had said, and they both laughed.

And he read *Moby-Dick* to her, and she remembered when he came to that haunting final passage:

> On the second day, a sail drew near, nearer, and picked me up at last. It was the devious-cruising *Rachel,* that in her retracing search after her missing children, only found another orphan.

He looked at her quickly, his large eyes dark and bright, and she felt tears in her own eyes, too. She had known that she was called an orphan, but had had only a loose understanding of what, in the human sense, the word meant. Now she knew.

Often the two of them would sit up very late into the night in that room on Wabash Avenue, long after the hour Mrs. Bonkowski had told Assaria should have been her proper bedtime, while Gabe talked, dreamed aloud to her, read his own and other writers' stories to her, and told her all his plans.

When Assaria reached age eleven, Mrs. Bonkowski decreed that their sleeping quarters in the room should be divided by a heavy burlap curtain. "It's only proper," she said. "It's either this, or two separate rooms, and Gabe says he can't afford a second room for you. I run a proper house here, and what *I* can't afford is talk."

But, sitting under the covers in their respective beds, Sari and Gabe would usually keep the curtain parted as they talked into the night. Finally, he would cry, "Taps! Soldiers rest! Lights out!" Then he would tuck her quickly into bed, close the curtain, turn out the light, and undress himself in the dark.

Who could have dreamed a father more wonderful than that?

Then came that glorious day in the early spring of 1923 when Gabe burst into the room, just before suppertime, full of news. "Guess what!" he cried. "I've got a new job! Working for a big paper in a big city, Sari — San Francisco! One of the biggest cities in the West! I sent them my stories, Sari, and they've hired me. As a reporter, a real newspaperman — for thirty dollars a week! I'm going to San Francisco!"

Sitting on her bed, and seeing his good, broad face so happy, she knew that she shouldn't be thinking only of herself, that she should be happy for him too, but the fact was that she was, all at once, worried. "Am I going to San Francisco, too?" she asked him.

"Of course you are!" he said. "You don't think I'd go off to San Francisco and leave you here, do you? We're going together, and we're going in *style*. We're going to San Francisco, and we're going in a Pullman car." And he had stepped quickly to where she sat, lifted her by the armpits to her feet, and swung her around and around.

As he swung her, her feet left the floor, and suddenly her whole body seemed to swell and fill with a strange rush of totally new excitement. What was this? She felt choked and dizzy, and deliriously happy all at the same time. Bright wings were fluttering inside her, crimson wings over which she had no control, and clinging to him, hugging her body tightly against his, she felt her eyes close and her head go hot, as though with fever, and suddenly without meaning to she was kissing him, kissing his cheeks, his ears, his eyelids, his throat, and then his mouth, her body pressed against him, arched and expectant — flying to him — and kissing him again, her mouth opening to him, her tongue searching for his.

Just as suddenly as he had picked her up, he set her down again, dropped his arms, and took two quick backward steps away from her. He stared at her, but his face was no longer happy. His eyes were wide, and his face was flushed, and he looked dismayed. "I've got to go out," he said. Then he turned on his heel, pulled open the door to the room, and was gone.

That night at supper, Mrs. Bonkowski said, "Where's Gabe? Why isn't Gabe here?" Then she threw Sari a quick, suspicious look. "Where's your friend Gabe? He's late for supper."

"He had an errand to do, I think."

"Well, supper can't wait for latecomers, can it?" Mrs. Bonkowski said. "If he's late, he's late, and that's all there is to it. I hope he isn't counting on me leaving something for him in the ice box. He knows the rules — no p.g.'s in the kitchen."

"He's got a new job," Sari said. "In San Francisco. We're moving to San Francisco."

Mrs. Bonkowski looked glum. "Well, that's the way of it, isn't it?" she said. "You get some good p.g.'s, and they up and leave on you. Just like that. Now I'll have to find somebody to fill that room. That's the life I have to live, taking in p.g.'s. I wouldn't of had to of lived this kind of life if Bonkowski hadn't of up and died on me."

Much later, after Sari had gone to bed and turned off the light, and he had still not come back, she finally heard him letting himself into the room and heard him taking off his clothes, as he always did, in the dark, and change into his nightshirt.

"Gabe?"

At first he said nothing, and from the other side of the closed burlap curtain she could hear the springs sag as he got into bed, and the rustle of the bedclothes as he pulled the sheet and blankets over him, heard him settle his head against the pillow.

"Gabe? You're not angry at me for something, are you?"

"In San Francisco, we'll have two rooms," he said finally, in a strangely gruff voice from the darkness. "In San Francisco, we'll each have our own room. We'll be able to afford that, on thirty dollars a week."

She didn't answer him, and after a while she turned on her side, away from him, facing the wall, listening to the steady rhythm of his breathing. She knew that she was all at once terribly unhappy, and the room seemed to fill with the sour smell of her mother's red scarf burning, its gold fringe twisting into ugly black worms. I want, she thought, someone to love me, someone to sing to me, but who can that someone be? All I wanted was arms to hold me, and if they can't be Gabe's, then whose? Everything seemed to have changed, to have turned upside down, and would never be the same again.

And she knew that she no longer thought of Gabe Pollack as her father, and had not thought of him as her father for a long time, and would not think of him that way again. Beneath the bedclothes she touched her body with her fingertips, and felt herself hurt there, and there, and there.

Gabe had told her that San Francisco was a big city, but she was unprepared for the city's busyness and scale. The biggest building in Terre Haute had been City Hall, but the huge gabled and turreted Ferry Building in San Francisco would have swallowed that. Buildings taller than any she had ever seen pierced the skyline, and the streets were noisy with trolleys and cable cars that were pulled along by invisible hawsers underneath the streets. At intersections, where two cables crossed at right angles, there was a stomach-wrenching moment when the grip man was required to pick up speed, then release his grip in order to pass over the intersecting cable, then grip his cable again when the crossing was passed. Terre Haute had been flat for as far as the eye could see, but San Francisco was a city of tall, steep hills — so steep that, on some of them, the sidewalks rose in steps. From the tops of the hills — Nob Hill, Telegraph Hill, Russian Hill were some of their names — there were views of the great blue bay filled with traffic of ships from foreign ports and the ferry boats that plied their way continuously back and forth between San Francisco and the Oakland Mole, which was the westernmost terminus of the east-west railroads. At the mouth of the bay was the Golden Gate, and the Pacific Ocean beyond, and, on clear days, a glimpse of the distant Farallon Islands. But what impressed her most about San Francisco was its sense of newness and cleanliness. In 1906, much of the city had been destroyed by a great earthquake and fire. But the city had quickly and enthusiastically rebuilt itself, and if the entire city appeared to have been constructed at the same time it was because it had been. San Francisco struck her as being all of one piece.

Of course Gabe's new job, as a general-assignment reporter for the *Chronicle*, kept him out long hours, and kept him moving about the city. He was forever being called to the courthouse, or to investigate a burglary in the suburbs, or to go to the scene of a barroom fight or murder on the waterfront, or a tong war in China-town. But that was all right. She tended to feel shy and uncomfortable in Gabe's presence now. The old easiness between them seemed to have been replaced with — what? An excessive politeness seemed to be what it was. At first, this new distance had distressed and confused her, but now that was all right, too.

She had decided to do something that would make him very angry.

He had found rooms for them both in a boardinghouse on Howard Street, but their new landlady was a far cry from the loquacious Mrs. Bonkowski. She was a Mrs. Tristram Dodge, a thin and mousy woman whose principal interest was her cat, a big tiger tom named Pussy, who draped himself across Mrs. Dodge's shoulders while she sat in her front parlor with her mending basket. Ignored by her landlady, Sari had all the freedom she needed to work on her plan. Gabe seldom came home for supper now, and often did not come home until after Sari had gone to bed. And in the mornings he was usually up and out of the house before it was time for Sari to rise and dress for school. On weekends, he often shut himself in his room, where Sari could hear him — he had a typewriter now — working on his stories. She missed their late-evening talks, but she knew that his work came first. Besides, she herself had not been idle.

She had waited for a week to tell him her news, wanting to surprise him with the solid proof of it. Then she had tapped on his door, and, when he opened it, she had handed him ten dollars.

"What's this?" he asked her suspiciously. "Where did you get this?"

"I have a job," she said. "And that's my first week's wages."

"A job? What kind of a job?"

"I'm an usherette at the Odeon movie theatre on Market Street. Ten dollars a week."

"You're too young. There are laws — "

"I lied about my age," she said triumphantly. "I told them I was fourteen, and they believed me. They gave me a uniform with a blue jacket and a white shirtwaist, and a little flashlight. I help show people to their seats."

"But what about your schoolwork?"

"The job is after school. Afternoons from three o'clock till seven, and Saturdays from noon to eight."

"Your homework — "

"That's easy. After I've shown the people in, I find a seat in the back row and do my homework with my flashlight."

"That's bad for your eyes!"

"Nonsense. I can read as well — even better — with my flashlight than I can with my bedroom lamp!"

Standing in the doorway, staring at the money in his hand, he said. "I don't want you to do this. I can't take this money from you."

"I just want to pay my share of the room and board," she said. "Why should you do it all when I can help? Isn't this what you're always saying about America? If a person works hard, he can get ahead? I just want to work hard and get ahead — just like you!"

He kept staring at the money, shaking his head.

"Besides," she said, "I get to see all the movies free!"

"No," he said. "You'll neglect your schoolwork, watching movies."

"But you only have to watch the movie once. When it comes on again, you already know the story. That's when I do my homework."

"No," he said finally. "I'm not going to let you do this."

"What?" she cried. "What do you mean? How can you not let me do it? I'm doing it already!"

"I'm your guardian. You're to do as I say."

"Well, I won't!" she said angrily. "I've spent six years doing what you wanted me to do. Now I'm going to do what I want to do for a change!"

"And if I forbid you?"

"Then I'll run away. I'll run away, quit school, find a full-time job, and you'll never find me, Gabe Pollack!"

"Job? What kind of job can you get — a girl of thirteen?"

"I'll become a prostitute, that's what I'll do!"

His hand, clutching the money, went up, as though he were about to strike her. "Where are you learning gutter talk like that?" he said. "At school? At the movies?"

"And I'll tell you something else," she said. "I won't just become a prostitute! I'll become the best damned prostitute in the world!" Then she had slammed the door in his face, run down the hall to her own room, let herself in, and bolted the door behind her.

Alone, she pulled the ribbons out of her hair, unbuttoned the top buttons of her blouse and, in front of her dressing-table mirror assumed the languid, smoldering pose of Blanche Sweet in *Anna Christie*, which had been playing just that week at the Odeon.

Presently there was a tap at her door, and his voice said, "I'm sorry, Sari. I don't want you to run away. Please don't run away."

But she was giggling so hard at her image as a prostitute that she couldn't answer him.

And so, every afternoon, she would run — run the twelve blocks from her school to the Odeon to save the nickel carfare — and change into her usherette's uniform to be ready to be at work with her flashlight by three o'clock. And, once a week, she would slip ten dollars under Gabe's door without comment.

These were some of the movies that she saw: *The Three Musketeers*, with Douglas Fairbanks; the *Four Horsemen of the Apocalypse* and *The Sheik*, both with the dashingly exotic Rudolph Valentino, the new film sensation; *Way Down East*, with Lillian Gish, whose wide-eyed, pinch-lipped look of injured innocence Sari also tried to imitate in her mirror; *Peck's Bad Boy,* with Jackie Coogan; *Where the Pavement Ends,* with Ramon Novarro and Alice Terry; and *A Woman of Paris,* with Adolphe Menjou and Edna Purviance . . .

These are only a few of the titles and performances that Sari remembers.

And of course she had lied to Gabe Pollack, at least a little bit, because some of her favorite films she watched two, three, or as many as half a dozen times.

"Only a B in history?" Gabe Pollack would say to her. "You're watching too many movies."

"History bores me. It's nothing but memorizing the dates of wars and the names of generals. Everything else is an A — and an A-plus in math."

The movies and the people who made them were very much on the public's mind in those days. Around that time, as some of you may remember, there had been a dreadful scandal involving a movie personality, and it had happened right there in San Francisco, in a fancy suite at the St. Francis Hotel. A popular movie comedian named Roscoe "Fatty" Arbuckle had been arrested in connection with the death of a young woman during a wild orgy at the hotel. The woman was said to have been a local prostitute, and there were other, darker implications of misdeeds involving illicit narcotics, illegal alcohol, and bizarre sexual practices. Apparently, the actual details of what had gone on were so shocking and ghoulish that even the most lurid of Mr. William Randolph Hearst's newspapers would not print them, and there was only whispered speculation about what might really have happened. The only consensus seemed to be to the effect that the girl's death had somehow been caused by Fatty Arbuckle's great weight. At Assaria Latham's school, her schoolmates, knowing that she worked at a theatre where Arbuckle's films had been shown — though no more, since all his films were now banned — naturally assumed that Sari must somehow know all the sordid facts. Of course she knew no more about the affair than anyone else. But it pleased her to think that the other girls suspected that she knew more than she was telling.

Meanwhile, during those years of the early 1920s, a new phrase had entered the American lexicon: "movie star." To be a movie star, Sari had read, it helped if a girl happened to be small. Somehow, small women seemed to fit better into the celluloid frames and, despite their appearances on the big screen, she read, many of the actresses she admired the most — the Gish sisters, Nita Naldi, Mary Pickford — were slightly built women. And Sari herself, as her fourteenth birthday approached, could see that she was going to be small, barely five feet three inches tall. Studying herself in front of her mirror in those days, practicing the mannerisms and expressions and gestures of the silent-film stars she had watched on the screen, Assaria Latham was able to see herself maturing into a tiny, almond-eyed, olive-skinned, almost Oriental-looking beauty with extraordinary thick, dark red hair, which she caught back with ribbons at the nape of her neck. She had not worked at the Odeon for long before she had decided that, with luck, becoming a movie star might be something that she could reasonably aspire to.

All over America, it seemed, pretty girls were being plucked from beauty contests and from amateur theatrical productions to be screen-tested and offered movie contracts. And it was all happening just a few hundred miles away, in Hollywood, California.

Naturally, she did not confide any of these ambitions to Gabe Pollack at the time. She knew he would thoroughly disapprove.

But Mr. Moskowitz, the Odeon's manager, she decided might prove a useful ally. He dealt directly with the men who distributed the films, as well as with the men who owned the theatre, who, in turn, were the same men who produced the movies. The theatre's full name in those days, in fact, was Loew's Odeon, and it was owned by Marcus Loew, Adolph Zukor, and Louis B. Mayer — producers all.

Mr. Moskowitz had told her that most usherettes did not last in the position long. They found the routine tedious, and the wages low. But Sari, always punctual, appeared to be a different sort. At the end of six months, he raised her pay by a dollar a week. After a year, he presented her with another, two-dollar raise, and suggested that the two of them might have dinner some evening. To this latter invitation — knowing that there was a Mrs. Moskowitz — Sari had responded with a polite demurral.

But it was with all these things in mind that Sari, who was by then sixteen and in her last year of high school in early 1926, spotted a small item in the afternoon paper and read it with interest.

TRYOUTS TONIGHT

The Bay Area Amateur Theatre Troupe will hold tryouts tonight for *She Who Is Seized,* a new romantic drama by the internationally renowned playwright Wilmarth L. Fears. The drama offers speaking parts for six female and five male characters, plus four walk-ons, according to Millicent Simmons, the troupe's president, who will also direct the production. Interested local thespians are invited to appear for readings and casting tryouts tonight at Miss Simmons's house, 815 Sutter Street, at 8:30 P.M.

That night, Sari went to Miss Simmons's address and was given two pages of dialogue to read. About thirty other people had shown up, and so Sari had not held out much hope that she would be chosen for any sort of part. But the next morning, to her everlasting wonder and surprise, she received a note from Millicent Simmons saying that she would like to cast Sari in the leading, and title, female role. "My dear, you will be perfect as Sabrina!" Miss Simmons wrote.

As Sari would later find out, the chief attraction of *She Who Is Seized* to Miss Simmons and her Amateur Theatre Troupe was the fact that its production rights could be acquired for a very low fee — fifteen dollars is the figure that comes to Sari's mind today. And, looking back, the play was a terribly silly piece of costumed and melodramatic claptrap. It told, in three crowded acts, the story of a wealthy and beautiful American woman named Sabrina Van Arsdale who was pursued across the face of Europe by a handsome Russian prince named Ivan Troubetskoy, or something like that. For three acts, and through many costume changes, Sabrina resisted the prince's blandishments and costly gifts and amorous advances as she fled from Moscow to St. Petersburg, from St. Petersburg to Paris, from Paris to Capri, and finally to a doge's palace on the Grand Canal in Venice. There where she had been hiding, protected by the doge, the prince, disguised as a peasant, at last succeeded in finding her, and burst in on her, brandishing a sword in one hand, and speaking lines Assaria would never forget: "Madam, I am mad with love for you! I am intoxicated with your beauty! I am made insane by love! If you continue to repel me, I shall destroy your loveliness with this blade, and then fall upon it myself!"

This was the cue for Sabrina, played by Assaria, to cry, "I am seized by love! I am your princess for all time!" And to fall into the prince's arms as the curtain descended.

"My dear, I want you to play this last scene with *passion*," Millicent Simmons, the play's directress, said to her. Miss Simmons was an ample, marcelled spinster of a certain age, much given to breast-beating gestures. But despite her age, Sari learned, Miss Simmons was considered to be frightfully daring and "Bohemian."

"You are not just seized by love here, you are seized by *passion!* Passion, sexual passion, of the deepest, most visceral sort! It is *lust* that you must express here. I want you to project all that feeling into those two lines! Let your voice *growl* — growl out those lines — with passion!"

Despite the creakiness of the material, and the director's almost impossible demands, the largely inexperienced cast had worked hard rehearsing the production, and when *She Who Is Seized* finally opened before an audience in the auditorium of the Odd Fellows Hall, one February evening, the play was an astonishing success. And Assaria, holding the hand of her young prince, was required to bow and curtsy her way through a total of thirteen curtain calls, to a standing ovation. The originally scheduled run of three performances was extended to eight, then to ten, then to twelve. No previous production of the Bay Area Amateur Theatre Troupe had ever achieved so long a run, and the play seemed to delight audiences of young and old alike. Gabe Pollack himself was assigned by his paper to do a story on the city's surprising new hit drama. ("You were very good," he said to her almost shyly after coming to see the play, and she did not tell him that the only way she had been able to perform the last scene had been to try to hold, in her head, the memory of the time he had held her in his arms and kissed her nearly three years before.) The story in the *Chronicle* created a new demand for tickets, and the play's run was extended four more nights. Then *She Who Is Seized* and its cast were invited to perform the play for the patients and staff of the Shriners' Hospital for Crippled Children. That story made the papers, too.

The grand climax to the dramatic history of *She Who Is Seized* came after that performance. Sweeping into the dressing room, Miss Simmons threw up her hands and announced, "My dears, I have some extraordinary, astonishing, absolutely breathtakingly wonderful news for all of you! We have been invited to perform for the students, parents, and faculty of Miss Katherine Burke's School! Need I tell you what this *means?* Miss Burke's is the educational emporium of San Francisco's most elite young ladies! It is to other schools in the city what Russian ermine is to muskrat! These are the daughters of Crockers, Floods, Fairs, Mackays, and Spreckelses, the flowering of the city's finest families, the backbone of the financial community and the heart of the *Social Register*! My dears, what we have enjoyed thus far is mere popularity. This, my dears, is *prestige*. Up to now, we have been casting our pearls before swine, the hoi polloi, the proletariat. Now we have been invited to perform our talents for the aristocracy! This is an equivalent to a command performance before the kings and queens of all the high courts of Europe. What can *possibly* follow this, my dears? Only — " and Miss Simmons placed one hand dramatically across her broad bosom, "Only — Hollywood!"

As it happened, however, the performance at Miss Burke's was the group's last. And it was after this that Sari was sitting backstage at her dressing table, removing her makeup, and looked up into her mirror and saw, standing behind her, one of the most beautiful girls she had ever seen. Tall and slender and blonde, the girl was about her own age, and even her Miss Burke's uniform — blue and white middy blouse, long, pleated, dark blue skirt — which had been starchily designed and crafted to reveal as little as possible of a girl's good looks, could not disguise this particular young woman's beauty. In a husky, throaty voice that seemed as honeyed as her hair, the girl said, "You were wonderful. You were absolutely wonderful. I had to come backstage and tell you."

"Thank you," Sari had said.

"Assaria Latham. What a beautiful name. What a beautiful name to go with such a marvelous talent. When you said those last lines, I felt I was going to faint."

"Well, thank you. Thank you very much."

"I want you to be my friend," the girl said. "Will you be my friend?"

"Well, yes — "

"Good. I want you to be my friend, and I want to be your friend. When can we meet? Can you meet me tomorrow after school?"

"I'm afraid I have to work after school."

"Saturday, then. Saturday afternoon."

"I also work Saturday afternoons," Sari said.

"Then Sunday. Nobody works on Sundays, do they?"

"Yes, I guess that would be all right."

"Good," the girl said. "I'll meet you at four o'clock on Sunday, at the Japanese Tea Garden in Golden Gate Park. We'll have tea." She touched Sari's shoulder lightly with her hand. "I'll see you then." She turned on her heel to go.

"Wait," Sari called after the retreating figure. "Wait — I don't even know your name!"

"I'm Joanna LeBaron," the girl said.

Assaria LeBaron, for the past several days and with increasing interest, has been watching the recent burst of activity in the trading of shares of the Kern-McKittrick Oil Company on the Big Board, as reported in the *Wall Street Journal*. Forty-six hundred shares were traded on Monday, fifty-seven hundred shares changed hands on Tuesday, and then, on Wednesday, sales of Kern-McKittrick jumped to ten thousand six hundred shares. During the course of all this, the price of a Kern-McKittrick share has risen from fifty-three dollars to fifty-nine and seven-eighths, an increase of well over ten percent. On Thursday morning, she had called Ed Neuberger, her man at E.F. Hutton and one of the few stockbrokers in town whom she can trust, and asked him about it.

"What's going on at Kern-McKittrick?" she had demanded.

"Rumors," he had said. "Nothing but rumors."

"What sort of rumors?"

"That they're about to announce a big takeover bid."

"And who — or should I say whom? — is said to be the target of this bid?"

"So far, there's nothing but rumors, Sari," he had said with some hesitation. "The whole street these days is nothing but rumors."

"Are you leveling with me, Ed? Because I'll find out if you're not. Because we're not talking here about rumors, we're talking about what smells to me very much like insider activity, which as you know is quite against the law."

"I'm not going to accuse anyone of breaking the law, Sari."

"Then why don't you find out what's going on?"

"Why don't you ask Harry Tillinghast?" he had said. "He's your relative."

"He is *not* my relative. Just because his daughter happens to be married to my son does not make him any sort of relative of mine!" And she had slammed down the receiver in his ear.

Then, not adding to her sense of fiscal composure, had come Thursday's letter from her sister-in-law, whom she *had* considered her relative and — until now — friend. In perfectly polite, but — to Sari, at least — rather cold and impersonal terms, Joanna had announced her intention to resign the Baronet Vineyards account, "due to a divergence in advertising and marketing philosophies," and had rather patronizingly offered to help Sari find new agency representation "across the street," as Joanna put it in her maddening advertising jargon. "So much for pacts made in blood!" Sari had said, crumpling Joanna's letter into a ball and tossing it into the wastebasket where it belonged. Obviously, Eric's sudden and unannounced trip to New York had had a great deal to do with this development, and Sari does not like any of it, any of it at all. To reporters from the *New York Times* and the advertising weeklies who have already begun calling asking for a fuller explanation, Sari has been issuing — through Thomas — a curt "No comment," until she can think of the properly worded statement to deliver to the press.

To her gratification, however, there have also been calls from other big New York agencies — including Benton & Bowles and Young & Rubicam — soliciting the Baronet account.

Now it is Friday, and Sari is swimming in her big indoor-outdoor pool. The pool enclosure projects from the back of the house, invisible from the street, at the lowest level, a floor below the one that contains Melissa's apartment. Most people in San Francisco do not know that the pool exists, and are unaware of its most remarkable engineering feature — a glass roof, which operates on electric motors and which can be opened to the out-of-doors in warm weather, or kept snugly closed on chillier days, such as this one. Swimming in her pool is the only sort of regular exercise Sari LeBaron is able to get these days, and she tries to do a daily stint of forty laps. Swimming is a mindless — and mind-calming — occupation, involving no more mental exertion than counting the laps as they go by, and this is one of the reasons why she enjoys it. Also, because it saves struggling in and out of a swimsuit, Sari LeBaron always swims in the nude.

Now her laps are done, and Thomas is waiting by the pool to help her out. A special lift, a sort of hydraulic breeches buoy, has been devised for this purpose, but then Thomas must help her out of this contraption, and into her chair, and cover her wet and naked body with an oversize bath towel, and then, when she has dried herself, help her into a thick terrycloth robe.

"Thank you, Thomas."

"A registered letter has just arrived, Madam. I thought I'd better bring it to you here."

"Ah," she says, and he hands her the letter. She sees immediately that it is written on the letterhead of Baronet Vineyards, Inc., and she tears the letter open. *Dear Mother*, she reads.

> *This letter is being addressed to all shareholders of Baronet Vineyards, Inc., and is to advise of a purchase offer we have received from the Board of Directors of Kern-McKittrick Petroleum, Inc., for our company. In its initial proposal, Kern-McKittrick offers 12.5 shares of its common stock for each share of Baronet stock we hold. Because of the generosity of this offer, and my firm support of it, I urge that a meeting of our Board and*

*shareholders be scheduled at the earliest convenient date for all
concerned in order to consider this matter.*

Sincerely,
Eric

"*Aha!*" she cries, in a voice that is a mixture of triumph and
dismay, and hands the letter to Thomas. "Just as I suspected! War
has been declared, Thomas — call out the Marines! Get my lawyers
on the phone, and get them over here just as quickly as possible!
Call out the National Guard! Get Gabe Pollack — I may need him,
too — tell him to get here as fast as he can! Call out the Reserves!
Order a freeze on any sales of Baronet stock — can I do that? Ask
the lawyers! But wait — first things first! Get Eric for me — no,
never mind, I'll get him myself," and she seizes the poolside telephone. "They'll find out who they're dealing with!" she cries.

"Eric?" she says when she has him on the line. "I am in receipt
of your little billet-doux. Let me just say that you, as of this moment, are dismissed as an officer of this company! Do you hear
me, Eric? *You're fired!* Peeper has taken over full responsibilities
for your job — as of this moment! Do you hear me?"

"Yes, and I'm one jump ahead of you, Mother," he says. "Another letter is on its way to you, in which I offer my resignation
from Baronet until this matter is settled."

"*Settled!* Resignation? Well, I haven't received that letter, and
you can't resign because you're *fired!* I want you to clean out your
desk and be out of that office and out of that building by five
o'clock tonight! No — make that three o'clock this afternoon! That
gives you two hours. If you're not out by three o'clock this afternoon, I'll call Security and have you physically removed! Do you
hear me, Eric? *Physically removed!*"

Marylou Chin is in tears.

As if — *as if!* — Eric is thinking, as if I didn't have enough on
my mind right now without having to deal with a hysterical woman!
He moves about his office, continuing to cram the contents of his
desk and files into a large valise.

"What about *me?*" she sobs. "What's going to happen to me?

I've sat here, taking your dictation, typing your letters, watching you do this, thinking to myself all the time, does he even *care,* even care one tiny little bit, what's going to happen to me? I have an aunt in a nursing home in Petaluma — I'm her sole support! What's going to happen to her now that you've done this?"

"For Christ's sake, M'lou!" he says. "You knew damn well what I was doing. You never mentioned an aunt in Petaluma."

"Aunt Grace — her sole support — but you don't care — no, no, not even the tiniest little bit . . .''

"Confront her, you said. You sat right in that chair two weeks ago and said to me, 'Confront her.' Your exact words. And that's what I've done, dammit, and now you give me this shit! I'm sorry, M'lou, but — "

"You — yes, you — you have the luxury of confronting her. But she hardly knows I exist! I've spoken maybe two, three words to her in my entire life! You can confront her, but all I'll get is a pink slip from the personnel office!"

"Listen, M'lou — I'll hire you back. As soon as I win this thing, I'll hire you back — you know that!"

"No, you won't," she sobs, "because you won't win. You can't win. She always wins, you know that. How stupid can you be? So — for me — it will be out with the garbage."

"Dammit, *I will win!*" he shouts.

"No. No, you rich men are all alike. You can quit, resign, go home to your mansion in Burlingame and clip your coupons and collect your dividends. You can retire for life. But me — but me —"

"Goddamn it, M'lou, I'm not going to take anymore of this! As if I didn't have enough on my mind right now!"

"You — yes, *you* — that's all you think about is you! Never about me, never about Aunt Grace — "

"Never in my life have you mentioned an Aunt Grace! Aunt Grace is not my — "

"No. Of course not. Why would I? Because you wouldn't care. And all the time you've been using me, and I've done my best to keep your dirty little secret from your wife!"

"Now, wait a minute," he says. "*Whose* dirty little secret are we talking about? It's your dirty little secret as much as it is mine."

"Oh, yes," she says. "Oh, yes. Who started this? Who asked me if I'd ever eaten at the Blue Fox? Who asked me to dinner with him at the Blue Fox? Whose idea was that? Who put his arm around me in the taxi and said I smelled of patchouli? Who said, 'Your apartment isn't far from here, is it?' Who said, 'Do you have a roommate?' Who said — "

"Oh, for Christ's sake," he says, yanking open his desk drawer and grabbing for his checkbook. "How much do you need to tide you over? How much is the goddamned nursing home?"

"*No!*" she wails. "No, I don't want any of your filthy money. You think you can buy off everybody with your filthy money. You — you're all alike. I never want to see or hear from you again in my entire life!"

"You look like hell when you cry," he says.

Seven

*W*HO KNOWS ALL THE SECRETS of the wine maker's art? Certainly not Sari LeBaron, as she would be the first to admit to you. Why is it that the nobler grapes of the finest red wines grow better in the foothills, while vines for the lesser whites and *vins ordinaires* thrive better on the valley floors? Some say it is because the soil in the foothills is "younger," more vigorous and limy, while the soil of the valleys is older, more acidic, having been washed down there from the mountain slopes for centuries. But others will disagree, and tell you that it is because the morning mists linger longer in the foothills, sweetening and fattening and adding delicacy to the fruit, while down in the valleys the mists burn off more quickly, exposing the fruit longer to the sun, and producing vines with tougher stalks and grapes with thicker skin. Why do some wine makers insist that the finest wines must be aged in charred barrels made of oak from the Nevers forest in France, while just as respectable wines can be achieved when aged in barrels made of stainless steel, or even plastic? The point is that no one knows the answers to these questions with any degree of certainty. They are all a part of the mystery and romance of wine making.

But Sari LeBaron does know that a great part of the mystery and romance of wine making is also backbreaking manual labor — as she herself learned at the bottling plant, working long hours packing corked and labeled bottles into their cases, lifting filled cases off the conveyor belt and onto handcarts to be trucked away. Wine making is both an act of faith and an act of will, it is an art of stewardship and proprietorship and the ruthless use of muscle — not just a sissy sampling and tasting and talking about "body" and "bouquet." This is something, she feels, that her sons have yet to learn. They've had it too easy. They have not been sufficiently toughened up. They were born to her, after all, somewhat late in life, when Baronet was once again on its merry way, with millions pouring in, with all the old debts paid off. Neither Eric nor Peeper ever knew what hard work was all about, and that is why she feels that it is not time to pass her stewardship along to them. In a business that she learned from the bottom up, she has forgotten more about the wine business than either of them ever knew.

This, at least, is what she tells herself, but of course it's only half the truth. The full truth would acknowledge that Sari enjoys the power that she wields — relishes it, luxuriates in it, lives it, breathes it — even more, now that she is an old woman and alone and considered a phenomenon in a business that is predominantly male, more than when she was younger and her husband was alive. What will happen to her company, you may well ask, when Sari dies and the ghouls from the federal, state, and local governments swoop down to bleed her estate for taxes? I wouldn't ask her that question, if I were you. Assaria LeBaron doesn't plan to die.

"I have a saint's name," Joanna had said to her that Sunday afternoon at the Japanese Tea Garden. "Surely I shall be martyred."

"A saint? Which saint?"

"*Jeanne d'Arc.* First, I want to tell you all about me. Then I want you to tell me all about you. That's important, if we're going to be lifelong, bosom friends, as I hope we are. First of all, my family's in the wine business, or at least it used to be. But now, with Prohibition, the wine business is dead in California. We still grow some grapes for the table, for grape juice and raisins and jams and jellies, and things like that, and they let us put up three barrels of wine a year for our personal use — isn't that a screech? It's lunacy, and so mostly my father is retired and lives on his investments. We're supposed to be rich, but don't get me wrong, I'm not a snob, though my mother sort of is one, and I don't care whether you're rich or not. In fact, I'm more or less a Marxist, and I think Karl Marx is the cat's pajamas. I believe in the equal distribution of wealth. My parents are Catholics, and my mother is *very* Catholic, but I'm not, though they made me get confirmed and everything. I don't believe in organized religions. I'm a maverick, a wild horse. I've been a maverick since I was fourteen. That's when I decided to be a free spirit. My absolute idol is Isadora Duncan, and I believe in free love. I think free love is the cat's pajamas, don't you? I went to see Isadora Duncan when she was here, and I became her absolute slave. I love that Russian man she married, the one they say may be a spy. I think he is one, don't you? I think it's an absolute screech that he can't speak a word of English, and she can't speak a word of Russian, and so the only way they can communicate is in the language of love. I absolutely adore all talented people, which was why I adored you in your play. My favorite writer is probably Sigmund Freud. I've read a lot of Freud, and I think most of what he says is the cat's pajamas . . ."

Sari had never met anyone like this girl, with her bright, rapid-fire delivery and ability to skip nimbly from subject to subject barely without a pause for breath. At first, she simply sat there, wide-eyed, listening to Joanna talk.

". . . Once a week, I fast. I eat nothing but a few sips of water. It's good for the figure, and it also helps me think more clearly. I make all my important decisions on my fast days. It was on a fast day that I met you, and decided that I wanted you to be my friend. I have an absolutely divine brother, Peter, who you must meet. He's twenty and divinely handsome, and you'll adore him. He's at Yale now, but he'll be coming home for the summer, and that's when you'll meet him. Peter and I do secret things together. We have a secret club, which nobody belongs to except him and me, but maybe we'll ask you to join it, too, if Peter approves. We'll see. I've never had a sister, but of course I've always wanted one. What's your sun sign?"

"Sun sign?"

"Your astrological sign. I think astrology is the cat's pajamas. When were you born?"

"May twenty-fifth."

"Oh, *no!*" she cried. "I can't believe it! This is an absolute screech! You're a Gemini, and so am I — June tenth. We're a double sign, the twins, which means that each of us is really two people. We have a dark side, and a bright side. We have a face we show for the world to see, and another face that is secret, private, and that we only show to ourselves and to certain special friends. We also have very emotional relationships, and we have artistic talent, and we're very sexual. Have you ever done 'it' with a man?"

"It?"

"Yes. Made love with a man."

"No. Have you?"

"Oh, yes," she said airily, "lots of times. I told you I believe in free love. I think sex is the cat's pajamas. Of course, it helps if you do it with champagne. But I gather that in the Fatty Arbuckle case, that got somewhat — out of hand."

"Really?" Sari said. "What happened, exactly?"

"Well," Joanna said, lowering her voice to a whisper, "from what I'm *told*, they'd all been drinking a lot of champagne. And Fatty Arbuckle tried to put an empty champagne bottle up — you know, up inside this girl. And when they tried to pull the bottle out, some of her insides came out with it. That was how she died."

"How awful!"

"That was the story I heard. The people who own the Saint Francis Hotel are friends of my parents, and I overheard them talking about it." Looking at Sari she had said, "But I can't believe that you've never done it."

"Well, I haven't."

"The way you did that last scene in the play — when you *flung* yourself into the prince's arms and told him you were seized by love — that was the sexiest scene I've ever seen on a stage!"

Sari giggled. "Well," she said, "the director, Miss Simmons, kept telling me to play it that way."

"Watching you, I was certain you were richly experienced. Well, if there's anything you want to know about sex, just ask me, and I'll tell you anything you need to know. If we're going to be lifelong, bosom friends, it's important that we tell each other everything. Is there anything?"

"Well — but no, I guess not."

"No. Go ahead. Ask your question. We're going to be friends, aren't we?"

"Well," she began hesitantly, "one thing I've always wondered is — how does it begin?"

"In my case," Joanna said, "I like to begin it with a glass or two of champagne. That's strictly personal, of course. But Daddy, being in the wine business, made sure before Prohibition started that we had enough wine to last us for years and years. We have a whole cellarful of wine, a whole roomful of champagne."

"No, you don't understand my question," Sari said. *"Explique-moi."*

"I mean, that scene in the play was a seduction scene. The prince was seducing Sabrina. I've watched hundreds of seduction scenes in movies — Ronald Colman trying to seduce Vilma Banky in *The Dark Angel*, Pola Negri seducing Charles Mack in *Woman of the World*. But in the movies they never show you what happens *next*. In the play, I never knew exactly what the prince and Sabrina would do after the curtain went down."

"Why, jumped straight into bed, of course!"

"Just like that? But, I mean — then, who starts it first? The man or the woman?"

"Makes absolutely no difference," Joanna said with a wave of her hand. "It can happen either way. You've seen a man's *thing*, haven't you?"

"Oh, of course." It had been a half-lie. Once, in the semidarkness of an early morning, through a parting of the curtain in their room, she had caught a glimpse of Gabe Pollack naked, seen a shapeless appendage, surrounded by a dark mat of hair.

"Well, it gets very big and hard, and then he — "

"But how does it *start?* Do you have to take off all your clothes to do it?"

"You don't *have* to," Joanna said. "But it's better that way. I believe in the skin-to-skin method."

"But how does it *start?*"

"It starts with" — and now they are both whispering, excited, giggling, their heads together over the teacups, and Sari is asking questions that she has often wanted to ask but has never found the right person to ask, and is now asking them of an almost total stranger. "It starts with — tickling."

"Tickling? Ah. That's what I meant."

"He tickles you. You tickle him. Down *there.*"

"*That's* what they don't show in the movies!"

"He tickles you — you begin to laugh — and then — but you've really got to try it for yourself, you know. And it would be best to try it with an experienced man — an older, experienced man. Meanwhile, you obviously know how to do the seduction part, and that's half the battle. You could give lessons in seduction."

"I'll give you lessons in seduction, and you can give me lessons in the rest of it!" Sari said.

Then, sitting back in her chair, Joanna said, "Of course, my mother says that sex should be saved for marriage, but she's very old-fashioned. Since I believe in free love, I don't suppose I'll ever marry."

And Sari realized that her new friend was ready to change the subject, and, it occurred to her, her new friend was perhaps not quite as worldly and sophisticated as she pretended to be.

"Will you get married, do you think?"

"Oh, I suppose so."

"Who will it be?"

"Probably — Gabe Pollack."

Joanna laughed. "Gabe Pollack. What a funny name. Is he handsome? Is he nice?"

"Oh, yes."

"Older?"

"Yes."

"Then you should do it with him first. That's my opinion, anyway. Are we becoming friends?"

"You know, I really think we are."

"My friends call me Jo."

"And me Sari."

"Sari."

"Jo."

"Then I think there's one important thing we ought to do," Joanna said. "I think we ought to make a pact in blood. Have you ever made a pact in blood before?"

"No."

"Neither have I, but I know how it's done. Here's how we'll do it." The bow on Joanna's blouse was secured with a bar pin. Undoing the clasp and removing it, she said, "First we each prick our right thumbs with the pin — just enough so there's a little drop of blood. I'll do it first, then you." They pricked their thumbs. "Now we press our thumbs together hard, so our blood will mix. Now, repeat after me the oath of eternal friendship. 'I, Assaria Latham —' "

"I, Assaria Latham —"

" ' — do solemnly swear that for now, and until the end of time, I am pledged in friendship to Joanna LeBaron, that in sickness and in health —' "

"In sickness and in health —"

" '— each will turn to the other for aid, comfort, and assistance, wheresoever in the world we may happen to be, to be forever truthful with one another, each denying the other no secrets, in a spirit of pure and lasting sharing, for richer, for poorer, through thick and through thin —' "

"Through thick and through thin —"

" 'From this day forward, forever and ever. Amen.' "

"From this day forward, forever and ever. Amen."

"Now you give the oath to me."

Sari had not been able to memorize and duplicate Joanna's oath exactly, and they had giggled over that, but it came out essentially the same, and as they sat there giggling over their empty teacups in the Japanese Tea Garden, Joanna said, "You know I feel as though I've known you all my life."

"So do I!"

"You're the sister I never had."

"I never had a brother or a sister."

"It's the oath that made the difference."

"Now," Sari said. "Tell me something. Remember that we've just vowed to be truthful."

"Of course. What is it?"

"How many times have you actually done it with a man?"

Joanna frowned and looked quickly down into her teacup, and Sari could see the color rising in her cheeks. "How many — *times?*"

"How many times. Forever truthful, we just said. No secrets."

"Well," she said finally, "I guess — twice. Twice and a half, because the other was — we'd both had too much champagne. But — " and she looked up at Sari with a grin. "Promise you'll never tell anyone! Promise you'll never tell any of the other girls at Burke's!"

"I promise," Sari said. Then they were both laughing.

"Oh," Joanna cried suddenly. "I've just had an absolutely outrageous thought. You must have outrageous thoughts sometimes, don't you? All Geminis have them."

"What is it?"

"I'd like you to make love with my brother. And let me watch!"

Now it was Sari who, despite herself, was blushing. "That *is* an outrageous thought," she said.

"Of course I'm only joking," Joanna said quickly, "even though Sigmund Freud is absolutely full of that sort of thing. But wouldn't that be the cat's pajamas?"

Sitting there, in the fading afternoon, whispering, giggling, two sixteen-year-olds, they had gone on and on, talking of everything in general and nothing in particular, sharing outrageous thoughts (dreams of going to Hollywood to become a movie star, et cetera, et cetera), while Sari felt herself being drawn closer and closer into the web of Joanna LeBaron's exaggerated charm. What was it about Joanna that drew Sari to her? Whom did Joanna remind her of? The Van Dusen Sisters, of course. Like them, she seemed a finished person. She was like them, but nicer.

Years later, it was possible to see why Joanna had gone on to become one of New York's most glamorous and successful woman advertising executives. She was a consummate bullshit artist.

"Well, where *is* Mr. Pollack?" Sari is demanding of his secretary. "You realize that this is Assaria LeBaron calling."

"Right now, Mrs. LeBaron, Mr. Pollack is on a PSA flight to Los Angeles, and obviously I have no way of reaching him. He has appointments in L.A. all afternoon."

"What is he doing in Los Angeles, when I need him here?"

"It's a business trip, Mrs. LeBaron. If he should happen to phone me, I'll tell him that you're trying to get in touch with him."

"Well, then let me talk to that other fellow, the one who works for him, the redhead, the reporter — What's-his-name. Oh, what *is* his name? You know who I mean!"

"Archie McPherson?"

"Yes. Let me talk to him."

"Hold on, and I'll try to connect you," Gabe's secretary says.

"Archie," she says when he comes on the line, and now she is speaking in an altogether different voice, sweet and cozy and persuasive, her motherly, her grandmotherly voice. "Archie, dear, how are you? But I don't know why I should even be calling you, because you betrayed me, didn't you? You told Gabe that I gave you that story about Melissa paying off the rock group, and you weren't supposed to do that, were you? That was supposed to be our secret."

"I didn't tell him, Mrs. LeBaron. He guessed it, and there was no way I could deny it."

"How many times have I told you to call me Aunt Sari? Well, it doesn't matter, Archie, and I forgive you. The story ran, and I liked it very much, and you'll still get your check. Don't worry."

"Thank you, Mrs. LeBaron."

"Please — Aunt Sari."

"Aunt Sari."

"Good. Now there's one other thing you could do for me, Archie. You still see Melissa, don't you?"

"Yes. From time to time."

"Well, I want you to go on a little fishing expedition for me, Archie, with Melissa."

"Fishing?"

"Yes. For information. From Melissa."

"Tell me what sort of information you'd like to know."

"Melissa made a very peculiar accusation to me the other night. It concerned her — parentage. She's made these sorts of accusations before, but never so — vehemently, I guess is the word."

"Her parentage?"

"Yes. That's all I can tell you now. But I need to know — it's terribly important that I know — whether Melissa has some — well, peculiar notions about me, and about her father. If you could take her out, and get her on this subject, and perhaps find out what these notions are, and how much she feels is based on fact, and how much is just — fantasy."

"I see."

"Then if you could relay this information to me, I'd appreciate it. This must be strictly confidential, of course, between you and me. Whatever you find out would not be for newspaper publication, you understand that."

"I understand."

"I consider you this town's fact-finder *par excellence.*"

"Thank you."

"If you get her a little drunk, she might open up. A few drinks might help. You see, a couple of months ago she made a completely unplanned and, unbeknownst to me until recently, trip to Switzerland, to Saint Moritz, where she was born. I'd like to find out what was behind that, if anything. If you get her a little drunk, and get her on the subject of Switzerland, she might tell you something that she'd never tell me. Do you understand?"

"Yes. I see."

"And you'll be well compensated for this one, Archie. Particularly if you learn anything — interesting. Have you bedded her down yet?"

"I beg your pardon?"

"Have you been to bed with her? If you did, that might help, too."

"*My God,* Mrs. LeBaron, I —"

"Don't be angry. I happen to think my daughter is a very attractive woman, and you're a very attractive man. Melissa is a few years older than you, perhaps, but most men find her attractive. People used to say she reminded them of the actress Joan Fontaine, and she's always shown rather a preference for younger men. Her sexual appetites are perfectly normal, and you shouldn't have any difficulties there. This is only a suggestion, of course. Unless, of course, you're gay."

There is a brief silence on the other end of the line. Then he says, "No, I'm not gay — not that it's really any of your business."

"Of course it isn't. I only mentioned it because most of the men in this city seem to be gay. Or so they say. And I only mention it because this is nineteen eighty-four, and I wanted you to know that I'm no sexual prude — about you, or about my grown daughter."

"Yes," he says gruffly. "Well, I'll see what I can do."

"Good. And remember Switzerland."

"I will. But I'm not promising anything."

"Thank you, Archie." A sigh.

She replaces the receiver in its cradle, but with the dead, dissatisfied feeling that somehow the conversation had not gone as well as it might have. Am I losing my touch? she asks herself. Am I losing control?

Somehow, this day, which had managed to start out badly, still is not going well.

Melissa, Melissa. Where did we lose sight of you? So much wrong advice along the way. Hard advice, hard taken. Come back, Melissa, come back. But how can you come back to a place you never seemed to be, never seemed to belong?

Perhaps it was being the first child, and for so many years the only child, and the fact that both mother and child had nearly died in childbirth, that had made them all too anxious with her, too much on the lookout for little signs of something that might go wrong. They had fussed over her too much, pampered her too much, indulged her too much, worried over her too much, given her too much. Perhaps that was it. In the beginning, the theory had been that this adorable child, this special child, should be given anything and everything it wanted, anything that money could buy. This had been in the 1920s, when the LeBaron fortune seemed limitless, and it had pleased Sari to shower the little girl with all the things she herself had never had, never even dreamed existed, as a child — the handmade dresses from Best's and DePinna and Magnin's, the dollhouse and furniture, the collection of dolls and other toys, every variety of stuffed and cuddly creature. Her nursery had been fitted out with a miniature theatre, complete with stage lights and movable sets, furniture and other props, designed for marionette performances. And in those days there had always been a nurse — a series of nurses — for Melissa.

But even as a toddler, she had been extraordinarily exigent. She would demand, for instance, that her playpen be filled with all her toys. Then, one by one, she would throw them all out, and then scream until all the toys had been returned to her, at which point the process would be repeated. Once, when one of the nurses had locked her in the nursery as punishment for something or other, she had gone to the window and thrown out all her toys. Then she had thrown out all the bedclothes from her bed, along with everything else she was able to lift and carry to the window. All of this lay festooned across the shrubbery in front of the house on Washington Street. By the age of three, Melissa's temper tantrums had become an almost daily fact of life.

"Miss Melissa is having one of her fits," Thomas would say. "She says she's going to hold her breath until she dies."

"Please don't call them fits, Thomas," Sari would say. "There is no epilepsy in this family. It's just — " But what was it?

At six years old, she was still wetting her bed regularly. Doctors were consulted. "Ignore her, and let her outgrow it," one of them had said, but it was becoming a hard problem to ignore. "Put her in a diaper and rubber pants," another doctor, Dr. Obermark, had suggested. "When she sees she's still being treated as an infant, that will shame her out of it." But that hadn't worked, either, and the minute the diaper was soaked, Melissa would scream until it was changed for her. "Have her nurse wake her up, once an hour, during the night, and sit her on the toilet — that will stop it," another specialist recommended, but it hadn't, and nurses did not remain long when bound to such a regimen.

"The child," said one of the nurses, "is simply rotten spoiled, Mrs. LeBaron. She is simply a spoiled brat. If I were you, I'd let her select one toy a day to play with. Then I'd have all the other things locked away. If she can't amuse herself with that one toy, then that's that."

"She'll just cry her lungs out."

"*Let her!*"

That nurse had been let go, and there had been others who were more compliant. Needing to keep their jobs, they tended to do what Sari — and Melissa — wanted.

Then had come the hard times of the 1930s, after Peter Powell LeBaron's parents died, and all the debts had appeared, and it had been necessary for Sari and Peter and Joanna to go out into the fields themselves to help return the land to vineyards. Much of the staff of the Washington Street house had to be let go, and the only ones retained were Thomas, for the housekeeping, Cookie, and Melissa's nurse. Perhaps that had aggravated the situation even more, because Sari had been gone all day, and it was hard to control the quality of the nurses, but someone had to look after the little girl.

At seven, the bed-wetting problem still continued, and at eight a new one had arisen: nail biting. "Mrs. LeBaron, the child's nails are chewed down to the *quick*. They're *bleeding*, Mrs. LeBaron!"

"Tape her nails with adhesive tape," one doctor said. Melissa just chewed through the tape.

Another doctor prescribed a foul-tasting substance that was to be painted on the nails. But the foul-tasting substance could be washed off with soap and water.

Every day, it seemed, there was a new problem. "Mrs. LeBaron, Melissa would not get out of bed this morning. She says she's sick, but she has no temperature."

"She's got to get out of bed to go to school."

"She's been in bed all day. She says she's never going to get out of bed."

Then, when she was ten, Melissa, who had never been a good eater, seemed to stop eating altogether. She began complaining of stomachaches when she sat down at the table, and dawdled over her food, pushing it around her plate without eating a mouthful, and Sari had watched with horror as the already thin child grew thinner and thinner. More specialists were consulted.

"Fill the child's plate, and set it in front of her for exactly twenty minutes," said Dr. Obermark, considered the finest pediatrician in the city. "If she hasn't touched her food by then, remove the plate. When she gets hungry enough, she'll eat."

But that had not worked, and Dr. Obermark, after two weeks, offered another formula. "Tell her she cannot leave the table until she cleans her plate," he had said, and so Sari had found herself sitting at the table with Melissa for hours as the child stubbornly sat at the table, staring at her uneaten food. And the more anxious Sari became, the less she ate, and soon it would be seven weeks since Melissa had taken more than a tiny morsel of food. Though her bowels rarely moved now, Sari had watched the girl shrink from ninety pounds to seventy. "Eggnogs," decreed Dr. Obermark. "One raw egg, beaten into chocolate milk, three times a day." But Melissa gagged over these concoctions and vomited them. "I'm going to give her liver shots," said Dr. Obermark, but Melissa fought these so hard that twice the doctor's hypodermic needle had broken off in her buttock.

"Melissa darling, you've got to eat!" Sari cried. "If you don't eat, you'll die."

"I want to die."

"Oh, Melissa, don't say that — we all love you so!"

"You don't love me. You only say you love me because you like to give me things."

"That's not true. It's the other way around — I like to give you things because I love you."

"Daddy doesn't love me."

"He loves you very much."

"Why doesn't he ever speak to me?"

"He's been so busy, darling. We've all been so —"

"You're not my real mother, and he's not my real father, is he? I know that. I'm adopted, aren't I?"

"Oh, Melissa — please don't say things like that! Things that hurt me so!"

"I'm adopted. I don't look like either of you."

"You're our darling little girl!"

From Miss Burke's School, where Melissa was enrolled, there were the regular disturbing reports from Miss Hays, the headmistress. "Melissa is a bright child, and achieves high scores on such tests as the Stanford-Binet. She has a high I.Q., and is perfectly capable of doing the work, but she is a social and a disciplinary problem. Yesterday, for instance, she locked herself in a cubicle in the washroom, and refused to come out until the last bell . . ."

"Mrs. LeBaron, Melissa has developed a new habit that is very disruptive to the classroom. She sits at her desk and rubs her legs together."

"Rubs her legs together?"

"Yes. We feel she is — masturbating, Mrs. LeBaron. It is very distracting to the other girls, and to her teachers. A very distracting habit and, we feel, an unhealthy one."

"I'll speak to Dr. Obermark about it right away."

"Mrs. LeBaron, in view of the fact that Melissa is continuing to be a social and disciplinary problem at school, I wonder if you have perhaps considered a special school for her. There's a school called Hedgerows in Pasadena, which specializes in —"

"No! I don't want to take her out of Burke's, and away from all her friends."

"Mrs. LeBaron, Melissa really has no friends here . . ."

On the question of where Melissa would go to school, Sari knew she stood on very firm ground. Over the years, the LeBaron family had shown considerable generosity to Miss Katherine Burke's School. She was certain the school would never expel a LeBaron daughter.

Then there was the imaginary playmate whose name, she explained to her mother, was Jober Rice. "No, not Joe Be*ryce. Jober Rice.*"

"Is Jober Rice a boy or a girl?"

"Neither. Just Jober Rice." Whenever she was reprimanded for anything, she would explain, "Jober Rice told me to do it."

"She is *much* too old for an imaginary playmate, Sari darling," Joanna said. "*Much* too old. That phase comes around age five or six. That can't be happening."

"But what can I do? She says Jober Rice exists."

At ten and a half, she began to complain of headaches, dizziness, and an inability to see clearly. "I need to wear glasses," she said.

"Are you sure?"

"I want glasses to wear in hotel lobbies."

"Hotel lobbies?" She often made bizarre statements like that.

She was taken to see a famous ophthalmologist, Dr. Heidt, who gave her a thorough examination.

"There is absolutely nothing the matter with her eyesight, Mrs. LeBaron," Dr. Heidt said. "She has perfect twenty-twenty vision, and I can find no physiological basis for the headaches and the claims of dizzy spells. I would not prescribe corrective lenses for her."

"But she says she wants to wear glasses."

"You can get her some frames with ordinary window glass in them, I suppose. I imagine that's an item you could find in the dime store."

And so, for the next two years, Melissa had worn her dime-store glasses constantly. They gave her an owlish, bookish look, which, Sari thought, did not enhance what was otherwise becoming a pretty face. And still the complaints of headaches, dizziness, and poor vision continued.

"What's that on my plate?"

"A lamb chop, darling."

Staring down at it through her glasses, she would say, "But why can't I *see* it? All I see is a fuzzy thing like a bear's paw."

At least she had started eating again, though pickily, and there were long days of hunger strikes.

"I'm afraid she's very sick, Mrs. LeBaron," Dr. Obermark said. "And the trouble is that she's very uncooperative. I think we should consider sending her to a hospital."

"A hospital?"

"There's a very good clinic in San Rafael. There's a possibility she might respond to electric shock."

"Oh, no!" Sari cried.

"These electric shocks aren't fatal, Mrs. LeBaron. In fact, after the first treatment she won't have any idea of what's happening to her. The treatments do not build up anxiety. In fact, they lessen it."

"Oh, no," Sari said. "Please, not that."

"Her disorder is psychological, Mrs. LeBaron."

One summer Sunday they drove out to the Colusa vineyard. Cookie had packed them a picnic lunch they planned to eat in the foothills of the Sutter Buttes, that sudden upthrust of rocky mountains that seems to rise, unbidden, from the middle of the flat Sacramento River valley floor. "Try to plan more little family outings with her," someone had suggested. But at her first sight of the Buttes Melissa began to scream, "Why are those mountains doing that? What are they doing there? They don't belong there! They're looking at me as though they want to kill me!"

"Those are the Sutter Buttes, dear — mountains that some earthquake heaved up in the middle of the valley thousands of years ago. I think they're actually quite dramatic, and quite pretty."

"I hate them! And they hate me! They're looking at me as if they're going to eat me. I want to go home!"

"We can't go home yet, darling. We haven't had our picnic. Let's pretend the mountains are a couple of lazy old dinosaurs, sleeping in the sun. Or a pair of camels, resting. Let's make up a story —"

"No! They're monsters! Take me home!"

"Now, Melissa —"

Then Melissa looked at her and said, "I'm a monster, too, aren't I, Mother? That's why you brought me here. So your monster could meet some other monsters."

"Melissa, *please.*"

"I hate it here! I want to go home! *Take me home!*"

"Her disorder is psychological, Mrs. LeBaron," Dr. Obermark repeated.

But then, before accepting this view, we must take into consideration Melissa LeBaron's parents. There are the parental influences that the psychologist would want to know about. Would Assaria LeBaron ever admit that she had ever been anything less than a perfect mother to this difficult child?

"Pick a card, any card," Melissa had said to her. "It's a trick."

Sari had picked a card, the jack of spades.

"Look at it, but don't show it to me. Now slip it back into the deck. Now, we shuffle them — " And then Melissa had fanned out the deck, face up, on the table. "Your card was the three of hearts!"

"No, Melissa, it was the jack of spades."

"Let me try it again." But once more the trick had not worked. Frustrated, Melissa had said, "Let me try it one more time." And still it had not worked.

"Melissa, why don't you practice your trick, and when you've got it right, bring it back and we'll try it. It's important to know how to do a thing properly before you do it."

But would a sensitive mother have said that? Should she — perhaps — instead — have pretended that the trick worked the first time and congratulated the clever child? The way, playing a board game with a child, a parent will often learn how to lose at checkers? It is too late to ask that sort of question now.

Then we must consider the influence of Melissa's aunt Joanna, which was important in its own way. In 1927, a year after Sari had married her brother, Joanna suddenly married a young doctor named Rod Kiley, and moved with him to Santa Barbara. Less than six months later, however, this marriage was over, though Joanna was four months pregnant with Rod Kiley's child. "A mistake, a mistake!" Joanna cried cheerfully to Sari, announcing the failed marriage. "I knew I should have stuck with free love!" By the time Lance was born, Joanna was divorced, had resumed her maiden name, and had moved back to San Francisco. During the hard period of the 1930s, when all of them were working to get the vineyards back into production and the debts paid off, Joanna and her son occupied a suite of rooms on the top floor of the big

White Wedding-Cake House at 2040 Washington Street. This was a matter of practicality, a matter of money. There was plenty of room, and the two small families, it was supposed, could live comfortably and independently under the same roof. And yet it was perhaps inevitable that certain problems should have arisen with this arrangement.

To Joanna's credit, she tried not to interfere with her sister-in-law's private life. And yet — and yet — there were times when it was almost impossible for Joanna not to voice an opinion about all the difficulties with Melissa. Little things:

"Sari darling, her temper tantrums are cries for help. You can't ignore them . . ."

"Dr. Obermark says . . ."

"I think Dr. Obermark is right. She should see a psychiatrist. I know the name of a wonderful man —"

"But not electric shocks! Not that!"

"It's the very latest technique, Sari."

"No, no."

"Sari, Melissa says that she and her friend Jober Rice are going to *murder* someone! I thought you ought to know."

And Sari, at the breaking point, crying out, "Jo, will you please stop trying to tell me how to raise this child! I'll either do it my way, with my own experts, or I won't!"

You see what I mean.

And it did not help matters one little bit that Joanna's little Lance was growing up to be a sturdy, clean-limbed little boy, normal in every way.

Which brings us to Melissa's father, Peter Powell LeBaron.

Peter LeBaron had many talents, but one cannot say that fatherhood was one of them, and one cannot say that he was a close or loving or demonstrative father with any of his three children. It was as though he erected an invisible distance, or shadow, between himself and them. Whenever any of his children entered a room where their father happened to be, you could sense and almost see that shadow falling, like a cloud passing across the sun. It was strange, but the gaiety and boyishness that had been part of his exuberant charm as a younger man seemed to have disappeared when he became a father. Where was the old playful, irreverent Peter? Sari often wondered. His old self had gone into hiding somewhere beneath this shell of quiet, withdrawal, and reserve.

There are several explanations for this, of course. One could argue that he was required to tackle fatherhood when he was too young, only twenty-one, and was unprepared for its demands. Or you could say that, in a sense, it was because he was forced to marry Assaria, though forced is the wrong word, because he seemed eager to marry her at the time. But you could say that he was also too young for marriage, not ready for it. Even during their engagement and the early months of their marriage, Sari had begun to feel it, though at first she would not admit it, this sense of a shadow, of a distance, falling across what was supposed to be her love and his.

Having breakfast in their suite at the hotel in Saint Moritz that fall of 1926, waiting for Melissa to be born, he had been reading the Paris *Herald Tribune,* and she had said to him, "Are you happy, Peter?"

Outside, the day was bright, and the sun was shining on the lake and on the pine trees along the shore, and sparkling on the distant snow-capped alpine peaks, and from below there was the soft *plop . . . plop . . . plop* of balls being lobbed back and forth across the tennis courts.

"Happy?" he said without looking up from his paper. "Of course I'm happy, darling."

"I want us to be happy," she said. "I'm going to work so hard to make ours a happy marriage, and to be a good wife."

"Why shouldn't we be happy? We're going to have everything in the world we want. Father is building us the house on Washington Street. You're going to have a staff of eleven servants at your beck and call."

"Eleven servants! It's just that I don't know how good I'll be at becking and at calling."

"Mother is selecting them, so you can be sure they'll be excellent."

"It's just — it's just that I want us to have more than just material things, Peter. I want us to have experiences together, to see things and learn things together. I want us to travel. I'd like it if we could go to China. I want us to walk the Great Wall, visit the Forbidden City, see the Palace of the Great Mogul. And then I'd like us to learn some foreign language, and then visit some little villages in faraway countries, and see whether we could talk to them in their own language, and whether we could understand them, and learn about their lives, and — that's the sort of thing I mean."

"We'll have everything in the world we want," he said.

"Everything, except — except, Peter, I don't know how to say this, but sometimes I feel so mixed up. Sometimes I wonder if we did the right thing. Did we do the right thing, Peter, getting married?"

He smiled. "A little late to ask that question now, isn't it?"

"That's not an answer, Peter."

"Of course we did the right thing."

"If you ever thought it wasn't the right thing, you'd tell me, wouldn't you?"

"Of course I would, but I'm sure I'll never need to."

But what she couldn't tell him was that, despite his being her husband, she still felt that she was living with a stranger, that somehow, in agreeing to marry him, she had allowed herself to become a prisoner, a prisoner with a life sentence that could never be commuted, a permanent possession of the LeBaron family, like one of the pieces of heirloom silver that her mother-in-law had explained were to be passed on from generation to generation.

Lifting the coffeepot, he said, "More coffee, darling?"

"Thank you, Peter."

He filled her cup. "Cream and sugar?"

"No," she said, and laughed. "I know I shouldn't mind, I know a bride shouldn't mind that she's been married nearly three months, and her husband still doesn't remember that she takes her coffee black."

"Sorry," he said. "Now, can I get back to my paper?"

"And a bride shouldn't mind, I know that, if her husband wants to read the paper. All men read the paper in the morning over breakfast. No, I don't mind. But can I ask you just one more question, Peter?"

"Of course."

"Do you love me, Peter?"

"Of course I love you. I love you very much."

"And I love you," she said.

Many years later, she asked Joanna about this. "You know, I think Peter loves me, Jo," she said. "He's never treated me with anything but kindness. But it's just — how can I put it, Jo? It's just that, when I first met him, there was real ardor — real passion, I guess you'd call it, between us. A thrilling, passionate kind of loving we experienced together. Then, later, it wasn't there. If there were another woman, a mistress even, I would understand it. I could accept that. But there isn't any."

Joanna gave her an odd, mischievous look. "Well," she said. "who knows? There may be another woman."

Having just said that she could accept it if there were another woman, it was hard for Sari to know what to say next, but she said it anyway. "Then who? Who could it be?"

"My dear, I haven't the slightest idea."

"Is love important, Jo? Is it important to be in love?"

Joanna smiled. "In my lusty youth, I used to think so. Now I think the answer is hard work."

How does one tell another woman, even one's best friend, that in fourteen years of marriage to a man, there has been no sex in the marriage, no sex at all? Though there was sex before. Now it is only endearments: "I love you, Peter." "I love you, too, Sari."

And so, for her, the answer had been the same — work, hard work, out in the vineyards on her hands and knees alongside her husband and the Chinks and the wetbacks and the Okies from the Dust Bowl, planting and transplanting vines, chip-budding the new stalks by hand with a grafting knife, and slowly getting rich again. ("How rich are we, Grandma?" Kimmie had asked just yesterday. "It seems that all Mother and Daddy talk about is money any-more." "Rich enough so that your Grandpa Tillinghast thinks he'd like to take over our company," she had answered.)

*   *   *

Then, in 1941, when Melissa turned fifteen, Sari made a discovery that cut like a knife through her heart, that night when she and Peter and Joanna were dining at the Mural Room.

About the same time, another disturbing event had taken place. Thomas had reported it to her. "I must speak to you right away, Madam," he had said.

"Certainly, Thomas."

"I went down to open up the pool enclosure," he said. "It's such a nice day that I thought Madam might enjoy her swim in the fresh air."

"Yes . . ."

"As I came to the glass door, I saw that Miss Melissa was sitting on the diving board. With Mr. Lance. They were both in a state of undress, Madam."

"Yes."

"And it was quite clear to me what was happening, Madam. Miss Melissa was instructing her cousin on how to perform the sexual act."

"A boy of twelve . . ."

"He had an erection, Madam, if Madam will pardon the expression."

"I see. And then what happened?"

"I made a very large noise opening the glass door, and they saw me, and they grabbed their towels and ran into the dressing rooms."

"Into the same room?"

"He ran into the gentlemen's, and she into the ladies'. I came immediately here."

"I see. Well, thank you, Thomas. I'll handle this."

She decided, for reasons of her own, not to apprise Joanna of this episode. Instead, she immediately sent for Dr. Obermark.

Dr. Obermark's face was very grave. "I would recommend two procedures, in light of what you've told me," he said. "With her history of hysteria and intractability, and her refusal to accept any form of discipline or to conform to normal patterns of restraint, I can only see this latest symptom as a warning to us that she is about to embark upon a career of compulsive promiscuity. I recommend, therefore, that her uterus be surgically removed for her own protection. I would also recommend that she be immediately examined, and treated, by a clinical psychologist. I have an excellent woman in mind."

Melissa was told that her appendix was inflamed, and would have to be removed. The same story, incidentally, was told to Melissa's father. On the domestic front, Sari handled things by tactfully suggesting to Joanna that, now that things were looking up financially for Baronet, it might be appropriate for Joanna and Lance to find another house or apartment in the city.

But somehow, someone — a nurse, perhaps? — told Melissa what had happened. Or, just as likely, she simply guessed.

A few months after her operation, she said, "Was I a difficult birth, Mother?"

"You were a darling baby."

"But I'll never know what birth is like, will I."

"Don't be silly, darling."

"Then why don't I menstruate anymore, Mother?"

"Not all girls do, Melissa."

"That's a lie! All girls my age menstruate!"

"Most girls would think it a blessing not to have to menstruate — not to have to get the curse. I know I would."

"Why do you want me to be a monster, Mother? Why do you want me to be more of a monster than I am already?"

The clinical psychologist whom Dr. Obermark recommended had the unlikely name of Dr. Lilias de Falange. She submitted Melissa to a battery of tests, followed by lengthy interviews, and at the end of that summer she sent out the following typewritten report:

> Subject is an attractive, intelligent, well-dressed Caucasian female, with a tendency to underweight, age 15 yrs., 7 mos.
>
> Interpretation of Rorschach session follows:
>
> Considering this child's response to Card V, we clearly have a situation of sexual obsession, as evidenced by fixation on Dd 22, the noted appendage of butterfly, which patient described as a "pulsating toothpick." That this response is sexual, no one can

doubt, but more importantly it demonstrates her conviction that penile insertion is dependent upon emaciation, and thus this shows her own bodily concerns are intimately linked to frigidity in sexual development.

Not only is this patient potentially frigid, she also has evidence of lacunae in affective responses generally noticed in absence of color remarks to cards VIII and IX. What seems to be occurring is a fear of loss of vital fluids. (Could she conceivably be frightened of the onset of menses?) But, more importantly, she seems to be showing a marked void in emotional reciprocity, resulting in a forced, rigid approach to the world, more commonly expressed as a masculine, sadistic front. In short, this child's feelings are truncated.

Patient shows a remarkably similar developmental pattern to that of Dr. Edward Lahniers' pioneering treatise on "vagabond youngsters," published last year in *Psychological Disturbances of Youth*. In that study he noted the forward progression of a syndrome in which supposedly "loved" children became antagonistic and disorderly towards those authority figures who were responsible for them. Why, he asked, does not affection beget affection? The answer, he found, lay in misaligned allegiances. The child identifies with or takes the part of (either positively or negatively) the parent who has secrets to hide from the other parent. In other words, the child develops symptoms which prevent the parents from recognizing or working out marital problems. The result is emotional mayhem, because so long as the child was serving as a "secret agent," chaos ruled in the home, but the chaos at least neutralized the child's basic fear of disintegration of the family unit.

Clearly this child is trying to protect secrets. Either she learns to stop being the victim, or she succumbs to chronic hypochondria, insanity, or suicide.

Attached to the report was a bill for five thousand dollars.

Looking back, were the measures Dr. Obermark recommended too harsh, too Draconian? Or does it matter, now that it's too late and the effects were irreversible? Looking back, does any of this matter? Does it matter that, five years later, Dr. Obermark was the same Dr. Otto Obermark, the prominent pediatrician you may have read about, who was arrested for sexually molesting an eight-year-old boy in the underground parking garage below Union Square, and was sent for two years to San Quentin? Does it matter that Dr. Lilias de Falange later ran off with a rodeo performer, moved with him to Albuquerque, and briefly made the papers when their month-old baby strangled itself in its crib, while Dr. de Falange was drinking in a saloon downstairs? Does any of this matter?

It was all years and years ago.

"Mr. Philip Dougherty is calling, Madam, from the *New York Times.*"

"Good Lord, has the *Times* gotten wind of Eric's shenanigans already?" Sari says. "I only had Eric's letter yesterday!"

"I believe this is about the other matter, Madam — LeBaron and Murdock resigning the Baronet account. Mr. Dougherty writes the advertising column."

"Oh. Well, tell him I'll have a prepared statement for him in half an hour."

Sari has known that some sort of statement will have to be forthcoming from her end of things. It was only a matter of time. At first, she has considered some sort of angrily worded statement, repudiating Joanna and her agency. "My sister-in-law has obviously gone soft in the head," she has thought of saying. Or, "LeBaron and Murdock didn't resign us. We fired them for gross incompetence." And yet, now, considering what Eric is proposing, and the fact that this, too, will eventually come to the attention of the press, the wiser tactic would be to diffuse any impression that a family feud might be brewing. One can sometimes accomplish more with honey than with vinegar, as they say. A more gently worded statement from Baronet's president seems to be in order. In five minutes, she has composed it.

> It is with genuine regret that Baronet Vineyards, Inc., announces its departure from LeBaron & Murdock, its agency for more than thirty years. "As evidence of the deep respect in which we continue to hold LeBaron & Murdock, what more powerful evidence can we hold up than the fact that, since 1952, when we first came to the agency, Baronet's sales have risen from 150,000 cases a year to over 3,000,000 cases a year," a Baronet spokesperson said today. "The parting of the ways comes as a

result of small but persistent differences in merchandising philosophies."

Baronet will be interviewing for new agency representation
over the next few months. No new appointment will be announced until these interviews have been completed.

And now, having done that, Sari has another idea. Why not, in
this new spirit of honeyed friendliness, telephone Joanna and read
the press release to her, and ask her what she thinks of it? The
idea appeals to her, because it contains an element of surprise.
Joanna won't be expecting to hear from Sari on a conciliatory note
at this juncture. She'll expect Sari to be mad as hell. As of course
she is.

"I just wanted to see if you approved of my wording, Jo," she
says when she has her on the phone, "before I ask Miss Martino
to dictate it to the *Times*."

"Why, I think it reads very *nicely*, Sari," Joanna says. "It's certainly kind of you to give us all the credit for your wonderful figures.
You had an awful lot to do with that yourself, you know."

"No, I believe in giving credit where credit is due."

"Sari, I'm really terribly touched, darling."

"Of course, I was a little hurt that you didn't give me any advance
warning that you were doing this," Sari says.

"But I thought I was just going through the proper channels,
telling Eric. After all, Eric is your advertising director."

"*Was*."

"Oh. Well, I'm sorry to hear that, Sari. But I'm not going to tell
you how to run your company."

"I can't have him on my payroll while he's plotting to sell my
company to someone else, can I? I presume by now you've had
his letter to the shareholders."

"Yes. This morning."

"May I ask you what you think of his proposal?"

"Well, I must say I find it very tempting," she says. "Harry's
offer seems generous, and Eric seems to think he might sweeten
it by a point or two when we get into negotiations. It would mean
a lot of money for all of us, and there's also another thing."

"What's that?"

"As you and I get older, Sari, it's been on my mind. You and I are now the senior stockholders, in terms of age. With a privately owned company like Baronet, if something should happen to either of us, the government could come in and place whatever price they wanted to on the stock. Our heirs could be taxed to the moon. We'd have no control. But if we were to become part of Kern-McKittrick, that's a publicly owned company, and the price of its stock would be established in the marketplace. We'd be providing much more security for our children, and your grandchildren. That's the point my lawyers have been making to me. What do your lawyers say?"

"I haven't met with them yet."

"What I think we ought to do," Joanna says, "even before we start listening to what lawyers think, is all of us sit down together, like civilized human beings, and talk this whole thing over. It doesn't have to be a *High Noon* shoot-out. After all, we're connected by blood as well as wine."

"And speaking of that," Sari says, "in any shareholder vote, we are going to have what I call a Lance problem. Or it could also be called a Melissa problem, if you remember the terms of Peter's will."

"Yes. I know exactly what you mean."

"Things could get very — unpleasant, couldn't they."

"Yes. But that's if there's a *High Noon* shoot-out. First let's meet and talk about it. Why don't I clear a few things off my desk, and fly out for the weekend? How would that be? Besides, it's been ages since I've seen you."

Sari is silent for a moment. Then she says, "But what about me?"

"Hm?"

"What about me? If you and Eric and Lance all vote against me, and if Melissa finds out she's legally entitled to vote more shares than she knows she owns, and votes it all against me —"

"Melissa must not be told. That would be —"

"But suppose I were to tell her?"

"You wouldn't do that, Sari. You'd do a lot of things, but you wouldn't do that."

"I would, if I thought she'd vote on my side!"

"You're still talking about a *High Noon* shoot-out. It hasn't come to that."

"And if she voted on my side, that would put the kibosh on you and Eric, wouldn't it? Because I'd also have Peeper on my side."

"Sari, we're quarreling. Let me come out to San Francisco for the weekend, and we'll meet and talk — like civilized — "

"Of course, Melissa could decide to vote against me. It would be just like her! Then where would I be?"

"Sari," she hears Joanna's voice saying, "you've worked so hard for the company all these years. I should think, at this point, that you'd be ready to slip out of your girdle, relax — maybe travel, take a cruise — relax, and enjoy your life."

"This company *is* my life! This company is my entire life! It's the only life I've ever had. You, Jo, of all people ought to know that. Jo — remember I did you a big favor once, long ago. Why don't I hear you saying that you'll take my side in this? Do you remember a pact made in blood? Whatever became of that, my fair-weather friend? Let me just say this — if you side with Eric in this thing, it *will* turn into a *High Noon* shoot-out, and I will tell Melissa everything she needs to know. *Everything*."

"Sari dear," Joanna says. "Please relax. I'll come out for the weekend. We'll talk."

Eight

"TELL US MORE, Joanna dear," Constance LeBaron said, "about this new little friend of yours." They were sitting in the red-plush breakfast room of the old LeBaron house on California Street.

"She is absolutely the cat's pajamas," Joanna said through a mouthful of fresh grapefruit. "She's small and dark, and absolutely beautiful, and she's the most divinely talented actress who's obviously going to become a simply famous movie star. Her name is Assaria Latham. Isn't that the most divine name?"

"Where does she go to school?"

"Public school."

"Public school! Really! Not Burke's or Hamlin's."

"Don't be a snob, Mother. Not every nice girl in San Francisco goes to Burke's or Hamlin's."

"And you say she lives on Howard Street. I didn't think people *lived* on Howard Street. Isn't that a little peculiar?"

"All struggling artists have to starve in garrets, until they achieve fame and recognition."

"Have you seen the neighborhood where this girl lives?"

"Nope," Joanna said, gouging out another grapefruit section. "But I'm going to. She's invited me."

"When you see the neighborhood around Howard Street, I think you may be in for a rude awakening," her mother said. Constance LeBaron was a woman who pronounced a word like "neighborhood" as though it were spelled *neighbourhood*. "It is not one of our more desirable residential districts. In fact, I'm not sure I should want you to go there alone."

"Oh, don't be such a snob, Mother. She's such a snob, isn't she, Daddy?"

"Joanna's always our little free spirit, isn't she, Mother?" her father said.

"And tell me again where you met this girl?" her mother said.

"At school. They did her play at school. It was a wonderful play, and she was the best thing in it."

"But don't forget," her mother said, "that next year is to be your debutante year. And with everything that will be going on for you then, this new friend of yours might not quite — fit in, if you see what I mean."

"Why not, I wonder?"

"What I mean is that she might not — feel comfortable with some of the other people we know."

"You don't know Sari," Joanna said. "She'd be at home in the humblest hovel or in the mightiest millionaire's mansion. You haven't seen her on the stage. I have."

"I assume that Mother and I will have an opportunity to meet this paragon," Julius LeBaron said.

"Yep. I've invited her here for tea next Sunday." She was intently squeezing her grapefruit into her spoon, determined to extract every last juicy polyp from the fruit.

"It is acceptable," her mother said, "when dining *en famille*, to pick up the chicken leg with one's fingers, or the chop at the end. It is also acceptable to squeeze a grapefruit into a spoon, as you're doing now, but only *en famille*. Never when dining out, or at a public restaurant."

"Oh, Mother!"

"It's important to remember these things, dear, as your debutante year approaches."

"This coming Sunday?" her father said.

"Yep. That's her day off."

"Day off from *what?*" her mother said.

"She works as an usherette in a movie theatre," Joanna said. "Did you hear the one about the nervous usher at the wedding? He said, 'Mardon me, Padam, but you are occupewing the wrong pie. Please allow me to sew you to another sheet.' Isn't it a screech?" She tossed her napkin on the breakfast table. "Well, I'd better be off or I'll be late. I have promises to keep, and miles to go before I sleep!"

And she was off.

"An usherette in a movie theatre," Constance LeBaron said after her daughter had left. "What next, I wonder?"

With a chuckle, Julius LeBaron said again, "Well, she's always been our little free spirit, hasn't she, Mother?"

Assaria's first impression of the house on California Street was of red plush — red plush everywhere, toy plush, cut velvet, and red damask window hangings. And gilt. Whatever was not coverable by plush or velvet was gilded — little gilt tables and uncomfortable-looking little gilt straight-backed chairs with velvet seats, and the walls were overwhelmed by huge mirrors in gilded frames. It was the kind of Nob Hill house you used to see a lot of in San Francisco in those days, but now see only rarely. It dated from San Francisco's earliest era of affluence, the Victorian age, and it had managed to escape the fire. And as Joanna took her around the house, it seemed to Sari quite literally a palace. She had never seen anything remotely like it, not even in the movies.

These were some of the things she marveled at that first day: The brass rods that gripped the crimson carpets to the stairs, thin from polishing; the heavy embroidered bellpulls in every room that were used to summon servants; these, she was told, were called "annunciators." There was one whole room called "the Library," lined floor to ceiling with books in identical morocco bindings, in cases with heavy glass doors, locked and secured by tiny keys. In a silver bowl in this room were what appeared to be nothing but dried petals — indeed, they were, dried tea roses, pikake and jasmine flowers and bits of vetiver root, Joanna explained — that, when stirred with one's fingertips, threw a sweet odor into the air. "A perfectly ordinary potpourri," Joanna said. Perfectly ordinary! In another bowl, a chocolate apple, which, when tapped, fell apart into perfectly shaped little slices.

Later, she would learn more about this wondrous house. The mirror gloss of the mahogany of the dining-room table was achieved by its being rubbed daily by the palms of the hands of Negro servants. ("White people's hands can't do it," Joanna said.) The creamy luster of the heavy silver chandeliers and tea sets could be maintained only by daily polishing. On a sandwich plate, there appeared to be a rosebud, but when Sari picked it up it unraveled into a thin strip of tomato peel that had been artfully fashioned to resemble a flower. ("Only decoration, silly! Not to *eat* it." Only decoration!) In this house, real flowers were never permitted to die. Unseen hands replaced them. Candles were not permitted to burn down to stubs, but were replaced at each new occasion for lighting them. Nothing was permitted to wear out, or to break or to disappear or to grow old or to lose its gleam, in this wondrous house, run by elves and magicians.

Order — that was what it was. It was order that arranged everything here, order that moved automatically about this house like shuttles across a loom, establishing precedence, sequence, consequence, giving every symbol of the house its place, and making all the symbols coherent and interrelated, smooth and finished. This, Sari decided, was what luxury meant — order, order everywhere. If the coverlet of a bed were to be turned down, it inevitably revealed a monogrammed satin blanket cover, and clean white linen sheets and pillow slips with deep embroidered hems. In this house, with its order, rude surprises were ruled out.

That first day, Joanna had taken her into the portrait gallery, with all the LeBarons, in order, painted as they looked, or may have wished that they had looked, when in their early teens. In front of one portrait of a strikingly handsome youth, Joanna had paused. "That's Peter," she whispered. "Isn't he just the cat's pajamas?"

In that other gallery, too, was the same wine barrel that now reposes in Sari's house on Washington Street, and Joanna had read the inscription on it, and explained its significance to her. "My grandfather's," she said. "They say if you were to drink it now it would blow your head off."

Then Sari was led into the red-plush drawing room, to be introduced to Joanna's parents — to Constance, a short, plumpish woman with a wide poitrine and blonde, marcelled hair, wearing a black dress and pearls, and to Julius LeBaron, a tall, pleasant-looking man with a high, balding forehead, who wore an open shirt with an ascot and a tweed Norfolk jacket. Immediately Sari decided that she liked the father better than the mother, who seemed a little nervous and distracted, and sat stiffly in her gilt chair, twisting and untwisting her long rope of pearls, and touching her hair. "Joanna tells us you are Jewish," she said. "How very interesting."

"It's true that my parents were Jews," Sari answered very carefully. "But I remember very little about them, and I've never had any religious training. I've never been inside a church or synagogue."

"And this man who is your guardian, this Mr. Pollack. I gather that he is also Jewish?"

"No," she said in the same careful voice. "Gabe Pollack is an atheist."

"And not a socialist, too, I hope! So many of them are, you know."

"No," she lied, for Gabe still spouted vaguely socialist ideas.

"How interesting. We, of course, are Romans."

At first, Sari thought Joanna's mother was saying that they were from Rome, but then she understood. "I see," she said.

"Well, I've always said that we in San Francisco are terribly fortunate to have such a nice class of Hebrew people. The Haases and the Koshlands, and the Fleishhackers and the Zellerbachs are all of the Hebrew persuasion, and we visit them. Are you by any chance related to those families, my dear?"

"No, I don't believe so," Sari said.

"Mother, I always thought you said it wasn't nice to talk about politics or religion," Joanna said.

"I'm just trying to draw your young friend out, Joanna dear."

"Well, I say it's hogwash. Have a piece of cake, Sari. It's a Lady Baltimore cake. Our cook makes it."

"And Joanna tells us you live on Howard Street," Constance LeBaron said, relentlessly pursuing the same conversational theme. "How interesting."

"Yes."

"South of Market."

"Yes, very historic," Sari said.

"Really? I've never heard south of Market described quite that way. Historic?"

"Now, Mother," Joanna's father said again.

"I'm only making small talk," Constance LeBaron said. And then, "Next year will be Joanna's debutante year."

"Yes, so she told me."

"It will be upon us before we know it, a very important time in a young girl's life. There will be many functions that she will be called on to attend. Important functions. The Bachelors' Ball, for instance. Have you heard of the Bachelors' Ball?"

"No, I haven't."

"It's very important. All the finest young men from all the finest families in the city put it on. To be invited is a great honor, and of course Joanna will be invited. There will also be many other functions, all of them important. Joanna will need many pretty new dresses for her debutante year."

"Personally, I think it's all hogwash," Joanna said. "I'm only doing it because my parents want me to. Most of the bachelors are fairies. Which is why they're still bachelors."

"Now, Joanna, don't be coarse," her mother said, and to Assaria she said, "I'm only mentioning all these things because Joanna tells us that you have become her best friend. And I think it's sometimes . . . helpful . . . if best friends come from the same . . . well . . . world."

"I think," Sari said, "that one reason why Jo and I have become good friends is that our worlds, as you put it, are different. We both have a lot to learn from each other."

"Hear, hear," said Julius LeBaron.

"Joanna tells us that you work as an usher in a movie house. How interesting."

"Yes. Isn't that what America is supposed to be about? Working to improve oneself and get ahead?"

"Hear, hear."

"Well, I suppose you have a point," Joanna's mother said, making a small face and twisting her pearls.

"Mother, I think we should leave the young people to their own devices," Julius LeBaron said. "I think you've done enough drawing out of Joanna's young friend. There's an opera on the wireless that I want to hear."

"Very well," Constance LeBaron said, rising stiffly from her chair. She extended a plump hand to Sari, and Sari noticed that two fingers on which she wore jeweled rings had grown to such a fleshy size that surely the rings could no longer be removed. "It's a pleasure to have met you," she said. "I hope you'll enjoy your afternoon."

"Now," Joanna said when her parents had left, "let's get out of here."

"Where shall we go?"

"Down to the cellar. Follow me."

She led Sari out of the drawing room, across a hallway to a door under the main staircase, and unlocked it with a key. "My parents don't know I have this key," she said. "Peter borrowed it from Daddy's key chain one day, and had two copies made, one for him and one for me." The doorway opened onto a steep staircase, leading downward. "Watch your step," she said. "Some of the steps are uneven." Down they descended into the darkness, as though into the belly of a ship, but instead of the smell of soiled humanity and seawater Sari remembered from years ago there was a smell of vinous sweetness in the air. "Isn't my mother an absolute screech? Don't pay any attention to any of the things she says. Nobody does, not even Daddy. Daddy liked you, I could tell, and Daddy's the only one who counts around this family. I could tell he thought you were the cat's pajamas." At the foot of the flight of stairs, now, there was illumination as Joanna screwed in a single light bulb. They were in a large room with a concrete floor, and on all sides, from floor to ceiling, the walls were lined with row upon row of dusty wine bottles, reposing in diamond-patterned racks. And there were also several pieces of furniture scattered about, furniture that had seen better days — an ancient, butt-sprung sofa, and a pair of overstuffed club chairs with springs dangling loosely from beneath their fringed bottoms. A number of empty, overturned wine cases had been placed around the room to serve as tables, and empty wine bottles had been put to use as candle-sticks. In the dim light, the room managed to create the shabby illusion of a formal parlor.

"The wine cellar," Joanna explained. "This is one of Peter's and my secret places. This is our clubhouse. Peter and I brought all this furniture down from the attic. Isn't this the cat's pajamas? Mother and Daddy never come down here. When they want wine, they send MacDonald down for it. MacDonald is our but-*lah*. That's the way Mother pronounces it — but-*lah*. MacDonald is the only one who knows our secret, and MacDonald won't tell because *we* know a secret about MacDonald. Want to know what it is? MacDonald sneaks ladies of the evening — I mean *real* ladies of the evening — into his room at night. Sometimes he sneaks in more than one at a time. We caught him at it, so we're blackmailing him, because if Mother or Daddy found out about it they'd can him, just like *that*. Now, first we light the candles — then we have our tea."

"Tea?"

Studying the rows of bottles, Joanna said, "Today, I think champagne, don't you? Since this is your first visit here. Of course, you can have whatever you want. Peter and I thought of opening our own speakeasy down here, but that might be *too* risky. Want a fag?"

"A fag?"

"A cheroot. We keep a pack of Camels hidden under the sofa cushion, here. Not even MacDonald knows about that . . ."

Sari declined the cigarette, but decided she was not going to decline the wine, and Joanna was now expertly twisting the cork from the champagne bottle. It came out with a surprising pop. "Of course, this really should be iced, but we have no ice. This room stays about sixty-two degrees, though, which is cool enough, and we have everything else we need. Glasses," she said, lifting up one of the wine cases, "are kept under here." She produced two wine-glasses, and filled a glass for each of them. Then, sitting on the old sofa, she tapped a cigarette from the pack, lighted it from a candle, sat back, inhaled, and blew out smoke, rather the way Sari had watched Lois Moran smoke a cigarette in *Stella Dallas*. Then she had lifted her glass and said, "Chug-a-lug. To friendship."

"To friendship." And Sari had her first taste of champagne.

"Isn't this the cat's pajamas?" Joanna said.

Later, after they had both had two glasses, and Joanna was pouring them a third, Joanna said, "But seriously, what do you think I ought to do with my life? I mean, you're all set. You're an actress, and you're going to go off to Hollywood and become a rich and famous movie star, but what's going to happen to me? Oh, I know what's supposed to happen. After my debutante year, I'm supposed to marry some rich man — preferably a Crocker or a deYoung — and settle down in Burlingame, and start having babies. But I don't want to do that, and I'm not going to do that. I don't want to just be a flapper. I know some girls at school who all they want to be is flappers. But I don't want to be that. What could I be?"

"Let's see," Sari said, trying to concentrate. "What could you be . . ." The champagne was beginning to fill her head with the most wonderful warm glow, and she could feel tiny beads of per-spiration forming on her brow, even in this somewhat chilly room. "Let's see . . . let's see . . ."

"It has to be something exciting, and it has to be something glamorous, and it has to be something important. Like a poet, like Edna Saint Vincent Millay. Could I be a poet, do you think?"

"Or . . ." Sari said. "Let me think. Or — how about a famous newspaperwoman? Chasing down exciting stories every day. Meeting all the important people who come through town — the President of the United States, the Queen of Rumania! Or — how about a famous lady novelist? I can see you writing the most beautiful romantic novels, Jo. You know all about love — "

"Love — and passion!"

"Or — no, wait, I have the best idea of all," she said, draining her glass.

"What's that?"

"A lady pilot! You could learn to fly a plane — they say it isn't hard. You could learn to fly a plane, and fly it all over the world! You could be the first woman to fly from here to Mexico! There are some airplanes, you know, that can land on water, and you could fly to the Amazon jungle, in South America, and land on the river — you could explore — you could discover lost Inca cities —"

"Oh, I love that idea!"

"And I love this champagne!"

"Oops — we're ready for another bottle."

"Whee!" Sari said, as another cork popped. "Think of it! Flying! Up in the air, over the mountains. Up where no one has ever been before! Whee! Chug-a-lug!" A little champagne sloshed from her glass onto her wrist, but she barely noticed it.

"Chug-a-lug."

"Up in the zither. I mean up in the ether. Oh, dear, I seem to be spilling —"

"Here, let me fill you up again. Don't worry, there's plenty more. And don't worry, champagne doesn't stain."

"Up!" Sari said. "High! And have you seen those airplanes that can write messages in the sky? You could write your poems in the sky!"

"And let them be blown away on the wind."

"But after you'd given them to the world. After the Queen of Rumania had —"

"Like putting a message in a bottle, and throwing the bottle into the sea . . ."

"But with a poem . . ."

"Gemini."

"This is the cat's pajamas," Sari said. "I feel like the Queen of wherever it is. Whee! We come from different worlds! But we're —"

"We should have music," Joanna said. And, from under another empty wine case, she produced a small wind-up Victrola and a stack of disks, and presently the room was filled with the strains of someone singing "I Want to Be Happy."

"I am happy!" Sari said. "I've never been so happy in my life! Is this what champagne always does?" And she had all at once started to laugh, and presently the laughter turned to hiccups. "Oh — dear," she had gasped. "Do you — really think — we should open another bottle?"

"Why not? This club caters to its members' every need."

"Chug-a-lug. Chug-a-lug-lug-lug. Here's to your debutante year!"

And then, a little later, after the Victrola had wound down and the music had stopped, a silence had fallen between them. Joanna, her feet tucked up underneath her, sat at one end of the big sofa, staring up at the dark, cobwebby ceiling. She had lighted another cigarette, and was blowing smoke upward into the air. Sari sat at the opposite end, staring into her half-empty glass. And why, suddenly, had a tear appeared in the corner of one eye, and coursed quickly down her cheek? She brushed it aside with the back of her hand, grateful that Joanna had not seen it.

"A penny for your thoughts," Joanna said.

"I was thinking — " she began. I am thinking, she thought, that I do not really belong here, in this strange household, where the mother treats her daughter's friend as though she were some unwanted germ, or insect. And I am thinking that if I don't belong here, then where do I belong? In Hollywood? Or on a mountaintop in Katmandu? And I am thinking, why did she feel it was necessary to tell her mother that I am Jewish, that I am poor, that I live on Howard Street, and work as an usher in a movie theatre — all facts that were guaranteed to displease her mother? Unless . . . unless . . .

"All Geminis have the two sides, the bright side and the dark side," Joanna said. "I'm sure you're like me. You like the high life, but you also like the low life."

Am I part of your adventures with the low life? she thought. Is that it? Is that why I was brought here, where I was immediately made to feel out of place? Or am I being used as a tool, an instrument, a weapon in this girl's private arsenal, from which she fights some mysterious, private battle with her parents? But she didn't say any of these things, and instead she said, "I was thinking how lucky you are to have two parents who love you. I hardly remember my parents at all." Two more unbidden tears came. She brushed at them.

"Parents can be a mixed blessing, believe me. Having parents isn't always the cat's pajamas. Don't be sad, Sari."

"And I was also thinking we should stop saying everything is, or isn't, the cat's pajamas," she said, with a small sniffle.

"Oh, you're *right!*" Joanna said, setting down her glass and clapping her hands. "It's such a cliché. I don't want to be a cliché. You see, that's why you're good for me! My parents have been trying to turn me into a cliché for years, and until I met you they'd damn near succeeded." She raised her right hand, and pressed the other across her bosom. "I, Joanna LeBaron, do hereby solemnly swear never to use that ghastly expression again. And as for *you —*"

"Yes?"

"You must promise to learn to smoke a cigarette!"

"Quick. Toss me the pack." She had caught it and, with some care and no small amount of trepidation, tapped out a cigarette and lighted it from the candle's flame, the way she had watched Joanna do. Now they were giggling again. "Besides," Sari said, "it is a scientifically known fact that cats don't wear pajamas."

"Neither do I. I always sleep in the nude."

"Not even Jewish cats who live on Howard Street."

"Oh . . . oh . . . oh!" They were rocking back and forth in their seats with laughter. "Why is that so funny?"

"I don't know! But it is!"

"We must always tell each other anything we don't like about the other. That's part of the pact," Joanna said.

"Part of the pact. More champagne?"

"Hell, yes!"

And, a little later — her voice a little low and woolly from the wine, and her speech a little rambling and discursive — Joanna was saying, ". . . and so there's this boy here in San Francisco, this Jimmy Flood. . . . My parents have him picked out . . . for me. They say the Floods are as good as the Crockers and the deYoungs, and the Floods are *Catholic.* Anyway . . . where was I? He's this boy, who goes to Stanford. Did I tell you his name is Jimmy Flood? Well, anyway, I said no . . . I said no, I won't. I said . . . free spirit. I said . . . love someone else . . . not Flood, not Jimmy Flood. That happens to be his name, you see. But . . . love someone else . . . unacceptable. We . . . this was in Woodside, and oh, my God, it was years ago. We — did you ever do this? We dressed up, pretended to get married . . . found my mother's old confirmation dress . . . white. Wildflowers for my bouquet . . . did you ever do that? I was only six or seven, seventh or third grade. I mean *second* or third grade. We dressed up. It was only make-believe, of course, but I wore my first lipstick. It came off all over him when we kissed. But this was another boy . . . this wasn't Jimmy Flood. Jimmy Flood is Jimmy Flood, who's an altogether different person . . ."

"Who is the boy you really love?"

"Unacceptable. By the way, have you gone to bed with Craig Pollard yet?"

"Gabe Pollack. No, not yet."

"Shouldn't wait too much longer," she said, swirling the wine in her glass. "Strike while the iron is hot."

"Hot."

"Or he'll lose interest."

"But when?"

"Must plan this very carefully," Joanna said. "What does he do when he comes home at night?"

"At night?"

"Yes. Had your dinner. Everybody's gone off to their room to bed. What's he do then? 'S important."

"Sometimes — he reads in bed."

"Ah," Joanna said. " 'S the perfect moment. Reading in bed. You tap on his door. Some excuse why you need to see him. Into his room, close the door behind you. Sit on the corner of his bed. 'S he got hair on his chest?"

"Hair?"

"On his chest, yes."

"I think so, yes."

"Good. Touch him there. Then say, 'How curly your chest hair is.' Something like that. Can't resist that sort of thing — men. Tickle him a little there. Then let your hand slide down, under the sheet, and tickle him a little more . . . there. Then on, everything takes care of itself."

"Are you sure?"

"Absolutely. Won't be able to control himself. Wild. With passion. Lust. At least if he's normal. He is normal, isn't he?"

"Oh, yes."

"Still madly in love with him, aren't you?"

"Yes, but — "

"Then watch this."

And then, in the candlelight, as though in an erotic dream, she had watched as, at the other end of the sofa, Joanna lay back against the cushions and began to lift and turn her hips in slow, undulating rhythms, and, in her husky, throaty voice, to murmur, "Oh, my sweet . . . oh, my sweet . . . tickle me there . . . oh, yes . . . oh, oh, oh. . . . . Oh, yes . . . more . . . yes . . ."

But hypnotic as this performance was, Assaria was suddenly stricken with a problem of far more urgent proportions. She had just lighted her second cigarette and immediately stubbed it out. "Oh, *Jo!*" she cried. "Jo — I think I — I feel so — "

Joanna quickly sat up and looked at her. "Oh, God!" she said. "You're *green!* Wait! Hold on! Cover your mouth with your hands!" And she jumped up and ran a little unsteadily in her stocking feet — she had long since kicked off her shoes — to a corner of the room, and ran back with a galvanized pail. "Here," she said, and held Sari's head over the pail while what remained of Sari's lunch, and a good deal of champagne, came up.

"See?" Joanna said. "Club caters to members' every need." She was stroking the top of Sari's head. "Don't feel bad. Happens to the best of us. Happened to me, even to Peter. Who has an absolutely hollow leg. Champagne should've been iced. My fault."

When she was able to look up from the pail that was gripped between her legs, she was instantly sober again. But her face was streaming with perspiration now, and she could feel locks of her damp hair hanging stickily across her forehead.

Joanna handed her a handkerchief. "Nurse Jo to the rescue," she said. Then she said, "I've just decided what I'm going to do with my life. I'm going to work for you, and you're going to work for me. I don't know how we're going to do that yet, but that's what we're going to do."

It was an apt enough prediction, as things worked out.

But it was at that moment that Sari realized the two of them were no longer alone in the room. A tall and slender young man was standing there, staring at them, his expression a mixture of confusion and anger and disbelief, and she immediately recognized the face she had seen upstairs in the portrait gallery that very afternoon, though the face was now more mature.

"Peter!" Joanna cried, running toward him. "What in the world are you doing here? You're supposed to be thousands and thousands of miles away in New Haven, Connecticut."

"I was expelled," she heard him say.

"Will you have another drink?" Archie McPherson asks her. They are sitting in the bar at Ernie's, and it is afternoon.

"No, thank you," Melissa says. "I'm really not sure why I accepted this invitation of yours, you know."

"Really? Why not?"

"Because I don't trust you," Melissa says.

"Oh?"

"That story you wrote, about me paying the rock group for their date. Where did you get it from?"

"I have my sources," he says with a smile.

"Oh, I'm quite sure you do. But what was your source for that one — in which I was quoted, without being interviewed or asked for a quote?"

"It was accurate, wasn't it?"

"More or less. As accurate as any newspaper stories ever are. Who gave it to you?"

"It could have come from any number of people."

"Name two."

"It could have come from one of the Odeon's board of directors."

"Impossible. Since I did what I did without consulting or informing the board."

"Or it could have come from Maurice Littlefield himself, or someone else in the group."

"Hardly likely. None of the group is what you might call smart. And Maurice is — sweet. But," and she taps her forehead with the tip of her index finger, "again, not clever enough to find a newspaper reporter to give his story to — particularly since I'd made it clear to him that what I was doing was a purely personal and private gesture. No, Archie McPherson, there's only one person who could possibly have given you that story."

"Who?"

"Don't think *me* stupid, too. My mother, of course. She's the only one I told about my plans, and the quote you attributed to me was substantially what I'd said to her. So I don't trust you, Archie. But I also feel sorry for you."

"Why's that?"

"You've chosen to play the role of double agent — working for Gabe's paper, and working for my mother as well. When Gabe finds this out, as my mother will make sure he does as soon as your usefulness to her is over, he'll give you the boot. Which is just what she is planning to have done. And that will be the end of you in San Francisco."

He looks uncomfortable. He is frowning now, and is bending his red plastic stirrer into little zigzag parallelogram patterns. "Where do you come off with this double-agent stuff?" he says at last.

"I know my mother. I know how she operates. She never approaches a problem directly. There has to be deviousness, and backstairs intrigue, and people have to be pitted against one another until they're at the breaking point, and she gets what she wants. Then she washes her hands of them. I feel sorry for you, because I can tell you're now coming very close to the last of your usefulness to Assaria LeBaron. Soon the Bay Area will see no more of you. How much is she paying you for your little services, anyway?"

"This is very insulting, what you're saying."

She waves her hand. "It doesn't matter," she says. "Whatever it is, I'm sure it's pitifully small potatoes. Just enough to make you feel that you're playing some important role in the future of the LeBaron family, and Baronet Vineyards, and that you're playing it on the side of the Big Enchilada."

"I thought we were friends, Melissa."

"You're right. We were. Which brings us to today. Why did you invite me for drinks today?"

"For drinks. And dinner, I hope."

"I'm not sure about dinner. That will depend upon whether or not you start telling me the truth. Let me guess. She suggested that you ask me to dinner to try to find out how I intend to vote. Correct?"

"To vote?"

"Yes. There's quite a juicy takeover bid for Baronet in the works, as I'm sure Mother told you, and Eric's spearheading it, with a lot of Tillinghast money behind him. Dear little Alix's father. Apparently Daddy doesn't want his little Buttercup's husband to be crucified for taxes when Mother dies, so he's offering to swap his stock for ours. Very clever of him. So, sooner or later, we're going to have to put Harry's offer to a vote. Already Mother's marshaling her forces for the battle, trying to find out who's on her side and get a head count of the enemy. We're in the Cold War phase now, but wait until Mother brings in her big guns! And your job is to find out which side I'm going to be on — right?"

"Honestly, Melissa, she didn't mention any of this to me."

"I don't believe you. And why, you may well ask, doesn't my mother simply ask me how I'm going to vote on the proposal? We live in the same house. Because that would be too simple, and that's not Mother's style. That would be like Hitler asking Czechoslovakia if he could have the Sudetenland. No, Mother prefers to gather her information through spies and secret agents. And by threats, real or implied. And by bribing border guards, like you."

"Melissa, believe me. The subject of a takeover — the whole subject of Baronet — never once came up between your mother and me. I swear it. If there were a Bible in this restaurant, I would swear that, on the Holy Bible."

"Then why this invitation? Then why this latest story in your paper?"

"Honestly," he says, "I think she told me what you'd done because she was proud of you. You'd been outvoted by the Odeon's board, and so you simply took matters into your own hands and paid the group's fee out of your own pocket. I think she felt you did the right thing, the decent thing, and I think readers felt the same way when they read the story. I think she thought you were too modest to publicize this personal charity yourself, and that she thought you deserved some sort of public credit for what you'd done."

"Hmmm," she says. "I don't believe that, either. It doesn't sound at all like the mother that I know and have been dealing with for more than fifty years. No, that story was designed to make me look either like an empty-headed Lady Bountiful — to a rock group, after all, not even a recognized tax-deductible charity — or like a damn-fool spendthrift. Either way, the story could be used to suit her purposes, you see. It could be used to illustrate the point that Melissa is a crazy airhead whose voice — or vote — should not be taken seriously in any shareholders' battle. You see, I know my mother very well. I know the Byzantine way her mind works."

"I honestly don't think that's it," he says. "I don't think it had anything to do with any takeover offer, or with Harry Tillinghast, or with any of this, which is all news to me."

"Ah," she says, with a little smile. "Then *that's* it. News to you. Perhaps she hoped I'd spill this can of beans to you, which I've just done, and so she's already succeeded. See how clever she is? She's even cleverer than I thought! And why wouldn't she simply give this story of the proposed takeover to you directly? Simple. So that when you scoop the entire country with this story, her hands will be clean! 'Who leaked this story prematurely to this reporter?' the others will all want to know. 'Not I!' she'll say. 'It was Melissa! Melissa's to blame, as usual! Old, unstable, unreliable Melissa, who should probably be placed in a loony bin. They don't let people out of the loony bin to vote at shareholders' meetings, do they? Well, when you next see my mother, give her my congratulations. Her little plot worked, as usual.''

"Melissa," he says, "I'll tell you what. I'll promise you, I'll swear to you, not to write a word about anything you've told me here this afternoon. I'll treat it as a matter of strictest confidence between us. How's that?''

"Actually," she says, "I don't suppose it really matters all that much. The lid's going to blow off this story in a few days, anyway. Wall Street has been full of rumors about it for the past week. Why so much sudden heavy trading in Kern-McKittrick stock? Have you been watching it? I have. So I don't suppose what you write about it will have the slightest effect on the final outcome of things. Except to discredit me, of course, which is part of her plan.''

"You're awfully hard on your mother, Melissa.''

"Hard on her? The truth is that I adore her, and always have. I often wish I had her strength, and her courage, her guts. I adored my father, too, worshiped him, but that was different, because I never knew him. He was never there. I worshiped my father in the abstract, as an idea, as a loving father who could never come close to me. I adored them both — my father in the abstract, and my mother in the essential reality. In religious terms, it's a little like the difference between the Son and the Holy Spirit. The Son was real, Jesus existed, but the Holy Spirit is only a theory, an idea, a ghost. I loved the fact that was my mother, and the ghost that was my father, but adoring her doesn't mean that I trust her. You see, my mother is a very rich woman, and she thinks — knows — that she can buy people. Most people. People like you, for instance. How much does a reporter like you make? Eighteen, twenty thousand a year? Don't tell me, I don't really want to know. But someone like you she can buy at bargain-basement prices. You're not the first she's bought, and you won't be the last. But she can't buy me. Not just because I have plenty of money of my own, but because I won't let her buy me until she levels with me.

So all she can do is try to manipulate me, through agents like you, but meanwhile she's stuck with me. That's why I feel sorry for you. When she's through with you, she'll dispose of you very quickly — like a used Pamper! But now she needs my vote. Even from the loony bin, she's going to need my vote."

"Incidentally, how *do* you plan to vote? Not that it's any of my business."

"No, it isn't. But the fact is I haven't decided, and you can tell my mother that. A lot depends . . ." She hesitates, and gives him a calculating look. "A lot depends on whether my mother finally decides to come clean with me. And a lot depends on how many Baronet shares I discover I am actually legally entitled to vote. And you can tell my mother that, too."

"Dammit, Melissa, I'm not going to tell your mother any of this! I've already promised to keep all of this in the strictest confidence."

"It will be interesting to see whether you keep that promise."

"A promise is a promise. Now, will you stop being so suspicious and have another drink with me?"

"No. Was that Mother's suggestion, too? Get Melissa a little drunk, and maybe you'll get her tongue wagging. I can just hear her saying that. Did she also say, get Melissa a little drunk, and then maybe get her to bed down with you? Melissa has healthy sexual appetites — don't we all? A little roll in the hay might get her to unbutton her lip. I can just hear her saying that, too."

He lowers his eyes. "That's not why I invited you to dinner," he says.

"Then why did you?"

"For one thing, because I find you a fascinating woman."

"Oh, I am, I am. Fascinating."

"And because I find the LeBarons a fascinating family."

"We are, we are. Quite fascinating."

"And because, to be honest with you, someday I might like to write the LeBarons' story."

"Well, you won't do that as long as Mother is around. If you found a publisher, she'd buy the publishing house."

"To me, it's a very romantic story. The young Gold Rush im- migrant . . . the story of a fortune made off the land in Califor- nia . . . the special conditions of climate that produce the grape, warm sunny days and cool, dry nights . . . the romance of the wine business. You see, I've done a certain amount of homework al- ready, Melissa."

"Romantic, yes. But there are a few rough edges to the LeBaron story, some pretty ugly and dirty undersides that you're not going to learn about from me. Plenty of dirty linen, plenty of family skeletons, believe me."

"Anyway," he says, "let's stop talking about mergers and ac- quisitions and family skeletons. Let's have a pleasant evening, and change the subject to something pleasant. Okay?"

"Very well," she says. "What shall that pleasant subject be?"

"You," he says easily. "Tell me about your holiday in Switz- erland last winter, for instance."

"Switzerland," she says. Then she lifts her napkin from her lap, folds it carefully, and places it on the tablecloth in front of her. Then she reaches for her Gucci bag, which she had placed on the floor, just beside her chair. "So that's it. I might have guessed. Sometimes I'm not as clever as I like to think. Switzerland. I'm going home. Thank you for the drink, Archie, but you're a shit. You're a shit, but I still feel sorry for you. I feel terribly sorry for the shits of this world. The stakes they are playing for are usually so pitifully small. My stakes are somewhat larger. Good-bye." She rises, with her bag, to go.

He starts to rise. "Let me drop you at your house," he says.

"No, thank you. I'll take a taxi. Taxis are cheap. Like this date."

Half-standing, he watches her as she turns and moves quickly across the restaurant toward the door, her thin Delman heels leav- ing brief impressions in the thick green carpet on the floor of Ernie's bar, small, resilient dimples that lose their shape immediately her heels have left them.

Finally, he sits down again, and calls to the passing waiter, "Check, please."

"Thank you, sir, but Miss LeBaron has asked that this be placed on her bill," the waiter says.

At this very moment, Gabe Pollack has just reached Assaria LeBaron at her house on Washington Street. "I'm in Los Angeles," he says. "My secretary says you've been trying to reach me."

"Yes," she says. "Gabe, this is very important. Harry Tillinghast is planning to make a takeover bid for Baronet, and Eric's behind him. Naturally, their object is to get me to bail out of the company. I'm going to fight this every inch of the way, Gabe. They're not going to do this to me, but there is one immediate problem. All the shareholders have received notices in the mail, and Melissa is having dinner with your Mr. McPherson tonight. I think it's more than likely that she'll mention something about it to him, and that he'll feel there's a story in it. All that is fine, Gabe, but I don't want a story yet. I'm meeting with the lawyers tomorrow, and there's a family meeting planned for over the weekend. If McPherson comes to you in the morning with a story on Kern-McKittrick, I want you to tell him to keep the lid on it until I'm ready. Will you do that for me, Gabe?"

"Sure," he says. "That should be no problem, Sari."

"Believe me, when I'm ready to go to the press it'll be a much bigger story than anything Mr. McPherson will be getting out of Melissa at tonight's dinner. And if you'll do that for me, Gabe, I'm sure you know what your reward will be."

"No — what?"

"You'll be the first newspaper in the country to have the story. You'll have the exclusive, inside track."

"If that's possible, that would certainly be very nice."

"I'll personally see that you get it, Gabe. *That* should sell some papers for you. I'll even go farther, if you'll sit on any story about us until I give you the high sign. You know I've never given interviews, but I'll give you an interview on this one — one that'll knock 'em off their feet. How's that for a return for the favor, Gabe?"

He chuckles. "Yes, I guess that would be really something," he says.

"Good. It's a deal. Besides," she says, "it rather amuses me that the first to get this story won't be the *Times* or the *Wall Street Journal,* but our little old *Peninsula Gazette!*" She replaces the receiver in its cradle.

While she has been talking, Thomas has been standing discreetly a few paces outside her door. Now he enters. "Madam," he says, "there was a letter today in Miss Melissa's mail that I thought you should know about."

"Oh? What sort of letter?"

"It is a letter from Switzerland, Madam. It appears to be from the Palace Hotel in Saint Moritz."

"I see."

"And it appears to be quite more than an ordinary letter. It is quite a thick packet. I didn't deliver it to Miss Melissa, because I thought Madam might wish to examine it first."

"I see," she says. "You're asking me whether I'd like to open it and read it first."

"I thought this packet might possibly contain information that would be of special interest to you, Madam."

"Yes." She hesitates, playing with a pencil. "You know I disapprove of doing things like this," she says. "I've never liked to do it. But yes, I think under the present circumstances, we should. These are very special circumstances, after all."

He nods. "I'll fetch it for you, Madam."

While she waits, she doodles with her pencil, and the doodles are the pie charts that she has been drawing and redrawing now for many days. When he returns, and hands her the letter, she sees that indeed it is very long.

"Have you read this, Thomas? Never mind — of course you have. It doesn't take twenty minutes to steam open a letter." She adjusts her reading glasses on her nose, and reads:

> *My dear Miss LeBaron,*
> *Thank you for your kind letter, and its interesting enclosure, and I apologize for the long time it has taken me to get back to you with a reply. We are just now coming to the end of our*

customarily busy and hectic winter season, and our staff is now preparing for what our British guests call their ''hols,'' a well-deserved rest until the hotel reopens for summer, in June. This gives me a chance to answer your letter in some detail, which I know you were hoping to have me do.

But first of all, let me tell you how pleased I was to hear that you enjoyed your stay with us. Let me tell you also that it was our distinct pleasure to have you with us as our gracious and most charming guest. I passed along your compliments and good wishes to Hans, your ski instructor, who in return sends felicitations to you. All of the staff agree with me that your visit was only flawed by the fact that it was much too brief! The staff and I all look forward to another, longer visit in the future and, in the meantime, send our compliments and greetings for a happy, healthy, and prosperous New Year!

Now, to get to the substance of the questions you pose to me in your letter. I confess, when you spoke to me in December here, I did not immediately in my memory (always faulty!) draw a connection between your name and the people you feel may have been your relatives who stayed at the Hotel in 1926. Too, the fact that the Hotel was in the throes of its busy winter season may also be blamed for my unfortunate mnemonic failure. But the photograph of the young woman you enclosed immediately ''triggered'' my memory, and I remembered the young woman as though it were yesterday! Also, a search of the Hotel's records and registry (kept as meticulously as possible since the Hotel's first existence in 1856) revealed that indeed Mr. and Mrs. Peter Powell LeBaron stayed with us in 1926 and also in 1927. It is particularly regrettable that I should not have remembered their party instantly, since theirs was an unusually long stay!

Remember, of course, that in 1926 I was only a young boy of twelve, working here for my father, being trained, as he was trained by his own father, in the hotel business from the ground up. That year, I worked in a variety of positions. I worked as a busboy in the dining room, as a waiter in the Bar, and occasionally helped out at the Concierge's desk, delivering mail and

*telegrams and newspapers to the guests' rooms. As a result, I
got to know many of the guests and their habits more than a
little well. . . .*

"What a windbag," Sari says, turning a page.

> *. . . The woman in the photograph you sent me is very def-
> initely Mrs. Peter Powell LeBaron. I remember her well, and
> our Guest Record Ledger shows that she and her husband oc-
> cupied Suite 91–93 on the fourth étage. It might interest you to
> know that this particular suite has also been a favorite of many
> notables over the years. Miss Mary Pickford and Mr. Douglas
> Fairbanks spent a part of their honeymoon there. It was also the
> suite which Miss Greta Garbo always requested, as did Marlene
> Dietrich and Miss Barbara Hutton, when she was Countess
> Haugwitz-Reventlow. Other more recent dignitaries who have
> occupied the suite include Arturo Lopez-Wilshawe and the Baron
> Alexis de Rédé, Salvador Dali, Lord and Lady Ribblesdale, Mr.
> and Mrs. David Rockefeller, Mr. Henry Ford II, Miss Christina
> Onassis, and the King of Qum . . .*

"And what a name-dropper!" Sari says. "The King of Qum!"

> *. . . Mr. and Mrs. LeBaron's traveling companion, Mrs. Mary
> Brown, who remained with them throughout their stay, occupied
> an equally fine apartement, Suite 87–89, on the étage below.
> Suite 87–89 has provided a "home away from home" for an
> equally distinguished list of notables over the years, including
> Miss Paulette Goddard, Mr. Alfred Hitchcock, M. Jacques Fath,
> the novelist Erich Maria Remarque, Count Theo Rossi, Miss Elsa
> Maxwell, Miss Audrey Hepburn, Baron and Baroness Thyssen,
> and His Royal Highness Prince Karim Aga Khan. The late Shah
> of Iran particularly fancied this suite, as did David O. Selznick
> and Lady Maureen, Marchioness of Dufferin and Ava. But on
> to my recollections of your relatives, which will interest you
> more . . .*

"About time!" Sari mutters.

> . . . *With the photograph you sent me in my hand, the memories of Mr. and Mrs. LeBaron come flooding back. I remember that Mr. LeBaron was a very tall, very distinguished-looking man, good-looking in a rugged American "Western" way. His wife was a tiny woman, but quite extraordinarily pretty, though she looked, in contrast to her husband, quite foreign. I remember that there was some speculation among the Hotel staff about what might have been her country of origin. Some speculated that she might have been Italian, but I remember that she was addressed by her intimates as "Saree," so there was some talk that she might be part Asian, perhaps Indian. She must have been quite young at the time — recently married, I believe — but in the eyes of a boy of twelve she seemed very mature, so poised, so dignified, so full of self-confidence and excitement, almost a* grande dame. *What I remember most vividly about her was her walk. For a woman of such small physical stature, she seemed to have extraordinary presence, and this was expressed in the way she walked. Coming down the short flight of steps into the dining room in one of her beautiful dresses, her walk was almost regal, like an actress stepping out onto a stage into the spotlight, and heads would always turn throughout the room as she made her entrance, and moved gracefully to her table, which was number 5, a wonderfully lithe and springy walk . . .*

And why are Sari's eyes suddenly misting? She shakes the letter, and reads on.

> . . . *The LeBarons' traveling companion, Mrs. Brown, was an altogether different sort, who struck me as a shy, solitary, almost moody young woman who seemed to prefer her own company to that of others. I recall that almost every afternoon, in every weather, Mrs. Brown would take a walk around the lake, alone, a distance of 8.5 kilometers. The threesome would frequently gather in the bar at cocktail time, and there would*

*be lively conversation, but it was always my impression that it
was Mrs. LeBaron who "sparked" conversation, who tried to
keep things gay and interesting, while Mrs. Brown played a
more withdrawn and passive role in their social intercourse. I
remember, too, that for all the LeBaron party's outward impression of gaiety and ease and friendship, they also somehow con-
veyed an impression of inner sadness, some infinite sadness seemed
to burden them. I don't know why I say this, because there was
no outward evidence of this, and yet I remember that many of
the staff noticed this, and commented on it, and speculated about
it. There was speculation, in light of the fact that no Mr. Brown
was traveling with Mrs. Brown, that she might have been recently divorced, and that this might have been the cause of Mrs.
Brown's apparent disaffection and dégagé air. It was suggested
that Mr. and Mrs. LeBaron might have accompanied Mrs. Brown
on this long holiday to divert her mind and raise her spirits after
a recent bereavement. And yet neither explanation entirely satisfied the gossips among the staff. American divorcées, we have
noticed, often style themselves by taking a maiden name as a
first name — Mrs. Vanderbilt Brown, for instance. While American widows customarily retain their husbands' first names —
i.e., Mrs. Thomas Brown. But Mrs. Brown styled her nomen-
clature "Mrs. Mary Brown," which did not lend itself to either
explanation, divorce or widowhood. But that it must have been
one or the other became clear as the weeks went by, and Mrs.
Brown's condition became apparent. Her condition also helped
explain the undercurrent of what I call sadness that seemed to
pervade the LeBaron party.*

*Because, you see, it was not your relative Mrs. LeBaron who
was pregnant during her stay here, and gave birth to a child
four months or so after arriving. It was Mrs. Brown. I know I
am correct in this because of an incident that happened. We had
learned that Mr. LeBaron's family were, or had been, in the
wine business in California. There are still a number of vineyards
here in the Engadine, some of them very old, and at one point
Mr. LeBaron expressed an interest in visiting one of these. But
here in the Old World the art of wine making is surrounded by*

superstitions and old wives' tales. It is said, for example, that wine must not be bottled during the dark of the moon. It is said that bottling done while a north wind is blowing will turn the wine cloudy, and that there must not be rain or cloudy skies. Even today there are cellar men who will turn pale with fear if a woman passes by their casks at certain times of the moon, and at any time at all if she is great with child. It is all very silly, of course, but our Old World vineyardists believe these factors will doom their harvest. It fell to my father to explain, as tactfully as possible, to Mr. LeBaron that while Mr. LeBaron and his wife would be perfectly welcome to visit one of our local vineyards — provided the phase of the moon were checked on first, of course! — it would be quite unwise for them to include Mrs. Brown in their company. This was explained to him simply to spare Mrs. Brown any embarrassment and discomfort. I remember this because I know that when Mr. and Mrs. LeBaron toured the vineyards, they toured alone. I am certain of this because I was selected as their guide to accompany them on their tour. I remember that when the tour was over Mr. LeBaron offered me a very generous pourboire of a hundred francs. As the son of the hotelier, I quite naturally would not accept this.

I remember that Mrs. Brown's baby was born during one of the winter months — December or January of 1926–1927. I remember because there were heavy snows, and there was a great deal of excitement surrounding the event. It is not every day that a baby is born at The Palace! I remember that it was a very difficult birth. If I recall, the baby was about to make a breech presentation, and our old hotel doctor — whose speciality was mending bones broken on the ski slopes! — felt he could no longer handle the situation, and Mrs. Brown was rushed to hospital in a sleigh. A sleigh had to be used because motor vehicles could no longer pass through the streets, due to the snows. At the hospital, we heard that surgery had been required — a caesarian section, I presume — and I remember that we at the Hotel were able to help by contacting the Red Cross and obtaining many demilitres of blood. Later, I remember hearing that both mother and child were very nearly lost. I wish I could tell you the sex of the child, but I cannot. I had no interest in it. To a young man of twelve years old, a baby is simply that — a baby!

I wish that there were more that I could tell you about Mr. and Mrs. LeBaron and Mrs. Brown. Our records show that they arrived at the Hotel on 17 August 1926, and departed on 1 March 1927, whether to return to America or for further European travel I do not know. In our Guest Registry we note any special preferences or requirements that our guests may have, in order that these may be attended to on future visits. I note that Mrs. LeBaron had a special preference for one hotel maid, Annelinde. I note that Mr. and Mrs. LeBaron liked a Continental breakfast — orange juice, croissant, and coffee — served in their suite at 7 A.M., and often came down for a fuller breakfast in the dining room around 9. I note that Mr. LeBaron wanted the Paris Herald Tribune *delivered with his Continental breakfast, and that he liked his shirts laundered without starch. The only notation I find on Mrs. Brown's card is that she liked her breakfast eggs cooked exactly three and one-half minutes.*

I note that Mr. and Mrs. LeBaron's address in the Registry is given as 1023 California Street, San Francisco. Mrs. Brown's is given as Bitterroot Ranch, Lakeside, Montana.

I hope, dear Miss LeBaron, that all of this will be of some assistance to you in your search for lost relatives, and in your project of constructing a "family tree," and if I can be of any further help to you please do not hesitate to call on my eager service.

Meanwhile, my staff joins me in wishing you amities and felicitations.

Sincerely yours,
Andrea Badrutt

"Well, Thomas," Sari says, putting down the letter, removing her glasses, and rubbing her eyes. "What should we do with this? Give it to her or burn it up?"

"You're asking my opinion, Madam?"

"Yes, of course I am."

"I think, under the present circumstances, you should give it to her."

"Here," she says, handing him the letter. "Seal it up. Put it on her mail tray in the morning. This will mean telling her the truth, of course."

"Yes, Madam. I see what you mean. Yes."

"But what if — ?"

"I know what you're thinking, Madam. But you've got to take that chance. Considering the present circumstances, considering what Mr. Eric is threatening to do, I don't see that you have any choice. If she knows the truth, there'll be at least a fifty-fifty chance that she'll vote her shares in your favor, and at least a fifty-fifty chance that you'll win. If she isn't told the truth, there's no way you'll be able to win at all. Your pie charts tell you that."

She sighs. "You don't think I should speak to the lawyers first?"

"Under the circumstances, I don't think the lawyers would advise you to do differently, if you're going to win. Look at the pie charts. Besides, this isn't just a legal problem, is it, Madam? It's a human problem, too."

"I could still lose."

"Isn't a fifty-fifty chance of winning better than no chance at all?"

"You're right. Of course. As always. I've always said that you could have become the president of General Motors if you hadn't decided to take up buttling."

"I think I'd rather be a butler, Madam," he says. "It's much more interesting."

PART THREE

The Takeover

Nine

SARI AND PETER had spent the first three full summers of their marriage — the summers of 1927, 1928, and 1929 — at Bitterroot Ranch in northwestern Montana with their little girl. The property consisted of three thousand wooded acres in Lake County, overlooking Flathead Lake, and with snowcapped mountains on both horizons, which Julius LeBaron had bought for a song — ten dollars an acre — before the war, when land in the Rockies was considered next to worthless. Now, the U.S. government would like to purchase Bitterroot for a National Forest, but Sari and Julius's other heirs have been holding out. The figure the government has offered is $500,000. Private developers have also shown an interest.

Bitterroot was, and is, in timber country, but it had been Peter's idea to clear the valley of trees for sheep ranching — Australian merinos were what he had in mind. And he had also planned to experiment with a new breed of beef cattle that had been developed in Texas, called Santa Gertrudis, noted for their hardiness in all kinds of weather and their thrifty growth on grass feeding. That, at least, had been his plan.

The main building at Bitterroot was a comfortable, ten-room log house, all on one level, set on an open hillside above the lake. There were several other outbuildings — sheds, toolhouses, and a cottage where the ranch superintendent, Mr. Hanratty, lived with his wife. Every morning, after a breakfast cooked for them by Mrs. Hanratty, Peter would set off to fell his daily quota of trees. Each tree felled was logged in a little notebook he kept in a pocket of his denim work pants, and each evening at dinnertime he would announce his tally. "Twenty-five today" . . . "Thirty-one today," and so on, and at the end of each of those three summers the daily tallies would be totaled. The totals were impressive — forty-five hundred trees one summer, forty-nine hundred the next, and so on, and so on, and clearing the forest seemed to have become almost an obsession with him, and Assaria often wondered about it. It seemed his only interest and yet it did not seem possible to her that he could ever succeed in clearing the acreage he had in mind in a lifetime of summers, particularly since he refused any outside assistance in his labors — even Mr. Hanratty's, when it was offered. He insisted that he was going to do it all himself. "Then," he would say, "we're going to retire here, and raise Australian merinos and try Santa Gertrudis cattle. It won't be too lonely, will it?"

"It's the most beautiful country in the world," she said. "But by then there may be more children — grandchildren, perhaps."

To this he would say nothing.

How does one treat a lover who isn't? How does one try to make him happy? One tries kindness, one tries congratulation. "Forty trees today! That's a record, isn't it? How wonderful!" How does one try to enter his remoteness, his solitary and brooding landscape, the discouragement and disappointment and determination to do nothing but wield an ax? She had felt this settling over them — felt it, but tried to dismiss it — even before they were married, and she had felt it in Switzerland, and tried to make a joke of it. Sadness, Andrea Badrutt had called it, and that was as good a word for it as any. Infinite sadness, impenetrable sadness, but what he had not detected was that it was Peter's sadness that had somehow become encapsulated within Peter's heart and in his mind, and that Sari, for all her attempts at gaiety, could not reach through to touch. "You don't regret this, do you, Peter?" she would say to him. "We did the right thing, didn't we?" "Oh, yes, of course," he would say. And then, at times despite herself, she would lose patience with him. "You agreed to this!" she would cry. "This was what you said you wanted us to do!" "Oh, yes," he would say. "Yes, I know." And she would find herself asking herself: *Is love important? Is it important to be in love?* Perhaps not, and perhaps love is nothing more than watching the man you love, the lover who isn't one, cutting down trees, and cheering when he recites the daily totals. Come back, she had wanted to say to him. Come back to the place we had once, to where we made love, and where you told me I was so lovely, and that you loved me. Come back, come back. But he wouldn't come back and, instead, she would watch him, shirtless, in his slowly diminishing pine forest with his ax, and the small brown mole in the fine hairs just above his belly button would fill her with more longing and sadness than could be satisfied in even the most soaring and mountainous landscape of love, much less love at its most banal. Why is the shower bath not draining properly? she would ask herself, and with her fingers she would stoop and scoop out a small dark wad of his hair, and her eyes would fill with tears.

"Ours is not a conventional marriage," he would sometimes say to her.

"But does that mean we couldn't try to make it one? I thought that was what we were going to try."

"Well . . ." he would say, and turn away.

"Make a life of your own," Joanna would say. "Hard work. That's the answer. Organization. Organize something."

And so that is what she had tried to do.

Sometimes, those summers at Bitterroot, she would come with him and watch him as he worked, stripped to the waist and sweating while she sat wrapped in a scarf or sweater against the chilly mountain air. The sun glistened on the muscles of his back and shoulders as he swung his ax, the splinters flying into the air, the sounds of his chopping echoing in the hills. It was also this hard physical exercise that kept him in such splendid physical shape, but vanity had nothing to do with what it was that drove him.

"There's more . . . to . . . lumbering . . . than just . . . knowing how to use an ax," he said between swings. "It's a very precise and mathematical art."

"Really?"

"Absolutely. For instance, before you start cutting down a tree, you have to decide exactly where you want it to fall. Then you plan your cuts accordingly. You have to take into consideration the wind direction, for example — things like that." He wiped his dripping brow with his forearm. "Here. Let me show you. Now suppose you tell me exactly where you want this tree to fall. Exactly."

"Let's see," she said, looking around. "How about over there, on top of that little flat rock. Is that too small?"

"Easy," he said, and began to swing.

She watched him as he swung at the bole of the big pine, chipping away fat, wedge-shaped splinters.

Presently the tall trunk of the tree began to sway, its branches rustling, agitating, protesting, as though making one last plea for its life.

He stepped back and looked up at the tree. He studied it, looking into the sun, his left hand bridged across his eyes. A wind had come up, and the trunk of the tree creaked and sighed in it, the branches lifting and whispering. "One more cut," he said. "This one's crucial."

He swung at the bole once more. There was a sharp *crack*, almost like the sound of a gunshot, as the heart of the bole snapped — Sari has often thought that when her own heart finally stops she will hear that same explosive sound — and the tree began to fall, slowly at first, then very fast. There was a crash, and it was on the ground, and its topmost branch, the finial where you would have placed an angel or a star if it had been a Christmas tree — lay precisely across the center of the small flat rock.

Assaria ran to see. "Bull's-eye!" she cried, clapping her hands. "Bravo!"

"Nothing to it," he said, panting and wiping his dripping brow with the back of his bare arm again.

"Let me get Melissa," she said. "Let's show her what her daddy can do!"

"No," he said. "I think I've done enough for today." He slipped the little spiral notebook from his pants pocket, and made a penciled notation. "That's thirty-three."

"She'd be so proud of you!"

"Maybe some other time."

"I wish you'd try to spend some more time with her, Peter," she said. "She needs more fathering, I think."

"Well, I can't help the way I feel," he said.

"But try. Just try. I mean, watching you do a trick like that would thrill her!"

"I'll try," he said.

But he had not tried.

The summer of 1929, they had stayed at Bitterroot longer than usual, into October. The warm weather had held, and the snows had held off, and Peter had wanted to take advantage of the bonus the weather was offering to get in as much lumbering as possible. One evening in mid-October, they had both commented on the astonishing sunset. The sun had gone down huge and red in the western sky, and the snowcaps flashed with such an intense and fiery color that it seemed for a moment that the entire world had burst into flames. The next morning, they learned that, in a sense, it had. In New York, the stock market had made its first precipitous plunge, and traders who had bought on margin could not cover their borrowings, and overnight thirty billion dollars of American capital had disappeared into what would be a deepening whirlpool of debt. Julius LeBaron had telephoned them that morning from San Francisco, and told them to come home immediately, where only the beginnings of the troubles they would have to face, and which you already know about, awaited them.

It would be more than a dozen years before they returned

to Bitterroot again, and by then the forest Peter LeBaron had been trying to level had grown up nearly as tall and implacable as before.

"You didn't come home last night," Gabe Pollack said to her. "I was very worried, Sari."

"I spent the night at my friend Joanna LeBaron's house," she said. "I — it was something I ate, I guess — but I got a little sick, and they let me spend the night." She didn't tell him that she had slept in her clothes under an army blanket on an old sofa in the LeBarons' cellar, that she had been spirited out of the house early that morning through the kitchen and into a service alleyway, with the disapproving complicity of MacDonald, the LeBarons' butler, and that she still had a splitting headache from the afternoon before.

"LeBaron? The wine people?"

"Yes."

"Well, you're really moving in high society, aren't you?"

That was a damn-fool thing for Gabe Pollack to have said, and he should have known better than to have said it. He had been working as a general-assignment reporter for the *Chronicle* for three years now, writing about the city's high life as well as its low, and he should have gained a better understanding of the city's somewhat arcane social structure, just as Sari would gain it in time. The LeBarons weren't then, and aren't now, members of San Francisco's high society. They were merely rich, and by 1926 it had been decided that to be merely rich in San Francisco was not enough.

I mean, San Francisco society at that point may not have been very old, but it had already decided who it was. It had had to. By the turn of the century, everyone knew that the Crockers and Tevises and Floods and Haggins and Spreckelses were rich, but did that make them society? If so, then how did you classify all the others? That woman in furs and jewels at the opera might be a Crocker, or she might be the madam of a Barbary Coast bordello who had just gone into real estate speculation. Society had needed someone to codify it, and fortunately by the year 1900 someone had come forth to do just that, borrowing heavily, almost abjectly, from earlier established models on the East Coast. If Mrs. Astor had needed Ward McAllister to help her designate who New York's "Four Hundred" were, so San Francisco had appointed Ned Greenway, a champagne salesman, to make a list of who counted and who did not and, in the process, to teach San Franciscans how to perform cotillion figures. For his West Coast equivalent of Mrs. Astor, Greenway had, in turn, appointed Mrs. Eleanor Martin, whose brother-in-law owned the gas company.

But it was more than to New York that San Francisco looked for social guidance. San Francisco also borrowed, deferentially, from older, more serenely established Eastern cities, such as Boston, Philadelphia, Baltimore, Charleston, Savannah, and New Orleans. Allegiance to societies of the Old South was reinforced by the fact that San Francisco was strongly pro-Confederate during the Civil War. By 1926, the year we are writing about, though Ned Greenway was long gone, membership in San Francisco high society was fixed, and fairly immutable. It didn't matter that most of the forebears of the city's elite had been rogues and ruffians of the worst order. It didn't matter that the original James Flood had been a bartender, or that Old Man Crocker had stood over his Chinese coolie labor force with a horsewhip while they built his Central Pacific Railroad, and paid them in cash so he didn't need to bother keeping books. What mattered was that the children and grandchildren of these men were considered ladies and gentlemen.

The LeBaron money was simply too new to admit them into the charmed circle, or for them to be regarded as anything more than upstarts. They hovered somewhere around the circumference of the circle, permitted to penetrate it at this point or that, but were never given unqualified membership in it. Everyone knew, for example, that Mario Barone, Julius LeBaron's father, had been an Italian immigrant who never learned to speak or write the King's English. Everyone knew that Constance LeBaron's mother, for all Constance's airs, had been a chambermaid at a downtown hotel and — or so it was said — even performed more intimate services for some of the hotel's gentleman guests. Then there was the fact that the LeBarons were Catholics, in a city where the best people worshiped at Grace Church Episcopal. But worst of all, perhaps, was the fact that the LeBarons, though they lived in the city, were really not City People. They were Valley People, they were farmers who had made their money from the sweat of their brows and the strain of their backs in vineyards in Sonoma, Napa, Livermore, Stockton, Lodi, and Modesto. They had not gone on into respectable businesses such as banking, commerce, railroads, shipping, or the professions. They had remained essentially country bumpkins, hicks. With Prohibition, they had turned from grapes to tomatoes — but what was the difference in that? Tomatoes were just another stoop-labor crop. No, Gabe should not have confused the LeBarons with high San Francisco society, as Sari herself would learn in due course.

Here are some of the things she would overhear about the LeBarons over the years:

Much snickering about Julius's grandiose name-change, and she would hear Julius and his son called, behind their backs, Sir Julius and Lord Peter.

She would hear them called the Wops and the Dagos.

She would hear someone say, "What was the name before it was LeBaron? I think it was Baroney or Baloney, or something like that."

"The Dagos are having some sort of a dinner party. But do we really want to go?"

"They're N.O.C.D. — Not Our Class, Dear."

"LeBaron men always marry *down*, don't they. They never marry *up*. Well, what can you expect from Dagos?"

"Mackerel-snappers . . ."

"The LeBarons? Oh, you mean those Valley wine people . . ."

"My dear, have you seen what Constance LeBaron has done with that lovely old house on California Street? All that gilt and red plush! How would you describe it? Middle European whorehouse . . . ?"

"I've heard that the girl Peter LeBaron is marrying is . . . Jewish."

"Well, what can you expect?"

"They say that Julius LeBaron has lost absolutely everything in the crash . . ."

"Well, what can you expect?"

"From rags to riches, and back to rags again, in one generation . . ."

"What can you expect . . ."

Over the years, Sari would hear these comments. She would take them with a grain of salt. They even, in a grim way, amused her.

But that night, when Gabe made his remark about the LeBarons and high society, she did not know any of this, and simply assumed that what he said was true, and was mostly impressed with the fact that he had missed her the night before. Somehow, she had thought that he would not even notice she was gone.

"I'm sorry I made you worry," she said.

"Of course I was worried. Anything might have happened. I thought of going out to look for you, but I had no idea where to look. I was terribly worried, Sari."

"I'm sorry."

"I mean, you're a big girl now, and you can do as you please, but if you're going to be gone all night at least let someone know. At least telephone. If I'm not here, at least leave a message with Mrs. Dodge . . ."

And she had also thought: Why, here I am. Alone in his room with him, and it is after dinner, and he is reading in bed, and now the rest of the scenario was hers to write. She closed his bedroom door behind her, and said, "Can we talk a little bit, Gabe?"

"Of course," he said.

She sat down on the corner of his bed. "I didn't mean to worry you," she said, "but something's been worrying me."

"What's that?"

"I'm almost seventeen, and I'll be graduating from high school in June. My friend Joanna is going to go on and be a debutante for a year, and do nothing but go to parties. But I can't do that, of course. So what am I going to do? Joanna keeps saying that I should go to Hollywood and become a movie star, but that takes money, and I don't have that much money, so what should I do? I'm sure Mr. Moscowitz would let me work longer hours at the Odeon — regular hours, full time — but then what?"

"I'm sure you'll find some nice fellow and marry him," he said.

"Yes," she said. "I've been thinking that, too. And I think I've found that nice fellow, Gabe."

"Who? Tell me about him."

"You."

"What?" He smiled. "Oh, no, no — "

"Yes," she said, leaning toward him, reaching out with one hand to touch him very lightly on the chest. "I love you, Gabe. I want to marry you."

"No, no." He took her outstretched hand in his, and pushed it away from him. "No, you're not serious."

"I've never been so serious in my life! Let's get married, Gabe. I'd make such a good wife to you, I promise! I'll work for a while, and then, when our children come, we'll have enough money for a place of our own. I know we can be happy, Gabe, because I love you. I love you so much. Please marry me, Gabe — it's the only thing I want."

"Listen," he said, still holding her hand, tighter now, but at a little distance from him in the bedclothes. "Listen, I love you, too — but not that way, Sari. Do you understand?"

"No."

He was sitting full up on the bed now. "You'll always be my friend, Sari — I hope. You're sort of like the daughter I'll never have. If ever you need anything, I'll be here, and if ever you're in trouble I'll do everything I can to help. But no — not marriage, Sari. Get that out of your head right now, do you understand? It's because I can't give a woman what a husband should give a wife in marriage. What more can I say? I can't say anything more than that. Please try to understand."

"Oh, Gabe, please! Make love to me, and you'll see."

"No." His voice was very firm now. "I can't give you what you want. It's that simple. It would be unfair to you even to try. A husband and a wife should be — but I can't be that to you. I used to think, perhaps — but no. I know myself, Sari, and I know you. You'll find someone, of course, but not me." He released her hand. "So go to bed now, dear Sari. And let's both try to forget this conversation ever happened. Good night, Sari. I'll see you in the morning."

"Oh!" she sobbed. "You don't love me one little bit!"

His face was sad now. "It has nothing to do with love. It's me."

She ran out of his room and down the hall into her own, and flung herself across the bed — confused, hurt, bewildered, and finally angry. Never had she been so angry in her life, and at so many things and so many people — angry at him, of course, and angry at Joanna for giving her all the wrong directions and advice, and finally and most bitterly furious at herself, ashamed of herself and hating herself for having behaved so foolishly, thinking: How can I have been so stupidly foolish and naive? Of course, that was not the way to seduce a man! Even the stupid character she had pretended to be in the play had been smart enough to know that! Sabrina Van Arsdale had not got her Russian prince by throwing herself at his feet, by throwing herself across his bed. She had run away, and let him chase her across the face of Europe — to Paris, to Capri, to the doge's palace on the Grand Canal. She would run away, too, to Hollywood, to New York, to the ends of the earth, to the moon, and then he would see how much he would miss her, how much he would worry about what might have happened to her, how many nights he would lie awake wondering where she had gone, wandering the night streets in search of her, sick with worry, wondering where she was . . . and then . . . and then . . . "Mr. Moscowitz, I want you to give me the names of all the top producers in Hollywood, all the top ones!" And then, when she had gone there and become a famous movie star with a white Rolls-Royce and a chauffeur and a butler of her own, and a mansion on Sunset Boulevard, Gabe would see her name in lights on all the marquees, and her face in all the movie magazines, and Gabe would know where she was and come, with his hat in his hand, to her house to find her. And her butler would answer the door — leaving it on the chain, of course, for Gabe would try to burst in — and say, "I'm sorry, Mr. Pollack, but Miss Latham cannot see you." And the door would close in his face.

She rolled over in the bed, staring straight upward at the ceiling with tear-filled eyes, thinking: Is love important? Is it important to be in love?

Sometime later she would remember a friend of his, another

young reporter from the paper, David Somebody, with whom he often spent evenings, having dinner and playing cards, he said, and she would have to ask herself if they also played at other things as well . . . but she could not even think about that.

Is there a point at which one needs to be in love, *must* fall in love, in order to fill some sort of vacuum?

In any case, three weeks later none of this seemed to matter because, by then, she had fallen in love with Peter LeBaron.

"We're going out on the *Baroness C* on Sunday. Can you join us?" It was Joanna LeBaron calling her on the telephone.

"On the Bering Sea?"

"No, silly. The *Baroness C.* It's our boat. Can you come with us?"

"Who is 'us'?"

"Peter and I, of course. We're going to pack a lunch, and go for a sail."

"That sounds wonderful," she said.

"Good. We'll pick you up at ten o'clock on Sunday morning."

The *Baroness C* turned out to be a thirty-two-foot sloop with a gleaming mahogany hull and a spanking white enameled deck that had been designed and built by the great Nathaniel Herreshoff himself, Joanna explained to her, even though Sari had until that point never heard of the famous Rhode Island yacht-builder. From the marina at the foot of the Embarcadero, they were ferried out in a dinghy to where the *Baroness C* was moored, and Peter scrambled aboard first, then helped the two girls and the heavy picnic hamper up onto the rocking deck.

"Mother thinks the *Baroness C* was named after her," Joanna said.

"But it wasn't," Peter said. "It just happens to be the third sailboat our father's owned. The first was *Baroness A*, the second was *Baroness B*, and so on."

While Peter moved efficiently about the boat, casting off the mooring, setting lines, and hoisting sails, Joanna explored the contents of the picnic hamper. "MacDonald's put together the most scrumptious goodies for us," she said. "Jellied eggs. Crabmeat sandwiches. Stuffed artichoke hearts. Aren't we lucky —"

"To have a butler we can blackmail," Peter said with a wink.

It was a habit they had, Sari had begun to notice, of finishing each other's sentences.

Soon they were under sail, gliding out across the Bay under a clear blue Sunday sky.

"I've never been on a sailboat before," Sari said.

"There's only one rule. Peter is the skipper, and you and I have to do everything he tells us to." But with Peter lolling at the tiller, and the boat gliding northward, its sails full in a good breeze, there seemed now very little to do except admire the morning and the distant green and wooded hills. There was no bridge across the Golden Gate, of course, in those days, and the northern suburbs of Marin County had not been developed. Sausalito was still a sleepy fishing village, and Belvedere and Tiburon were still virtually uninhabited, accessible only by boat. Soon the city was just an outline on the horizon behind them, and the shore of the upper bay — San Pablo Bay — was a wilderness reaching down into the water. "We've got to see that you get some proper sailing gear," he said to her.

She had hoped they wouldn't notice. Both Peter and his sister were wearing khaki shorts, loose, short-sleeved shirts, and canvas shoes, and Sari, in her middy blouse and skirt, had felt a little overdressed for this outing. "Well, I wasn't sure —" she began.

"Kick off those silly shoes," he said.

She did as she was told and kicked off her black patent-leather pumps.

"And take off those silly stockings."

Obediently, she rolled down her white, knee-length hose, and now she was barefoot.

"Now take that silly bow out of your hair," he said.

She removed the bow and shook her hair loose.

"Now that's more like it," he said.

"Our skipper isn't always so mean and bossy," Joanna said. But Peter wasn't looking mean and bossy. He was smiling at Sari, and his smile was wonderfully warm, and she smiled back at him a little shyly.

"Jo says you want to join our little club," he said. "The notorious California Street Wine Cellar Club."

"I'm afraid I'll need to learn the rules for that, too," she said.

"The only rule —" Joanna began.

"Is that there are no rules," he finished. And there was something in the way he said this that sounded so — what? Abandoned, almost, and Sari suddenly had the excited feeling that she was being invited into a loose and careless world of sensuous pleasures and no responsibilities. The very ease with which Peter LeBaron lay back across the stern of the sailboat, one bare arm resting on the tiller, seemed to suggest this, and so did the stillness and ease with which the *Baroness C* cut through the water. From her only other journey across the water, Sari remembered the endless churning of engines below the deck, night and day. But here the motion was effortless and smooth and still, and the only sounds were the gentle lapping of water against the boat's hull and the sigh of the wind and the occasional snap of the sails. Putting her head back, and letting her loose hair fly in the breeze, she had thought: I could sail on like this forever.

As though she had been reading her thoughts, Joanna said, "Let's try to do this every Sunday for the rest of the summer."

"Of course, I'm afraid our first meeting wasn't very auspicious," Peter said.

"No. I'm afraid I'd drunk much too much champagne."

"My fault," Joanna said. "Bad bartending."

"And I'd just been booted out of Yale."

"What happened, anyway?" Sari asked.

"A gross miscarriage of justice," Joanna said. "Too furious-making, really."

"A misunderstanding —" Peter began.

"On the part of Yale University!" Joanna finished for him. "A university that should be stripped of its credentials!"

"Well, that's putting it a little strongly, Jo," he said.

"It isn't! Tell her! Tell her what happened."

Peter shrugged. "It was nothing, really, but what happened

was —" And he had begun a rather rambling explanation of what had occurred in New Haven earlier that spring.

What it all amounted to, it seemed, was a misunderstanding between Peter and his department head. He was majoring in chemistry because, he explained, as soon as Prohibition was repealed — and it was bound to be before too much longer — the family would probably go back into wine production, and science was going to play an important part in the future of California wine making. Wine making was becoming more and more a science, yet it would always also remain an art. How else to explain why the most brilliant scientists at U.C. Davis could apply all their knowledge and come up with an inferior wine? And why could the most ignorant farmer create a wine that was superb? These were questions that might never be answered.

"Isn't Peter brilliant?" Joanna interrupted.

But that had nothing to do with the misunderstanding between Peter and his department head, he continued. Three days a week, in chemistry class, there was a two-hour lab period, and in these lab periods each man was assigned a lab partner. Peter's partner was a chap named Walters, who happened to be a wisenheimer whom nobody liked.

"Wisenheimer is too good a word for him," Joanna put in. "The man is a total and utter creep."

Anyway, in this one experiment that they had been assigned to do, Peter had performed all the right procedures. And yet, for some damned reason or another, he had not been able to produce the proper result. And so, after the class was over, Peter had simply opened Walters's desk and copied the results off Walters's paper. The department head had challenged this. "You could not possibly have come up with this result using these procedures," the department head had said. They had called it cheating, but it wasn't cheating, was it?

"Absolutely not," Joanna said.

Not when you got your result from the guy who was your own lab partner, even if he was a wisenheimer. Weren't partners supposed to help each other out?

"Absolutely yes," said Joanna.

Anyway, Peter had denied everything, and so the department head had asked him to repeat the experiment in the presence of a faculty member, and he still hadn't been able to produce a result that matched his procedure, and so they kicked him out. And so that was all it was, a misunderstanding.

"Isn't that the most ridiculous thing you ever heard?" Joanna said. "Who gives a rat's rear end about a silly old chemistry experiment, anyway?"

To Sari's untrained ears, it all sounded rather complicated, but she also agreed that it sounded pretty unfair.

"It was, no doubt about it," Peter said. "Anyway, Pop's working on getting me into some other college in the fall. I'll probably finish up at Stanford."

"Which is actually —" Joanna began.

"A much better school," Peter finished.

"Meanwhile, Daddy's being very stiff-necked about it," Joanna said. "It seems that Yale had to go and write him this silly letter. That was what made me see the most violent shade of red — that letter. All about how Peter 'fails to regard the consequences of his actions.' Did you ever hear of anything so ridiculous? Peter — of all people."

Peter laughed. "Well, it's all water over the dam now," he said.

"Yes, darling boy, and now you have a whole extra month of summer vacation," Joanna said.

"Pop wants me to look for a job."

"That's ridiculous, too. Aren't parents a bore, Sari?"

"It's been so long since I've had any that I've forgotten," she said.

"Oh, I'm sorry. I forgot. But maybe you're lucky. Parents can really be a terrible bore at times."

Peter still leaned back against the tiller, a dreamy look in his eyes. Then, with his free hand, he fished into his shirt pocket and produced a harmonica, and began to play "I Want to Be Happy."

"Now, the most important thing we have to do is find the absolutely perfect spot for our picnic lunch," Joanna said, her eyes scanning the shoreline. "It has to be absolutely perfect and secluded." The shore ahead of them was rugged now, lined with large rocks that descended in a steep cascade into the water. "There —" Joanna pointed. "There's a little beachy stretch between the rocks. Let's drop anchor over there." Peter hugged the tiller closer to him, and the boat responded, and when they were perhaps twenty yards from the beachy stretch, he lowered the anchor and began furling the sails.

"Before we eat, a swim," Joanna said.

"Oh, dear," Sari said. "I didn't bring a swimsuit."

"Who needs one? We swim in the buff. It's healthier, and there isn't a prying eye for miles and miles."

"You mean we wear — *nothing?*"

"Of course. *Au naturel.* Don't tell me you're *shy,* or something!"

"But Peter is —"

"Don't be a goose. Peter is my brother, and you're my best friend. Remember what we swore — no secrets."

Peter lowered a rope ladder from the side of the boat, and now he and Joanna were nonchalantly shedding their clothes, and so what was there for Sari to do but try to imitate their nonchalance and start removing her skirt and blouse and dropping these garments, as Joanna was doing, in a little pile on the deck? But when Sari undressed, she still could not quite bring herself to look at the other two.

"Last one in is a rotten egg!" Peter cried, and dove into the Bay. Joanna and Sari followed him, together.

"There's a sea serpent here who sucks girls under the water," Peter shouted, and ducked, his bare feet surfacing briefly above the water, and Sari felt his hand grip her ankle and tug her under. She came up sputtering and laughing. He did this to Joanna next, and soon they were all doing it to one another, and the water, which had seemed icy cold at first, began to seem less so. Then they were clambering up the ladder and into the boat again.

"We don't even have to dress for lunch," Joanna said, shaking her wet hair. "We wear sarongs like they do in the Islands." She handed Sari a large beach towel. "And look," she said, opening the picnic hamper, "MacDonald has even included a bottle of wine."

"Aren't we lucky —" Peter said.

"To have a butler we can blackmail," Joanna said.

And, after lunch, as the three of them lay on their stomachs on the deck in the sun that was beginning to lower through the Golden Gate, Sari decided that she was getting used to these wild and indifferent and irresponsible new friends who lived surrounded by this golden haze of money. Peter was cradling his harmonica against his mouth again, playing snatches of show tunes, but Sari could still not bring herself to look at him.

Then, when it was time to lift anchor and sail back across the Bay, there was a problem. The mainsail would not feed into its channel on the mast properly. A line was fouled at the head of the mast. "Nothing to do but shinny up the mast and straighten it out," Peter said, and, from the corner of her eye, she saw him expertly starting up the mast.

When he reached the top, she finally allowed her eyes to travel upward to him, where he worked on the fouled line. With her left hand, she bridged her eyes to watch him as, naked and gleaming, he clung to the swaying masthead like a panther clinging to the trunk of a slender tree, the sun behind him, framed in the bright sunlight.

She realized that Joanna's eyes were reaching in the same direction. "Peter really is a kind of genius," Joanna murmured. "He's afraid of nothing. He can do anything."

Was this when Sari decided that she was in love with him, this indistinct blur of body rocking in the afternoon sun?

Ask her. But she won't tell you.

I think it was.

The next Sunday it rained, and their second outing on the *Baroness C* had to be canceled, and Sari kicked the stairs and cursed the rain all the way to her room.

Then the true summer holiday began. Sari still had her afternoon job at the Odeon, but now she had begun to think of looking for a job that would be full-time. "Oh, don't," Joanna said. "You don't really need the extra money, do you? This way, we can have girly lunches together — you don't need to be at the theatre until three. And all your evenings will be free to have fun, and in the mornings you can sleep late, late, late — the way girls our age are supposed to do!" Joanna rattled off a long list of things that the three of them would do that summer. "We'll drive out to Stinson Beach, and Half Moon Bay. We'll take a picnic lunch to Seal Rocks. Perhaps we'll drive down to Carmel. . . . And Peter's very keen on taking the *Baroness C* out to the Farallons. That will be exciting — even a little dangerous, you know, because we'll be on the open ocean . . ."

They had done some of these things, as a threesome, driving around San Francisco in Peter's snappy little Stutz motor car, which he had painted fire-engine red ("We're Flaming Youth!" Joanna liked to cry out to other motorists as Peter sped past them on the highway), and when he and Joanna dropped Sari at the theatre, it was sometimes possible for her to sneak them in, free, to see whatever movie happened to be playing. When she did this — between her chores of showing patrons to their seats with her flashlight — Sari would come and sit with them.

But, increasingly, outside obstacles began to interfere with Peter and Joanna's summer plans.

The proposed trip to the Farallon Islands, for instance, never came to pass. "Daddy's had the marina lock up the *Baroness C*'s sails and tackle, and ordered her into drydock," Joanna said. "Really, Daddy's just being too beastly to poor Peter."

"Why did your father do that, Jo?"

"It's the whole Yale thing, of course. And Daddy found out that Peter's been taking out the boat."

"Isn't it Peter's boat?"

"Of course it is, really. But officially it belongs to Daddy."

"And Peter's been taking it out without permission?"

"What difference does that make? Oh, it seems that Daddy had promised the boat to some friends of his that Sunday we all took her out. The friends arrived at the marina — and no *Baroness C!* So now everybody's sore as hell at everybody else, and poor Peter gets to shoulder all the blame. It isn't fair."

"Poor Peter . . ."

"And Daddy says if Peter ever does a thing like that again, he'll take the car away from him. Can you imagine? We'd all be simply grounded. Isn't Daddy being just too beastly?"

"If I were Peter, I'd start doing things that were designed to please your father."

"Peter won't. Peter has too much pride. It's all so silly. It's not that Daddy gives a rat's rear end about sailing. He just wants to own a sailboat because sailing's *stylish*. What a snob!"

Soon other roadblocks were appearing that were also altering arrangements for scheduled get-togethers.

"Sari darling, I can't make it for lunch today. It seems Mother's scheduled dressmaker's appointments, back to back, all day long. Oh, I hate this debutante business! I don't want to be a debutante at *all*. I'm only doing it because Mother absolutely *insists*."

Sari, innocently enough, had assumed that one ball gown was all that was required to be a debutante. A different gown, it seemed, would be required for each of the many functions Joanna would be attending during her debutante year — a gown for the Bachelors', another for the Cotillion, and others for each one on the long list of luncheons, teas, cocktail parties, dances, and little dinners to which she would unquestionably be invited — a full year of entertainments. Each of these outfits required many hours of consultations and fittings with the dressmakers, and each gown had to be accessorized with shoes, gloves, handbags, and hats, even stockings and underwear, requiring still more hours of shopping. Then there were the consultations with florists and hairdressers and corsetieres and caterers, and long sessions with photographers and cosmeticians and stationers. The agenda of Joanna's appointments seemed endless, endless . . .

"Sari darling, I can't make it for lunch today, either. I'm devastated. But there's this photographer from New York named Hal Phyfe whom Mummy says is absolutely the cat's — whom Mummy says is supposed to be the absolute tops, and Mummy insists on having him photograph me. I'm dreading it, but there's no way out of it where Mummy is concerned . . ." When did Mother become Mummy? Sari wondered. "But look, Peter is free — why don't the two of you have lunch? Poor Peter! He's so at loose ends.

All his friends are off to Europe, or at Tahoe, and Daddy won't let him do any of those things. Daddy is being absolutely relentless about Peter getting a job. . . ."

She and Peter had lunch in a small French restaurant on Telegraph Hill.

"Are you looking for a job?" she asked him.

"Don't have to. I have one," he said.

"Really? How exciting. What are you doing?"

"Clerking for a law firm on Montgomery Street."

"Wonderful!"

"I'm there right now — helping prepare briefs, searching titles, settling estates and trusts, filing suits and underwriting quitclaim deeds on underpensioned debentures, torting out the torts and summonses and serving pensions and suspensions, and otherwise helping with the ancillary legalistic forensics of the prosecutor's prosthesis. I'm having a hell of a time."

"I don't understand."

He grinned and touched his finger to his lips. "Ssh," he said. "Our secret. That's what my father *thinks* I'm doing. Actually, as you can plainly see, I'm having lunch and spending the afternoon with you."

"Oh," she said, a little disappointed. "So you don't have a job."

"No, but my father thinks I do, and that gets him off my back. Having lunch and spending the afternoon with you is much more fun. You're good company. I like you."

"I like you, too," she said. And then, "Why am I good company?"

"You're a good listener," he said. "That's an important thing in a woman — that she be a good listener. What shall we do after lunch? Shall we nip up to Muir Woods and look at the big trees?"

"I have to be at the theatre at three," she said.

"Oh," he said. "I'd forgotten about that." And now it was he who seemed disappointed.

"I could go with you to Muir Woods on Sunday," she said.

"Sunday? Oh. Well, I don't know. We'll see . . ."

After lunch, he drove her to the Odeon in his car. *Ben-Hur* was playing. "I'd actually like to see that film," he said.

"If you like, I'll sneak you in."

"Okay . . ."

She sneaked him in, pretending to collect a ticket from him at the entrance to the auditorium, and, when the theatre had filled — the movie was playing to sell-out audiences — she came and sat beside him in the dark, in the only remaining empty seat, which he had saved for her. During the famous, exciting chariot-race scene, she reached out and covered his hand with hers. He did not respond. He did not take her hand in his, but he didn't withdraw his hand, either, and merely left it there, resting coolly across the armrest of the theatre chair. Clearly, he didn't mind her hand covering his. Was this a sign?

"Sari dear," Joanna was saying on the telephone, "all hell has broken loose here. Daddy's found out that Peter really doesn't have the job with the lawyers that he said he had. Daddy actually called the lawyers up to check on him! Wasn't that the nastiest thing to do? And on top of everything, I can't meet you today because of more photographs Mummy wants taken. But Peter's free. See what you can do to cheer poor Peter up. The pressure's really on him now . . ."

But then, all at once, the pressure was off again. Julius and Constance LeBaron were leaving for the Islands. In the East, the Islands mean the Caribbean, but in California the Islands mean Hawaii. Julius was taking Constance, who was close to a nervous breakdown from all her shopping, on a three-week holiday. They were sailing on the *Lurline*. The children would have the California Street house to themselves. The pressure was not only off, it had disappeared.

"The three of us will meet tonight at eight o'clock in the Mural Room at the Saint Francis," Joanna said. "Peter's made a reservation. After dinner, we'll decide what else to do — but it'll be something *wild*. Flaming Youth. I may be a few minutes late, because there's something going on at the Burlingame Country Club. But I'm going to tear myself away from that. See you later . . ."

Sari and Peter arrived first, and Sari was impressed to see that the headwaiter recognized Peter, bowed to him, and called him "Mr. LeBaron," and "sir." They were led to one of what were considered the best tables, on the aisle, in the front of the room. When they were seated, Peter poured a little whiskey into each of their water glasses from the silver flask he carried in his jacket pocket. By now, Sari knew that everyone in America was doing this, and nobody paid any attention to it. They clicked glasses. "Joanna really hates this debutante business," Peter said.

"Do you think so? I'm really not so sure. I think she rather likes it. After all — buying all those beautiful dresses?"

He frowned and shook his head. "No, she hates it. Hates the whole thing. You mustn't be fooled by what things seem to be . . ."

"What do you mean?"

"Jo is a Siren. She weaves spells. She lures people toward the rocks."

"Yes, I've noticed a bit of that."

And then, when some time had passed and Joanna still had not appeared, Peter said, "Where the hell is she, anyway? She's nearly half an hour late."

"She mentioned something in Burlingame," Sari said.

"Yeah, that's what she *said.*" And then, suddenly, he said, "Do you think she's seeing somebody?"

"Seeing somebody?"

"Some man? Somebody we don't know about?"

"Oh, I don't think so, Peter."

"Well, *I* think so," he said, and his look was dark and almost angry. "I damn well think so."

"I'm sure she'd have told me if there were someone — special."

"What makes you so sure? What makes you think you can trust her? What makes you so goddamned sure?" He splashed more whiskey in his water glass.

"We promised each other that we'd —"

"And what makes you believe her goddamned promises?"

"Well, she did mention a Flood boy."

"That nitwit! What would she see in him, for God's sake? What would she see in that goddamned nitwit? All that goddamned nitwit wants is to be able to say he's slept with every girl in San Francisco!''

Sari hesitated. "Maybe we should order our dinner," she said. "And not wait for her."

He consulted his watch, which he wore in his vest pocket, suspended from a gold chain. "Well, let's give her fifteen more minutes," he said.

But easily twenty-five more minutes had passed, and Joanna had still not arrived, when the headwaiter approached their table. "Mr. LeBaron, sir," he said. "Your sister just telephoned. She said she has been unavoidably delayed, and will not be able to join you for dinner. She says she will see you at home, later this evening."

When the waiter had departed, Peter slammed his wadded napkin on the table. "That bitch," he said. "Now I'm sure of it. She's seeing somebody, and she's keeping it from me, and she's keeping it from you. Sari, I want you to find out who this bastard is."

"Well, I'll try, but I really don't think —"

"I want you to find out who my sister's seeing," he said. "I want you to find out everything you can about this bastard. His name, what he looks like, where he lives, where he went to school, how she met him, what she's doing with him, where they go. *Everything.*"

"I'll try. But I don't think —"

"Dammit, why do you keep contradicting me? I know I'm right." Sari had never seen him so angry. "Find out everything about this bastard," he repeated. "I want to find out who's screwing my sister."

"I said I'd try," she said quietly.

"Good." He glared fiercely at the white tablecloth. Then he said, "Let's get the hell out of here."

"Please don't be cross with me, Peter. For whatever it is."

"Dammit, I'm not cross. I just said let's get out of here." He began signaling for his check.

"Where shall we go?"

"Somewhere. Anywhere. I don't care."

Then, for a time, they drove aimlessly and a little wildly about

the dark city in his open car, up and down the steepest hills —
Fillmore Street Hill, Powell Street Hill, Lombard Street Hill — driving too fast, and skidding around corners, bouncing against the
curbs of sidewalks. He was not drunk, Sari decided. He was only —
what? Upset about something.

"What's upset you so, Peter?" she asked him. "I mean, after
all, suppose she *is* seeing someone? So what?"

"Because she's doing it behind my back. Because she's lying to
us, and keeping her dirty little secret from us, and that means she's
doing something she's ashamed of." Then he said, "Let's go back
to my house. We'll catch her when she comes in, catch her red-
handed when she comes in, and tell her what we know."

They drove back to California Street and let themselves into the
quiet house whose master and mistress were thousands of miles
away across the Pacific Ocean. MacDonald, in his tailcoat, had
appeared. "Can I get you anything, Mr. Peter?" he asked.

"A bottle of champagne," Peter said gruffly.

MacDonald nodded and disappeared on padded, slippered feet.

"She hates our mother," Peter said.

"Really, Peter? Why do you say that?"

"Because it's true. Hates her with a vengeance. Hates even being
in the same room with her. That's one reason for you, you know."

"A reason for me?"

"Of course. Mother doesn't think you're quite — suitable to be
Jo's friend. Jo chose you as her friend as another way to get back
at Mother."

She considered this unwelcome notion. Clearly, he was still in
an unpleasant mood. "Well," she said at last, "I thought Joanna
genuinely liked me."

"Oh, she likes you all right. But she likes you even more because
Mother disapproves."

MacDonald reappeared now with a bottle of champagne in a
silver cooler, and two glasses on a silver tray. He set these on a
low table between them, shifting a bowl full of cymbidiums to
make room for them.

"My mother is an alcoholic," Peter said. Sari said nothing, and
MacDonald began filling their glasses. In the bottom of each cham-

pagne glass was a fresh strawberry. "It's true, isn't it, MacDonald?" Peter said. "My mother is an alcoholic. Tell Miss Latham that it's true."

MacDonald pursed his lips. "Well, Mr. Peter. Will there be anything else, sir?"

"No, thanks."

MacDonald withdrew on the same quiet, slippered feet, and now they were alone again in the red damask room, in this still, perfectly ordered house where fresh flowers were never allowed to die or even to fade in their crystal bowls, where Negro maids polished the mahogany tabletops with the palms of their hands, where no one seemed to have to lift a finger even to wind the eternally ticking clocks, where everything seemed so patterned, and yet where there now seemed to be also so much confusion. Peter scowled darkly at his champagne glass, and took a sip. "I nurse my drinks," he said. "That's what makes the difference. That's why I'll never be an alcoholic."

"Why is she — that way, do you think?"

"Because she hates my father. Everyone in this house hates everybody else. This house is full of hate. Except for Jo and me."

"But I don't understand. If Joanna hates your mother so, why is she going through the debutante thing, which she also says she hates?"

"Don't worry. Jo has Mother wrapped right around her little finger."

"Really? It seems to me the other way around."

"Jo always knows what she's doing."

"She's spent more time with your mother these past few weeks than she has with me. Why — if she hates your mother so?"

"Jo always has a plan. With her, there's always a plan."

"I still don't understand."

"There's a lot about this family that's hard to understand," he said.

From a distance now, in the house, there was the sound of a ringing telephone, and Peter sat sharply forward in his chair. "That'll be her," he said. "That'll be Jo calling. Wait and see."

Presently MacDonald reappeared. "That was Miss Joanna, sir," he said. "She says to tell you that she won't be coming home tonight. She's spending the night with friends in Burlingame."

"I see. Thank you, MacDonald."

"Will there be anything else for you tonight, sir?"

"No thanks. Good night, MacDonald."

When he had gone, Peter said almost triumphantly, "Well? You see? That sort of proves it, doesn't it? She's sleeping with someone else!"

"Someone *else?*"

"Some guy. She's got to be!" And the look in his eyes was so fierce and wild that it almost frightened her. Then she was angry.

She set down her champagne glass. "Look," she said, "I don't know, and frankly I don't care. What Joanna does is her business. It's late, and I'm tired. Will you take me home?"

He held out his hand. "Wait," he said. "Don't go."

"I know I'm supposed to be a good listener," she said, "but I'm bored with this conversation. I don't care who your sister's sleeping with. Or if she's sleeping with anyone at all. Take me home."

"Wait," he said. "I've got an idea. Let's you and I sleep together! Let's you and I have sex! That would show her, wouldn't it? That other people can play her little game?"

She stood up. "That's a stupid, disgusting suggestion," she said. "If you won't drive me home, I'll take the streetcar."

"But wait — think about it!"

"I don't even like you, Peter LeBaron! I think you're a stupid and disgusting man! You think you can get away with anything with all your money. Well, you can't. I hate you, Peter LeBaron!" Then she picked up her wineglass and flung the contents, strawberry and all, into his face. "That's what I think of you!"

She had taken the streetcar home, struggling to hold back tears, certain that she would never see either of them again.

But the next morning he telephoned her. "I'm calling to apologize," he said. "I'm really sorry. I'd had too much to drink. I behaved like a cad. Please forgive me, Sari. I'm really terribly, terribly sorry, Sari, about last night."

"You behaved," she said evenly, "as your sister might put it, like a rat's rear end."

"I know. And I'm asking you to forgive me. Will you? Will you just give me another chance — one more chance, Sari? Please?"

"Well. Perhaps."

"Tonight? The same place? The Mural Room? Let me show you that I'm really not a rat's rear end."

"Let me think about it."

"Please. I know there's no excuse for what I said and did, but I have been going through kind of a rough time lately."

"I understand all that."

"So — will you?"

"Well — all right."

"I'll stand on my head to get you to forgive me."

That night they met at the Mural Room, and he seemed so cheerful and eager to please her that the previous evening seemed to have occurred years ago, and to have involved an entirely different person. After a few minutes, the headwaiter approached them, and said, "Your dinner is served, Mr. LeBaron."

"Thank you, George." Then he rose from the table, and gestured to her to follow him.

Mystified, she also rose, and followed him out of the restaurant, into the lobby of the hotel, to the elevators.

"Where are we going?"

"You'll see. Sixth floor, please," he said to the elevator operator.

On the sixth floor, he produced a key and ushered her into a suite of rooms overlooking Union Square.

"Oh, Peter!" she gasped.

The room seemed to be filled with flowers — roses, calla lilies, birds of paradise. In the center of the sitting room, a round table draped with a long white cloth was set for two, with serving dishes under silver lids, and a three-branched silver candelabrum with its candles lighted.

"Oh, Peter!"

"Just an ordinary little hotel suite," he said. "I said I'd stand on my head to get you to forgive me. Now, watch me." And he kicked off his shoes, sprang forward on his hands, and stood on his head in the center of the room. "I'll do more than that," he said. "I'll walk on my hands." And he began walking about the room on his hands, his stockinged feet high in the air, his trouser legs flopping about his ankles. He looked so ridiculous that she began to laugh. "I'll do this all night if you say so."

"There's a monster here who tickles the feet of people who walk on their hands," she said, and reached out and tickled the soles of his passing feet.

"Oh!" he yelped. "How did you know I'm ticklish?" and he back-somersaulted onto his feet again. "I can't stand to be tickled!"

"Are you ticklish here?" she said, laughing, tickling his chest. "And here?" tickling him under his arms.

"Stop, stop," he moaned, and suddenly, gasping, he was holding her in his arms. "Oh, Sari," he said, "I want — I want — so much!"

"What do you want?"

"So much that I can't have. What do you want, Sari?"

"I want someone to love me. Someone to love. I love you, Peter . . ."

"Oh . . . oh," and now he was kissing her, and she felt her own body, of its own accord, of a mind of its own, grow limp and breathless, pressing against him, arched and expectant.

"Your beautiful nipples . . . I couldn't take my eyes off them that day on the boat . . . little pink points." Now he unbuttoned her dress and was kissing them, first one, then the other, curling his tongue around them. "Let me show you the only way to drink wine," he whispered. "Let me show you the wine expert's way," and she watched with amazement as he reached for the bottle of chilled wine on the table, filled a glass, and then dipped first her left breast, then her right, in the glass, then licked the nipples clean while a fire of excitement shot through her like a volcano erupting. With her breast in his mouth, his eyes traveled up to hers.

"Oh, Peter," she sobbed. "I love you so. I love you more — more than the world. Do you love me, Peter?" Then, in one motion, he picked her up and carried her into the bedroom, where the coverlet was turned down and the sheet folded back in a clean white triangle.

"Love me, Peter!"

At first, there was a little pain, but then, wonder of wonders, she began feeling herself liking it a little, just as Joanna had told her she would, and when it was over she lay damp and spent in his arms, damp, and spent, and loved. "All my life," she murmured, and she thought: Now we will get married. Marriage is what happens next. We are in love, we will get married, and we will have his beautiful children, all my life. Then she discovered that there were tears in his eyes. "What is it, Peter? What's wrong, my love?" She ran her fingers through the fine hairs of his chest, and kissed his eyes, finding that even the taste of his tears thrilled her.

"I've done a terrible thing . . . a terrible thing," he said.

"No, you haven't. It was lovely and wonderful, and I wanted it too, Peter."

"No . . . you don't understand."

"I want us to be happy," she said. "Like the song." Under the covers, she began to tickle him again, and soon he was laughing despite himself, and then they were making love all over again, and it was even better than the first time. After that, he appeared to sleep.

As she lay beside him in the big bed in the darkened bedroom, nested against him, spoon fashion, while their uneaten dinner in the sitting room outside grew colder under the hotel's silver warming lids, she let only one thought drift through her mind. She let the thought pass, waft past like a slightly chilly breeze, then disappear, banished, but not unobserved. The thought was: If Joanna always has a plan, is this a part of it? Is this why she has been arranging for us to spend so much time together? Is she testing us, testing me, testing Peter, experimenting with us to see what will happen when the two reagents are placed together and heated in the retort — what fumes will rise, whether an explosion will occur? Is this all a part of some mysterious Joanna plan?

"We must never tell Joanna about this," she whispered. "Promise me. Never."

But there was no answer, and she let the thought drift away into the clouds of foreverness and forgetfulness, where it belonged.

Instead, she thought: It is simple. He loves me. Next, he will ask me to marry him, and I will say yes.

Their clothes lay in a heap on the floor by the bed. Reaching down, she found Peter's tweed Norfolk jacket, picked it up, stepped out of bed, and slipped it on. It reached halfway to her knees. On tiptoes, she walked out into the sitting room of the suite, where two low table lamps were lit, and where the table was still set for their dinner. The candles on the table had guttered out. She lifted one of the warming lids: cold asparagus. She picked up a spear, and nibbled it. She lifted another lid: rissolé potatoes. She replaced that lid, but a third lid revealed baby lamb chops, which would be excellent cold. She sat down at the table and selected a chop with her fingers.

Sitting there in Peter's baggy jacket, overlooking the Square and the lighted city, the chunky palm trees that dotted the Square with the tall Dewey Monument at its center — the monument with the loosely draped lady at the top of her pedestal — and having her own quiet, solitary dinner and eating a baby lamb chop with her fingers; everything about it all was somehow — well, somehow like having a picnic on the deck of a sailboat in a sheltered cove, but tonight it was infinitely more rewarding, more fulfilling and romantic, she thought.

Looking out at the Square, she thought: I am that loosely draped lady, she is me. See how surely and squarely she stands, chin tilted upward, resolute, proud, secure in her world, unafraid of the future. See how she seems to be spreading her wings, preparing to fly, borne by the wind. She is me. Oh! She is me.

And she thought: It is simple. He loves me. Next, he will ask me to marry him. That is what happens next to lovers. And I will say yes.

But, as a few of us know, it did not happen quite that way, not quite that way at all, at all, at all.

"Sari, I've arranged to come to San Francisco on Friday," Joanna is saying. "I'm taking the eleven o'clock, so I should be in the city by one. I'll be staying at the Stanford Court."

"Nonsense," Sari says. "You'll stay here, of course. There's plenty of room. I'm not going to have you staying at some hotel."

"Well," Joanna says with a little laugh, "that's very nice of you, but I think I should warn you that I'm more than likely going to take Eric's side in this — if it should come to a vote, that is. And I don't want to feel I could be murdered in my bed!"

"Nonsense again. There's no reason why we two can't meet and discuss this thing like two adult, civilized human beings."

"That's what I'd like, Sari. Just a nice, adult, preferably pleasant family discussion of the situation. Not a formal stockholders' meeting. Just a discussion of the pros and the cons."

"Exactly."

"And I think Eric should be present when we do this," Joanna says. "I think Eric should be able to present his side."

"Well, Eric and I aren't speaking at the moment," Sari says. "So I'm afraid that's out of the question."

"Sari, I'm sure Eric will come if you ask him. At least ask him, Sari. I think it's important that everyone concerned be present when we meet — Eric, Peeper, Melissa, and you and I."

"What about Lance?"

"Lance won't be able to make it," she says. "But he and I've discussed it, and he will go along with whatever I decide to do. Which I'm sure comes as no surprise to you, Sari."

"No," she says a little sourly. "No surprise at all."

"Then what shall we plan?"

"Let's plan on dinner here at the house Saturday night," she says, "if that suits everybody."

"And you'll try Eric."

"Yes."

"And no lawyers — nothing like that, Sari."

"Just family."

"Who knows?" Joanna says. "We might just all end up having a good time. Wouldn't that be nice — for a change?"

"And it's settled — you're staying here. I'll cancel your hotel reservation. And Jo — give me your flight number. I'm going to send Thomas out to the airport to collect you."

                        *   *   *

"Well," she says to Thomas a little later. "Did Melissa get that letter?"

"It was on her breakfast tray, with all her other mail, this morning, Madam."

"Then why the hell haven't I *heard* something from her?"

"When I picked up the tray, all the mail was gone."

"Then why no reaction from downstairs?"

"Perhaps Madam should —"

"What?"

"Initiate a conversation with Miss Melissa."

"On *that* subject? No! Then she'd know immediately that we'd steamed open the letter and read it. Then she'd really be on the warpath with me!"

"Yes, Madam has a point."

"There's not that much time to waste. We're going to try for a family meeting. Here. Saturday night."

"I know, Madam. Have you invited Miss Melissa yet?"

"No . . ."

"Why not do that now? Madam might get some hint, from her tone of voice."

And so, while Thomas watches, Sari picks up the interhouse phone and taps out Melissa's code on the buttons, and Thomas listens as his mistress says, "Melissa darling, how are you today? . . . Oh, fine, just fine. Darling, can you come up for dinner Saturday night? Joanna's going to be here from New York, and we thought we could all discuss this takeover proposal of Eric's and Harry's . . . yes, all of us. . . . You can? Oh, good. Seven-thirty, very casual. . . . And — how's everything else? Ah . . . good."

She replaces the phone. "Sweetness and light," she says to Thomas. "All milk and honey. Butter wouldn't melt in her mouth. She'd *love* to come! Dammit, Thomas, what in hell is Melissa trying to *pull?*"

"Well, I will keep my eyes and ears open, Madam. At the moment, that's about the only thing we can do."

Ten

*I*T *IS FRIDAY MORNING,* and Sari and her lawyers are meeting in her downtown office on Montgomery Street. Jacobs & Siller have sent not one, but two, of their senior partners over to discuss the situation on the theory, perhaps, that two heads are better than one, or, more likely, that two heads mean they can double their fee. The lawyers' names are Jonathan Baines, Esq., and Simon Rosenthal, Esq., and Messrs. Baines and Rosenthal have just finished explaining to Sari, who proposed this meeting, that there is really very little they can do. Sari is thinking: senior partners! They both appear to be no more than eighteen years old, and Mr. Baines has a beard, like a hippie.

"You see, Mrs. LeBaron," Mr. Rosenthal is explaining, "the way your husband's will was written, you and your sister-in-law each control thirty-five percent of Baronet Vineyards. Clearly, your late husband wished to divide the rest of the shares proportionately and fairly among members of the next generation. Thusly, of the remaining thirty percent of the company, fifteen percent was bequeathed in equal shares to your children, and an additional fifteen percent was bequeathed to your sister-in-law's children.''

"I know all this,'' Sari says impatiently. "But fifteen percent to Lance doesn't seem fair, when each of my children only gets five.''

"Unfortunately,'' he says, "your sister-in-law had only the one child. But we must assume that your late husband intended this will to be fair and equitable, one that would preclude any family conflict or dissension. The will was very likely written with the thought in mind that Joanna LeBaron might have further issue.''

"At age forty-six? Not bloody likely!''

"Well, your late husband's last will and testament was written in nineteen forty-five, when she would have been — uh — thirty-five or thirty-six, and when your late husband still might have supposed, or taken into consideration, the possibility of future issue.''

"Well, what can we do? Who can we sue? Can we break the will?''

"Of course, that is a possibility, Mrs. LeBaron,'' Mr. Baines says, "but I think a rather remote one. Don't you agree, Si?''

"Your husband died in nineteen fifty-five —'' Mr. Rosenthal says.

"Dammit, I know when he died!''

"— and his will was probated, without contest, later that year. The provisions of this will have been operative since then, and we don't think it likely that a court would look kindly at an attempt to break, as you put it, an instrument the provisions of which have been operative for nearly thirty years.''

"And on what grounds could we attempt to break the will, Mrs. LeBaron?'' Mr. Baines says.

"Fraud!''

"Fraud?''

"Fraud — deceptions — lies.''

"What sort of lies, Mrs. LeBaron?''

"Never mind. What I want to know is how I can win this thing. That's what I brought you here for. I'm not going to let them take my company away from me.''

"Unfortunately, Mrs. LeBaron,'' Mr. Rosenthal says, "in view

of the way in which your late husband apportioned his estate
among his heirs *per stirpes* —"

"Don't use expressions like *per stirpes* with me. Speak English."

"Unfortunately, the way the Baronet shares were divided under
your late husband's will, if your sister-in-law votes in favor of
the acquisition, as you indicate to us she will, and if her son,
Lance, votes with her, and they are led by your son Eric and Mr.
Tillinghast, they will have fifty-five percent of the share votes,
Mrs. LeBaron. If that is the way these four shareholders align
themselves, there is no way that you could win. It is a lost
cause."

"Dammit," she says, "I hire you people to help me defend my
case, and you start out telling me you're going to lose it for me!"

"Mrs. LeBaron," Mr. Rosenthal says, "this is not a *case,* and you
are not a *defendant.* This is an offer to buy, and you are one of the
proposed sellers. In Wall Street terms, this is a takeover bid, and
your company is the target."

"Means the same thing, doesn't it? Just words."

"All we could do," Mr. Baines says, "since our firm serves as
trust officer for your late husband's estate, and if the Kern-
McKittrick offer is placed before a shareholder vote, is be present
at this shareholders' meeting. Naturally, we would have no vote
ourselves, nor could we in any way influence the vote. But we
could be present at the meeting to make sure that everything is
conducted legally, and that the shareholders' interests are properly
protected. In fact, I think we should be at this meeting, don't you,
Si?"

"Definitely. Make sure that there isn't any hanky-panky."

"Not that I can see that there would be," Mr. Baines says. "It
seems like a perfectly straight and aboveboard offer. A clean bid,
as they say."

"Then let me ask you one thing," Sari says. "What if Melissa is
not my daughter?"

"Hmm?"

"You heard me. If Melissa is not my daughter, then what?"

"Not your daughter. Well —" Mr. Baines says.

"Adopted, or something."

"Well," Mr. Baines says, riffling through some papers in the open briefcase on his lap, "since Melissa LeBaron is designated in Peter LeBaron's will as his five percent heir *per stirpes,* I don't see that it makes any difference whether she was adopted or not. She is still one of the heirs *per stirpes.*"

"And," Mr. Rosenthal adds, "Melissa LeBaron's vote hardly counts in the takeover bid at all. With or without her vote, you are already outvoted."

"So I'm defeated. Powerless. I've as good as lost control."

"Which brings us, Mrs. LeBaron, to a recommendation on our part. We know you feel strongly about the matter, but we feel strongly also, as your advisers, that we should advise you to accept the Kern-McKittrick offer."

"Never!"

"There is even a rumor circulating that Harry Tillinghast is willing to increase his offer by five tenths of a point."

"Five tenths of a point! Peanuts."

"You are a solely family-owned company at the moment, Mrs. LeBaron. In the event of your death, or your sister-in-law's death —"

"I'm perfectly healthy, thank you!"

"In the event of your death, the government could step in, and place any sort of appraisal it chose on your estate —"

"You're going to tell me all about taxes, aren't you? Well, I've heard all those arguments."

"But your heirs —"

"I don't plan to have any heirs."

"Everyone has heirs, Mrs. LeBaron."

"I'll be the first one not to."

"We've been in communication with Joanna LeBaron's lawyers at Cravath, Swaine and Moore in New York. They strongly recommend that she accept the Kern-McKittrick offer. We also recommend that you do."

"Harry Tillinghast's in the oil business. What does he know about making wine?"

"I'm sure you'd still be able to exercise a certain amount of control."

"I want full control! I want the control I've had since Peter died. I want to keep my company. If I can't, this meeting is over."

Mr. Baines begins snapping his briefcase closed. "Well, we've given you our best recommendations," he says. "There's nothing more we can say."

"You've wasted an hour of my time to tell me there's nothing I can do."

"The only thing I can suggest that you do," he says, "is what you can accomplish with your personal powers of persuasion in terms of the others in your family. Meanwhile, keep us abreast of developments."

When they have gone, she buzzes for Gloria Martino. "See if you can get Eric on the phone for me," she says.

In Burlingame, Alix LeBaron is lying under a towel on her massage table, having a pedicure performed on one end of her anatomy and a massage performed on the other. As usual, she lets the telephone ring five or six times before reaching a bare arm out from under the towel to answer it.

"Well, Belle-mère," she says, "I hardly expected to hear your voice. I didn't think you were speaking to anyone in this household. Except Kimmie, of course. Kimmie's somehow the only one in this household who's managed to escape your wrath."

"I was wondering if I could speak to Eric," Sari says.

"Eric is playing the golf this morning, Belle-mère." Alix is the kind of woman who always calls golf "the golf." "May I take a — *ugh!* — a message for him? Forgive me if my voice sounds funny, but I'm simply being pounded to death by this brute." She winks up at the ample, peasant face of the Swedish masseuse. She realizes that Sari doesn't have the faintest idea what she is talking about, but doesn't care.

"I was calling to see whether you both could have dinner with me tomorrow night, Alix. Joanna's coming into town, and I thought a nice little family dinner would be pleasant. Very casual. Nothing dressy."

"Well, this is a switch, isn't it, Belle-mère? One minute you discharge Eric from the company, and the next minute you ask us to dinner."

"I just thought a little family dinner would be pleasant. See if we can perhaps iron out some of our differences."

"I see," Alix says. "I can't speak for Eric, of course, because he's out playing the golf. But I do know that we happen to be free."

"Then will you come?"

"Are — *ugh!* — are you inviting Daddy, too? Because this merger thing is all essentially Daddy's idea."

"Well, actually, I hadn't planned to."

"Daddy's a stockholder too, Belle-mère."

"I know, but this isn't to be a meeting of the stockholders, Alix. Just a little family dinner."

"Isn't Daddy family? He's my father."

"I know that, but —"

"I think Eric would be much more willing to come if he knew that Daddy were going to be there."

"Very well. We can invite Daddy."

"And Mummy?"

"Daddy and Mummy. Shall I expect you then? At seven-thirty?"

"I'll have to check with Eric. Call you back, Belle-mère." With another long reach, she replaces the receiver in its cradle without saying good-bye.

Soon she is back to her musings. Having her massage always makes her pleasantly drowsy, and from the table where she lies — on her stomach now — being kneaded, prodded, and poked by Helga, she can see a spray of red rambler roses arching just above her window sill. Roses are red, violets are blue, angels in heaven don't get to screw. The sun is shining on the roses. In San Francisco, there is fog. She heard that on the TV this morning. That is one reason why Alix is glad she lives in Burlingame and not in the city. The fog, the fog, the soggy, soggy fog. The heat from the Valley does it. The heat from the Valley sucks in the cold fog from the ocean through the Golden Gate. Or something like that. It gets sucked in through the Golden Gate and stays there while here, barely ten miles further south, the sun is shining, which is why you get red rambler roses here, and not there, and why you also get geraniums and lemon and verbena and palm and, if you're lucky, a banana tree. She has had a particularly satisfying morning.

It has been, needless to say, a bit of a bore in recent days, having Eric around the house all day. I married you for better or for worse, but not for lunch, she had told him. But today, at least, he has the golf, and that is a relief, and in this morning's mail there had been his bank statement, and she had opened it and found a check for $10,000 made out to Marylou Chin.

She had immediately hopped into her little white Porsche and run downtown and had the check Xeroxed — both sides, of course — and then come home, put the check back into the statement, and put all his mail on his desk.

Then she had telephoned Marylou Chin. "Miss Chin, this is Alix LeBaron speaking," she had said.

"Yes, Mrs. LeBaron. How are you?"

"I'm well. Have you been sleeping with my husband?"

There was a brief, incriminating pause, and then Miss Chin had said, "Certainly not. What a thing to say!"

"You're lying," Alix had said. "I know you have. I have the proof."

"What sort of proof?"

"Proof enough."

"Mrs. LeBaron, if you won't tell me what you're talking about, I'd like to terminate this conversation. Good —"

"A check for ten thousand dollars," Alix says, and adds, "among other things."

"When Mr. LeBaron was forced to leave the company, I was also terminated. Mr. LeBaron was kind enough to offer me that money to help tide me over until I could find another job. It was a loan."

"Rather a *large* sum of money, don't you think, Miss Chin? To *tide you over*, as you say."

"I have an aunt, my aunt Grace, in a nursing home. There's no one to take care of her but me."

"A *likely* story!" Alix had said. "The old aunt-in-the-nursing-home routine. You're lying, and you know it."

"Mrs. LeBaron, I am telling you the truth. If you want, I can —"

"How long have you been fucking my husband?"

"Mrs. LeBaron, I am not going to listen to —"

"Well, you'd better watch out, is all I can say. Because I have the proof, and I know you're lying, you lying little sluttish little whoring Jap cunt." Then she had hung up the phone, feeling thoroughly vindicated. Lying Jap cunt.

"Helga, work a little more on that little roll of fat right around my tummy," she says. "Really work hard on that today."

"Is no roll of fat. You imagine."

"I'm not imagining it! It's there! I saw it in my mirror this morning."

And so they had come home from Bitterroot that autumn of 1929 to find Julius LeBaron's affairs in a shambles. "What am I going to do?" he said to them in a dead voice, as though the answer lay in their blank faces. He had been heavily into the market, and had been buying on margin, and had been forced to sell it all to cover this, and now the creditors were pressing him, and the banks were calling on him for more collateral to cover loans. The brokerage house where he did the majority of his business had collapsed, and his broker was out on the street, and the banks — the Crocker Bank, the Wells Fargo Bank, the Anglo-California Bank — the same banks whose presidents had invited Julius LeBaron for lunch in their boardrooms six months ago, were now demanding more collateral, which he didn't have. "What am I going to do?" he kept asking in that dead, bewildered voice.

"We will pray," Constance LeBaron had said. "We will pray to the Blessed Virgin to intercede for us. We will pray, Father, we will make a novena. *Ave Maria, gratia plena . . .*" Sari could tell that Constance LeBaron had been drinking. And the prayers went upward into the ether, into the crystalline rooms of heaven while Constance LeBaron did her beads. "Blessed Mother, Mother of Mercies, Mother of Miracles and Holy Mysteries, send me a red rose to show me my prayers are being answered . . ." But no red rose had appeared, and no miracle occurred.

Later — days, weeks, because time seemed to telescope upon

itself during that period when Sari and Peter spent most of their time in the Washington Street house, still new, still unpaid for, as they would find out later, worrying and wondering what was going to happen next — a message had come for Sari. "Mrs. LeBaron, Mr. LeBaron, senior, wants to see you at once. He says it's urgent."

She had gone to the California Street house, which now seemed suddenly to have become very dark, as though even the gilt and red plush had become covered with a dark patina of age and overuse. He had been sitting in the shadows in his chair, looking out the window into the fog, and she had entered the room from behind him.

"Sari, are you strong?" he had asked her. "Are you strong enough to carry Peter, and the little girl?"

"Carry him?" Why had there been an air of unreality, of theatricality, about this meeting with her father-in-law? It was as though losing his money had changed Julius LeBaron utterly, turned him hollow, into a walking ghost, and she had felt strangely that she was not speaking to a man she knew, but to another actor on a stage.

"One reason why I approved this marriage while, as you know, Mother strongly opposed it, was because I believed that you were strong. Peter is not strong. Of the two of you, Peter is the weaker vessel. I have always known that. Can you carry him, Sari, when I am gone? I mean carry him, support him, back him up, be his backbone? As you know, Peter never finished college, he has no training, no profession, no capacity for hard work. What will become of him? You must help him."

"Physically, Peter is very strong," she said.

"I'm not talking about physical strength," he said. "I'm not talking about cutting down trees. Inner strength. Courage. Gumption, guts. Will you provide those things for him, Sari? Stand behind him — carry him?"

"I'll try, Papa Julius."

"Is that a promise?"

"I promise, Papa Julius."

"I've always tried to keep my promises to you, haven't I, Sari?"

"Yes, Papa Julius."

"Then you must keep this promise to me. Carry him. Somehow."

"It's a promise, Papa Julius," she had repeated.

He had turned his head toward her slightly, and she had seen that there were tears in his eyes. "You're a good girl, Sari," he said. "If only things hadn't — happened as they did — things might have been different. But that's crying over spilt milk, isn't it? That's past. That's water over the dam, water under the bridge, and we can't change what's past, no more than the leopard can change his spots. But you were good to do what you did, Sari, and I want you to know I'll always be grateful."

"Thank you, Papa Julius. Please don't cry."

He brushed at his eyes with the back of his left wrist. "I think Joanna's in her room right now. Will you see if you can find her, Sari, and send her down to see me?"

"Joanna is strong, too," she said. "We'll do our duty for each other. We promised to." But once more she had felt as though she were reciting lines of dialogue, written for her by someone else.

By the summer of 1930, after a brief, misleading rally, Wall Street prices had broken again, and begun a long decline that would last for years. With world production falling, with unemployment in the United States passing four million, and with breadlines everywhere, the harsh realities of the Great Depression had become daily facts of life. Every day, it seemed, the economic news in the newspapers was more alarming, and there was even more disturbing talk of revolution. Wealthy Americans who had come out of the crash with anything at all were moving to Europe, in fear of their lives. By now, the banks owned Julius LeBaron's house on California Street, though they permitted him to live there until the house could be sold. But that might be never, since no buyers had appeared for the big house. And the latest threat was that the banks were considering razing the house and turning it into a parking lot.

Every morning, now, Constance LeBaron went to mass and took communion, while her husband remained alone in the house, brooding in his chair, considering who knew what fatalistic possibilities. Constance had begun having visions. In one of these, her own mother had risen from her grave and come to confront Constance as she sat at her dinner table. Her mother had spoken to her in an alien tongue, but Constance had understood the message. The Blessed Virgin was punishing her, her mother said, for touching her private parts when she was a child. In another vision, the Blessed Virgin herself had appeared out of a gin bottle, holding a red rose high in the air, and when Constance had tried to seize the rose, the Blessed Virgin had said to her sternly, "Go to Calvary!" In still another vision, Constance herself had been bodily transported to the shrine at Lourdes, where, in the grotto, the Virgin appeared once more, and delivered the same message. It was hard to interpret what any of these experiences meant.

Sometimes, Constance would ask Sari and Peter to accompany her to mass because Joanna, following her divorce, had been on poor terms with the Church. Sari, of course, was not a communicant, though she went through the proper motions of the mass. Before marrying Peter, Sari had gone through a brief period of religious instruction, but she really understood little of the intricacies and mysteries of the Catholic faith. In return for this, and the promise that any children would be raised as Roman Catholics, the Church had agreed to marry Sari and Peter — but in the chancel, not in the nave. And their cause had been helped by the fact that the LeBarons' family priest, Father Quinn, had just been designated a monsignor.

One Saturday morning in July of 1930, Constance telephoned and asked if Sari and Peter would take her to mass. When they arrived at the house, Constance explained that she had just had another vision. Her dead mother had reappeared — this time in her bathroom mirror while she was putting up her hair. Once more her mother had berated her for touching her private parts with her fingertips when she was a little girl, but this time she had added some new information. The cause of the Great Depression, Constance's mother had explained, was Joanna. Joanna's brief marriage three years earlier and her divorce six months later had brought all this disaster about. Not only that. "My daughter is to blame for all the sins of the world," Constance said. "All the sins of the world. My mother told me so. In heaven, my daughter is called Satana, the whore of California Street."

"Now, Mama LeBaron, I wouldn't take any of this too seriously," Sari said.

"In heaven, my mother has breakfast with the Blessed Virgin every Thursday. She sits on the right hand of God."

Sari could tell that Mama LeBaron had been drinking again. There was liquor on her breath, and her hair, perhaps because the preparation of her coiffure had been interrupted by the vision, was in disarray. How was it, she began to wonder, that at a time when there didn't seem to be money for anything else, there was still money for gin? But she hadn't asked that question.

At the Church of Our Lady of the Cadillac — as the Cathedral of Saint Peter Martyr was often affectionately called, since most of its parishioners had at least once upon a time been wealthy — they arrived a little early, while Sari and Constance knelt, in prayer, at Constance's customary pew. In her prayers, Sari also let her thoughts fly heavenward in behalf of this benighted family. Oh, Lord, she said, if there is a Lord, let Thy mercies descend upon these unhappy people who, through the years, have bestowed so much grace on Thee. Lord, if there is a Lord, let a little of Thy grace and wisdom and compassion and forgiveness shower itself upon these, Thy humble servants, in their need. Dear Lord, if there is a Lord, remember their kindness and their devotion to Thee, and let, oh, just a little bit, of Thy kindness and devotion fall upon them, and give them peace. Lord, dear Lord, if there is a Lord, give us — something!

Then, all at once, Constance LeBaron began to shout. "Where is Peter? Where has he gone?" she cried.

"Hush, Mama LeBaron. He's in the confessional."

"But why has he been in the confessional so long? What does he have to confess about?"

"Peter often makes long confessions, Mama."

"He has nothing to confess! Peter is a saint, and we are in Saint Peter's church! It is my daughter who is to blame for all the sins of the world, she who is called Satana, the whore —"

"Mama, Mama, please."

Peter stepped, just then, into the pew beside them, and Sari gave him a worried look, and the mass was about to begin. The priest was at the altar, and made a sign of the cross as high and as wide as his arms would reach, and a great hush of worship fell over the cathedral. *"In nomine Patris et Filii et Spiritus Sancti . . ."* But now Constance LeBaron had begun to shout again, "Where is peace for me? Indulgence . . . absolution . . . *is there any eternal life for me?*

"Agnus Dei, qui tollis peccata mundi —" while the other congregants in the church tried to resist turning in their seats to see what was causing this disturbance, tried to concentrate on the solemnity of the mass, and on the sanctity of the man, God's messenger on earth, whom He had selected to perform it. And now Mama LeBaron was on her feet, moving toward the center aisle, and Sari was reaching for her sleeve to restrain her. "Where are you going, Mama?" she whispered. "To Calvary! I am going to Calvary! It is because of my impure thoughts! This is why my daughter is known in heaven as a whore! I am going to Calvary to curse the Holy Ghost who entered me and caused me to give birth to a whore!" The priest stopped the mass and was staring at Mama LeBaron as she staggered toward the altar. "Mama, please!" Sari cried, starting after her. On the altar, someone, some generous-hearted parishioner, had placed a small bouquet of red paper roses. "A red rose!" Mama had cried. "The Blessed Virgin has heard my prayers and sent me a red rose. The Blessed Virgin, who has breakfast with my mother in heaven every Thursday, and sits on the right hand of God! *Give me my rose!*" But, reaching out for the paper flower, she stumbled and fell against the altar rail. Beside her, both Sari and Peter helped her to her feet again. "Come, Mama," Sari whispered gently. "Mass is over, and it's time to go home."

As they moved slowly down the aisle, the priest behind them raised his arms once more, and blessed the congregation, including the departing member, and began the mass again. *"In nomine Patris et Filii et Spiritus Sancti . . ."*

Pacem.

*   *   *

That night, a little after ten o'clock, there was a telephone call from the Sonoma ranch. A neighboring farmer, noticing the LeBarons' old Packard parked for hours in the drive, and no lights whatsoever coming from the ranch house, had gone out into the ruined vineyard with a flashlight to investigate. He had found them, lying roughly side by side, each with a gunshot in the temple, and Julius LeBaron's pistol lying on the ground between them. The instructions for their burial had been found on Julius's desk in the house on California Street.

And so, a murder and a suicide, and presumably ineligible for interment in holy soil, they had chosen a mode still employed by certain Ligurian peasants to this day, and had asked to be translated into walnut trees in the corner of the vineyard where they died. Church technicalities would not permit them to enter heaven together. But this way, perhaps their souls would wander into some less explicit universal landscape of stars and trees and harvests, and perhaps forgiveness, looking for peace and redemption and transfiguration in some distant Parnassus or Elysian Fields, or in temples of even more dubious design.

"We're ruined," Peter said to her, looking hopelessly at the array of evil-worded legal documents that was spread out across his desk. "There's nothing left. Not even life insurance. He'd borrowed on that, too. All that we can find are a couple of savings accounts, in Mother's name, totaling about ten thousand dollars, to be divided between Joanna and myself. We're going to have to sell this house."

"How can we sell it?" she said. "We don't even own it yet. And nobody wants to buy a house like this today."

"Then what are we going to do?"

"We still have the land, don't we? How much land do we have?"

"Thousands of acres," he said. "Thousands and thousands of acres that no one will want to buy, either. We're land poor."

"Then what we'll do is go out there and start planting grapes. Prohibition is going to end. It's only a question of waiting for enough states to ratify the new amendment. We'll go out and plant grapes, and within a few years we'll have a harvest. When Prohibition ends, we'll be back in the wine business. We're young, Peter, and we're strong, and we'll work hard, and Joanna will help us. That's what we'll do. It's what we must do.''

"All that will take money. Vines . . . labor . . . cooperage. Where will the money come from? We don't have the money."

"Gabe Pollack will help us," she said. "We did him a favor once. He'll help us now."

This was true. Gabe Pollack is an old man now, and he doesn't like to boast or take more credit than is his due, or even like to talk about such things much. But it was true that, in 1928, when the LeBaron fortune had seemed well-nigh limitless, Sari and Peter had lent Gabe enough money to buy a struggling little newspaper in Menlo Park called the *Peninsula Gazette,* when it came up for sale.

And had it pleased Assaria Latham LeBaron, a wealthy matron all at once, wife of the millionaire, to play the role of Lady Bountiful to Gabe Pollack, whom, once upon a time, she had envisioned coming hat in hand to her Hollywood mansion, begging for forgiveness, begging for mercy, for having spurned her advances? Oh, more than likely. But Sari is not really a vengeful sort. Actually, it was Sari who had first learned of the newspaper that was for sale, and who suggested that she could lend him the money to buy it. You see, Sari had never forgotten her debt to Gabe.

And the older he got, the more thrifty and frugal Gabe became with his money, a regular magpie. In the summer of 1929, when no one had any notion of the disasters in the offing, Gabe had looked at his balance sheets and decided that enough was enough. "My stocks have more than tripled in value since I bought them," he had said. "And that's good enough for me." And so he had sold everything at the top of the market. For cash. Of course, you could argue that the actions of men like Gabe helped bring on the crash. True enough. But it didn't alter the fact that, as the Depression deepened, Gabe Pollack was a reasonably rich man.

That, however, is really not the point of all this. The point is that, though he and Sari would always have their differences over the years, he would always love her. And she would always love him. That love provided the core, the quick, of their relationship. They would always try to help each other out, through all calamity. Isn't that, after all, the simplest definition of love — the little sacrifices we make for one another day by day?

And so Gabe had lent them a hundred thousand dollars. Or maybe is was two hundred thousand. Gabe doesn't remember, doesn't want to remember, and it doesn't matter because his loans were all repaid in due course, years ago.

Eleven

HERE IS THE MENU, Madam, that Cookie proposes for to-night's little dinner," Thomas says. "She suggests a cucumber velouté to start, followed by turbans of sole with crab stuffing. Then potted squabs, with peas, mushrooms, and onions, and wild rice. A salad of Bibb lettuce and mandarin oranges, and, for dessert, a dacquoise." Sari's current Cookie is somewhat fancier and Frenchier than others have been.

"Oh, good," Sari says. "A dacquoise. What is that, anyway?"

"I believe it's a light almond layer cake with buttercream filling."

"Well, it sounds fine. In fact, it sounds quite elegant. It almost sounds like one of those grand dinners we used to have before Peter died. Now let's work on the seating. Do you have the place-cards?"

"Right here, Madam." He wheels her chair across the hall, and into the formal dining room, where Gloria Martino — who has a touch with such things — is already working on the flowers.

"Do you like these tulips?" Miss Martino says. "They're the first I've seen in the markets this spring, and I thought they were awfully pretty. I thought I'd do everything in white, yellow, and green, and then we could use your white, green, and gold Spode."

"Very nice, Gloria."

"I'm wiring the tulips, so they won't flip-flop."

"Now, let's see," Sari says, studying the dining-room table. "I think I'll put Joanna on my right, since she's come from the farthest away. And I'll put Eric at the other head of the table. That should please him, don't you think?"

"Did Melissa tell you she's bringing a friend?" Miss Martino asks.

"No! She most certainly did not. Who is this friend?"

"It's a Mr. Littlefield."

"Littlefield — the name rings a vague bell. But she wasn't supposed to do that. Tonight's dinner was supposed to be just *family*."

"It does help balance the sexes a little better, Mrs. LeBaron," Miss Martino says. "Otherwise, it would have been five women and only three men."

"But nine is an awkward number. Well, I suppose we just have to chalk it up to Melissa's perverseness. Besides, we're trying to be nice to Melissa these days, aren't we?"

"That thought also crossed my mind," Miss Martino says.

"Well, then, let's do it this way," Sari says. "We'll put Alix on Joanna's right, then Peeper, then Melissa, who will be on Eric's left. That way, we use Melissa as a kind of buffer zone between Eric and Peeper. Then" — pointing to the other side of the table — "let's put Mildred Tillinghast on Eric's right, then Mr. Littlefield, and then Harry Tillinghast, who will be on my left." Though they are certainly old enough to conduct themselves properly at a dinner party, Sari has decided against inviting her twin granddaughters. She wants this to be an adult dinner party, and, besides, she does not want the gentlemen at the party to feel overwhelmed by members of the opposite sex.

"Do you think white candles or ivory, Mrs. LeBaron?"

"Ivory, I think, Gloria. The smart decorators all over town are

making their clients use black candles. But I'm old-fashioned. Is
Joanna up yet, Thomas?''

"Oh, yes, Madam. Up and gone. She's having breakfast downtown with Mr. Eric.''

"Hm. Well, I guess we've got to allow members of the opposite
team to go into their little huddles.''

"Do you think the lime green damask —?''

"No, I think the white with the gold monograms —''

And so it has gone, throughout the day, as the White Wedding-
Cake House at 2040 Washington Street prepares itself for an evening's entertainment and festivity such as it has not seen for some
time. Out of the vault in the cellar comes the best and the heaviest
silver, the pistol-handled knives and the three-pronged dinner forks,
the matched silver epergnes that will be filled with flowers, the
heirloom silver candelabra with their candles fitted into flared crystal bobeches, the Baccarat wineglasses, the enameled place-cards
and their silver holders, the white damask napkins with the fan-
shaped gold monograms, ''ALLeB,'' the looping serifs of the letters
artfully intertwined, the silver service plates, followed by the Spode.
It is decided that Thomas will wear his dinner jacket tonight, instead of his customary white coat, and will announce the courses.
This, naturally, is all to impress the Tillinghasts. Sari selects a dress
of green watered silk.

And now they are all here, all of them, all gathered in the
drawing room before dinner, for cocktails, with all the lamps lighted,
with the candles in the sconces lit, with bowls of fresh flowers
everywhere, and a cheerful blaze in the fireplace with its high
marble mantel.

From her command post at the center of the room, Sari surveys
her dinner guests. Mildred Tillinghast, as usual, is wearing too
much jewelry — a diamond dog collar, diamond chandelier ear-
rings, a diamond bracelet, and her famous emerald-cut diamond
solitaire, which is so heavy that it inevitably slips downward into
the palm of her hand, and has to be twisted back into a position
where it can be displayed. It is Harry, Sari thinks, who likes to see
his wife go out in the evening decorated like a Christmas tree; as
a self-made man, he believes in showing off what he has made.

"You look very pretty tonight, Mildred," Sari says. "I like your dress." Lifting one fold of her skirt slightly, Mildred says, "Jimmy Galanos. Your house looks beautiful, as always, Sari. You have such good taste. I've always said that about you — Sari has such innate good taste." Was there something a little condescending in that word, *innate?* Never mind.

Melissa is wearing a very simple, long black belted sheath, which flatters her, and has also kept her jewelry simple — two jet clips at her ears, nothing more. Melissa does have innate good taste. But Sari does not know what to make of her young man, Mr. Littlefield. He seems very young indeed. He seems not even to have begun to sprout a beard, and is a rather underfed-looking creature with frightened-looking eyes, wispy hair neither long nor short, and a manner of not seeming to want to talk at all. He is not the least bit attractive, not the least bit sexy, though Sari has learned from Thomas this afternoon that Mr. Littlefield appears, at least temporarily, to have moved into Melissa's apartment downstairs. What Melissa sees in him Sari cannot imagine, and all Melissa has said about him is that he has "tremendous talent." Talent at what? Not talent at dressing, surely, for though he is wearing a dark blue suit that looks brand-new, it looks as though it had been tailored for a somewhat larger person, and his black wing-tip shoes are of a style Sari has not seen men wear for years. The shoes look somehow familiar and so, all at once, does the suit. Melissa has outfitted this young man in Peter LeBaron's old clothes! Clothes that have been packed away since 1955 in the basement storage caves! Though he is standing a little distance away from her, Sari can suddenly smell the distinctive scent of mothballs. Melissa, Melissa, what are you up to now?

"Hey, man," she hears the young man say to Peeper, "you look just like that other guy over there."

"Eric's my twin brother," Peeper replies with a smile.

The twins, handsome as always, have not yet to Sari's knowledge greeted each other. In fact, they are standing at opposite sides of the room, Peeper chatting with Littlefield and Melissa, and Eric in conversation with Joanna. And yet, looking at both boys, Sari is struck by an oddity that she has been aware of all their lives. Even though they had never been dressed alike as children, somehow they always turned up looking as though they had — almost as though an extrasensory sartorial message passed between them. If Eric came down for breakfast wearing a brown tweed jacket, Peeper would appear a few minutes later from his own room, in brown tweed. Tonight, though the two had dressed for dinner miles apart — Eric in Burlingame and Peter on Russian Hill — it is their neckties that are not quite, but almost, identical: dark red, with small, darker, figured patterns. It was a riddle Sari would never solve. Now she watches as — ah, good for him! — Peeper takes the initiative, and crosses the room toward his brother. "Hey, Facsi," she hears Peeper say, "remember me, your old facsimile? I haven't heard from you in days. You're not sore at me for something, are you?" Good old Peeper.

But with dismay she watches as Eric spurns Peeper's outstretched hand, and sees Peeper's open, handsome face fill with an expression of deep hurt. "So you are sore at me," he says.

"Not sore at you, you ass. Just amazed at your goddamned insensitivity."

"Why? What've I done, Facsi?"

"You seemed to expect me to do handstands over your being made co–marketing director. Did it occur to you that it meant taking half my job responsibilities away from me?"

"But Mother said —"

"*Mother said.* That's our little mama's boy. And I suppose you're going to take her side in Harry's bid for the company?"

"I wouldn't go for anything she didn't want."

"Well, I'm sick and tired of working for my mother. And so would you be, if you were half a man."

"I'm half of you, Facsi," she hears Peeper say quietly. "We were a split cell."

"Oh, cut the crap," Eric says. "If you ask me, you got half a brain."

Now Peeper's face is red. "Well, bugger off, Eric!" he says sharply.

"Boys! Boys!" Sari cries. "We're not going to have that sort of talk in my house tonight. This is to be a pleasant little family dinner." She thinks that the evening is getting off to a somewhat rocky start, and she signals to Thomas. "More drinks! More drinks for everybody."

"Of course, we're all dying to know what you think of Harry's offer," Mildred Tillinghast says. "That's the burning question on everyone's lips."

Overhearing this, Harry says, "And maybe you've heard I'm prepared to sweeten it a bit, Sari."

"No business talk tonight," Sari says firmly. "Tonight is for fun. Tonight is just party."

"Of course, you have wonderful business sense, Sari," Mildred says. "I've always said you have an innate business sense."

Raising her glass, Sari says, "I'd like to propose a toast — to Joanna, who's come all the way from New York to be at our little family gathering tonight. Welcome home, Jo."

"Hear, hear . . . welcome home, Aunt Jo."

Alix LeBaron, languishing on one of the long sofas in front of the fire, wearing a white knit caftan of nubbly wool and many gold chains and bracelets, looks as though she is waiting to be photographed by *Town & Country*. She is also clearly trying to catch Peeper's eye. When he finally turns to her, she says, "Well, Peeper, it's about time you said hello to me."

"Oh, hi, Al," he says easily, and she rewards him with a sulky smile.

It is clear to Sari that Alix is trying to make some sort of play for Peeper. "Alix," she says, "how is Sloanie coming along with the orthodontist?"

"Oh, it's endless, Belle-mère," Alix says.

"Mother," Peeper says, "didn't there used to be a beautiful Baccarat millefiori paperweight on this table?"

"It had an accident," Sari explains, careful not to look in Melissa's direction.

"Ah, that's a shame," he says. "I loved that little piece."

"Maids," Alix agrees. "They break everything."

Of all the expensively dressed and coiffed and groomed people in this room, Sari thinks — with Mr. Littlefield something of an exception — it is Joanna who is the wonder of the world. Though her blonde hair is now silver, the famous dark blue eyes still flash, and the dark double eyelashes, aided now no doubt by mascara, still create an extraordinary effect. The skin, for a woman of Joanna's age, is still remarkably smooth and clear, and the voice is even deeper and richer. A truly beautiful woman, Sari sometimes thinks, never really ages to the point of losing her beauty. It has something to do with the facial bones, the cheekbones in particular, and of course the eyes. It doesn't matter what Joanna wears — one hardly notices clothes on her — because one so quickly becomes caught up in Joanna's face, and the way her hands move. She is a toucher — always reaching out to touch, with just a dab of a gesture, the person she is talking to. She even sits youthfully, legs crossed at the knees, leaning forward, her chin in her hand, listening to what the person she is talking to has to say. She is, Sari is forced to admit, nothing short of miraculous, and she is weaving her spell now as she always did, holding the room with her famous charm. "Wheel me a little closer to Joanna," Sari whispers to Peeper, who is standing closest.

"Now, I want to propose a toast," Joanna says. "To Sari, my oldest and dearest friend. Sari, I just want to say that whatever the outcome of all this is, you'll always be that to me."

"Hear, hear . . . to Mother . . . to Sari . . . to Belle-mère . . ."

"The old wine barrel in the portrait gallery," Joanna says. "That was what touched me most, when I came into this house again and saw that there. Grandpa had it in his house in Sonoma, and Daddy kept it on California Street, and then Peter brought it here. It's a symbol of continuity, isn't it, but not a monument. It's still simple, still a simple, classic example of the cooper's art. When I walked into this house yesterday — your beautiful house, Sari — and saw the old wine cask, I thought for a minute I might burst into tears. And everything else — the portraits of the children, all of us, in the long gallery. It would keep the house young, Daddy used to say. And it has, Sari, it has, and of course Peter carried on that tradition, too. This house is so full of so many memories for me — my brother's pipe collection, the Roman bronzes in the front hall, the elephant's foot with all his walking sticks, all the things he loved — I finally felt home again. I finally felt that some things don't need to change. That's what you've maintained here, Sari —

an island of continuity, of permanence and tranquillity in a sea of change. But the old wine barrel said it to me most."

There is a silence, and then Eric says, "Lovely. I'd like a copy of that little speech, Aunt Jo."

"But it's not a speech," she insists. "It's what I feel, and what I mean. You know what I mean, don't you, Sari?" She laughs. "Or is the old advertising copywriter coming out in me? I always wanted to find some way to use that barrel in Baronet's advertising, but was never clever enough to figure out how. Of course, we don't handle the Baronet account anymore."

"It was you who resigned it, don't forget," Sari says. "That wasn't my idea."

"But we're not to talk about business."

You see? That is Joanna's cleverness. She knows that they are not to talk about business, and yet she steers the talk around to business anyway.

"I'm still getting calls from agencies who want to pitch for the account," Eric says. "But of course, since I'm no longer with the company, I refer all those calls to Peeper."

"Hey, I was wondering how those guys got my private number," Peeper says.

"No business talk, remember?"

"But, Sari," Mildred Tillinghast says, "what *do* you think of Harry's offer? Don't you think it's exciting?"

"No business . . ."

"Just give us a tiny little hint of what you think of it!"

"The old wine barrel. People who come to the house for the first time think it's a very peculiar thing for me to keep — and an even more peculiar place to put it!"

"The portrait gallery . . ."

"Sometimes it weeps. In certain kinds of weather."

"And when I was a little girl, Sari, on California Street, I used to put my ear up to it, like listening to a seashell, and sometimes there would be little gurgling sounds. Grandpa's wine was trying to talk to me."

"Wine keeps changing. It never dies."

"Sometimes the barrel feels warm to the touch."

"Just think. Over a hundred years old."

"Nearly a hundred and thirty . . ."

"What would we find, I wonder, if we were to open it?"

"At every party, there would be someone who'd want to open that barrel!"

"The bung's so calcified into the bunghole now, it would take a sledgehammer to open it . . ."

Thomas is moving about the room again, taking more drink orders, and a housemaid is passing hors d'oeuvres, mushroom caps filled with sour cream and caviar. "What's this stuff?" Sari hears Mr. Littlefield ask Melissa.

"That's caviar, dear. Sturgeon roe — salmon eggs."

"Fish eggs?"

"Don't eat it if you don't want to, dear."

"The portraits," Joanna says. "How was yours done, Sari? I forget."

"Your father had it painted from a photograph of me that was taken when I did that play."

"Oh, that play! That's how we met, of course, when you brought your play to Burke's. How I loved that play!"

"Oh, it was an awful piece of claptrap."

"But *you* were what made it wonderful! If you hadn't married Peter, you could easily have gone on to Hollywood and become a great film star. That's what I always thought."

"Where's the john?" she hears Mr. Littlefield ask Melissa.

"Out the door there, down the hall, and to your right."

"Just think — everyone in this room is hanging out there in that gallery," Joanna says, and Sari thinks: You have to hand it to her. She tries to keep the conversation bubbling on, even through the rocky patches.

"Well, *I'm* not there," Alix says. "My children are there, but I'm not, and neither are Mummy and Daddy. Because we're not considered *family*."

"Well, we'll have to rectify that, won't we, Sari?"

And Athalie isn't there, either. Where is Athalie? Forget Athalie, forget she ever existed. But she did exist. She did.

Mr. Littlefield has returned from using the facilities, and Sari cannot help but notice a change that seems to have come over him. His face is flushed now, and his hands are twitching, his head bobbing up and down in strange little jerking motions. He is trying to light a cigarette, with a match, and it takes him four matches before he can get the flame and the tip of the cigarette to come together. He looks all at once quite unwell, and Assaria LeBaron propels her chair toward him, determined to discover what this allegedly tremendously talented young man does for a living, and what his relationship might be with Melissa. "I hope all this family talk doesn't bore you, Mr. Littlejohn," she says.

"Littlefield," and with more little jerks of his head, he says, "Nice place you got here. Like, man, this is a real mansion."

"Well, yes, I suppose —"

"I mean, like, thanks for asking Melissa and I up," he says. And then, "I gotta go to the john again," and he steps out into the hall once more, the cigarette clenched between his teeth, and his hands thrust deep into the pockets of his borrowed suit jacket. Sari thinks that surely he is ill, and that perhaps among his problems is one to do with his bladder.

"Did you know my brother, Harry?" Joanna is saying.

"Only slightly. But of course, everyone knew him by reputation."

"A good reputation, I hope."

"Oh, the very finest."

"Together, he and Sari made an unbeatable team." Then, in a quieter voice, she says, "Tomorrow, I'd like to go out to the Sonoma vineyard and see Mother and Daddy's graves, see the trees. Peter always thought it was barbaric, the way they wanted to be buried, but I always thought it rather — poetic. Would anyone like to go with me? Sari? Melissa?"

And now Mr. Littlefield has returned from the bathroom again, and this time his appearance is almost alarming. His face is now very flushed, and his eyes are quite large, and the twitching of his hands and the jerking of his neck muscles are more pronounced. Surely this young man is very ill, Sari thinks. Melissa has noticed something, too, for she sees Melissa whisper something to him, an anxious expression on her face. Then Sari notices another extraor-

dinary thing. Mr. Littlefield has an erection! Its unmistakable size
and contours are quite obvious against the trouser leg of Peter
LeBaron's old blue suit. She wonders if others in the room will
notice it, or whether, since now the others are all standing, while
she, of necessity, is seated and therefore at eye level with his condition, it will escape their observation. To Thomas, who has just
handed her a fresh drink, she whispers, "Is dinner nearly ready?
You know I dislike a long cocktail hour."

"I'll speak to Cookie, Madam."

"After Mother and Daddy died, Peter and Sari and I went out
into the fields," Joanna is saying to Harry Tillinghast, "and we got
down on our hands and knees with the field hands, and started
planting vines . . ."

"Remarkable."

This, of course, is one of the annoying things about Joanna. She
tends to take over and start controlling the conversation, which
Sari herself should be doing. If Sari is not careful, she will have
surrendered the hostesship of her dinner party to the tyranny of
wit and beauty, but she is so busy trying to keep her eyes from
traveling back to Mr. Littlefield's aroused state that she can think
of nothing to say. Interrupting Joanna, she makes a statement that
even embarrasses her with its banality. "Well, I hope everybody
has a good appetite because we have quite a nice dinner planned,"
she says. "Cookie has worked very long and hard . . ." And she
finds herself blushing, thinking: *Very long and hard.*

There is a little laugh from Joanna, and Sari knows that Joanna
has noticed the Littlefield situation, too — Joanna, who notices
everything. Joanna winks at her, and then turning to the young
man, says, "Are you from San Francisco, Mr. Littlefield?"

He stares at her dumbly, as though he has not understood the
question. Then he repeats, "San Francisco?"

Melissa says, "Maurice, I think —"

Joanna laughs brightly again. "Melissa, dear," she says without
a trace of sarcasm, "where do you find such *interesting* young
men?"

"Maurice is —" Melissa begins, but she is interrupted by Thomas,
who has stepped into the room to say, "Dinner is served, Madam."

Thank goodness, Sari thinks, as the group makes its way through the portrait gallery toward the dining room, with Thomas propelling her chair. At least Mr. Littlefield's peculiar problem will soon be concealed under the folds of the table linen.

The dinner begins smoothly enough. Sari has memorized her seating chart, and directs each guest to his place, and Thomas has stationed himself just slightly behind the hostess's chair, where, in his role as her majordomo, he will supervise the service. Mr. Littlefield has picked up one of the white napkins and is scrutinizing, farsightedly, the heavy gold embroidery. "What's this?" he says.

"It's your napkin, Maurice," Melissa says a little sharply.

"No, I mean what's *this?* It says *Alleb* on it. What's that mean, *Alleb?*"

"That's my monogram," Sari says. "A-L-Le-B.''

"A cucumber velouté," Thomas says, as the soup course arrives.

While the soup is being served, Sari notices that Mr. Littlefield has managed, with difficulty, to light another cigarette, and she also sees that he has lighted the end with the filter tip. She whispers to Thomas, "An ashtray for Mr. Littlefield, please."

Beside her, on her left, Harry Tillinghast is saying in a low voice so that the others cannot hear, "You made a very serious mistake, Sari, when you fired Eric the way you did. I've always admired you as a businesswoman, but that was a mistake."

"Well, what would you have done, Harry, if your marketing director had decided to organize a palace revolution against you? Pin a medal on him?"

"In my opinion, that was a mistake in judgment, Sari, and counterproductive."

"Well, it was my decision to make. Besides, we're not going to talk about —"

"Did you drop your napkin or something, Allie?" she hears Peeper say to Alix, who is seated on his left, and she looks down the table in time to see Alix's hand quickly withdraw from where it must have been touching Peeper's knee. Oh, dear, she thinks, what can be done to divert this evening from what suddenly threatens to become a disaster? She takes her first spoonful of soup, and the others follow her lead, except for Mr. Littlefield, who is still smoking his cigarette with the wrong end lighted. This creates an acrid smell, like burning rubber, that mingles unhappily with the gardenia perfume from the scented candles. "A toast," she says, a little desperately. "To all of us! To long life, peace, and happiness!" And lifts her glass.

"Is this Baronet wine?" Mr. Littlefield asks, and the room falls silent. It is a question that, somehow, has never been asked at Assaria LeBaron's table. "Well, is it?" he asks again.

"No, actually it is a Monbousquet, nineteen seventy-nine," Sari says at last. "French. Our wines are inexpensive jug wines. *Vins ordinaires.*"

"But of course they wouldn't always have to be," Harry says. "Baronet possesses the vines, and the capacity, to produce truly noble wines. Under a different label, of course. Have you ever thought of that, Sari?"

"Yes, thought of it and immediately dismissed it. I know my market, Harry."

"But there's a whole new upscale market that could be tapped. Young urban professionals —"

"I know all about yuppies," she says. "But I also know my market. What do you know about wines, Harry?"

"Quite a bit, as a matter of fact. I've had my office do a study on it. Demographic profiles —"

"Yes. Studies. Demographic profiles. But I've learned this business from the ground up, as Joanna says. I've fought off the larks —"

"Larks haven't been a problem for years, Sari. Pesticides took care of them."

"Yes, and do you know I miss them? They were beautiful birds with a beautiful song. Beautiful, voracious birds."

Turning to Mr. Littlefield, on her right, Mildred Tillinghast says, "I hope you'll forgive all this talk about the family business, Mr. Littlefield."

Sari cannot let this comment pass. "It's not *your* family business, Mildred," she says sharply. "At least not yet!"

"But, Sari, Harry and I own stock!"

Down, down, she can feel her evening descending, ineluctably, into the widening whirlpool of discord she had so hoped to avoid, and the downward descent seems to be gathering a momentum that she can no longer control.

Turning back to Mr. Littlefield, Mildred says, "What business are you in, Mr. Littlefield?"

"Business?"

"Yes. What do you do?"

"I'm a rock star."

"A rock star. How very —"

"Oh, my God!" Sari cries, because she has just realized who Mr. Maurice Littlefield is. "You're the one who killed the snake!"

"Bugger bit me!"

Once more, the table falls silent.

"Tell me," Sari says, trying, if it is still humanly possible, to rescue the evening, "how did you and Melissa meet?"

"We didn't meet, exactly," he says. And then, his face still hotly flushed and his eyes wide, still not having picked up his soup spoon, he begins, "Listen, let me tell you a story, lady, a story about that snake that will knock you off your feet!" The silence at the table becomes one of shock at the enormity of this gaffe. But, unaware that he has committed one, he repeats it, and in a much louder voice. "I mean, this will really knock you off your feet!"

"Maurice," Melissa says in a low, warning voice from across the table.

"Wait! Let me tell it. The snake's name was Sylvia. I mean that was its name, Sylvia, and there was this girl in the group named Marty, in I think Omaha, and this Marty she really loved that snake. She used to tie it around her, she used to wrap it around her, you know, her neck, and she used to even stick it down under her dress to make it look like, you know, she had these big tits, and she'd play with that snake — crazy, man! — like she really loved it, and it was like that Sylvia really loved this Marty, and she'd wrap herself around this Marty like she really loved this Marty, and Sylvia never done nothing to hurt this Marty, see? So in I think Omaha we had this gig, and this Marty was out on the stage with Sylvia and I — Sylvia, who was this snake — and Marty was wrappin' the snake around her, stuffin' it inside her dress to make it look like these big tits, you know? You know? You know? And — *whee!*" He is shouting now, and he flings his head back, and the cords of his thin neck stand out. "Whee! There goes my head! Hold me down, Major! Hold me down, Captain Marvel, 'cause I'm up on the ceiling, I'm up in the stars, I'm out in space, man! Whee! I'm climbin', man, climbin' to the fuckin' stars, man! *Ace me out!* Ace me out of a fuckin' sp-i-i-i-n! Sing to me, sugar! Sing to me, Lucius! Dance on the head of my dick, Lucius! W-o-o-o-o-o-o! This is Star Wars, baby, and here comes Darth —"

"*Maurice!*"

"W-o-o-o-o-o-o-o-oo! I'm trippin', man!" And all at once his head topples forward, his whole body sags, and his head falls into his soup bowl, sideways, with a soft splash.

"My dress!" Mildred Tillinghast cries, half rising and gathering the folds of her Galanos skirt about her knees.

"My Spode!" says Sari. And yet, miraculously, the soup bowl from her treasured set of porcelain, so thin that through it you could see the outline of a bird's foot, remains unbroken from the apparently inconsequential weight of Maurice Littlefield's head. Meanwhile, all the men at the table are on their feet to assist the young man out of his velouté.

Melissa has also risen. "I'll handle this," she says in a taut voice. "Stand up, Maurice!" she commands. "*Stand up!* I'm taking you downstairs." She pulls him slowly to his feet, and soup dribbles from his face down across his shirt and jacket and necktie while Sari and Thomas exchange looks of mutual consternation.

"I'll be right back," Melissa says, and there is silence from the rest of the table as, with one hand firmly grasping the young man's elbow, she steers him on an unsteady course out of the dining room.

"Well!" Sari says at last. And then, determined not to lose control of the gathering, she says to Thomas, "Just remove his place setting, Thomas. Mildred, you and Harry can move a little closer together. I know it means husband next to wife, but the circumstances are a bit — unusual, I guess you'd all agree. Mildred, is your dress all right?"

"Yes — I think so. Was it something I said, Sari, that made him do that?"

"I doubt it," Sari says. And then, "Tell me — I want to know what each of you thinks — is Claus von Bulow guilty? I think he's innocent — either innocent or stupid to have kept the hypodermic needle. Peeper, what do you think?"

"I think . . ." And for the next few moments, everything is a forced babble of chatter, as everyone tries to put behind him or her the Littlefield episode.

"I'm prepared to sweeten my offer, Sari," she hears Harry Tillinghast, on her left, say to her. "Thirteen point two five shares per."

"I thought it was thirteen a little while ago."

"I'm sweetening the sweetener, Sari."

"It's still chickenfeed. My company's shares are worth a damn sight more than thirteen point two five of yours."

"*Your* company, Mother?" Eric says.

"We're not here to talk business! This is not a business dinner. How often must I remind you?"

Now Melissa has returned to the dining room, and takes her seat at the table again. "I'm terribly sorry," she says. "It's entirely my fault. I was trying something, an experiment, and it didn't work. It's really a tragic story. It has all the classic ingredients. Born and raised in some dreadful little East Texas town — an alcoholic mother, and a father who was a wife beater and a child abuser. Ran away from home when he was ten. Got into drugs. But underneath all the sordidness, there is this really remarkable natural musical talent. That's what I hope to rescue somehow. But the problem is shyness — a terrible shyness. It affects him in front of audiences. So he'll take an upper to feel better, and then a downer to bring him down from the high, and then he'll snort a line of cocaine to bring him up again, or sniff some amyl nitrate. I'm trying to rehabilitate him, that's all, because of the very real talent that's there — trying to let that talent come out. I thought, perhaps, if he could join a normal family for a nice, normal little dinner party —"

A normal family, Sari thinks.

As though reading her thoughts, Melissa adds, "A supposedly normal family, anyway. But obviously he wasn't ready for it. I even dug out an old suit of Daddy's for him to wear, so he'd look at least halfway decent. But he wasn't ready. He just wasn't up to it. Anyway," she says, looking around the table for reassurance, "he's my little project right now — to try to rehabilitate him, to try to get him to stay off the drugs. And it's only because of the — I assure you — really extraordinary natural musical talent that he has, talent that it would be such a shame to see wasted. I'm going to keep trying. I'm not going to give up yet. But tonight was a mistake, and I apologize."

From the others at the table, she sees only looks that express varying degrees of skepticism.

"The child has been hurt, damaged, all his life," she says. "I can't help it, but my heart always goes out to the damaged children of this world!" There is silence as each person at the table thinks, in his or her own way, of Melissa's troubled childhood. "They need so much, and receive so little," she says. "All they ask for is a little love, and faith, and kindness, and reassurance and understanding. Anyway, that's all I'm trying to provide for this poor, lost little boy." Then, almost defiantly, she adds, "And I don't care what any of you think!"

Finally, Joanna says, "Melissa and her little projects. You've always had them, haven't you, dear? Well, I for one think it's very Christian of you. I say bravo, Melissa."

"Anyway," Sari says with unnecessary enthusiasm to fill the silence that follows, "let's not let any of this spoil our dinner."

"Turbans of sole, with a crab stuffing," says Thomas quietly, announcing the next course.

By the time the dacquoise has been served, it is almost possible for Sari to believe that the peaceful, pleasant gathering she had imagined is actually occurring. But then it is Harry Tillinghast — Harry, who will not let go of a subject until he has wrestled it to the floor — who feels he must go back to his favorite topic. Remarking on the sweetness of the buttercream filling in the dessert, he finds an occasion to make a bad pun about the sweetness of his stock offer. "We all know how Sari feels about it," he says, "but what about the rest of you?"

"Personally, I find it quite generous," Joanna says.

"Dammit," Sari says sharply, "my company is not for sale!"

"*Your* company, Mother?" Eric says again.

Sitting forward in her chair, Joanna says, "Sari dear, just tell me one thing, and then I promise we'll get off the subject. Just tell me why you *care* so much about all this. I think that's the thing that none of us quite understands."

"Care?" Sari says. "Why do I care? You're a fine one to ask me that! How would you feel if someone were trying to take your ad agency away from you?"

"Actually," Joanna says, "I plan on retiring in another couple of years. I'm really rather looking forward to it, and I've got my successor all picked out."

"*You,*" Sari says. "You, of course — but you were different. You were born with a golden spoon in your mouth, but I wasn't. I used to run twelve blocks to school to save the nickel streetcar fare! I care because this company is the only thing I've ever owned."

"But don't you think you're being a bit melodramatic, Sari? I mean, after all, you do own other things. You have children, grandchildren, all the money in the world, a beautiful house —"

"Children are a duty and a responsibility. So is money, and so is a house. All those things need to be nourished and cared for. But work — work is where the nourishment comes from. It's what keeps you alive while you take care of the other things. You — you all had your Catholic faith, which I never really understood, but which I know helped you through the bad times. This company has been like a faith to me — a spiritual support — a comfort through all the disappointments and disasters — the larks —" And now tears — real or feigned, who can tell with Sari? — have welled in her eyes, and she dabs at them with a corner of her monogrammed napkin. "I named it, you know. I named it Baronet. When the larks destroyed our first harvest in nineteen thirty-three, Peter said to me, 'We've lost it. It's gone. We're finished.' And I said to him, 'We're *not* finished! The grapes are gone, but not the vines! We'll try again, we'll take the gamble. All farming is a gamble — the rain, the sun, the elements, the birds. It's all a gamble, but if you're going to be a gambler you have to stay in the game to win. We'll win,' I said. 'Wait and see. Let's give ourselves a new name. Let's call ourselves — Baronet Vineyards! Baronet! It has a lucky sound. With a new name, maybe we'll have new luck,' I said to him. And we did. We won. They've called me a tough old broad — I've heard them — but it's only a life of work that's made me tough. How can you ask me why I care? How can you ask me to give it all up without a struggle?"

Sari LeBaron lowers her face into her cupped hands. "You see," she says, "all I am asking is to be allowed to die with my boots on."

While she has been speaking, Peeper has risen from his place at the table and moved to stand behind his mother's chair. He places his hands on Sari's shoulders, and squeezes them tightly.

She covers his left hand with her right one, and whispers, "Thank you, Peeper."

Only what you can accomplish with your personal powers of persuasion, her lawyers, Baines and Rosenthal, had said to her.

Eric is the first to speak. He clears his throat, and then says, "Harry, I think we should call this whole thing off. It's just not worth it, Harry. It's not worth what it would do to our mother. Let's call if off."

There is a brief silence, and then Alix LeBaron shrieks, "*Call it off?* You mean you're changing your mind? You mean you're *backing out?* You do that, you son of a bitch, and I'll slap a separate maintenance suit on you so fast you won't know what hit you!"

"Now, Buttercup —" Harry Tillinghast begins.

"I mean it! I'll slap a separate maintenance suit on him so fast he won't know what hit him! Because I know what he's been up to! He's been getting it on with that little bitch Jap secretary of his!"

"That's a goddamned lie, Alix!"

"It's not! I've got the proof! A canceled check for ten thousand bucks!"

"That was for —"

"Aunt Grace in the nursing home? I know all about that one, too — the old nursing-home line!"

"Alix, you're ruining my party," Sari says.

"You stay out of this, Belle-mère! This is between Eric and me."

"And stop calling me Belle-mère while you're making nasty accusations to my son! I see now that it's not your father who's behind this whole takeover scheme — it's *you!*"

"None of this is true, Alix," Eric says. But Sari can see that the small forceps scar on his left temple has begun to redden, which only happens when he is angry or upset. Or frightened.

"It is true! She admitted it to me! I confronted the Jap bitch with what I knew, and she admitted it!"

"I don't believe you," Eric says, but the forceps scar is now quite red, and his eyelids are twitching.

"*Tell it to the judge!*" Alix screams.

"Alix, I'm taking you home," Eric says.

"*No!*" She is sobbing now. "I don't want to go home with you! I want to go home with Mummy and Daddy! Mummy . . . Daddy . . . please . . . take me home!"

"Now, now, Buttercup . . ." Harry Tillinghast says, as between them he and Mildred Tillinghast support their loudly weeping daughter, and escort her to the door.

When they have gone, Peeper turns to Sari and says, "I wouldn't worry too much about what she says, Mother. These adultery things are damned hard to prove. I mean, unless she's got photographs or something. She doesn't have photographs or something, does she?"

"Goddamn it," Eric says, flinging his napkin on the table. "So you believe her too!" He pushes his chair back hard and jumps to his feet. "I'm getting out of this goddamned fucking rats' nest!" And he, too, is gone.

Now the number at the dinner table is reduced to four — Sari and Joanna at one end, and Peeper and Melissa at another, with empty chairs separating the participants. Their dacquoise has been barely touched, nor will it be, and Sari's Cookie will forever wonder what was wrong with it, nor will she ever prepare it in her life again for anyone.

Thomas, who has been waiting in the vestibule just behind the kitchen door — waiting for a moment of peace to descend upon the hostess's table — appears now to say, "Coffee is served in the drawing room, Madam."

"Thank you, Thomas." And, when he has gone, she says to no one in particular, "Well, a new little wrinkle has been added to our problem."

Peeper looks at his uneaten dessert for a moment or two, and then mumbles, "Better be on my way, too. Early golf date in the morning."

"Of course," Sari says. "Good night, Peeper. Give me a kiss."

And now, as the three women move toward the drawing room, and the promise of coffee and a nightcap — which Sari suddenly very much needs — Joanna, still trying to rescue something from the ruins of the evening, says, "Oh, good. A hen party! Now we can really gossip." But her heart is clearly not in this suggestion, for she adds, "I keep wondering, if Peter were alive, would he have been able to prevent all that? He was always such a wonderful . . . peacemaker. I'll never understand why Peter did what he did."

In the room they are now entering, right there in front of the marble fireplace, stands the little Regency games table, with a top that flips about on a swivel to reveal all sorts of little secret compartments where one could hide one's chips, like cards up a sleeve, an early nineteenth-century device for cheaters and charlatans and crooks. And Sari could swing the tabletop open to reveal the place where a square of green blotting paper lies . . . And there, too, suddenly — there is no correlation — is the vision of Peter eating his breakfast roll above the tennis courts at Saint Moritz, eating his breakfast numbly and automatically, a kind of passive eating, as though there were nothing of importance left in the world to do. Peter, trying to face the consequences of his actions, but unable to do so, and responding only with emotional emptiness, the life drained out of him, a vacuum whose depths she kept trying to explore, and plumb, and fill somehow, but always — almost always — without success.

Peter. The *peacemaker?* Well, hardly that, unless with peace you assume defeat. King Croesus of the Lydians consulted the oracle at Delphi, and the priestess told him, "You will cross a river, and a great nation will be defeated." And so, when the neighboring Persians were giving him trouble, Croesus crossed the river into Persia, where his armies were totally destroyed by the enemy. When he returned to the oracle for an explanation, she replied, "I didn't say which great nation would be defeated when you crossed the river."

In the drawing room, over the coffee cups, Joanna is saying, "If you retired, you could travel, Sari. You could take a cruise. You used to say you wanted to go to China. You could do all that now, things you never did because Peter hated to travel . . ."

Sari says nothing. Melissa says nothing. Thomas appears to collect the finished coffee service, and to place a fresh bucket of ice on the drinks cart. Melissa goes to fix herself a drink.

"Fix me one, too," Sari says. "Scotch. Rather stiff, I think."

"Will there be anything else this evening, Madam?" Thomas asks.

"No, I don't think so."

"Oh, Thomas," Joanna says, as he is about to leave the room, "you know what a stickler I am for detail. Will you remind Cookie for me that I'd like my breakfast egg cooked for exactly three and a half minutes?"

Thomas looks quickly at his mistress, and their eyes meet, and lock briefly, and then they look — very briefly — toward Melissa before Thomas decides that this is the moment to nod to Joanna's request, and to withdraw.

Melissa sits back on the small Empire sofa, her legs crossed at the knees under her black sheath. A touch of ankle shows. With her drink in her left hand, she fishes with her right for a cigarette from the silver cigarette box and lights it with a small cloisonné lighter. Exhaling a thin stream of smoke, she says, "Aunt Joanna. Or should I call you Mrs. Mary Brown? Or should I call you Mother?"

Joanna leaps to her feet. "You broke your promise!" she cries at Sari. "You broke your solemn oath! *I should never have trusted you!*"

"*I did not!*" Sari says. "Melissa, tell her that I didn't tell you this!"

"She didn't tell me," Melissa says. "I found out. With the help of a man who remembers when I was born in Switzerland. And under the terms of the will, I believe this means I am entitled to half of Lance's shares — not just five percent, but seven and a half percent more, or twelve and a half percent all told. 'Fifteen percent of said shares in said company shall be divided, equally, among any and all living issue of my aforesaid sister, Joanna,' is the way the will reads. And so, Joanna, you and Lance and Eric and Harry don't control fifty-five percent of the vote, do you? You only control forty-seven and a half percent. The swing vote belongs to me, doesn't it? Which way will I vote, I wonder? For one of you two bitches or the other? Of course, I will have to ask myself, how would my father have wanted me to vote?"

The other two women say nothing.

Twelve

SHE HAD WANTED her debutante year. It was as simple as that. To Sari, she had pretended to make light of the whole thing, pretended it wasn't important, pretended she was merely going through the motions of it all to please her parents. But she had wanted it. She had wanted the Cotillion and the Bachelors' Ball. She had wanted the attention, and her photograph in the papers, and she had wanted the escorts and the filling out of dance cards and the parties — the dances and the luncheons and the teas and the balls that would go on throughout all that 1926–1927 season. She had wanted every little bit of it.

By the spring of 1926 she had ordered — from Tiffany's in New York! — the special, engraved, white-on-blue stationery which was for answering invitations and writing thank-you notes. By July, she had received her special engagement calendar, bound in blue leather, with the words embossed in gold on the cover, "My Season — Joanna LeBaron." The engagement book had come from

Tiffany's also. ("So much more posh, don't you think, than something from Shreve's?" she had said to Sari. "Everyone else is using Shreve's.") By the time the engraved invitations began fluttering in, she would be prepared to start making entries in the pages of this diary in her round, precise, boarding-school hand. She would be prepared to write "accept" or "regret" on the corner of each invitation, and prepared, no doubt, to pin all the invitations — the accepted and regretted — around the frame of the mirror above her dressing table on California Street, each invitation a small, private conquest and a little battle won. But of course, by the time the invitations would normally have started to come in, Joanna was otherwise engaged in another part of the world.

Looking back, it is easy to see that she could barely contain her excitement about it all, even as she pretended to disparage it, saying things like, "Of course, it's all a lot of nonsense, isn't it? It's all utter rot. I'm only doing it because Mother wants it — she's such an utter snob." But she had wanted it for *herself,* and the wardrobe of gowns and suits and afternoon dresses that every debutante had to have, and the flowers arriving from Podesta & Baldocchi, and the young men from the stag line saying, "May I cut in?" Even though, in the end, because of what happened, it was not possible for her to have all of it, she had wanted just as much of the whole ritual as she could have — if not all, then at least half of it.

She had missed the Bachelors', and she had missed the Cotillion, the two events for which her most important gowns had been designed, the balls her mother had labored on for years, toiling on all the right committees, seeing to it that her father gave to all the proper causes — all that money and effort had gone to waste. But she had made the most of what was left — the smaller parties in the city and on the Peninsula, during the spring and early summer. And, in June, her parents had given a big dinner dance for her at the Burlingame Country Club, under a blue-and-white-striped tent.

In retrospect, it is all rather ironic because now that Joanna LeBaron is who she is, the Dragon Lady of Madison Avenue, the Medea of Media-land, she would probably never admit to having been a debutante at all. If she started talking about her debut with some of the high-powered men and women she deals with now,

Sari sometimes thinks, Joanna LeBaron would be laughed right out of the Graybar Building. Such are the jokes life plays on one. "Why weren't you honest with me?" she should have said to her. "Why didn't you say that all you wanted was your debutante year?" Oh, but Joanna had wanted even more than that.

Now it is midnight, and Sari LeBaron is alone. Joanna has stalked off angrily to bed, declaring that she will be taking the first plane back to New York in the morning, refusing to believe that it was not Sari who told Melissa their secret ("I knew I should never have trusted you!"). And, without another word, Melissa departed for her apartment downstairs. Attending, perhaps, to Mr. Littlefield.

It is past midnight, and Sari is alone in her quiet house, trying to put her noisy thoughts in order. What will happen now, she thinks. It is no use. She cannot think. She could, if she chose, summon Thomas for company — for consolation and, perhaps, advice. He would get out of bed and come down to be with her. All she needs to do is push a button, ring a bell, and he will appear. But she will not do that. It would not be fair to him. He and all the others have worked too hard this evening — and for this.

And it is not Thomas's problem, is it? It is her own. Whatever happens, she thinks, this is going to be my last hurrah.

In her chair, she propels herself through the empty rooms of her house. Ah, it is all so pretty, flowers everywhere and still so fresh! In the drawing room, the satin draperies are pulled closed, and there is all her French furniture and the intricate needlepoint rug, handmade for an Irish viscount, and that lady there in the portrait over the cream-colored sofa was a courtesan of some French king or other, and was painted by Jean-Marc Nattier, very valuable, it has been said. The hems of the satin draperies sweep the floor, and between those two windows is a Louis XIV escritoire, very rare, and lacy with giltwork, and against the opposite wall stands the seventeenth-century coromandel screen, fourteen folding panels. The rosewood piano in the southwest corner of the room is by Bösendorfer, and has ninety-two keys instead of the customary eighty-eight, a piano built for the Austrian concert stage. There, on the Louis XVI commode, is the collection of jade — boxes, animals, and bibelots.

In the dining room, the rosewood paneling of the walls serves as a backdrop for the mahogany Biedermeier table that will expand to seat thirty-two, and the Biedermeier chairs are covered in plum-colored watered mohair. On the dining-room mantel is a pair of Chinese Ming yellow vases, considered priceless. And then into the portrait gallery: Melissa. . . . The wheels of Sari's chair move silently across the polished parquet. Possessions — the Sevres candlesticks, the Flemish tapestries, the half-dome of leaded glass above the elevator cage, the pair of Second Empire commodes — money bought only possessions, and very soon the possessions possessed you; you could not give them up. The LeBarons had bought her, and now she possessed them, or at least part of them. And that of course was another part of Joanna's secret. She wanted to possess things, and to possess people, too. Looking about her, Sari thinks, oh, the greatness of my possessions! Oh, the greatness of this house! And how can I be unhappy in the midst of all these things, all this luxury, when all I have to do is push a button, ring a bell, and what I want will appear as if in a miracle. Gabe Pollack, giving her away at her wedding, had said to her, "This almost seems a miracle. But this is America, where anything is possible. Only in America could this happen."

"MacDonald brings ladies of the evening into the house." This is Joanna speaking. "Sometimes two at a time! One of them died here, and he had a devil of a time getting her out. Peter found out about it, and that's why MacDonald lets us have our secret cellar . . ." Was any of this true? Or was it all a fantasy? Did any of these things really happen?

"I Want to Be Happy!" It was the song playing on the phonograph in the LeBarons' wine cellar, and the song Peter had played on his harmonica on the deck of the *Baroness C.* It was a song she had often heard him whistling to himself when they were together, but these were not the words she had wanted to hear him say. She had wanted him to say, "I love you, Sari. I love you with all my mind and soul and heart and body. I want to run away with you to China, and walk along the Great Wall with you. I want to spend my life with you, to be with you always, to make you happy.

I want to love you always, to share everything with you. I love you so much that I want to shout it from the rooftops, and tell the world how much I love you. I want to marry you . . . will you marry me?"

But he had not said these things, not even while, not even after, they committed the act of love together. He had remained bright and cheerful — oh, sometimes moody, of course, when he complained about how hard his father was being on him — but at the same time detached and elusive and somehow unattainable. "This is Sari Latham," he would say, introducing her to one of his friends. "My sister Joanna's friend." Was that all she was to him? His sister's friend?

Oh, sometimes he would throw her a sly, private wink, acknowledging that he and she shared a little secret from Joanna, but was a wink enough?

"What do you want to do with your life, Peter?" she had asked him.

"Oh, I want to be happy, of course. I want a good life, with a good job — probably in the family business. I have to finish college first, of course . . ."

And love? He did not speak of love.

One night, when Joanna was off at one of her subdebutante parties — "kids' parties," he had called them — he had driven her to Half Moon Bay, and they had climbed up across the dunes and down to the beach, and he had spread a blanket for them, and played his bright show tunes on his harmonica. They had had the beach to themselves, and Sari had begun tickling him again, and, laughing and wriggling under her persistent fingers, they had found themselves making love again, under the stars with the surf crashing behind them. But that was the way it always seemed to happen. Love was something they found themselves doing. It was unplanned love, love without desperate secret meetings in carefully planned places. It was something he enjoyed doing, it seemed, when the time and circumstances were right, but he also enjoyed sailing and playing his harmonica and driving fast in his red car. Did all men make love in this disengaged fashion? She really didn't know the answer. Were all lovers like this? She had no one with whom to compare this idle, handsome, virile, and uncommitted lover she had found.

"I love you, Peter," she had whispered to him when it was over. "Very much."

"You're very sweet," he said.

"Will we get married, do you think?"

"Married? Huh. Well, who knows? Perhaps. But I have to finish college first. And my father's even threatening not to send me back to college if I don't get a job this summer."

"Are you looking for a job?"

"Well, I can't just get any job, can I? I can't just get a job pumping gas. Can you see that? Peter LeBaron pumping gas? My life is really a bit messed up these days . . ." And they were off again on another subject.

And then, one day, on another beach — it was Stinson Beach this time — they had all three joined hands and run across the beach and into the waves. And as their running feet splashed into the surf, Sari had thought: This is the moment. He will release Joanna's hand now, take me in his arms, and shout, "Jo, Sari and I are in love! I'm in love with Sari! We wanted you to be the first to know!"

But that hadn't happened, and their hands remained joined as they dove together into the ocean. And he remained that bright, golden blur of boy on the top of the mast, his outline indistinct against the sun behind him. And she was still the loosely draped lady on the top of the Dewey Monument, poised, ready for flight, her chin up, on tiptoes, waiting to be kissed.

"Is it your friend Joanna who interests you so in the LeBaron household?" Gabe Pollack asked her. "Or is it the son? I hear he's very good-looking."

"Gabe! Jo is my best friend," she lied to him.

"You're moving in pretty fancy company," he said. "But this is America. In America, there are no social barriers between the rich and the poor . . ."

In early July of that year — 1926 — Sari and Joanna met at their favorite place, the Japanese Tea Garden in Golden Gate Park, and Joanna had immediately said, "I have something very serious to talk to you about, Sari," and from the expression on her face Sari knew that it was indeed serious. For a terrifying moment she had thought that somehow Joanna must have found out about her and Peter. But how could she have? Unless he —

"What is it?" she asked.

"I've — I've gone and gotten myself gravid," Joanna said with a forced little laugh.

"Gravid?"

"Preggers. Pregnant," Joanna said.

"Oh, my God," Sari whispered. "Who?"

"*Enceinte.*"

"How many periods have you missed?"

"Four. As of this week."

"Oh, my God, Jo!"

"It sort of blows my debutante year into a cocked hat, doesn't it?" she said. "Not that I care about that, of course. It's just —" But there were tears in her eyes now, and a little sobbing sound came involuntarily from her throat. "Oh, Sari, what am I going to do?"

"Who is the boy, Jo?"

"I can't tell you. I won't."

"I thought there were never going to be any secrets between us," she said, knowing even as she said it that she had already broken her side of that promise.

"This is different. I can't tell you."

"Is it the Flood boy?"

"No! I told you I'm not going to tell you who it is!"

"Why not? He'll have to marry you."

"No. He won't. He can't. It's my problem. I'm going to have to solve it some other way."

"You mean he's already married?"

"No! Stop asking me these questions! I told you I can't marry him, won't marry him, don't want to marry him."

"Well, tell me this. Does he know?"

"Yes. No. I don't know. Maybe he suspects, but it doesn't matter because I can't marry him."

"But he'll *have* to marry you, if —"

"Stop talking about getting married! I told you I can't marry him!"

"If you've told him, then what does he offer to do about this?"

"Nothing."

"Nothing?"

"No, because I haven't told him, not in so many words. But as I say, maybe he suspects."

"Then you must *tell* him, ask him what —"

"I *can't* tell him!"

"Why not?"

"Because I say I can't, that's why!"

"Then what — what are you going to *do*, Jo?"

"I don't know!" she sobbed. She made balls of her fists and pressed them hard against her eyes. "Oh, Sari, please help me . . . I don't know . . . I tried . . . I never thought, from just a few little times . . . I never thought . . . afterward, I thought I was being so careful, with the douching and everything. . . . They said douching with vinegar, that was supposed to do it, wasn't it?"

Sari had never heard this and experienced a flutter of panic over her own situation. Vinegar?

"Oh, Sari," Joanna said. "Just say you'll help me. Please say you'll help me. I'm so frightened, Sari!"

She put an arm around her friend's shaking shoulders. "Of course I'll help you, Jo," she said. "Any way I can. But how —?"

"My debutante year," she said. "That was supposed to begin right after Labor Day. That's a joke, now, isn't it? Labor Day?"

"Tell me this," Sari said. "Have you told your parents?"

"Yes."

"And what do they say?"

"Frantic! Frantic. They want to send me away, give the baby up. But I won't, I won't do that! Oh, Sari, just say you'll help me. We made a solemn pact — a pact in blood! Just let me hear you say you'll help me, Sari!"

"I've already said I'll help you, Jo," she said quietly. "I'll help you in any way I can. Now tell me everything your parents said."

Joanna had made the mistake of telling her mother first, and Constance had immediately become hysterical. Monsignor Quinn had been summoned to the house, and Julius LeBaron had been called home from the office. "Is it Jimmy Flood?" he had demanded. "If it is, I am going to the telephone this minute and call his father, and —"

"Oh, no!" Constance LeBaron had wept. "Not the *Floods*, Father — please! We'd never be able to hold our heads up in this town again. Oh, please don't do that!"

"It's not Jimmy Flood!" Joanna had cried.

"The thought of abortion may have crossed your minds," Monsignor Quinn had said. "But you must not let it. That is against the written word of God and the Holy Church, and is out of the question."

"I don't want an abortion!"

Monsignor Quinn had crossed himself and repeated, "It is out of the question. Do not utter that word, Joanna."

"Tell us who the father is!" her father had said.

"I won't!"

"Please tell us, Joanna," Monsignor Quinn said. "That is the only way any of us can help you. We want to help."

"No."

"She must be sent away," Constance LeBaron had said. "She must be sent away as soon as possible, and as far away as possible. She will have the baby, and it will be put up for adoption. Can the Sisters of the Good Shepherd help us there, Quinn?"

"I won't put the baby up for adoption!" Joanna had said.

"You will damn well do what we tell you to do, young lady!" her father had roared. "You're a minor, and we are your parents, and you will do as we say!"

"I won't!"

"You *will!*" her father said, raising his arm as though to strike her.

"Her debutante season," Constance LeBaron had sobbed.

"If you try to make me give my baby away, I'll go all over town — right now — and tell everybody that I'm pregnant with an illegitimate baby! How will you hold your heads up in this town after that? I'll tell them I'm pregnant by Immaculate Conception!"

Monsignor Quinn crossed himself again.

"You wouldn't do that to us!" her mother had said.

"Oh, wouldn't I? Just wait and see!"

"Oh, Father, Father," Constance LeBaron had sobbed, and it was not clear whether she was talking to her husband, or to the Holy Father, or to Father Quinn, who had only recently been made a monsignor. "What are we going to do?"

"First, let us pray," Monsignor Quinn said, raising his hand to offer the Benediction. *"In nomine patri . . ."*

"I think her parents have offered her the best advice," Gabe Pollack said when she told him all of this. "Their faith prohibits abortion, and abortions are very dangerous anyway — particularly, I'm told, at this late stage in her pregnancy. I think you should try to persuade her to do what her parents propose."

"But she says she won't give up the baby. She says the baby is going to be a LeBaron, and she wants it raised as a LeBaron."

"Which does she want to be — a mother or a debutante? She can't have her cake and eat it, too."

"Joanna is very stubborn," Sari said.

"I think your parents are right," Sari said when they met the following day. "I think you should go away, have the baby, and then let it be placed out for —"

"No," she said, shaking her head. "I won't do that. I've made up my mind."

"I just don't see any other solution, Jo."

"I do," Joanna said. "I have another plan."

"What's that?"

"I'll agree to part of their plan. I'll go away for a while. And you'll go with me."

"Me?"

"Yes. You and Peter."

"Me . . . and Peter . . ."

"Yes. You could marry Peter. Why not? He's crazy about you,
I can tell. Then you'd go off on your honeymoon, to some faraway
place — Europe, perhaps. A week or so later, I would join you
there, wherever it is, and have my baby there. The baby is due in
December. After it's born, I could come home. I'd miss the first
half of the deb season, but I'd be back here for the second half.
You and Peter could stay on in Europe for a few months longer —
long enough so that it would seem as though the baby could be
yours and Peter's, conceived and born on your long honeymoon."

"That's a crazy idea, Jo!"

"Is it? I don't think so. You'd raise my baby as your own. My
baby would still be in the family, raised by the two people I love
the most, you and Peter. It wouldn't be like giving up my baby to
strangers, which I won't do, anyway."

"Marry Peter . . ."

"Crazy about you. I can tell."

"Oh, no, Jo."

"You promised to help me. Won't you help me?"

"But — has anyone spoken to Peter about this?"

"Yes. I have."

"And what does he say?"

"He agrees. Peter," she said, "will do anything to ensure my
happiness."

"Well," she said almost angrily, "if Peter wants to marry me,
he could at least ask me!"

"He will. As soon as he's sure you'll say yes."

"And what about your parents?"

"They'll agree. I'll handle them. They'll agree, if I can tell them
that you'll say yes."

"Let me think" she whispered. "Let me think . . ."

Joanna reached out and covered her hand with her own. "You
see," she said, "I want to keep my baby near to me, even if my
baby never knows who I am. Is that so strange, Sari — to want to
keep this little new life that's growing inside me close to me, always,
even though it never knows that I'm its mother? But I'll know,
and you'll know, and Peter will know — but that's all. It'll be our

secret, Sari, our wonderful little secret, a little baby that will belong to all three of us. No one else will ever know."

"But your parents —"

"They'll know, of course, but they'll never tell another living soul."

"No, I suppose they wouldn't."

"Help me, Sari. You promised to help me. Help me now."

"Let me think."

"Yes, but there isn't much time to lose. *Please.*"

"Well, I'll be damned," Gabe Pollack said when she had explained Joanna's proposal to him. "She *does* get to have her cake and eat it, too! That little girl is smarter than I gave her credit for. She gets to keep the baby, more or less, and gets to be a debutante as well!"

"But what do you think of it, Gabe?"

"It's a quid pro quo situation, isn't it," he said. "You do her this favor and, in return, you get to marry one of San Francisco's richest and most attractive young men. It's almost like a business deal, isn't it? But then, this is America, land of the deal."

"But what do you *think*, Gabe?"

"I think —" he began. Typical of him, she could see, trying to intellectualize the situation, trying to see it from every side. "I think," he said at last, "that she is asking a great deal of you. She is asking you to be the substitute for a part of her life. She is asking you to pay for one of her mistakes. In return, she's offering you her brother as a reward. But because there's money involved, I think she'll always think that you owe her the greater debt. Do you love him, Sari?"

She hesitated, suddenly embarrassed to confess the depth of her feelings to him. Their romance still seemed too one-sided to discuss it openly with Gabe. "I find him very . . . attractive," she said at last.

"Is that all?"

"He's very nice."

"And he's rich."

"Yes."

"Does he love you, do you think?"

"I don't know. I know he likes me. But is love important, Gabe? Is it important to be in love?"

He shook his head. "I can't answer that for you," he said. "But there's a saying that anyone who marries for money works hard for a living. So I hope there's more to it than that."

"I think there is," she said.

Finally, he said, "I can't advise you in this, Sari. I can't tell you what you should or shouldn't do. I think that this is something you've got to work out between yourselves — you and Peter LeBaron."

"Yes," she said. And then, "Of course, I used to think that someday I'd marry you."

"I've spoken to Father Quinn," Joanna said to her parents, "and he thinks this is an excellent solution."

"Quinn," her father said, "always favors any solution that's quick and easy, and keeps the Church's hands clean."

"I'd hoped for something so much better for Peter," Constance LeBaron said. "There are so many attractive girls — girls of good family — in San Francisco. Peter could have had his pick."

"I *like* Sari," Julius LeBaron said. "And there may be an advantage in the fact that she's not from our so-called social set."

"What would that be, pray?"

"Think about it a minute, Mother. Sari is definitely from the wrong side of the tracks, as they say. When she and Peter get back to San Francisco with their baby, and when people begin counting backwards on their fingers, as they're bound to do — well, somehow it's more understandable, more acceptable, for a young man of good family to have taken up with a woman of easy virtue, than for a —"

Joanna smiled. "Than for a young woman of good family to *be* a woman of easy virtue," she said. "I wondered how long it would be before someone came up with that little point."

Julius LeBaron's face flushed. "Well, you know how people talk." he said.

*   *   *

"What do you want me to do, Peter?" she said to him. They were in Julius LeBaron's study in the house on California Street, and this meeting had been arranged for them, and they were to make their final decision.

He was not looking at her, but staring miserably into space with an utterly stricken expression on his face. For some reason, she realized, he seemed more shattered by what was happening than anyone else. "Do?" he said at last in a dead voice. "Do? We've got to do what will make my sister happy. That's all there is to do."

"Do you love me, Peter?"

"Love you?"

"Yes. Just because you've been to bed with me doesn't mean you love me. I know that."

"We've got to help Jo," he said. "How did all this happen, Sari? A week ago, I thought I was the luckiest man on earth. But now — now I just don't know."

"Well, we're here to decide whether to go through with what she proposes. Or not to."

"I've got to help her. I've got to do my duty. She's my sister —" There were tears in his eyes, and he clenched his right fist and pressed his knuckles hard against his teeth.

"Peter," she said, and then, almost desperately, leaning toward him, she went on, "I love you, Peter. I love you so much. You're the only man I've ever slept with, and that means something, doesn't it? I love you enough for both of us, Peter, I'm sure of that, and I'm sure I can make you happy. I'm going to make you love me, Peter — I will, wait and see. I'm going to make you love me, and I'm going to make you happy. Will you let me try? I'm willing to try, Peter, if you are, and if you let me — I'll try. I'll try so hard. Will you?"

"Yes."

"Well, then tell me what you want me to *do!*"

"Marry me," he said at last. And then, "For my sister's sake."

"And for our sakes, too!" she cried. "We have to be happy, too, don't we? Don't we deserve to be happy, too? Don't we at least deserve a chance — a chance to try?"

"Yes," he said. "I'll try."

And so, the following week, an item appeared in the society pages of the *San Francisco Chronicle:*

PETER POWELL LeBARON WEDS
THE FORMER MISS LATHAM

In a small ceremony attended only by family and close friends, Mr. Peter Powell LeBaron was married to Miss Assaria Latham of Terre Haute, Ind., in the chapel of the Cathedral of St. Peter Martyr, San Francisco.

The bridegroom, long considered one of the city's most eligible bachelors, is the son of Mr. and Mrs. Julius LeBaron of 1023 California Street. Mr. LeBaron is the president of LeBaron Vintners, Inc., wine producers in the Napa, Colusa, and Sonoma Valleys until Prohibition. The bride's parents are both deceased. She is the legal ward of Mr. Gabriel Pollack of San Francisco. The bride wore an heirloom gown of white Valenciennes lace, and carried a Bible garlanded with white orchids and stephanotis. Miss Joanna LeBaron, the bridegroom's sister, was her only attendant.

Following a small reception at the LeBaron home, the bride and groom departed for an extended European honeymoon. Later this month, they will be joined by Miss Joanna LeBaron, who will undertake several months' travel and study of art and history abroad.

Now it is nearly one o'clock in the morning in the White Wedding-Cake House that was being built for them while she and Peter and Joanna were waiting for Melissa to be born in Saint Moritz, and still Sari has not gone to bed. She wants, desperately, to speak to Melissa now, but cannot. Mr. Littlefield's presence in Melissa's apartment precludes this. Perhaps, even now, the two of them are making love — why not? Sari would have nothing to say against this. And so, instead, she pens Melissa a short note:

Melissa dearest,
I know you are thinking that there is a great deal of explaining to be done, and I am very much prepared to tell you everything

you need to know. Please telephone me as soon as you receive
this.

Much love,
A.L.LeB.

She will have Thomas slip the note under Melissa's door in the morning.

Surely, once the special circumstances surrounding her birth are explained to her, Melissa will be reasonable, because now, more than ever, Sari needs Melissa on her side. "You will be reasonable, won't you, Melissa?" she says to Melissa's portrait now. "You'll vote on the side of the woman who sacrificed so much to raise you, and not on the side of the mother who gave you up — won't you?" But the enigmatically smiling portrait offers no reply. "You'll help me win this fight, won't you, Melissa?"

Wheeling herself away, Sari tells herself: *I'm going to win.* I'll win, she says, because I was strong enough to make a man love me who was afraid to love me, strong enough to make a lover out of a lover who wasn't one. I'll win because I have the strength, because I have the faith, because I have the will.

Watching her, the house seems to sigh.

We are your house, the house says. Without you, Sari, we would not exist. We were your wedding present.

"Not that I asked for you, or needed you!" she says.

But without *us*, Sari, *you* would not exist, the house says.

Thirteen

BARONET VINEYARDS, INC.
934 Montgomery Street
San Francisco

NOTICE OF SPECIAL MEETING
OF SHAREHOLDERS

A special meeting of shareholders of Baronet Vineyards, Inc., will be held in Suite 617–619 of the Fairmont Hotel, San Francisco, California, on Monday, April 30, 1984, at 9:00 o'clock a.m. for the following purposes:

1. To consider the acquisition offer by Kern-McKittrick, Inc., of your Company for 13.25 (thirteen point two five) shares of Kern-McKittrick per each one (1) share of Baronet Vineyards now outstanding.

2. To conduct a shareholder vote on above offering.

3. To transact any other business that may come before the meeting.

Shareholders of record at the close of business on March 4, 1984, are entitled to notice of and to vote at the meeting or any adjournment thereof.

March 15, 1984

By Order of the Board of Directors,

William C. Whitney
Secretary

It is important that your shares be represented at the meeting. Even if you expect to attend the meeting, PLEASE SIGN AND RETURN YOUR PROXY PROMPTLY.

"Well, the fat's in the fire!" Sari says to Gabe Pollack. "This is it! Here we go!" Her tone is almost jubilant, and Gabe knows that now that the fight is actually at hand, with a date, place, and time for the showdown settled, this fact alone has done much to buoy her spirits. Everything that has gone before has been as dust in the mouth. But now that the fighters are actually in the ring, have exchanged the perfunctory gloved handshake, and are squared off to do battle, Sari is in her element. "Have some more coffee," she says to him. It is Monday morning, and they are in Sari's drawing room, sipping coffee and enjoying a plateful of Cookie's sweet rolls, like old times. "Even if I lose, Gabe," she says, "and I may, I'm going to go down fighting. There's fight in the old girl left, Polly, and I've still got one or two pieces of heavy ammunition I haven't brought out. There's some fight left, and even if I don't win there'll be casualties, wait and see. The casualties won't be all on our side, either."

"What's your secret weapon?" he says with a little smile.

"Never mind!" she says with a wink. "If you tell what your secret weapon is, it's not a secret anymore, but I've got one and it'll be a real crowd-disperser that will turn this little meeting of theirs into a rout! It'll send lawyers running to their casebooks, it'll — but never mind. Whatever happens, this is going to be my last hurrah."

"Well, I wish you luck," he says.

"Don't. Don't wish me luck. I don't want luck. I want success.

Wish me success, if you want to — success with my last hurrah!"

He raises his coffee cup. "To success, then," he says.

"And now, on top of all this, get a load of this new development, Polly," she says, and hands him another piece of the morning's mail. He takes it and reads:

Law Offices
BARTLESS, MATHER, BROOKS & KLINE
Two Embarcadero Center

Assaria L. LeBaron, Esq.
2040 Washington Street
San Francisco, California 94109

re: Estate of Peter Powell LeBaron, Deceased

Dear Mrs. LeBaron:

This firm has been retained as counsel by your niece, Miss Melissa LeBaron, in a claim Miss LeBaron will be making against the Estate of your late husband, Peter Powell LeBaron, based on the recent disclosure to our client that she is the natural daughter of your late husband's sister, Ms. Joanna LeBaron of New York City.

As I am sure you are aware, under the terms of your late husband's Will, our client was specifically bequeathed five percent (5%) of all outstanding shares of Baronet Vineyards, and an additional fifteen percent (15%) was to be divided equally among all living issue of Joanna LeBaron. It will be our client's claim, therefore, that she is rightfully entitled to an additional seven and one-half percent (7½%) of outstanding Baronet shares at the time of your husband's death.

Further, it will be our contention that our client is rightfully entitled to any and all dividends paid on said 7½% of shares and which have thus far been unrightfully paid to our client's half brother, Mr. Lance LeBaron of Peapack, New Jersey. In this regard, it would be helpful to have from your office a full accounting of dividends paid, whether in cash or stock, to its shareholders of record since October 10, 1955, the date that our client became a beneficiary of the Estate.

Let me add that our client is fully aware that this is a family situation of some delicacy. Therefore, it is her wish and ours that all shares and monies due our client should be delivered to our client promptly and *in specie* fully, in order that litigation may be avoided. Meanwhile, until this matter is settled to our client's satisfaction, we have advised our client to avoid direct communication with other members of her family.

Sincerely yours,
J. William Kline, Jr.

"When did I get to be an 'Esq.'?" Sari asks.

"It's a form all lawyers seem to use nowadays," he says, handing the letter back to her. "Well, this is a hell of a note, Sari."

"Isn't it?" she says, her eyes sparkling. "Isn't it wonderful? What a damned fool I've been, Gabe! Why didn't *I* think of this?"

"I don't understand," he says.

"Don't you *see?* I've been so busy thinking about voting shares that I never even thought about *dividends.* Do you see what she's asking for — half of Lance's dividends for the past thirty years, *half of his entire income!* Do you realize how much that would amount to, Gabe? Millions! Millions and millions! Plus interest! If she's smart she'll ask for thirty years' interest on top of it all! Lance can't pay it, of course, nobody could, and there's no way she could try to get that kind of money out of me. She'll have to sue Lance, and if she wins she could send Lance LeBaron straight to the poorhouse. Then Lance could probably sue Joanna. Then maybe Joanna could try to sue me, though I can't see what she'd base a case on. Failure to disclose? *She's* the one who's failed to disclose. Don't you see, Gabe? This company is going to be so tied up in lawsuits that you won't be able to see the sky for the legal paperwork, and nobody is going to want to touch us with a ten-foot pole till it's settled, and that could be years! Oh, I almost hope that Harry Tillinghast wins his takeover bid. Then *he'll* inherit this whole can of worms. But the fact is that until this is settled nobody's going to want this company but me — *me!*"

"I see what you mean," he says.

"Gabe, this is simply the best thing that could happen to me at this point," she says. "And the damned thing is, why didn't I think of it? Dividends!" She waves the lawyer's letter in her hand. "And this is only the beginning. Hand me that," she says, pointing to a small pocket calculator that sits on a table. He hands it to her.

"Let's see," she says, "let's figure how much she stands to collect. Let's say, in round figures, Lance has been getting six hundred thousand a year, and Melissa wants half of that — that's three hundred thousand, times thirty years. That's nine million! Plus interest, cumulative interest —"

"The letter doesn't mention interest," he says.

"If they're smart, they'll ask for it. So, let's see —" She begins punching more figures into her calculator.

Watching Sari like this, greedily poking away at the little calculator, totting up sums of money and achieving totals that surely will never change hands, is not, Gabe thinks, to see Sari at her most attractive. In fact, as he sits there sipping his cooling coffee, there is almost something a little depressing about it all, and he can remember a pretty young girl, flushed from her first success on a stage, with whom it is hard to reconcile this old woman who sits opposite him now, licking her lips as millions are added to more millions of dollars. Yes, this morning Sari suddenly looks old, old and desperate, and even ugly in her thirst for power. He looks at his watch, and decides he must think of some excuse to go.

"Lance will be wiped out!" she cries gleefully. "*Wiped out!* At least twelve million, with interest — maybe more!"

"I wonder what Peter would have said," he says.

"Who knows?" she says breezily. "But isn't it funny, isn't it ironic, that Peter should have been — should have died — just when our company began to move into the really big time, in nineteen fifty-five? That was the year the really big money started to come in again."

Gabe Pollack shifts in his chair. "Well, it looks like you've got your secret weapon," he says.

"Oh, I've got one or two more arrows in my quiver," she says with another wink. "But I'll tell you this — I've never felt more sure of winning this thing than I do right now. And the press! Think of the field day they'll have with this! The illegitimate daughter, the mystery father, the daughter suing the man who turns out to be her half brother! Then the half brother suing his own mother! Maybe there's some way they can *both* be wiped out, Gabe."

"Well, that would be nice," he says a little dryly, "to have them both wiped out. But speaking of the press, Archie McPherson is already dropping little hints about a story. He knows something's up, and if he knows, then others will be finding out, too. When do I get my story, Sari?"

"Just give me a few more days," she says, "and I promise you you'll have it. You'll have it, and it will be an exclusive. Your name will be in all the papers, too! Now tell me, Gabe, when I answer this lawyer's letter, should I bring up the matter of interest they may have overlooked?"

"I'd let Melissa deal with her lawyers, if I were you. In fact, I don't see why you need to answer that letter at all. You're a family-owned company. You don't have to reveal any figures to outside lawyers at all."

"Wait for them to subpoena them, do you mean? But don't you see, I want them to have these figures. I want them to know how much is involved. I want to get these lawsuits started — right away!"

"Well," he says, "do what you want. You always have." He rises, a little stiffly, from his chair. "I've got to go."

"I'm certainly going to mention the interest business to Melissa."

"You're not supposed to communicate with Melissa."

"Oh, bull-do! Bull-do and double bull-do, Pollywog!"

"Well," he says a little lamely, "keep in touch."

"Give me a kiss," she says, and he pecks her on the cheek. "Dear old Pollywog," she says. And then, as he is going out the door, she calls after him, "Don't act so glum! I know you're worried that I'm going to use my *final* secret weapon. Don't worry — it doesn't look now as though I'm going to have to!"

Immediately, when she is alone, she seizes a pen and stationery and writes another note to Melissa. This is against the lawyer's instructions, of course, but Sari doesn't give a damn. Sari has no intention of obeying lawyers whom she isn't even paying. *Dearest Melissa*, she writes:

> *I think your legal maneuver is absolutely brilliant! I could kick myself for not having thought of it myself, but I've been so preoccupied with the Tillinghast business that I haven't been thinking clearly.*

If you pursue this matter of Lance's dividends, be sure to ask for cumulative interest. *You're going to be richer than Gordon Getty!*

Meanwhile, I have a proposal for you. How would you like to help run Baronet — with me, as a team. We could do it, you know, with what we now know you control. I'd be prepared to offer you a very important and powerful position in the company. Think about this, and let me know.

XXXX

A.L.LeB.

P.S. I know we're not supposed to have "direct communication." How about banging once on the radiator pipes if you're interested, and twice if you're not? Smoke signals, I'm afraid, would bring the S.F.F.D. screaming down Washington Street!

Then she adds, as a calculated afterthought, *Remember that I always loved you as though you were my own.*

Now it is night again, and the big house is silent. There have been no thumps on the water pipes, no smoke signals, no word whatsoever from downstairs. All Thomas can report is that he has not seen Melissa go out, and that Mr. Littlefield is apparently still there. He used the swimming pool, alone, for a short time this afternoon. With Melissa in the apartment, it is difficult for Thomas to search the place for clues as to what the two are up to. All Thomas can do is leave a pair of breakfast trays just inside Melissa's door in the morning, and pick them up, outside the door, when they are finished later on. Sari has tried telephoning Melissa several times, but Cora, Melissa's maid, who answers, will only say that Melissa is "unavailable," or "taking a nap," or "on her other line." What are they doing, plotting down there? Sari tries to imagine them in an orgy of illicit drugs and sex, but that is not Melissa's style.

It is night, and her dinner is finished, and the guards across the street at the Russian Consulate have changed, exchanging their stiff salutes. The curtains on the Washington Street side of the house have been closed, and only the curtains on the north side, facing the Bay, have been left open to take in the famous view. Sari is alone now, and feeling a little lonely. She would like some company, but there is suddenly no one. Gabe, she got the distinct impression, was more than a little disapproving of the new stratagems she outlined this morning. Gabe, she sometimes thinks, has never really understood her. No one has. Gabe cannot understand, for instance, how a woman who has so much, so many possessions, can ever be lonely . . . desperately lonely.

For company, now, there is only Thomas, and Thomas, when he has no news to impart, can be more than a little boring.

Her secret weapon. She moves now, in her motorized wheelchair, into the portrait gallery where the secret of her secret weapon reposes. In December of 1941, the world was suddenly at war again, and Peter had tried to enlist in the navy. He was only thirty-six, but had been turned down because of high blood pressure, which he found it hard to believe he had. And that was the year and month of Melissa's fifteenth birthday, and she had sat for her portrait in the family tradition.

Thank heaven the artist had persuaded Melissa to pose for her portrait without the infernal glasses, and the true, fresh beauty of her face and eyes had been captured and shone through without optical impediments.

"When did she get to be a beauty?" he had whispered when the portrait had been delivered, and she had replied, "Why, she's always been a beauty, you silly man. You've just been too busy to notice. She's got the LeBaron looks."

Sari had suggested hanging the portrait between Peter's and Joanna's portraits — the two members of the most recent generation — but suddenly and quite irritably Peter had said he did not want it there.

"Why not? There's such a nice resemblance to the two of you."

"I said I don't want it there! I want it hung on the opposite wall. Do as I say, Sari."

"Well," she had said easily, "it really doesn't matter to me where it's hung. We'll hang it wherever you want it, Peter."

And so it had been hung on the opposite wall. But there was something about Peter's behavior that puzzled her, disturbed her, nagged at her. It was one of her sadnesses that Peter and Melissa had never seemed able to become close to one another, that Peter had never been able to accept her as his own. Was that what it was? Was that why he wanted Melissa's image placed as far away as possible from his own? The question nagged at her for the rest of the day.

That evening, as it happened, they had arranged to dine with Joanna in the old Mural Room — gone now, replaced by a fancy dress shop — of the St. Francis Hotel on Union Square. It would have been an uncomfortable evening for Peter under any circumstances. One had only to look around the restaurant to see that he was one of the very few young men in the room. Already, San Francisco was becoming a city of women, of widows and waiting wives, of rowdy servicemen passing through on their way to the Pacific, and young men in civilian clothes were looked on with suspicion and distrust, as though they might be German spies. And here was handsome, healthy-looking Peter Powell LeBaron, who refused to believe that he could have high blood pressure, having dinner with his sister and his wife.

It was supposed to have been vaguely a working dinner, and they had wanted to discuss what course the company might take now that America was at war. It was agreed that little could be decided until it was clear what direction the war was taking and, meanwhile, to see to it that supplies of Baronet wines were shipped to officers' and servicemen's clubs around the country.

"We're a working man's wine," Joanna said. "And who's working harder now than our boys in the service? You might suggest that to your advertising people, Sari."

"Not a bad idea, Jo," Sari said. "Not bad at all."

After that, Sari had tried to keep the conversation light and inconsequential, since she had noticed several women in the room had been giving Peter disapproving looks, and he himself looked unhappy. A new musical called *Lady in the Dark*, which had been a huge hit on Broadway and which poked gentle fun at psychoanalysis, was coming to San Francisco. Should they try to get tickets to see it? What would be the role of Soviet Russia in the war? President Roosevelt's budget for defense was eleven *billion* — surely eleven billion dollars would be enough to win the war. What role would Hungary play? Yugoslavia? The Scandinavian countries?

Then Joanna had mentioned that she had had a letter that morning from Rod Kiley, the young physician she had married briefly in 1927, following her debutante season. He had written to tell her that he had enlisted in the Army Medical Corps, and had been given a commission as a captain. He was being sent overseas, though he couldn't say where, and was writing to explain why their son, Lance, might not be hearing from him for a while. (Four years later, he would be dead from shrapnel wounds in the Battle of Okinawa.)

"I never understood why you didn't stay married to him, Jo," Peter said. "He seemed like such a —"

"Such a nice chap, yes," Joanna said, finishing his sentence for him. "Oh, he was certainly *nice*. Just terribly old-fashioned. You know, a Puritan Yankee New England type, with ideas about marriage that went back to the Victorian era, or even before. For instance — believe it or not — he couldn't get over the fact that he hadn't married a virgin. To him, I was some sort of damaged goods."

"But how could he have possibly known that?" he asked her.

"Well," she said, "it was rather obvious."

"But how? It isn't really that easy —"

"To tell? Perhaps not with some women. But in my case, it was."

"How?"

She paused for a moment, looking straight at him. "Don't you know?"

"No."

She lowered her eyes. "My caesarian scar," she said.

He suddenly reached out — for what? — for something, and his hand struck his wineglass, knocking it over, shattering it, and red wine spread across the white tablecloth like blood. "Oh, dear!" Sari cried, reaching for a napkin, but Joanna said nothing, did nothing, but simply sat there with a small, oddly contented, curiously satisfied smile on her lips, and then, in a flash, it had come to Sari — the answer, and all the pieces of the puzzle fell into place at once. Of course, of course, Peter was Melissa's father, of course, of course, Melissa was Peter and Joanna's child. *"Tickling . . ."* *"I've done a terrible thing . . ."* *"I don't want her portrait hung there . . . Do as I say . . ."* And it struck her with such suddenness and swiftness that she lost her breath, and what felt like a rush of fever surged up through her cheeks and forehead and lodged behind her eyeballs, as she looked at first one, then the other of them. Waiters appeared from all directions, dabbing at the spilled wine with napkins, picking up pieces of broken glass, and gathering up the stained tablecloth at the corners to replace it. Sari excused herself and went to the ladies' room.

There she washed her hands and face, reapplied her makeup, and ran a brush several times through her dark red hair. Then she studied her reflection in the mirror, thinking: I am no different, but now everything is different. "Peter fails to regard the consequences of his actions," the president of Yale had written to his father years ago. But I love Peter. Even though Peter never loved me. All I ever wanted was someone to love me. "Can I get Madam anything else?" "No, thank you." When she left the ladies' room, she handed the matron an extravagantly large tip — twenty dollars. When she returned to the table, the others were ready to leave. Joanna was going on to a theatre party.

In the car, going home, Sari reached out and rolled up the window between the back seat, where she and Peter were sitting, and their driver. She was wearing the new breath-of-spring mink coat that he had given her for Christmas, and in the ladies' room she had splashed a great deal of My Sin on her throat and shoulders — Peter's favorite scent, and it was Joanna's scent! — and the back of the car was suffused with the odor of her perfume and the new furs. "I know," she said in a low voice. "I know the secret now. You're Melissa's father."

"Stop it!"

"No. I want you to listen to what I have to say."

"Stop it!" And he made a lunge toward the handle of the car door, but she seized his elbow.

"*You* stop it," she said. "What are you going to do — throw yourself out of a moving car into Powell Street? Act like a man, for God's sake! If you thought you were man enough to try to sign up and fight a war, you can be man enough to listen to what I have to say."

"No . . . no," he moaned.

"Just tell me one thing. Do you still love her?"

"Love . . . she's my sister." He sagged back into his seat. "No . . . no . . . but I've hurt her so terribly."

"You've hurt each other. But it seems to me she's hurt you more than you've hurt her."

"No . . ."

"Yes! Didn't you see what she did tonight? Did you see how she manipulates you? Do you see how she still wants to possess you, to keep you obsessed and ridden with guilt? Her caesarian section! Could it ever have been clearer to you than it was tonight, the kind of cat-and-mouse game she has been playing with you all these years? Peter, I don't care what happened years ago. You were both young, children really, and it was the nineteen twenties, when everyone was experimenting with things, trying new things, taking chances, taking risks —"

"It only happened when we'd both had too much to drink. We didn't know what we were doing."

"I'm not interested in your excuses." She was still gripping his elbow, and the words were pouring out of her, flooding out. "You and I took chances, too. We never thought of the consequences, and neither did you and she. I'm not saying that I forgive you, because there's nothing to forgive. I've done some hard thinking in this last half hour, Peter, and what I'm talking about is what's happening *now* — not what happened fifteen years ago. That's all in the past, water over the dam, and I understand all that, I accept it. But what's happening now is what we both saw tonight — how she uses an old mistake to own you, to keep her claim on you, to keep you forever belonging to her and from never belonging to me or to anyone else, not even to yourself! Don't you see? That's why she wouldn't give up the baby. She wanted to keep the evidence — the evidence of your love — and to be able to keep flinging that evidence in your face, day after day, year after year. What kind of love is that? It isn't love. It's torture."

"Don't hate her," he said, covering his eyes with one hand.

"Of course I don't hate her. But now you can see — now we can both see — how she uses that old mistake to keep you in her power, like a kind of slave. Tonight she finally tipped her hand, and lost the game."

That night, in her room, she changed into a long peignoir of white silk, and splashed more My Sin on herself. Then she went to the bar, fixed nightcaps for them both, and carried their drinks to his room, where he lay in his bed in his Sulka pajamas, looking ill and exhausted. She handed him his drink, and sat on the corner of his bed with hers.

"I just can't believe that she told you this," he said.

"She didn't. I guessed it. Tonight, when she made you spill your wine."

"We were just kids. We never thought —"

"Hush. I told you the past doesn't matter."

"Was it my fault? Was it? I was a nice boy, wasn't I?"

"That doesn't matter, either. What matters is that you and I got married, which was what she wanted. We raised Melissa, for better or for worse, which was what she wanted. It seems to me that we've more than paid back any old debt you may have owed to her."

"In the wine cellar. We'd have too much to drink. We drank too much in those days, perhaps. And then —"

"There you go. The past again. What matters more is the present, and the future, our future. We happen to be husband and wife, and we happen to have your daughter."

"I never believed Melissa would be born. I was sure something would happen, and she wouldn't be born."

"But she was."

"Perhaps now is the time to give Melissa back to her?"

She laughed softly. "I hardly think so," she said. "I think Melissa has enough problems right now without being told she has a new mother. You and I made a commitment to her, and I think we've got to keep it, Peter. Besides, Jo doesn't want Melissa back. She wants you. That's what became very clear to me tonight. You know, I asked her once why our marriage was so — passionless. I asked if she could explain your — distance. Separate bedrooms. I asked her if she thought you had a mistress, and she gave me an ambiguous answer, implying that you did, implying that she knew something that I didn't — which of course she did. So you see, that's the way she likes to think of herself, as your mistress. Forever. Your kept woman, and you're her kept man. What kind of love is that? Very second-best, it seems to me."

"I swear to you I never touched her again! Not after —"

She had raised her finger to her lips. "That doesn't concern me," she said. "Not now."

He clenched his fists and turned his head against the pillow. "It was the goddamned wine cellar!" he said. "That goddamned wine cellar, and that goddamned MacDonald letting us spend all that time there together! He must have known —"

"What concerns me," she went on, "is why we've never been a real husband and wife together. That's what baffled me until now. Now I think I understand it maybe a little bit. Joanna's and your secret was in the way. Because I'm your wife, and I'm a woman who loves you. I began loving you that night you had our dinner sent up to the suite in the Saint Francis, and we made love. Isn't it funny? In the same hotel where we had dinner tonight. I even remember the number of the suite — it was suite six-oh-nine and six-eleven. After we made love, and you fell asleep, I put on your baggy Norfolk jacket, sat looking out over Union Square, ate a lamb chop, and fell in love."

"I remember I ordered lamb chops. And asparagus —"

"— and rissolé potatoes. And I've loved you more and more over the years, Peter, loved you even more knowing that something was terribly wrong, and not knowing what it was or what I could do to help you — searching for ways to help you, and never finding them, looking for a path that would lead us . . . somewhere besides to our separate bedrooms. But the path was always blocked. By whom or by what I couldn't tell. Out of this frustration, I found myself loving you even more . . . desperately. It's been like a kind of . . . blackmail, hasn't it, this threat that she's held over you? But now that the secret's out, the blackmailer can't hurt either of us anymore, can she? We're free. We're free to love each other again, Peter, and we can if we want to. I want you to have a real wife, a wife who loves you, not just a blackmailing mistress. I want you to have the love you deserve, not second-best." He reached out and covered her trailing fingers with his own.

"It's kind of exciting, isn't it?" she said. "It's like starting over with a whole new life! It's like getting married all over again, with no secrets to hold us back!"

It would be pretty to be able to say that their old passion had been rekindled that night, and that their marriage had become complete, but the truth is somewhat different, even though — as the lawyers say — he returned to his spouse's bed that night. Their marriage did not become complete because Peter was no longer complete, if he ever was. A cloud, a shadow, a distraction, would continue to fall across him at times, even during lovemaking, and his eyes would half-close, and he was miles away. It was as though the damage to him had been too profound, and the scars would not heal.

Had Peter really been in love with Joanna? Sari never asked that question. Had he ever really been in love with anyone? Certainly Sari could never bring herself to ask him that. And what had he done to satisfy his own physical, venereal yearnings, if any, during those long years — the years Sari sometimes speaks of as the arid years, the dry years, of their marriage? What hasty, panting, illicit encounters may have taken place in sordid hotel rooms, or in parked cars, or in the back rows of movie houses, or even in the gilded boudoirs of Mme. Sally Stanford's famous San Francisco establishment, where all manner of exotic delights were served up for the randy sons of the city's elite? Who knew? Sari never asked him, and did not want to know. She had had enough of family secrets, and did not want to find out any others.

What happened was that Peter began withdrawing more and more from the day-to-day operations of Baronet, and turning more of this over to Sari, though he retained the title of president of the company.

And what also happened was that Sari did her best to divert him when she saw the clouds across his eyes appear, and one of his dark moods descending. She found him, for example, one morning alone in his study cleaning his service pistol. "What are you doing?" she asked him.

"Just cleaning my gun," he said.

"What for?"

"Needs cleaning."

"That seems like a dreary thing to do on a beautiful Sunday morning! I was thinking — let's do something we haven't done in years. Let's drive out to Seal Rocks, take a picnic lunch, and watch the seals."

They had done this.

Not far from Seal Rocks, there is an oceanside amusement park with a Ferris wheel — the largest Ferris wheel in the world, it was said, when it was first put up. After their picnic lunch above the rocks, they had gone to the amusement park and bought tickets for the Ferris wheel. Up, up, and down and around they had gone on the wheel, screaming with excitement with all the other passengers as the wheel spun faster, and moaning when the wheel stopped to let passengers disembark, and their little chair was left suspended, rocking back and forth, in the sky.

But even then, though the secrets had been aired, the spirits exorcised, the ghosts put down, that cloud, that shadow, that look of dazed distraction would fall across Peter LeBaron's face — even there, on the top of a Ferris wheel overlooking a Delft blue ocean, it would happen. She would never see that bright blur of boy swaying from the head of a mast again. Never.

"Isn't this wonderful!" she had cried, seizing his hand.

Wonderful.

If only Joanna would move away to some distant city, Sari had begun to think, that might help things. As it turned out, such an opportunity was not far in the offing.

Let me tell you something about Peter Powell LeBaron that will perhaps help explain him to you, for I also knew him well. You may have heard from gossips in San Francisco that Peter LeBaron, for all his boyish charm and almost-Valentino looks and seeming golden promise, was not bright. I take exception to this. He was certainly not bookish, and was no intellectual, and as we know he never finished college, but he was far from stupid. On the other hand, he possessed qualities that could be exasperating, as this story illustrates.

This is a story that I doubt even Sari knows, since she was not present at the time. But she will perhaps not mind my telling it at this point, since it reveals something of his character and temperament. It was in the late twenties, 1928 or '29, before the crash, and Peter and a companion were driving — too fast, of course — down El Camino in his red Stutz on their way to a party. They must not be late. Just outside Redwood City, a medium-size Border collie suddenly darted out from beneath a hedge and into the road. There was no time to brake, and Peter's front wheels struck the animal. He sped on.

"Shouldn't we stop? See if he's hurt? See if we can find the owner?" his companion urged.

"Stray mutt," Peter said, still speeding on.

"It was a nice little Border collie. It might have a tag —"

"No, just a stray mutt," Peter said.

The dog might have been killed, or only slightly injured. It might indeed have been a stray, or then again, more likely, it might have been some family's treasured pet. We'll never know.

That was Peter LeBaron. Short-sighted. Irresponsible. Spoiled. An aging youth.

Sari made only one allusion of what she had discovered to Joanna, and that was years later, after Athalie was born, and the twins, and by that time certainly Joanna knew that Sari knew, and that Sari had won. It had been at the cemetery, after Peter's funeral, and Joanna had been behaving very badly, very melodramatically, weeping far too much. The priest had raised his hand in the sign of the cross as the first shovelful of earth was cast into the grave, and Joanna, sobbing, had suddenly lurched forward, as though about to fling herself across her brother's casket. This was after

Sari's accident, of course, and she was now in a wheelchair, but she nonetheless reached out and seized Joanna's arm firmly, and whispered, "Stop this. If I can be brave, so can you." "I've lost him, I've lost him!" Joanna sobbed. As more shovelfuls of earth fell, and the priest intoned the final words, other mourners, with Gabe Pollack at Joanna's elbow now, led the two women away. "You lost him a long time ago," Sari whispered fiercely. And then, looking up at her, she said, "Just tell me one thing, Jo. Did your mother ever know?" Briefly, Joanna looked at Sari, and her streaming eyes had a frightened look, like that of a treed animal. Then she lowered her eyelids, and said, "Mothers always know everything."

And now, alone in the house, the house has begun to creak and sigh. A storm, bringing rain and fog, is blowing in across the mountains of Marin through the Golden Gate. One by one, the swagged tiers of amber lights from the bridge begin to disappear as the fog descends. The house sighs as though ghosts are taking possession of it. There are ghosts here, of course, and the ghosts and their secrets are hanging there in the portrait gallery.

Fourteen

"I'M AFRAID WE LOST THE BABY, Mrs. LeBaron," the doctor said. She was still drowsy from the anesthetic. "I'm terribly sorry."

"Lost?"

"Her lungs were filled with fluid, Mrs. LeBaron. She never started to breathe. In effect, she drowned."

"Drowned. Athalie." If it was a girl, they were going to call it Athalie. If it was a boy, it was to be Peter, Jr. This was in 1943.

"May I see her, please?" she said.

"Your husband is here," the doctor said. "He'd like to have a word with you."

"Well," she said, trying to arrange her face in as brave an expression as possible when he came into the hospital room, "we tried, didn't we? We did our best."

He kissed her on the forehead.

"Ask them to bring her in to me," she said. "I just want to look at her. Just once."

"No, Sari."

"Why not?" she said, pushing herself up on her elbows. "I know she's dead, but I just want to take one look at her. I just want to say good-bye."

"No, you won't want to."

"I do! Why can't I? Why can't I say good-bye to my baby?"

"There was much more wrong with her than what the doctor told you," he said. "Her heart —"

"What? He said fluid — her heart —"

"I've ordered the casket sealed. Later, when you're feeling better, we'll have a little service for her."

"Her heart," she said, and sank back against the pillows. It was the heart she had felt with her fingers, beating inside of her. "Athalie . . ."

"Forget Athalie. Forget she ever existed. That's the best thing," he said.

"But she did exist! She lived inside my body for nine months."

"Forget . . ."

"But we'll try again, won't we? Tell me we'll try again."

"We'll try again."

Joanna had come to visit her in the hospital. She had not particularly wanted Joanna's visit. She had begun to look at Joanna in a somewhat different light. She no longer trusted Joanna, pact in blood or no pact in blood. All those little suggestions on how she should raise Melissa during Melissa's troubled childhood no longer seemed helpful and solicitous and caring. They seemed like simple interference.

"It's nothing but a temper tantrum," she would say to Joanna. "Ignore her, leave her alone."

"But you can't ignore the child, Sari darling, don't you know that much about bringing up a child? Her temper tantrums are cries for help. Sari darling, I really think a child psychiatrist —"

"Jo, once and for all. Are you going to let me raise this child or not?"

"But Sari darling, remember that you owe me a rather large debt."

"Debt? What debt is that?"

"Peter."

"And, Jo, you also owe a rather large debt to me — remember that? Melissa. Isn't the score even?"

"Sari, we made a pact. A pact in blood. Always to help each other. We should not be talking about debts."

"No, we shouldn't be."

Today, instead of having that kind of a shapeless, pointless argument, Sari would probably have simply said to her, "Shut up! Mind your own business! Get out of my house. You got to have your cake and eat it, too!"

Now, standing by her hospital bed, Joanna said, "Sari darling, I'm just so terribly sorry about the baby. But in a way it's a blessing, isn't it? It could never have led a normal life."

"It had a name," she said. "Her name was Athalie LeBaron."

"The best thing to do is forget Athalie. Forget she ever existed."

She turned away from Joanna, her cheek against the pillow. "Was that your advice to Peter?" she said. "Athalie did exist." But she was feeling too weak to fight.

And when, at the end of that week, she came home from the hospital, she had — out of some almost forgotten instinct or impulse — flung a scarf across the mirror above her dressing table so that *Malchemuvis*, the Angel of Death, would not see his handsome reflection in the glass and be tempted to visit her house again.

Then, in the spring of 1945, the twins were born — two happy, healthy, beautiful baby boys, Eric and Peter, Jr.

Joanna came to see the babies, and immediately scooped them up in her arms with, it seemed to Sari, almost too much an air of possessiveness and protectiveness. "Is this little Peter?" she said to the small, bald head that was nestled against her left shoulder.

"Yes."

Peter had let out a small, plaintive cry.

"Oh, he cries, little Peter does, just like a little peeping frog," Joanna exclaimed. "Should his name be Peter or Peeper, do you think?"

"My son isn't a frog," Sari said.

But somehow Joanna had been able to make the nickname stick. And so Joanna managed to name one of Sari's children.

* * *

Still, with the birth of two fine twin sons, that should provide
our story with a happy ending, the happy, obstetric ending.
But our story doesn't end there. Every day, right before our very
eyes, under our very noses, accidents happen, mistakes are made.
The newspapers are full of these stories. They fill the files of the
psychologists. Years ago, in an obscure mill town in northern Ohio,
a worker in a steel mill is laid off his job because of hard times.
To fill his days, he whittles a crude slingshot, fastens to it a stout
strip of rubber sliced from an old inner tube, and presents this
plaything to his two young sons, showing them how they can use
it to dispatch empty beer cans lined up on a fence rail in the
backyard, much the way their father taught them to swim in the
Cuyahoga River and taught them to skip flat pebbles across the
surface of a pond. The two brothers are close, but they are young
and excitable, and three days later the older boy aims the slingshot,
playfully, at his younger brother. No harm was meant, but the
younger boy's eye is lost, and the sight of that single, bloodied
eyeball, dangling by the thinnest filament of muscle tissue from
his brother's head, and the brother's look of, at first, sheer surprise,
will not go away and reappears forever in the older brother's dreams
and nightmares. The half-blinded brother becomes a priest, ad-
ministering to the sick and elderly. And is it guilt over his brother's
disfigurement, that vision of the dangling eyeball that will not erase
itself, that causes the older brother to become a motorcycle racer,
experimenting with one daredevil feat after another, until, inevitably, he is thrown from his bike into a concrete retaining wall
beside a levee in California, and his own face is left brutally scarred,
with most of his lower jaw torn away? The sight of him after the
accident turns his wife permanently from him. Is this why, one
night sitting alone in a drive-in theatre in Texas in 1972, during
a showing of *Deliverance* — during the famous sodomy scene, in
fact — he quietly reaches for the automatic rifle on the passenger
seat beside him and begins shooting at the moviegoers in their
cars? Before he has finished, five lie dead — two women, a man,
and two teenagers on their first date — and four others are injured.
Is this why the older brother is now waiting on Death Row, while
the younger, half-blinded brother has been placed in charge of an

important parish in Detroit? Where, in this chain reaction, does the blame lie? Who must account for this physical and emotional carnage — the wife who would not let her husband touch her, the father who whittled the slingshot for his handsome and beloved sons, the owner of the mill that laid the father off, the producers of films like *Deliverance* that fill our screens with so much unnatural sex and violence, our loose gun-control laws, or our increasingly depersonalized society? You tell me.

During Sari's pregnancy with what would turn out to be the twins, Melissa seemed even more disturbed than usual about what was going on. "Do you *have* to have this baby, Mother?" she asked her again.

"Have to? Well, the fact is that I'm going to," Sari said. Though Melissa was now eighteen, Sari had been advised by the doctors and other experts whom she consulted that this appeared to be a classic case of sibling rivalry, albeit an inappropriate one for a girl of Melissa's age. "Her place and position, as the baby in the family, are being threatened with usurpation by the new infant," one of these experts had explained.

"Do you *have* to, Mother?"

"I'm very happy about it," she said. "Don't you think it will be fun to have a new little baby brother or sister?"

("Try reassuring her that, as the firstborn, she will always occupy a special position in the family," the same Expert had advised.)

"You'll always be special, Melissa," she said. "You're our first-born. In fact, I'm going to count on you for a great deal of help with this baby."

"I don't want you to have it!"

"Why not?"

"I'm frightened, Mother."

"What's there to be frightened of? The doctor says I'm perfectly healthy."

"You're not my real mother, are you?" Melissa said.

"Melissa, we've gone over this hundreds of times. Of course I am."

"I'm adopted, aren't I?"

"No, you are not adopted. Please, no more of this silly talk."

"Then why am I different?"

"Different? Every person is different from every other."

"Was I a difficult birth, Mother?"

A pause. "You were a beautiful baby," she said. And then, "Giving birth to a baby is never exactly easy."

"I'll never know that, will I? If I want a baby, I'll have to adopt one. The way you adopted me. Adopted people only get to adopt their babies because their blood is bad. I read that."

"Well, that's absolute nonsense, Melissa. Now please let's —"

"Don't have it, Mother. I'm frightened. The Sutter Buttes."

"What about the Sutter Buttes?"

"I'm afraid this baby is going to be a monster. Like the one I saw at the Sutter Buttes."

"The Sutter Buttes are nothing but a bunch of brown old hills."

("I would recommend, Mrs. LeBaron, that when your baby is born you be very attentive when the baby is in Melissa's presence," the Expert had said. "She should not be permitted to be alone with it. There is a possibility that she might try to harm it." And then, "I think I detect two heartbeats.")

But then, when the twins were born, the Expert was proved quite wrong. Melissa was overjoyed with the babies, as overjoyed as if they had been her own. Soon she was helping to feed and dress and diaper them, taking them out for walks in their twin carriage, lifting them in and out of their cribs and playpen, and lavishing so much obvious love and attention on them that all Sari's apprehensions quickly evaporated. In fact, the twins seemed to make Melissa happier and more relaxed than she had ever been in her entire life. It is a miracle, Sari thought, as within six months Melissa announced that she no longer wanted the various tranquilizing drugs that had over the years been prescribed for her by Experts. On her own, thanks to the advent of the twins, Melissa seemed at last to be growing up.

The only symptoms that remain of what was once diagnosed as "neurasthenia" are a certain tenseness of manner, a shortness of temper, a tendency to embrace sudden, short-lived, and sometimes inappropriate enthusiasms, and a periodic drinking problem.

*				*				*

Then, just before Christmas of 1945, Peter telephoned Sari at the Montgomery Street office. "Something terrible has happened," he said in a choked voice.

"What is it?"

"Joanna. She's just been rushed to Mercy Hospital."

"What's wrong with her?"

"Her maid found her. They think she tried to — tried to commit —"

"Oh, God. How is she?"

"They say — they say she's going to live."

"Thank God. You must get over there right away, Peter."

"I can't — can't face it, Sari."

"Then I'll go," she said quickly, and hung up the phone.

"I'm her sister-in-law," she said to the nurse at the desk outside the Intensive Care Unit. "How is she?"

"We had a close call," the nurse said. "But we're going to make it. We pumped her stomach out. Sleeping pills."

"Intentional, do you think? Or an accident."

"We don't know. They tell us there was no note left. She's awake now, if you'd like to go in to see her."

"Yes."

"Just for a few minutes. We're still a little uncomfortable."

"Joanna dear," she said in as tender a voice as she could muster. "It's me."

"Oh, Sari," she said, turning her head toward her. Joanna's still-beautiful face was gray, there were dark circles under her eyes, and her hair was damp and matted about her forehead. "I'm so sorry."

"What happened, Jo?"

"I was so discouraged and depressed. There seemed nothing left for me to live for."

"Jo, don't say that. You have everything."

"No. It's you who have everything. You have Peter —"

"Nonsense. You also have Peter, and you have me. We love you."

"You have the business. Years ago, when we used to go out and work with the field hands, I used to feel a part of things, a part of your lives, a part of the business. But now we're all becoming rich again, and there's nothing for me to do. Lance is off at school in the East, growing up. I'm all alone, turning into a bored, useless, middle-aged rich person. You have your job. You have your adorable little twin babies . . . I have nothing. Even our friendship doesn't seem what it was."

My adorable little twin babies, Sari thought. Is there possibly a connection between them and this? In Joanna's plan, perhaps I was not supposed to have any adorable twin babies. But instead she said, "Would you *want* to do something for the company, Jo?"

"What could I do? I have no talent. I have nothing."

"Perhaps we could think of something," Sari said.

"In school, my teachers used to say I was creative . . ."

"If you're interested, we'll think of something."

Joanna closed her eyes. "Peter . . . why didn't he come?"

"He's in Sonoma today," she lied. "We're still trying to reach him."

With her eyes still closed, she smiled a wan smile. "I have a saint's name," she said. "I'm bound to be martyred."

That afternoon, Sari dictated an interoffice memorandum to her husband. He was, after all, the president of Baronet, and this was a matter of company business that she was proposing.

TO: P.P.LeB.

FROM: A.L.LeB.

I spent some time with your sister at the hospital this morning.

One of the things that seems to be on her mind is her feeling of being "out of things" in terms of Baronet, whereas in the 1930s we all worked together in the vineyards, etc. Joanna feels that now that her son is nearly grown she is in danger of becoming an indolent woman of leisure, and she expressed an interest in being given something to do.

You may recall that several years ago your sister made an astute suggestion on how we might advertise our wines to servicemen during the war. This suggestion was never followed up, but it was a good one. And I think you will agree with me that Joanna has a keen creative mind.

You also know that you and I have both expressed dissatisfaction with our present advertising agency in New York, and that those fellows on Madison Avenue sometimes seem to have no idea of what goes on in our vineyards and wineries in California. Joanna, meanwhile, grew up in the wine business and knows it well.

My proposal is this: that Joanna be placed in charge of our advertising for at least two years, on a trial basis, and that funds be set aside for her to open her own New York agency, with Baronet as her principal account. This would of course require her relocation in New York, but that should present no problem.

I believe this would give your sister the "shot in the arm" she appears to need so much at this point in her life. And I believe she'd do the job well. A further advantage of such an arrangement might be that, whereas advertising agencies charge commissions of 15% of billings, Joanna might be persuaded, as a "family," or "in-house" agency, to charge a lower percentage.

Please let me know what you think of this suggestion, and whether we should put the proposal to her when she has recovered from her current illness.

And so that was how Joanna LeBaron became the Media Maven of Manhattan.

"Melissa has found out," Joanna is explaining to Eric on the telephone from New York. "This is exactly what I was afraid would happen."

"How did she react?"

"Angrily. Bitterly. Bitter at me, bitter at your mother."

"Who told her?"

"Your mother, of course. Who else?"

"That was a shitty thing to do."

"Yes. Shitty. But typically Sari. She denies it, of course, but obviously she felt she had nothing to lose by giving Melissa the facts — and everything to gain. So there we are."

"Well," he says, "now that she has the facts, what's she going to do with them?"

344 The LeBaron Secret

"Your guess is as good as mine, Eric. I've been trying to reach her on the phone for the past two days. Obviously, she's not taking or returning calls."

"Obviously."

"Do you think you might have better luck getting through to her, Eric?"

"When she's in one of her moods, I'm not sure."

"Will you try? It would be helpful if we knew how she intends to vote."

"I'll try, Aunt Jo. It's just that I'm not very hopeful."

"Otherwise, I guess we'll just go into our meeting on the thirtieth and let the chips fall where they may."

"Yes."

"And, frankly, I'm not hopeful about any of this, Eric, now that this has happened. Unless you can somehow manage to persuade her otherwise, I'm terribly afraid that Melissa is going to take your mother's side."

"What makes you think that, Aunt Jo?"

"Sari LeBaron has been trying to poison Melissa's mind against me for years," Joanna says.

This last, about poisoning Melissa's mind, is a damned lie, and Joanna knows it's a damned lie. But, Sari sometimes thinks, in the years since Joanna has become the Medusa of Madison Avenue, the Hecate of Hucksterism, she has built a very lucrative career on lying — on exaggerating and inflating the merits of her clients' products, and falsely denigrating and ridiculing the claims of her clients' competitors: "Nine out of ten hematologists recommend Bonzo Mouthwash . . ." "Are you still using old-fashioned Grippo for flu symptoms, when you could be dancing under the Miami moon after one dose of doctor-recommended Flu-Go?" "Kills Lice by the Millions on Contact!" Lies. Garbage. Lies are Joanna's stock in trade. At least, in Baronet's advertising, Sari has never pretended that her wines were anything other than what they were: plain, old-fashioned, no-frills wines for the working man. And when it comes to Joanna's claim that Sari was trying to poison Melissa's mind against her, the truth is the exact opposite. One example will suffice.

It was in the summer of 1955, when the twins were ten, and were spending the month of July at a boys' camp in Maine. Soon they would be on their way to Bitterroot, where the whole family was to spend the month of August, and Melissa — so changed, so improved — was helping Sari plan a homecoming party for them. Melissa was twenty-eight now, and Sari had begun to wonder whether she would ever marry. And yet, at the same time, she had grown accustomed to Melissa's presence in the household, and enjoyed her companionship. That morning on the Montana ranch had been clear and golden. The sun was reflected in silver half circles on the lake and, while Peter worked outside at clearing his trees, the mood of the two women in the ranch house was buoyant and expectant as they planned the little family party. "I wonder if they'll have changed much, after their month at camp," Melissa was saying, and Sari said, "They're probably brown as berries, and grown another inch or two."

Then she suddenly laughed and said, "Melissa, do you remember years ago, when I found out I was pregnant again, you were so upset about it?"

"Of course I remember."

"Why was that, I wonder?"

"I was frightened, Mother. Of course, when the twins were born, and everything was all right, I saw I shouldn't have been, but at the time I was terribly frightened."

"Frightened of what?"

"Frightened that the baby would be born a — monster. Deformed. And frightened that you were going to die."

"Whatever put that notion into your head?"

"It was something Aunt Joanna said."

"Joanna?"

"She told me that if you had another baby, it would be born deformed. She told me that if you had another baby, it would probably kill you. I used to have nightmares about it."

"Why in the world would Joanna have said a thing like that?" she said.

"She said you were too old. She said you were past your child-bearing years. She said it would be like Athalie. But even worse."

"I was only thirty-five . . ." But suddenly she was so angry that she could no longer speak, and her anger had a color — crimson — that seemed to spring up in a swordlike shaft from her groin to the ceiling of her brain. Finally, she said, "I'm going out to pick some wildflowers for the table."

She followed the sound of Peter's ax-strokes until she found him where he was laboring at his clearing in the woods, and she paused a little distance from him to watch him — bare to the waist, still tall, arrow-straight, muscular, and slender. The drops of perspiration flew from his forehead and shoulders in the same arcs as the pearly chips from the tall pine he was felling. A thought floated across her mind. He was fifty years old. From the early 1930s until after the war, they had not visited the ranch at all, and during those years much of the land he had cleared previously had turned into forest again, and in the years since he had managed to clear perhaps eighteen acres of the four hundred he planned for his sheep range, along with the new undergrowth that sprang up inexorably year after year. He always insisted on working alone, refusing the help of Mr. Hanratty, the ranch superintendent. Even though old, Hanratty was an excellent woodsman. "I want the feeling of personal accomplishment," he would explain to her, "and I want the exercise." But now, as she watched him, she saw that there would never be a sheep range, that he could never possibly live to finish the project he had undertaken, not if he lived to be a hundred. She saw it all as his delusion, his obsession, another form of his self-punishment, and she saw it all as somehow connected with Joanna.

She stepped closer to him. "Peter," she said, "how do you ever intend to finish this unless you get some others in to help you?"

The question seemed to irritate him, and he paused, frowning, leaning on his ax, and mopped at his brow with a red-checked handkerchief. It must have been a question he had begun to ask himself, and Sari knew she should not have asked it.

"It's coming along," he said finally, and resumed his chopping.

In the middle distance, Mr. Hanratty passed through the clearing, on his way to some errand or other, and Sari smiled and waved at him, but Hanratty was not on her mind. She was trying to decide how to tell Peter what Melissa had just told her, or whether in fact to tell him at all.

But, as though he had been reading her thoughts, he said, panting, between swings of his blade, "Had a — phone call — from Jo this morning."

"Oh? What did she want?"

"Wants to — have Lance — come out here for the rest of the summer."

"Really? Why?"

He paused once more, and mopped at his brow again with the handkerchief. "Lance is between jobs, and has been staying with her. But it seems she's got to go to Japan on business, and wants to let her servants go for the month and close the apartment. She wants to know if we can take Lance."

"Well," Sari said, "we can't."

"Really? Why not?"

"Because I don't want Lance here. If she wanted to send Lance out here, she should have asked me."

"I thought the twins would enjoy it," he said. "Having an older fellow around — someone closer to their age than you or me."

"Well, I don't want him here. He can't come."

"Well," he said, "I'm afraid I already told her we'd be glad to have him." And he resumed his chopping.

"What?" she cried. "You told her he could come without even consulting me? I'm going back to the house right now, and telephone her, and tell her that he can't come. That he's not welcome, that I don't want him."

"Ah, you wouldn't do that, Sari."

"I certainly would, and I certainly will. That bitch has some nerve —"

"Don't be so hard on Jo, Sari. It hasn't been easy for her, raising the boy without a father."

"And what about me?" she said. "I'm sick and tired of doing everything Joanna wants! I've raised her daughter, haven't I? I've raised enough of her damned children. I'm sick and tired of cleaning up after your sister's dirty little messes. Your sister is nothing but a plotting, conniving woman who wants to create dissension between us. First it was Melissa who was dumped on me. Now it's Lance. Well, I won't have it, Peter."

"Now, Sari, you don't mean that." He was circling the tree now, studying it, analyzing the cuts he had already made, planning the next ones. "Jo's your best friend."

"I certainly do mean it," she said. "And with a friend like that, I don't need enemies. All she wants to do is to drive another wedge between us. Don't you see? It's all she's ever wanted."

There was another blow of the ax, and the tall pine quivered, its limbs lifting and sighing in the wind, its needles whispering in a kind of protest. "I told Jo we'd help her out," he said.

"*Why?* Why do we have to help her out? Haven't we helped her out enough? Is it —" she began, as the ax fell again, "— is it because you think she's better in bed than I am? Is that it? Is it because she's the better lay?" She was screaming at him now, as the ax fell again. "*Or is it because Lance is your son, too?*"

The tree began to fall, and she saw it tumbling toward her, tried to run, then stumbled and fell as the tree crashed upon her. "Oh, my God!" she heard him cry. "Oh, my God, Sari!"

Mr. Hanratty, who had heard her screams, came running, and between them the two men tried to raise the weight of the tree that had fallen across her legs, and all she could hear was Peter sobbing, "Oh, Sari! Oh, my God, Sari!"

Later, from what she dimly recognized was a hospital bed, she opened her eyes and saw his face bending over her. "Oh, God, I'm sorry, Sari," he was saying. "The wind shifted, and then you ran — right into the path of the fall —"

"No," she said. "It wasn't the wind. It was my fault. I shouldn't have said that. It was all my fault."

"Don't say that," he said. "It was an accident, Sari — I swear to you it was!"

She closed her eyes. No, she thought, perhaps it was not her fault or his fault.

It was Joanna's fault.

Fifteen

*F*ROM THE FRONT PAGE of the *Peninsula Gazette:*

KERN-McKITTRICK TAKEOVER BID
SPARKS FAMILY FEUD

San Francisco, March 28. A complex family-business drama is unfolding in the boardrooms of two of California's most prestigious corporations, and in the drawing rooms of two of the Bay Area's wealthiest families. Pitted against each other, furthermore, are two of the city's toughest street fighters, oil magnate Harry Boyd Tillinghast, and Assaria Latham LeBaron, president and chief executive officer of Baronet Vineyards, Inc., and dowager of the LeBaron wine clan. Tillinghast's Kern-McKittrick Corp., it seems, would like to get into the wine business, and has made Baronet shareholders a $56 million stock offer to prove it.

The issue is complicated, however, by a couple of factors. For one, Harry Tillinghast's daughter, Alix, is married to Assaria LeBaron's son, Eric, 39, of Hillsborough. And Assaria LeBaron has flatly rejected the Tillinghast offer as "chickenfeed" — that's $56 million worth of chickenfeed, mind you.

Related Factors

Sparks began to fly in the LeBaron family in February when Baronet's New York ad agency, LeBaron & Murdock, Inc., re-signed the Baronet account, claiming "differences in advertising philosophies." LeBaron & Murdock is owned by yet another family member, Mrs. Joanna LeBaron Kiley, Assaria LeBaron's sister-in-law, who is known professionally as Joanna LeBaron.

Insiders, however, claim that the differences were more than philosophical, and that the real reason for the split was Baronet's refusal to pay full commissions on advertising placed through the agency, and Baronet's contention that it is entitled to "family prices."

But that intra-family dispute may also have been sparked by Assaria LeBaron's earlier announcement that her son Peter P. LeBaron, Jr., would be appointed co-director of advertising and marketing for the company, along with his twin brother, Eric. Eric LeBaron was reported as having been unhappy with this arrangement, which his mother defended as "bringing new strength to the Advertising-Marketing Division."

Eric LeBaron's unhappiness is said to explain his support of the Tillinghast takeover bid, which is also supported by Joanna LeBaron Kiley, another major Baronet shareholder. Thus, two sisters-in-law are pitted against each other for control of the company, and mother is pitted against son. Eric LeBaron has been dismissed by the company. His brother, Peter, remains, and will presumably support his mother in the struggle.

Family Secret

Baronet Vineyards, the nation's largest purveyor of inexpensive jug wines, has long been a wholly family-owned company, and its assets a closely guarded family secret. A number of take-over moves in the past have been unsuccessful. However, when the Tillinghast organization was able to acquire 2,000 shares of Baronet last year, Kern-McKittrick was able, as Assaria LeBaron puts it, "to get its toe in the door — and a very unattractive toe, at that. Oil and water don't mix, and neither do oil and wine." Kern-McKittrick operates oil-producing fields, primarily in Kern, Tulare, and Fresno Counties.

Due to the wine company's traditional secrecy, it is difficult to place a value on its stock, which has never been traded in the marketplace. However, the Tillinghast offer is currently 13.25 shares of Kern-McKittrick common for each share of Baronet common. And since Kern-McKittrick is currently traded on the

N.Y.S.E. at around $50 a share (it has reached as high as $56 in recent weeks, as rumors of the takeover have circulated on Wall Street), it is possible to figure that Harry Tillinghast estimates Baronet's stock as worth about $662 a share.

This, Assaria LeBaron insists, is much too low. Her company's shares, she says, are worth at least $1,000 a share, for which Harry Tillinghast would have to up his bid to at least $80 million in Kern-McKittrick stock. "Does he take me for a fool?" Mrs. LeBaron told the Gazette yesterday. "When he was allowed to buy in, he paid $700 a share. Now he offers $660. Does he think we've gone down in value?" Mrs. LeBaron accuses Mr. Tillinghast of acting in bad faith.

The matter will presumably be settled at a shareholders' meeting scheduled for April 30.

Unexpected Complications

To date, Baronet Vineyards is owned by only seven shareholders. Assaria LeBaron is said to control roughly 28,000 shares, and her sister-in-law is said to own an equal amount. An additional 12,000 shares are owned by Joanna LeBaron's son, Lance, 55, of Peapack, N.J., a sportsman and horse breeder. Peter LeBaron, Jr., is said to own 4,000 shares; his brother Eric owns 2,000 shares, and Harry Tillinghast presently owns 2,000 shares. However, an unexpected complication has arisen involving the shareholdings of Miss Melissa LeBaron, socialite and art patroness.

Miss LeBaron was raised in San Francisco as Mrs. Assaria LeBaron's daughter. But in the course of sorting out the LeBaron holdings in preparation for the takeover battle, it was revealed that Miss LeBaron is, in fact, the daughter of Joanna LeBaron Kiley by a previous marriage. Under the terms of her father's will, Melissa LeBaron was left 4,000 shares of Baronet stock outright. But the will also stipulates that the 12,000 shares which Lance LeBaron now holds were to be divided equally between Joanna Kiley's children. Melissa LeBaron is now claiming that this was not done, and that she is legally entitled to 6,000 additional shares from her father's estate. With 10,000 shares under her control, Melissa LeBaron could well provide the "swing vote" in the dispute. Miss LeBaron refused to be interviewed for this article, and all queries were referred to her attorneys, who had no comment.

Legal complications arising from this latest family revelation could easily stall the Kern-McKittrick takeover in its tracks.

"Stay That Way"

"This has always been a family-run company for four generations, and it's going to stay that way," Assaria LeBaron told the Gazette. "If anyone has any sense they'll see it my way, and keep Baronet what it is. Meanwhile, this is getting to be ridiculous. Nobody in the family is speaking to anyone else. Once I win, and get this all behind me, I'd like to get back to my real business, which is making and selling wine."

Mrs. LeBaron, a septuagenarian, is a well-known local philanthropist. It was she who principally underwrote the restoration of the Odeon Theatre, and she is active in urban renewal projects in the area south of Market Street. She is also the "Flying Grandmother" who last winter made headlines when, though she has no pilot's license, she took the controls of her company's Boeing 727 and flew the aircraft under the center span of the Golden Gate Bridge.

Mrs. LeBaron is also the owner of the San Francisco Condors baseball team, currently in spring training at Candlestick Park.

Baronet Vineyards was founded by her late husband's grandfather, Marc LeBaron, a French immigrant, in 1857. Her husband, Peter Powell LeBaron, Sr., was killed in a hunting accident at the family's Montana ranch in 1955. Since his death, Mrs. LeBaron has run Baronet almost single-handedly, and has earned deep respect as a tough trader and a shrewd but honest fighter in the business community.

"I love it, Gabe!" Sari says. "It's perfect. I got all the quotes, and I don't mind being called a tough trader or a fighter at all. I also like that 'shrewd but honest' part. In fact, I think the whole thing's very pro *me*, don't you?"

"That's what you wanted, isn't it?"

"And we even got in a plug for the Condors! They'll love that. And we've made the LeBarons French instead of wops. Old Julius would have loved *that* — though he'd have preferred it if it'd said 'French aristocrat.' When did this hit the stands?"

"Six o'clock this morning."

"Ha! We've already had calls from *Time* and *Business Week,* asking who Joanna's first husband was. They find no record of it. Ha! I told the truth. I said I didn't know. I told them to ask Joanna. Ha! So I put the ball right back in her court, on that one."

"I'm glad you like the story, Sari."

"I do. Congratulate Archie for me."

"I'm sure he'll be pleased to hear that he can still be of some use to you," he says without a trace of sarcasm.

"Now, Gabe. You know that at first I thought the best thing to do was to try to destroy Melissa's credibility. Then I changed my mind, and decided I needed her on my team. That's a woman's prerogative, isn't it, to change her mind?"

"Absolutely, Sari."

"Now, even if Melissa won't return my calls or answer my letters, she'll read this and certainly see the light — right on the front page! You've scooped the country, Gabe. Suddenly, I'm very optimistic."

"Good," he says.

"Miss Martino has already had calls from the network news. What do you think, Gabe? Should I go on TV with this? Should I do *Good Morning America,* and the *Today* show?"

"That would be up to you, Sari."

"If there's one thing I've always been able to do, it's present myself to the public. I think what I'll tell them is that all I'll consent to do will be a segment on *Sixty Minutes.* I think *Sixty Minutes* has more credibility than those morning spots, don't you? And they'll come to the house to tape it. With the others, I'd have to go to New York. What should I wear for *Sixty Minutes?* Something simple, I think, simple and businesslike. And I think I'd like to do it with Harry Reasoner, and not one of those other bozos. I definitely won't do it if it's Mike Wallace . . ."

Gabe Pollack is smiling. Sari is a star again.

After Peter's funeral, she had also been a star, the principal mourner, the chief recipient of the condolence letters and telegrams — from heads of industry, the mayor of San Francisco, the governor, from Chief Justice Earl Warren — all of which she would answer on embossed and monogrammed black-bordered stationery. And after all the guests had gone, and the hand-wringing and kisses and murmurs of sympathetic words were over, she and Gabe had been alone at last in the big house on Washington Street, and the Wedding-Cake House had suddenly seemed very empty, and Sari had found herself feeling very dispirited. She had draped her black mourning veil across the mirror in the drawing room.

"*Malchemuvis.*"

"Yes."

"You loved him, didn't you, Sari?"

"Yes. No. Off and on. On and off. He was a difficult man — to get to know. For a long time, it was like living with a stranger, a shadow, or a ghost, and I couldn't find out what was haunting him, haunting us. And then I found out, and it helped me bring him back to life — for a little bit, at least. From time to time. But the ghost never really went away. It kept coming back to haunt us with what it knew. Joanna. Did you see her at the grave? What a ridiculous woman."

"An evil woman, do you think?"

"No, not evil. Just ridiculous. Ridiculous, but very effective."

"I still don't understand it," he said.

"What?"

"A hunting accident. He never hunted, did he?"

"No. He chopped down trees. Back in the nineteen thirties, he used to carry a pistol, but that was just for the morale of the field hands when there were labor troubles — threats of strikes, scab labor coming in, that sort of thing. He never used it. I used to carry a pistol, too, for the same reasons, and I used my pistol more than he did, but never on a human being."

"Then how did it happen?"

"That morning, he seemed perfectly normal. A little more withdrawn than usual, perhaps. My accident upset him terribly. He blamed himself. He told Mr. Hanratty that he was going out to hunt some rabbits. Rabbits! Rabbits were never a problem at the ranch, not that I knew of. And when they found him, it was as though he had tripped over a fallen log, and the pistol had accidentally gone off into his chest. He was lying on his face, on the other side of the fallen log. It wasn't an accident."

"Why do you say that?"

"I found this," she said, and wheeled her chair to the Regency games table, spun its top around, and lifted the piece of blotting paper from one of the secret compartments underneath. "Hold it up to the mirror, and you can read it," she said.

He went to the mirror, and gingerly lifted one corner of her dark veil to expose a small triangle of glass. *I can no longer face this life,* he read.

"His handwriting. I found it on his desk. I haven't shown it to anyone else. He must have started to write a note, then changed his mind."

"No note was found."

"No note. Only that. It's not even addressed to anyone."

"He destroyed the note."

"Destroyed it. Burned it, perhaps. Who knows. But he changed his mind, and didn't finish it."

"I wonder why."

"Perhaps because he didn't want to place the blame on anyone. That would have been nice. But I think more likely he remembered that as a suicide he couldn't be buried in consecrated earth, as he was today. He remembered his mother and his father."

"But why would Peter have wanted to take his own life? That's what I can't understand."

"Oh, Gabe," she said almost desperately then, "I don't know. Sometimes I think I don't know anything. Today, in the church, I thought I don't even know who I am. I felt I had no right to take part in what was going on, and I couldn't understand even a little bit of it. I felt I was all alone there, lost in some terrible limbo, with even a name that was made up from some Kansas towns I've never seen. *Deus noster refugium* — but we're Jews, aren't we, Gabe? The Romans persecuted us, didn't they? We're Jews, wanderers, auslanders, strangers in a strange land, aren't we? And I thought, how did I ever become a part of this? I don't belong here. I belong in some different land of milk and honey, and orange groves and cypress trees and cedars of Lebanon, but I know nothing about that land, either. But why am I here, not there, and how did I get to where I am? How did I lose everything, my faith to boot? I had no business partaking in that High Requiem Mass today, genuflecting to an image of Christ on the cross. I had no business being there, and yet I was there. Has my whole life been a deceit and a hypocrisy? How did I become nothing — nothing at all — with no feelings left, and nothing to believe in, not even myself? Is Peter in heaven now? Is Athalie? Are Julius and Constance? Where will I go? I don't know. Who am I?"

Who is she? She had heard that question whispered, and so had Gabe, particularly in the first months after she and Peter had returned from their long, long wedding trip in Europe, with a new baby. Where did she come from? Terre Haute, they say. *Terre Haute?* And what a strange name — Assaria! And who is that man who was her guardian, Gabe Pollack? A Jew, they say. And she a Jewess? It's hard to say. From her looks, it could be either or. Were she and Gabe Pollack lovers, do you think? Hard to say, but isn't he — a bit minty, as we say? But who is *she?* And fifteen months for a honeymoon, and a baby! And that baby — it looks to me a good deal older than the LeBarons are saying it is! How old do they say? Four months? If I know anything about babies, that baby is closer to eight months old. That means, of course, that she was pregnant when she married him — and all in white! He had to marry her, of course. LeBarons always marry down. Look at Julius and Constance, for all her airs, pretending to be a real O'Brien, when the world knows. . . . Well, after all, what can you expect? They're Valley people. Mackerel-snappers. Cat-lickers. Dagos. Wops. Well, I'll say this for her. She caught a rich one. Caught him is right. Caught him with his pants down.

That was the way San Francisco talked when she and Peter first came home with Melissa. The past grows silent. It doesn't go away.

"Who am I, Gabe?"

"Well, I'm a member of my own little persecuted minority," he said.

"What do you mean? Oh, you mean — *that*. At least you can consider yourself part of a *group*. I'm nothing."

"In the final analysis, everyone is a minority of one. As God said to Moses, 'I am that I am.' "

"But what did God mean by that? Unless it was a riddle. That's what I feel I am — just a riddle."

"You loved Peter very much, didn't you?"

"I used to think I loved you," she said.

"But you loved Peter, Sari. I want to hear you say that. It's important to me."

She smiled a little absently. "Oh, we had our passionate moments," she said. "Is love important? Is it important to be in love? How many times I've asked myself that question."

"The answer, I think, is yes."

"Gabe, I'm a little frightened about staying in this house alone tonight. Will you spend the night with me? It doesn't have to be anything more than that. Just spend the night here so we two outcasts and orphans can be outcasts and orphans together."

Sixteen

*A*ND NOW, AT LAST, the day has come. It is April 30, and
the shareholders of Baronet Vineyards are gathered in a sixth-
floor suite of the Fairmont to decide on the business at hand. The
hotel has helpfully cleared one room of bedroom furniture, and
replaced this with a long conference table and comfortable swivel
chairs, an even dozen of them, and at each place a fresh pad of
yellow legal foolscap has been set, along with a new ballpoint pen,
glasses, and individual thermos carafes of ice water. In the sitting
room next door, urns of coffee and tea have been set out, with
cups and saucers and platters of fresh Danish pastries, croissants,
and raisin buns. In what had been the bedroom, the atmosphere
is all very businesslike. Outside, in the sitting room, Sari thinks,
there is an almost festive party air. The hotel has even sent fresh
flowers to the room, and a large basket of fresh fruit reposing in
a nest of green shredded cellophane. Outside, diagonally across
the street, Sari can see the garish facade of the Standard station

that occupies the site on California Street where the old LeBaron house once stood.

All these little extra frills and special touches have, of course, been arranged by Sari's office, for this is to be no ordinary stockholders' meeting. Normally, stockholders' meetings have been loose, informal affairs held in Baronet's old-fashioned boardroom, with everyone sitting around drinking Coca-Cola out of plastic cups. But Sari has chosen the Fairmont because she wants the meeting to be held on neutral territory. She has chosen this suite because it is prettier and more intimate than some of the hotel's standard meeting rooms. Not that this is expected to be a cozy little gathering of old friends. It is more like a council of war.

Assaria LeBaron is deliberately avoiding eye contact with any of the others in the room. Let them wonder, she thinks, what she will do first. Instead, she watches as the black court stenographer, who has been engaged to record the proceedings for posterity, deftly removes her little machine from its impossibly small black case, extends its slender tripod legs, and sets the machine upon the tripod. With this small gadget, with its handful of little symbols, she will record every syllable that is spoken and then, magically, transform her symbols back into written words. A small packet of white stenographic tape appears, folded accordion fashion, and is fed into the machine by the young woman's efficient, crimson-lacquered fingers, a tape that will soon be filled with impossible-to-decipher symbols — impossible, that is, for everyone but her.

She is a beauty, this black woman, with skin that has an almost purple hue, and a long, aristocratic neck, and the profile of Nefertiti. Her bearing is that of an aristocrat beyond aristocracy, an Ethiopian princess, secure in her breeding, her beauty, and her high art. This princess-priestess wears her glistening jet-black hair pulled tightly away from her face, and secured in a bun in the back. Her hair has the glossy sheen and luster of a black walnut veneer, and a clever trompe l'oeil paint job cannot be ruled out. Her high cheekbones have been blushed with the faintest persimmon color. Within this perfectly sculpted head are encapsulated all sorts of arcane transliterative powers and sciences. She frowns disdainfully at her machine, and then her nostrils flare imperiously as she seats herself in front of it, and poises her long, slender fingers above its keyboard. "May I please have," she says, "the names and positions of everyone at the meeting, starting with the gentleman seated at the head of the table, and then moving clockwise around the table?" Her fingers are ready for the responses.

"William C. Whitney," says Bill Whitney, the prissy little secretary of Baronet's board. "Secretary, Board of Directors, Baronet Vineyards, Incorporated."

"Harry Boyd Tillinghast," says Harry, who is seated on Bill Whitney's left. "Baronet shareholder of record."

"Eric O'Brien LeBaron, shareholder," says Eric, who is next.

"Eldridge R. Nugent, representing Mrs. Joanna LeBaron Kiley, attorney with the firm of Cravath, Swaine and Moore, One Chase Manhattan Plaza, New York City," says Joanna's lawyer, and the young black woman's fingers move noiselessly across her keyboard, her face expressionless.

"Joanna LeBaron Kiley," says Joanna. "And I think I should add that I am known professionally as Mrs. Joanna LeBaron. I, too, am a LeBaron shareholder of record. And I'd like to put on the record here that, though my son, Lance LeBaron, cannot be present at this meeting due to the press of business, I have here my son's power of attorney and executed proxy. In any voting that should occur at this meeting, I will be voting my son's shares for him."

"Noted," says Bill Whitney.

Typically Joanna, Sari thinks. Can't just give her name, rank, and serial number like everybody else. Has to make a little speech.

"Jonathan Baines," says the first of Sari's lawyers, who is seated on her right. "I am an attorney with the firm of Jacobs and Siller, San Francisco, and I represent Mrs. Assaria LeBaron."

The responses now turn a corner of the table, and come to Sari, seated at the other head opposite Bill Whitney. She says in a clear voice, "Assaria Latham LeBaron, president and chief executive officer of Baronet Vineyards, and shareholder."

On her left, her second lawyer says, "Simon Rosenthal, attorney, also of Jacobs and Siller, and also representing Assaria LeBaron."

I have two lawyers to Joanna's one, Sari thinks. This ought to give me at least a psychological advantage.

"Peter Powell LeBaron, Junior," says Peeper. "Vice-president for advertising and marketing of Baronet Vineyards, and shareholder."

Now the responses arrive at an empty chair. No one has failed to notice that Melissa has not appeared. The meeting was called for nine o'clock, and it is past that hour now. And so the roll call skips Melissa's place, and moves to the last gentleman at the table, Melissa's lawyer, Mr. Kline, who is playing with a pencil and doing his best not to seem concerned by the situation. "I am J. William Kline, Junior," he says, "an attorney with the firm of Bartless, Mather, Brooks and Kline. Our firm represents Miss Melissa LeBaron, shareholder, who should be arriving at any moment."

"Do you hold Melissa LeBaron's proxy, Mr. Kline?" Bill Whitney asks him.

"No, I do not," he says. "But when I spoke to my client last night, she assured me she would be here. I suspect —"

"Traffic," says Sari. "There's heavy traffic on the bridge. I heard it on the radio this morning."

"What bridge?" says Eric crossly. "Where's she coming from, anyway? Isn't she just coming from Pacific Heights?"

"Well . . ."

"Meanwhile," says Bill Whitney in his prissy voice, adjusting his spectacles across the bridge of his nose with his left pinky, "while we're waiting for Miss LeBaron, I have a suggestion to make to the meeting. As I'm sure we all realize, today's meeting will involve certain — ah — divergences from our normal procedures. The correct tallying of share votes will be particularly important today." You can say that again, Sari thinks. At meetings in the past, nobody had paid much attention to how many share votes each stockholder had because everybody just voted to support her policies. "Since any voting that will be done today will be done in the thousands of shares," Bill Whitney continues, "I suggest that each individual shareholder be given one vote for each thousand shares held. Thus, the holder of two thousand shares would be given two votes, a holder of four thousand shares would have four votes, and so on. I believe this would simplify things. Are there any objections to this proposal?"

No one speaks.

"Very well," he says, "then that is the way we will proceed. As soon as Melissa LeBaron arrives, that is."

"May I suggest," says Harry Tillinghast, "that this meeting does not intend to wait for Melissa LeBaron forever?"

"No," says Bill Whitney. "But I think we can be a little flexible, Mr. Tillinghast."

"Thank you," says Mr. Kline. "I assure you my client will be here at any moment."

"And in the meantime," says Sari, "*I* have a proposal to bring before this tribunal."

"This isn't a tribunal, Mother," Eric says sharply. "This is a shareholders' meeting."

"Well, tribunal, kangaroo court, whatever you want to call it," Sari says.

"Sari darling," Joanna says from across the table, "please don't make jokes. We're here to discuss serious business."

"What is your proposal, Mrs. LeBaron?" Bill Whitney asks.

"Well," she says, "as you all know, Melissa is presently laying claim to six thousand additional Baronet shares under the terms of her father's will, plus the four thousand shares she already owns. Am I correct, Mr. Kline?"

"Correct."

"Very well. These additional shares have not yet been delivered into Melissa's custody, and it will be her contention that they are still unrightfully being held by Lance LeBaron. Correct?"

"Correct."

"Very well, then. Since it may be some time before Melissa's claim is settled, and there may be lengthy litigation before it can be, there seems to me to be no question that the matter will be resolved in Melissa's favor. After all, my husband's will was quite specific, and there are no ambiguities. Four thousand shares were left to Melissa outright. Twelve thousand shares were to be divided equally among Joanna LeBaron's children. Melissa and Lance are both Joanna LeBaron's children. Therefore, Melissa is legally entitled to half of that twelve thousand. Correct?"

"That is our position, Mrs. LeBaron," Mr. Kline says.

"Therefore, in light of the obvious eventual outcome of this, I propose that for the purposes of this meeting, Melissa LeBaron be conceded the right to vote the full ten thousand shares which she will at a future date own, and that Lance LeBaron be permitted to vote only the six thousand shares to which he will be eventually entitled."

There is a whispered conference between Joanna and her lawyer, and hasty scribbles on the pads of yellow legal foolscap.

"Are you putting this in the form of a motion, Mrs. LeBaron?" Bill Whitney says.

"Yes. I so move."

"I second the motion," says Peeper.

"Moved and seconded," says Bill Whitney. "Very well. We'll vote in the same clockwise order. Remember, one vote per thousand shares. Mr. Tillinghast, how do you vote?"

"Against the motion," says Harry.

"Eric?"

"Against," says Eric.

"Mrs. Kiley?"

"Against."

"In favor," says Sari.

"In favor," says Peeper.

"Mrs. Kiley," says Bill Whitney, "how does Mr. Lance LeBaron vote his proxy?"

"Lance LeBaron," Joanna says carefully, "abstains from voting on this matter, since it involves the number of shares he is entitled to vote. A vote from my son on this motion would not be proper. In fact, it seems to me that it would be quite improper."

"I agree," says Bill Whitney. "However, that leaves us with a tie-vote situation." He consults his yellow pad. "Thirty-two votes in favor, and thirty-two against."

"However," Joanna says, "I believe that in any situation such as this one, a failure to vote is recorded as a vote against the motion. Melissa LeBaron has failed to vote. Therefore, as a shareholder of record of four thousand shares, her vote must be entered as four votes against."

Mr. Kline slams his fist down hard on the table, but says nothing.

"You are of course correct," Bill Whitney says, touching the frames of his glasses again with a fingertip. "My oversight. Therefore, the motion has failed, thirty-six to thirty-two." He gives Sari a disappointed look. "Sorry," he says.

"And now," Joanna says, "I would like to make a motion." She consults her watch. "This meeting was called for nine o'clock. It is now nine twenty-five. Melissa is already nearly half an hour late. I move that we adjourn for exactly fifteen minutes, and if Melissa has not appeared within that time, that we proceed without her."

"That seems reasonable," Bill Whitney says. "Shall we vote with a show of hands? All in favor?"

All hands go up except Sari's, and, when she sees that Peeper's hand is also up, she tries to pull it down, but it is too late. She gives him a venomous look.

"The motion is passed, thirty-six to thirty-two," says Bill Whitney, and he gives Sari another sad look. He, at least, is on her side, though he has no vote. If Eric and Joanna come to power, they will fire this poor horse's ass, and he knows it. At least, with Sari, he knows he has a job. A thankless job. But a job.

Mr. Kline also looks unhappy.

"Failure to vote is a vote against!" Sari cries. "Melissa's vote has to be counted against this motion!"

"I already have counted it, I'm afraid," Bill Whitney says with the same apologetic look. "The votes against were your twenty-eight, and Melissa's four."

"It is now nine thirty-two," Joanna says. "Melissa has until exactly nine forty-seven to get here."

The little group moves out into the sitting room of the suite, where the coffee urns and pastries are, but no one seems to have an appetite for any of this.

"Well, Sari dear," Joanna says, "I guess you could say I've won rounds one and two, couldn't you?"

"You are a miserable, conniving, thieving woman," Sari says. "You are a ruthless, selfish sneak. I don't know why it's taken me so many years to see through you. When we get back into that room, shall I mention what went on with you and Peter? Shall I let that black goddess punch that into her little machine and into the record? Shall I?"

Joanna turns on her heel and crosses the floor to join Eric and Harry on the opposite side of the room, and of course — she is not a stupid woman — Sari knows she should never have said that, never have said that at all. I am losing my control, she thinks. No, she thinks, I've already lost it. Turning to Mr. Kline, she says, "Have you tried to reach her on the telephone?"

"There's no answer at her apartment," he says.

I am dying by inches, Sari thinks. I am dying by inches, but I've lived by miles.

"Pick a card, any card," Melissa says.

He draws a card from the deck, and looks at it.

"Don't show it to me. Now put it back in the deck. Now, we shuffle them . . ." The telephone that has been ringing steadily all morning has just stopped ringing again.

"Don't you ever answer your phone?" he says.

"Not today I don't." She shuffles the cards, and then spreads them out on the table, face up. "Your card," she says, "was the seven of diamonds."

"Gee, how did you do that?" he says. "That's a neat trick, Melissa!"

"Once you know how to do a thing properly, it's easy," she says. "But that's a childish game. Let's try a more mature one. A simple hand of draw poker." She gathers up the cards, shuffles them once more, and deals them each five cards. She picks up her hand and looks at it. "I'll stick with the hand I've got," she says. "But you can discard and draw three more, if you want."

He discards three cards, and draws three new ones.

Melissa places a dollar bill on the table.

"I'll see you on that," he says, and covers her dollar with one of his own.

"I'll raise you five," she says, and adds five dollars to the pot.

"Fine," he says, and fishes a five-dollar bill out of his wallet.

"I'll raise you a hundred," she says, and from her purse produces a new hundred-dollar bill, and adds it to the little pile.

He hesitates, studying her face.

"Will you see me on that?" she asks.

He lays down his hand. "Three deuces," he says.

She spreads out her hand. "Three jacks," she says. "Sorry, Maurice, but you lose. You also lose literally as well."

"What do you mean?"

"I mean it's over. The gravy train has come to the end of the line. I realize that I'm a rich woman, but my resources are not the bottomless pit you seem to suppose. I'm through sending good money after bad. I've given you money, and I've seen you blow it on pills and poppers and coke and hash. I've tried to give you what I thought you needed — another chance. It hasn't worked. You've blown it, Maurice. I'm through with you. I'll give you twenty-four hours to pack up your stuff and get out of my house."

His eyes narrow. "And if I won't go?"

She gathers up the cards and scoops up the money from the table. "You're a bum deal, Maurice," she says. "If you won't go, I'll call the police and have you physically removed. Either you go peacefully, or I'll call the police. Do it whichever way you want. Dealer's choice."

In the suite at the Fairmont, Joanna LeBaron says, "Well, shall we give her five more minutes — on the theory that she's operating on Central Standard time? I'm willing, if everybody else is. But really, this is ridiculous. She's just wasting everybody's time. If the rest of us could make it to this meeting on time, why couldn't she? I came all the way from New York for this, and I was hoping to make a three o'clock plane. If I have to wait for the seven o'clock, I won't get home until after midnight. And I have an important business meeting in the morning."

Typical Joanna, Sari thinks. Always playing the prima donna. The overworked lady executive. *Her* business meetings are always more important than anyone else's. Of course. *Always.*

"I agree we've waited long enough," Bill Whitney says, and the little group files back into the meeting room.

"Now," Bill Whitney says when they are all seated, "we come to the principal business at hand. Mr. Harry Tillinghast has tendered an offer to buy our company from its shareholders. As all of you have been notified, this offer consists of thirteen and a quarter shares of the Kern-McKittrick Corporation common stock for each single share of Baronet Vineyards common stock. Now, I realize that a problem has arisen involving the number of shares to which Melissa LeBaron is entitled, and the number of shares to which her cousin, or I should say half brother, Lance LeBaron, is entitled. But I am also given to understand that this dispute will soon be settled in an equable and friendly manner between Miss LeBaron and Mr. LeBaron. Am I correct, Mr. Kline?"

"That is correct."

"I think, therefore, that we can set this dispute aside for the purposes of our meeting today. To do this, I suggest that we consider Melissa LeBaron, for the purpose of today's meeting, as the owner of only the four thousand shares to which she is unquestionably entitled, and about which there is no dispute. As for the twelve thousand shares which Lance LeBaron presently holds, six thousand of these shares are held by him beyond question, and without dispute. Am I correct, Mr. Kline?"

"Correct. About these shareholdings, there is no question and no dispute between my client and Lance LeBaron."

"Therefore, I suggest that for the purposes of this meeting we limit Mr. Lance LeBaron's entitlement to only those six thousand undisputed share votes, and that Melissa LeBaron be limited to her four thousand share votes which are undisputed. Will your client accept this arrangement, Mr. Kline?"

"My client accepts. She has so indicated to me in a letter dated April nine."

What's this? Sari thinks. Where did this letter come from? "May I see this letter?" she asks.

"Certainly," he says. He reaches for his briefcase, snaps it open, and withdraws a letter which he passes down the table to her. She glances at it briefly, waves her hand, and passes it back to him.

"Therefore," Bill Whitney continues, "a motion is in order that, in any balloting that may occur today, Mr. Lance LeBaron be entitled to six proxy votes. Does anyone so move?"

"I do," says Sari.

The motion passes unanimously, and Sari thinks: Good! That's six less votes for their side.

"I feel," says Bill Whitney, "that by leaving disputed shareholdings out of today's balloting, we can speed and simplify matters, leaving the dispute to be settled at some later date."

"Agreed."

A greed, Sari thinks. She can see a voracious greed in the eyes of everyone at the table. Isn't that what all this boils down to — a greed?"

"There will, therefore, be a total of seventy-four shareholder votes taken today. A simple majority of thirty-eight votes will be needed to pass or fail any motion to accept Mr. Tillinghast's offer, or to reject it. Are we ready to begin balloting? Do I hear a motion?"

"I move —" Joanna begins.

"Excuse me," Harry Tillinghast says, pushing back his chair. He stands up and clears his throat authoritatively. "I have something to say," he says, "before we start balloting. I am hereby increasing my offer to fifteen shares of Kern-McKittrick common for each share of Baronet common." He sits down abruptly.

There is a polite silence in the meeting room. Eric sits with his fingers steepled, looking pleased with himself. Obviously, this "surprise move" has been well rehearsed in advance. Then Eric says, "I move to accept."

"Twenty-eight votes *not* to accept," says Sari.

"Four votes not to accept," Peeper echoes dutifully.

"Ladies — gentlemen," says Queen Nefertiti in her regal voice, "I cannot accurately record the proceedings of this meeting with all of you talking at once. Please. One at a time."

"Two votes to accept," says Harry Tillinghast in an important-sounding way, as though the room should be awestruck that he is voting for his own proposal.

"Failure to vote is a negative vote," Sari says again. "That's four more votes not to accept from Melissa."

"Please, please —" If Bill Whitney had a gavel, he would pound it, but he has no gavel. "Will our meeting come to order — please?"

"Be sure you count Melissa's vote as *negative*," Sari says, pounding on the table with her fist. "Negative. She's not here, she didn't show up, so it's negative."

"Please . . . please," Bill Whitney repeats, consulting his legal pad, "this poor young woman here," indicating Nefertiti, "is trying to get all this down. Now, so far —" Nefertiti is back at her keyboard.

"Negative from Melissa!"

"So far," he says, "I have recorded thirty-six votes against the proposal — from Mrs. LeBaron, from Mr. Peter LeBaron, and, of course, Melissa. I have heard only four votes in favor, from Eric LeBaron and Mr. Tillinghast. Joanna LeBaron Kiley, how do you vote? A simple majority of thirty-eight votes is needed to pass or fail this motion."

Joanna sighs, and puts down the pen with which she has been scribbling, scribbling, and gives Sari a long look. The air between them becomes charged with electricity as Sari stares back at her just as hard and just as long from across the table, and then silently lets her lips carefully form the words: Peter. And you.

"Please record my twenty-eight votes against the proposal," Joanna says at last. "And my son, Lance, voting by proxy, also casts his six votes against."

With almost a look of relief, Bill Whitney says, "Then the motion has failed, seventy to four."

Eric rips the sheets of yellow paper from the pad on which he has been making notes, wads them into an angry ball, and hurls this in Joanna's direction across the table. "Thanks a lot, Aunt Jo," he says. "So much for loyalty. So much for promises. Fuck you, Aunt Jo. Fuck all of you. I've had it with this fucking family, and I've had it with this fucking company." He pushes his chair, hard, away from the table, and starts to rise as if to go.

"Wait, Eric," Joanna says, reaching quickly across the table to take his hand. "Don't you see why I had to do this? Whatever else she is, your mother is my oldest friend. I couldn't stand by and let this happen to her. Haven't you seen what this whole thing has been doing to her? She's become almost deranged by it." Her throaty voice is full of little histrionic catches now. "I couldn't just stand by — and witness — your mother's destruction."

Sari thinks, What is happening? She has still not quite recovered from the amazed discovery that she has won the battle, and won it by an overwhelming majority. But now what is happening? This was to have been her last hurrah, and now it is suddenly becoming Joanna's! Here is Joanna, talking about derangement and destruction! Sari cannot permit this! She cannot allow Joanna to make this final, grand, magnanimous, pitying gesture. Once more, Joanna has upstaged her. "Joanna," she begins.

"Go to your mother, Eric," Joanna says in that famous husky voice. "Make your peace with her. She loves you very much, and she's getting old. If we'd won, the family would have been divided forever. What happens to this company doesn't matter. What matters is that we be a family again, and that we love each other again."

Huh, Sari thinks. Now she's trying to kill me with kindness. *Is love important?* No! The power of your personality!

"Go to her, Eric. Go to your mother now. Do it now."

Eric has not moved, but Sari sees that his forceps scar has grown quite red. "Thank you, Joanna," she says. "Thank you for your concern about my mental health, and about my age — which is the same as yours, of course — and thank you for voting on my side in this. Eric — of course I love you. Dammit, I always thought of this as simply a business disagreement between us. It's just that this has always been a family business, and I wanted to see it stay that way, at least during my lifetime. After I'm gone, I don't care what any of you do, because I won't be around to know it. Now I have an announcement to make to all of you." Her eyes travel around the room. "I know there's been disagreement about the way this company is being run, and I know there's disagreement about what direction we should be taking. I also know I'm not getting any younger, and that I've held the post I hold for a long time. And so I would like to announce my resignation as president and chief executive officer of Baronet Vineyards effective June first of this year. I'd like to appoint, in my place, my son Eric. And I'd like to appoint my son Peter as executive vice-president, a post we've never had before. Eric and Peeper — I hope you can work together in these posts as partners, as a team, and as brothers. The way, in school, they used to do each other's homework, and take exams for each other — to the eternal confusion of their poor teachers! They never knew I knew this — but I knew. And they came through school with flying colors. They'll run this company with flying colors, too. Boys, God bless you — and success!"

Her eyes cross the table to Eric's, but his eyes are lowered, staring hard at the square of tabletop in front of him.

See? Not a dry eye in the house. Not even her own. Joanna is not the only one who can make a grandstand play.

A curtain line: "As for me," she says, "I don't intend to die without my boots on. I will assume the position of chairman of the board."

But of course no curtain falls and, instead, the silence that follows is disturbed only by the rustling of papers and the snapping open and shutting of lawyers' briefcases.

Finally, Bill Whitney says, "Do I hear a motion to adjourn?"

"I so move," Joanna says.

"Seconded . . ."

"All in favor . . . ?"

And Nefertiti begins dismantling and refolding her little stenographic machine.

Harry Tillinghast is the first to rise. "Well, you won," he says to Sari. "I won't say I'm not disappointed with the outcome of this. But I will say that, by kicking yourself upstairs, I think you've done the next-best thing."

"Will that make your little Buttercup happy?" Sari snaps. "Having her husband become the new president of Baronet? I know that she's the one who's been behind this whole thing from the beginning."

"That's not true," he says. "This was strictly Eric's and my idea. If you're planning revenge, Sari, leave my daughter out of it." Then he bows slightly. "Ladies . . . gentlemen . . . good day."

And now the four lawyers and Nefertiti and Bill Whitney have all left, and only the four of them remain — Sari, Joanna, and the twins. Only family.

"Well," Sari says, "it's your company now, Eric and Peeper. And I suppose I know what to expect. After a suitable period of mourning for the departed president, I'll hear that the Baronet account has gone back to Joanna's agency. Right?"

"That's been discussed," Joanna says.

"And the next thing I know I'll be seeing ads for your fancy new upscale label — Château Baronet — in magazines like *Vogue* and *The New Yorker,* and I'll be reading about the wine you can trust, and the wine you can bank on. Right?"

"It's one of the things we'd like to try," Eric says.

"Well, I wish you luck," she says. "As board chairman, I won't have much to say about operations, will I? So you might as well get going and start doing what you want to do right now."

"We'd still like to be able to consult with you, Mother. We'd still like you part of the decision-making process."

She snorts. "Decision-making! Well, I won't be counting on it. You plotted against me, Eric. You and Harry and Joanna plotted against me. Why should I believe anything you say now about decision-making?"

"You're being melodramatic again, Sari," Joanna murmurs.

"Why did you both plot against me?"

"Well, for one thing," Eric says, "when you took away half my job and gave it to Peeper, I was mad as hell. How did you think I'd feel when you did that?"

"But *I* was cross with *you.* For letting Harry get his big toe in the door. Without consulting me. I thought you should be —"

"Punished? Well, I simply decided not to take my punishment lying down. For a change."

"You even tried to lure Melissa into your plot!"

"Well, when Aunt Jo told me the true facts about Melissa —"

"Aunt Jo told you — *what?*"

"When Aunt Jo told me that Melissa was her child, not yours, then naturally —"

Sari is deliberately not looking at Joanna. "So," she says, "your aunt Jo told you this."

"Naturally, if Melissa found out that she had a lot more shares to vote, her vote would make a big difference. It was simply something we had to take into account. We knew that if you told Melissa the truth about whose daughter she was — which you did — it would cast quite a different light on the situation."

"I did not tell Melissa anything," Sari says evenly.

"Oh, Sari, stop lying," Joanna says. "Of course you did. You had nothing to lose by telling her, everything to lose by not telling her. If Melissa had been kept in the dark, our side could have claimed fifty-five percent of the stock, and you'd have been outvoted. You had to take the gamble — by telling her."

Sari looks at Joanna now. "But that's not why you switched sides at the last minute, is it?" she says.

"I've already explained why I switched sides."

"Look," Peeper says, "the fight's over, isn't it? The way I see it, both sides won a little, and both sides lost a little. Didn't we come out with almost a tie score? So why are we still fighting? Can't we all shake hands now and get out of the ring?"

"I'm not so sure the fight's over," Sari says. "There's still one thing that worries me, Eric. It's Madame Buttercup. Is she still threatening to slap a separate maintenance suit on you so fast you won't know what hit you, as she put it the other night?"

"Well," he says, spreading his hands, "it's no secret that things haven't been so great lately between Alix and me."

"A separate maintenance suit could cast something of a pall over the new president of the company. Is there still a Chinese lady in the picture?"

"No," he says. "That was a mistake. It's over."

"Good. I've never pretended to be particularly fond of Alix. But I am fond of the little girls, particularly Kimmie. I see a little bit of myself in Kimmie. I like to think that maybe, in the next generation, it will be Kimmie who will be taking over. It would be a shame if Alix tried to take Kimmie away from us."

"Alix and I are trying to patch things up," he says.

"Good. I also think Alix is a woman who will do what her father tells her to do. And I think her father is going to tell her not to start slapping separate maintenance suits on people. Not now that she's going to be the wife of the president of Baronet. Now, as the retiring head of Baronet — and as your mother, Eric — I have one final suggestion. Why don't you and Peeper kiss and make up? Why don't you go out now and buy yourselves a few drinks and start figuring how you're going to divide up responsibilities in this company? Why don't you both go out and get pleasantly sloshed together?"

Peeper — always the easier-natured of the pair — is the first to rise. He goes to Eric and puts his hand on Eric's shoulder. "I'm game," he says. "What do you say, Facsi? Like old times, all for one and one for all? What do you say?"

Eric grins sheepishly, stands up, and accepts his brother's outstretched hand. And, for a few seconds, the brothers throw soft punches at each other's shoulders. Watching them, Sari is suddenly very happy. She feels she is in control again.

Then they are gone, and Sari and Joanna are alone.

"I know you have a plane to catch," Sari says. "Don't let me keep you."

"Oh, I have plenty of time," Joanna says, glancing at her watch. "It's not even noon."

"All packed?"

"All packed. You know me. Organization."

"Yes."

"Well."

"Well." Then Sari says, "Why did you break your promise and tell Eric about Melissa? That was supposed to be our secret. Yours, mine, and Peter's. We made a solemn pact."

"And why did you break your promise, and tell Melissa about me? On the score of broken promises, I'd say we were about even."

"Joanna — for the last time — I told Melissa nothing."

"Sari, please don't lie anymore. Of course you told her. How else could she have found out?"

"Very simply. She found out on her own."

"How?"

"Last winter, when she was in Paris, it seems she also went to Saint Moritz. At the Palace Hotel, she got acquainted with Andrea Badrutt, the son of the man who owned it when we were all there. She showed him a picture of me when I was young, and asked him if that was the woman who had the baby there. He wrote to her that it wasn't, that the woman who had the baby was a blonde who called herself Mrs. Mary Brown, and liked her eggs cooked exactly three and a half minutes."

Joanna says nothing, but stands and moves toward the window.

"So you're the one who broke a promise, not I," Sari says.

"And yet this morning you were threatening to tell our secret to everyone."

Sari laughs softly. "Well, I was ready to haul out my last piece of heavy ammunition," she says. "But I didn't have to. You got the message and ran up the white flag. You surrendered, and switched your vote."

Now it is Joanna who is laughing. "Sari, Sari," she says. "Do you really think that's why I voted the way I did?"

"Of course. I scared the bejesus out of you."

"Sari, why would I have been frightened of a thing like that?"

"The scandal. Your reputation. The word, I believe, is incest."

"Oh, Sari darling. You really are so foolish. You could never have proved any of these — allegations of yours. Surely you know that."

"I could have given it to the papers — let them print it. Let them ruin your good name."

"Darling, darling Sari. I'm astonished at your naïveté. Do you think any newspaper in the country would print an unproven and unprovable allegation such as the one you're making? If they did, I could sue them, and sue you for defamation of character, and I'd win! I could take this whole company away from you. Really, what you say is too laugh-making. No, darling, your silly, hysterical little threat had nothing to do with the way I voted, I assure you."

"If it wasn't that, what was it?"

"Sari, you see I know you so well. I know how you manipulate people, and I've learned how to manipulate you. The fact is, I never wanted to get involved in anything with Harry Tillinghast. I dislike the man, and I certainly don't need his money. On the other hand, I've wanted to see Eric run this company for a long time. I figured that if I pulled a surprise move, and pretended to back down out of sympathy and concern for you, you'd be thrown completely off your guard. You'd have to do something to save face. The only thing that you could do would be to resign. Well, you didn't quite do that, but now Eric is where he should have been all along."

Sari pounds her fists on the arms of her chair. Joanna is trying to upstage her again. "I don't believe you!" she says. "You did it because you were scared spitless I'd spill the beans. Spill out your whole nasty little secret!"

Joanna shrugs. "Think what you will," she says. "It doesn't matter. I got what I wanted." And then, as though she is reading Sari's thoughts, she says, "I know you, and I know that the one thing you cannot stand is to be upstaged. Particularly by me."

"That's another lie! I have absolutely no use for you!"

"Switzerland," Joanna says quietly. "The three of us together there. My beloved brother, and my best friend, and me. Now look at us."

"Best friend and oldest enemy!"

"When I was having the baby, and was having so much difficulty with her, and when I almost died. You were both there. I began hemorrhaging, and you both gave blood. Your blood was in me, the blood that saved my life. It made me feel so incredibly close —"

"You're laboring under another misapprehension," Sari says. "Peter and I did not give you blood. We offered, of course, but our blood was the wrong type. The blood came from the Swiss Red Cross."

"Peter told me he gave blood."

"Well, if he did he lied to you."

"Peter would never have lied to me!"

"Well, I suppose you could go back and look up records if you don't believe me, but I assure you neither of us gave blood."

There is a worried look in Joanna's eyes now. "Anyway," she says, "I felt so incredibly close to you both that winter. And now look at us — at each other's throats."

"And so you supposed we were going to go through life together — a happy little threesome, strolling off into the sunset! Well, the trouble was that when we struck that bargain, you didn't level with me. You wouldn't tell me who the baby's father was. Years later, when I found out, I saw how you'd weighted the deal in your favor. It was supposed to be that if I'd raise your baby, I'd get Peter LeBaron as my reward. You didn't tell me that the real reason you wanted to keep the baby was that you wanted to use the baby to keep Peter for yourself. To keep him guilty and ashamed and beholden to you forever — dependent on you to keep his secret, the secret of the terrible thing he'd done to you!"

"The terrible thing he'd done," Joanna says. "Our nasty little secret, you called it. But, you see, I never thought of it that way. I loved Peter, Sari. I was in love with him. Call it unnatural love if you want, but I was in love with him. I tried, later, to replace him. Tried it with Rod Kiley. It didn't work. Nothing could ever replace Peter for me. Nothing ever has. And he loved me. Of course, he knew he was the baby's father, because he knew that there had never been anyone else for me but him, and that if there had been I'd have told him. Just as if there'd been anyone else for him but me, he'd have told me. We were that close."

Sari stares at this woman who is suddenly a stranger. "I think I'd like a drink," she says at last. "I had the hotel stock a full bar for our meeting in that cabinet over there. Will you fix me something, Jo? Do you remember how I like to make a martini?"

"Certainly." She moves toward the cabinet. "A full bar. This has certainly been the fanciest Baronet stockholders' meeting I've ever attended . . ."

She returns with their drinks and hands Sari her glass. "Well, here's to the old days," she says. "Chug-a-lug."

Sari says nothing, and takes a swallow from her glass. "So," she says, "there was never anyone else for him but you."

"No one. There was never anyone but me. He never touched — touched in love — another woman. If he had, he would have told me."

"I see. Of course, I managed to produce three children by your brother. How do you suppose that happened? By immaculate conception?"

"I said 'touched in love.' You told me once that yours was a sexless marriage. You asked me if I thought he had a mistress. I knew what the answer was, but of course I couldn't tell you then. The answer was that he was always in love with me. Don't forget, darling, that you were brought into this family as a convenience — to help Peter and me out of a rather embarrassing little pickle. If you thought there was a question of Peter loving you, ever — well, there's a fool born every minute, darling. The only one he ever touched in *love* was me."

"Then how — how do you explain Athalie and the twins?"

"Very simple. He wanted a male heir. Perpetuating the family was always very important to Peter, and to me."

"And when you and Peter discovered you'd accidentally started a little family of your own, I was invited in to bail you out."

"Well, that's a rather coarse way of putting it, darling. But yes." Carrying her drink, Joanna moves to the window again, looking out on the street, the Pacific Union Club across the way, and the cathedral beyond.

"I think what you and Peter did together destroyed his capacity for love," Sari says. "He never recovered from the shock of what had happened."

"Oh, Sari, Sari," Joanna says, laughing softly. "You understand so little. Peter and I did what we did only once. Ours was really a platonic love — love on a higher plane."

"Only once? Peter told me that you and he had had — intimate relations — a number of times. He said it would happen when you both got drunk. He blamed MacDonald for leaving you alone so much."

She laughs again. "You mean the butler did it? Peter told you that? Well, maybe it happened — twice. I really don't remember, it was all so long ago. It was what we called 'touching in love,' and that was when he promised me he would never touch another woman in love again. Ours was a pure love, you see."

"Pure love! After Athalie was born, why did you try to prevent the twins from being born by working on Melissa — telling her that if I had another baby it would be a monster, worse than Athalie?"

"I was concerned for your health, darling. My best friend's health."

"Bull-do. You were concerned that I was finally taking Peter away from you. That was all you were concerned with! You were simply jealous — jealous because I was having another child by him."

"Well, perhaps I was — a little. After all, I'm only human. The main thing I wanted was for Peter to be completely happy."

"Human! I think you're the monster, Jo! Or crazy — if you actually believe all these things you're telling me."

"No, Sari. You see, you still don't understand. You don't understand how close Peter and I were. We were like one soul."

"*One soul!* What if I told you that during that spring and summer while you were getting ready for your debutante season, Peter and I were having quite a passionate love affair?"

"I wouldn't believe you. It isn't true."

"Well, it is. While you were off at the Burlingame Country Club dancing your little feet off, and shopping with your mother for bags and hats and gloves and beaded ball gowns and silver satin dancing slippers, Peter LeBaron and I were having a love affair!"

"That's not true. I deliberately arranged for you and Peter to be alone together — to test him. To see if anything would happen. I even arranged for you to see each other naked — remember? To test him. But nothing happened — he told me so. He passed the tests."

"I'm afraid he failed them rather miserably, and told you a lot of barefaced lies!"

"Peter never lied."

"While you and Peter were busy being one soul, Peter and I

were making love — in a suite at the Saint Francis. On the beach at Half Moon Bay. Any place we could find!''

"You're lying now, Sari, darling. I know you are. Because I asked him, and he swore to me that there was never anything between you.''

"Well, so much for Peter's word of honor," Sari says, "because what I'm telling you is true.''

"You're just trying to upset me. But you can't. I knew Peter too well. He could never have deceived me. I'd have seen right through it if he'd tried.''

"I'm not trying to upset you. I'm just trying to get you to face the truth of what Peter LeBaron was.''

"I don't believe you. You see, Sari, that's always been one of your problems. You've never been able to believe that Peter was never in love with anyone but me. Never. You've never been able to face the fact that he was never in love with you. Dear Sari, I'm sorry, but it's time you accepted it now.''

"He may not have been in love with me, but we certainly *touched in love,* as you put it, a number of times — long before the whole idea of marriage even came up. While you and he were busy being one soul.''

"No. It's not true. He would have told me. You see, there were little secret things we did. Champagne —''

"You mean he dipped your breast in his champagne glass?''

Joanna turns sharply away from the window toward Sari with a little cry, and her hand flies up to her mouth. *"How did you know that?''*

"Because he did the same thing to me," she says. "He said it was our special little secret thing.''

Joanna stares at her, a look of horror on her face. Then she sits down quickly on one of the chintz-covered hotel chairs, her head in her hands. For several minutes, neither woman says anything, and the only sound in the room is the noise of the Powell Street cable car making its way up the hill with a load of screaming tourists hanging on all sides. As she watches Joanna there, huddled in the chair in the harsh late morning sunlight, her attitude of despair and dismay seems so profound that Sari cannot help but pity her.

And suddenly the years seem to melt away, and they are girls again, giggling in the Japanese Tea Garden in Golden Gate Park. *I, Assaria Latham, do solemnly swear that for now, and until the end of time, I am pledged in friendship to Joanna LeBaron . . .*

Gotten myself gravid . . .

That in sickness and in health, each will turn to the other for aid, comfort, and assistance, wheresoever in the world we may happen to be, to be forever truthful with one another . . .

She was the most beautiful girl Sari had ever seen.

Perhaps her commitment to Peter and his memory could be forgiven as a form of sickness. Perhaps loyalty to an old oath and an old friend mattered more than shattering her forlorn delusions.

Finally, Sari says, "I'm sorry, Jo. But I've never lied to you. Perhaps it's time we both accepted the fact that we both loved Peter. And that he was unfaithful to us both. And that neither of us owned him."

"Oh, Sari, Sari," Joanna says at last with her fists pressed tightly against her eyes. "There's only one thing I can say to you."

"What's that?" Sari asks her.

"You — you are the cat's pajamas."

"I think I'm ready for another drink," Sari says. "I think we should both get quite roaring drunk."

Seventeen

"*MISS MELISSA IS WAITING* to see you in the south sitting room, Madam," Thomas whispers to her as he helps her out of the elevator.

"Aha."

Thomas wheels her in to where Melissa sits, cross-legged, in one of the Belter chairs, a magazine in her lap. Thomas parks Sari's chair and hastily withdraws.

"Well, Melissa," Sari says. "May I ask what kind of games you're trying to play?"

Melissa's smile is faint. "Games?" she says.

"Where were you during the meeting? A rather important matter was at stake — the future of our company, that's all."

"I decided not to go."

"I see. You decided not to go. Do you know that the rest of us waited nearly an hour for you? Including a court stenographer who's paid God knows what an hour? Your lawyer was very upset, and so was I."

"Lawyers are paid to be upset," she says.

"That's a rather cavalier attitude to take. But typical. As it turned out, the business at hand was carried out in a matter of minutes — after we'd all cooled our heels for nearly an hour, waiting for you."

"I know. Eric telephoned me and told me what happened."

"I see. You'll take telephone calls from Eric, but you won't come to the phone for me, or even answer my letters. I can see which side my bread is buttered on, as far as Miss Melissa is concerned."

"I'm sorry, Mother. I was certain that there'd be ugliness at that meeting, and I just didn't want to get involved in it."

"Well, it's water over the dam now. I notice that you still call me 'Mother.' "

"Force of habit," Melissa says.

"I see," Sari says. "Well, state your business. I have a busy day ahead of me. Turning over the reins to Eric isn't going to be a simple matter. What can I do for you? But if it's mothering you want, remember you've got a new mother now."

Melissa uncrosses her legs. "Yes," she says. "Just as I've suspected for years. I've suspected she was my mother for years."

"What made you so suspicious, pray?"

"Oh, little things. The resemblance in the portraits, for one thing. The way she used to try to take over the mothering of me from you when I was a little girl, for another. Little hints and hunches. The way she sometimes used to look at me, for instance."

"I see."

"Now, of course, I'd like to know who my father was. Do you know?"

Sari hesitates. "Joanna never told me," she says. In a literal sense, this is the truth.

"I know there was a Flood boy she used to date — Jimmy Flood. But he's dead now. Could it have been him?"

"Joanna would never tell me," she says again. "This is a matter you must take up with her. But if she wouldn't tell me, I doubt she'll tell you."

"Then I thought it might be Lance's father. But then I found out she didn't even meet him until after I was born."

"That's true. He was from Pasadena."

"Perhaps I'll never know."

"Perhaps — not," Sari says.

"Of course, she may not even know herself. If she was sleeping with more than one man at the same time, how would she know for sure?"

"If that were the case, she probably wouldn't."

Melissa sighs. "Well, if you don't know, perhaps nobody knows."

"Perhaps not."

"Well, the other thing I wanted to tell you is that I'm going to be moving out," Melissa says.

"Moving out?"

Now, this is something that Sari is totally unprepared for, and at first she is not certain that she heard Melissa correctly. "Moving out from where?" she asks.

"From here. From this house. From my apartment downstairs."

"But — why? That apartment is to be yours for the rest of your life. It's in my will. Whatever happens to this house after I die, that apartment is to be yours for as long as you like."

"I don't want to live here anymore. After all, we're not even related to each other."

"That's not true! You're —" But she stops herself. "Are you planning to move in with Joanna — is that it? Because I'm quite sure Joanna won't take kindly to having a middle-aged spinster daughter move in with her, no matter what her legal —"

"I'm not planning to move in with Joanna. I've found a lovely apartment on Telegraph Hill — a view of the Bay and both bridges, terraces — Michael Taylor is going to do it for me."

"But you've always lived with me, Melissa!" Sari says. "Why are you doing this to me now? Why?"

"I'm not doing anything to you, Mother. I'm doing it for myself. It's time —"

"Time for what?"

"Time for me to move on. To be out on my own. My life is

more than half over, and it's time I figured out what I'm going to do with the rest of it. The first thing I'm going to do is have a house of my own."

"Do these plans have something to do with young Mr. Littlejohn?"

"No. Maurice Littlefield was a lost cause, I'm afraid. He'll be leaving San Francisco tomorrow."

"Then why? I don't understand."

"It's just something I have to do."

"Something you have to do. That's not a reason. Is it something I've done or said to upset you? The rent you pay — a hundred dollars a month — you could never find anything as cheap as that anywhere else in the city. Where else could you —"

"It has nothing to do with money. I have plenty of money. And when I get my share of Lance's stock —"

"You may have to sue him to get that, you know!"

"No, I won't have to sue him. Lance and I have talked, and he wants to do the right thing. There's no disagreement between us. It's just a matter of transferring shares from one account to another."

"What about the dividends for all those years? Dividends since nineteen fifty-five. You're entitled to those, too, you know! Those — plus interest."

"I know. But I'm not going to ask for that."

"But that's foolishness! You're throwing away millions and millions of dollars! Your lawyers are fools if they let you do that!"

"I don't want to send Lance to the poorhouse, Mother."

"Why not? To hell with Lance! It's your money. You're entitled to half his dividends since nineteen fifty-five, plus interest."

"Well, I don't want any of it. I happen to be rather fond of Lance."

"Rather fond! Rather *too* fond, if you ask me — if you recall a certain episode a number of years ago!"

"Oh, Mother," she says wearily. "That's another thing, another reason. I'm tired of all that."

"Tired of what?"

"Tired of Thomas spying on me, and reporting back to you on every move I make. Tired of having my letters steamed open and read."

"I don't know what you're talking about!"

"Don't you? A letter that's been steamed open, and then sealed again, looks a little different from a letter that's never been opened. I've seen letters like that often enough to know what's going on here."

"That's ridiculous! If Thomas has done anything like that, I shall speak to him and have him put a stop to it."

"And having people like Archie McPherson sent out on fishing expeditions with me, to find out how much I know about this or that. I'm tired of all that, Mother. Tired of it, and ready to make a life of my own."

"It's just that you were always a special child, Melissa. We always felt that you needed to be treated with special care. Please don't go, Melissa . . ."

But what, you may well ask, is going on here? Over the years, Assaria LeBaron — to close friends and confidants such as Gabe Pollack and Thomas — has managed to convey the impression that having Melissa living under the same roof with her has been something of a burden, a personal cross she has had to bear. You might think that Assaria LeBaron would heave a great sigh of relief that Melissa wants to move out, and yet here she is begging her to stay. Is it possible to become dependent on one's burdens? This is a tricky question, but the answer is yes.

"Special," Melissa says. "For years I knew I was special, but I didn't know why. I didn't know who I was, and no one would tell me. Now that I know who I am, I want a life of my own. It's as simple as that."

"It won't work," Sari says. "I know you, Melissa. You'll be terribly lonely. Before you know it, you'll want to come back. In just a few weeks, you'll begin to miss this house and want to come back. Wait and see."

Melissa smiles. "We'll see. But meanwhile I'm not going that far away."

"Then why go at *all?* If you know you're going to come right back?"

"I don't think I *am* going to come right back, Mother."

Now Sari hesitates again. She is running out of arguments with this difficult child. Finally, she says, "This house wants you to stay. It was built for you, you know — built for me to raise you in." But on this issue the White Wedding-Cake House, which sometimes seems to speak to Sari, remains noncommittal, ambivalent. Then Sari says, "But what about me? I'll be all alone, rattling around all alone in this big house, with no one to talk to, nothing to do — not even an office to go to anymore. All alone, getting older, all by myself —"

"Am I such fun to be with, Mother? Every time we're together, it seems we end up in a fight."

"Does it always have to be that way?"

"It's like a bad habit that can't be broken. We're like positive and negative electric charges."

"But do we *have* to be like that? Couldn't we try to be friends?"

"Maybe a little distance between us will help."

"Oh, please don't go. *I'm used to you, Melissa.*"

"Used to poor, difficult, temperamental Melissa? I should think you'd be glad to see me go."

"I'm not. I'm devastated."

"I know I'm no rose to live with, and I know I was an exceptionally difficult child."

"No. Not always. Sometimes, perhaps. But not always."

"And I know why I was. Would you like me to tell you?"

"Yes!"

"After all those head-shrinkers over the years, I think I finally learned something. I know exactly what was behind that brattish, monsterish, nasty little girl who insisted on wearing funny glasses, who pretended to be frightened of the Sutter Buttes, who wouldn't eat —"

"You lacked self-esteem, someone said."

"It wasn't that. It was because of you and Daddy. I always knew that there was something terribly wrong between you and Daddy.

But I didn't know what it was. Now, of course, I do. But I used to think to myself, if Melissa LeBaron is a good little girl, and does everything she is supposed to do, and is always Little Miss Merry Sunshine, there'll be no reason for Mother and Daddy to stay together, will there? If Melissa is no problem, it will be easy for them to go away from each other, get a divorce, and then I'll lose them and be all alone — sent to a foster home or an orphanage. But, I thought, if Melissa is a bad little girl, if Melissa is a *horrible* little girl, their worry about that horror will hold them together like a kind of glue."

"When you were little, and would ask me to tell you a story, I'd always say, 'I have two stories — one about a good little girl, and one about a bad little girl.' You always wanted the one about the bad little girl."

"I got very good at being a bad little girl, didn't I? I'd think: Whenever they think of separating because of whatever is so wrong between them, one of them will say to the other, 'But what will we do about Melissa? Melissa is such a problem to herself that she can't be left alone.' And so I made myself the problem, the unsolvable problem, that would force you to stay together, and the minute one problem was solved I'd think up a new one for myself. And it seemed to work. And all the time I told myself: If Melissa is a good little girl, they'll say to themselves: 'We can separate, we can divorce, because Melissa is no problem.' "

Sari reaches out now and touches Melissa's hands, which are folded in her lap. "Now, look, Melissa," she says. "We're not quarreling now, are we. We're talking like two sensible adults about things we should have talked about for years. We're talking like two friends. So don't move out. Stay with me. I need you."

"And then you had your accident, and I thought: Good, he can never leave her now. He's responsible for what happened to her, and his guilt will make him stay. She's too dependent on him now — he'll have to stay. You see, he was the one I was afraid would go away and leave us. I loved him so — this father who turns out not to have been my father at all. Perhaps that was why he never seemed to love me back. Who was I? Nothing but his poor sister's illegitimate child, whom you and he had been forced to raise."

"I think Peter loved you very much," Sari says.

"And then he killed himself."

"A hunting accident — that was the coroner's verdict."

"Nonsense. He never hunted. In fact, I think I killed him."

"What in the world makes you say that, Melissa?"

"I think I killed him as surely as if I'd pulled the trigger. Do you remember how he never seemed to like to look at me? Do you remember how he never seemed to want to speak to me? He seemed to treat me as though I were some sort of terrible family mistake — and I guess I was. My presence almost seemed to embarrass him. That summer of nineteen fifty-five we were all at Bitterroot, and the twins were coming home from camp in the East, and we were all excited — at least I was. It was only two weeks after your accident, and the doctors were still saying that they thought you'd be able to walk again. Everyone was trying to be optimistic — why did I choose that moment to be hateful? I was a grown woman then and should have known better than to do what I did, but perhaps my badness had become a habit. He was going out one morning, to cut down more of his trees, I supposed, and I said to him, 'Daddy, are you excited that the twins are coming home?' And without looking at me he said something like, 'Of course I am.' And then I said to him something like, 'Why are you always so happy and excited to see the twins, but never happy and excited to see me?' He said nothing. Didn't answer me, and wouldn't look at me. And so I asked him the question again, and still he wouldn't answer me. And then I suddenly got angry, lost my temper, and I said to him, 'What kind of a father are you, anyway? You tried to kill her, didn't you? Even if she's not my real mother, you tried to kill her. What kind of father would try to kill a person? I hate you.' And that was the day he did it."

Sari says nothing. There is, of course, a piece of green blotting paper in the Regency games table that she could show her, the handwriting on it so faint and faded as to be almost illegible. But Sari decides to keep that secret to herself.

"It's an irony, isn't it," Melissa says. "The father I wanted so much to keep I ended by destroying."

Perhaps all three of us should share the blame for that, Sari thinks, if that's what happened — Melissa, Joanna, and myself. The three women who loved him. If that's what happened.

"Anyway," Melissa says with a little smile — Melissa's beauty still shines when she smiles, Peter's beauty, Joanna's beauty, and we are talking only of physical beauty here — "I've been on quite a little journey of self-discovery over the past few months. So maybe you can see why I'm eager to take the next leg of the trip on my own."

"Well, at least tell me one thing," Sari says. "If you had come to the meeting this morning, which side would you have voted on?"

"Well, I certainly wouldn't have voted on the side of a woman who gave me away, who wouldn't acknowledge me, a woman who didn't want to be my mother, who handed me off to another woman to raise. That's one reason I didn't come this morning. I didn't want to look at her."

"Well, it's good to know you'd have voted on my side."

"No. I wouldn't have done that, either. I couldn't bring myself to vote on the side of a woman who had me sterilized."

"That was done on the advice of experts!"

"Experts! Haven't you lived long enough to know that there are no experts? Only know-it-alls and charlatans and cranks, and people who see a way to get a piece of the action."

"Dr. Obermark! You had been found in a — in a sexual situation with Lance, your half brother —"

"Don't try to blame Dr. Obermark," Melissa says. "You were the one who gave permission for the operation. You were the one who told the lie to me. I was old enough to understand, if you had told me, but you didn't. That's why I wouldn't have voted on your side today."

"And yet that's what you ended up doing — do you know that? Your failure to vote was counted as a vote against the takeover. So there!"

"Yes, so there. I know all that. So it didn't matter anyway. And, frankly, Mother, that was the final reason why I didn't come this morning. I didn't give a damn whether Kern-McKittrick took over the company or not. I still don't.''

"How can you be so ungrateful? Do you know that the only reason why you're here is because of me?"

"None of us asked to be born."

"They wanted to give you up for adoption. That's what would have happened if it weren't for me. I agreed to take you when no one else would. If it hadn't been for me, you'd have grown up in an orphanage or a foster home. If it hadn't been for me, you wouldn't have any of your money. Everything you have you owe to me, including that emerald ring on your little finger!"

Melissa rises. "And you see? Here we are quarreling again. As always. I've got to go."

"I won't let you leave!" Sari is shouting now, and even Thomas, waiting in the vestibule beyond a closed door, can hear her, and we can imagine Thomas wincing at the terrible things that are being said, but it is not Thomas's station to interfere. "You're an alcoholic and an irresponsible, immoral woman! If you leave, I'll tell you what will happen. You'll get drunk and find yourself in bed with some unsuitable man, some gigolo who'll want to marry you for your money. Within two months — I predict this, Melissa! — you'll come crawling back to me on your hands and knees, begging me to take you in!"

Melissa moves toward her. With her free hand, she slowly twists the square-cut emerald solitaire from the little finger of her left hand, and drops the ring in Sari's lap. "That," she says, "is to repay you for everything you've done for me."

Sari looks briefly at the ring. "You're a miserable, ungrateful child, and I hope your fortune-hunting gigolo takes you for everything you're worth! You're a drunken, dissolute woman!"

"Good-bye, Mother."

"If you leave, I'll cut you off without a cent in my will. I won't leave you a blessed cent! Why should I? You're no kin of mine — no kin whatever!"

"What are you afraid of, Assaria LeBaron?" Melissa asks. "Are you afraid that the old ghosts in the portrait gallery will come out of their frames to haunt you? Is that what you're afraid of? My father's ghost? My grandfather's ghost? Athalie's ghost?"

"I forbid you to leave this house!"

At the door, with one hand on the knob, Melissa says, "You can't forbid anymore. Don't forget, you're no longer in control."

"Get out!" Sari screams. "Get out of here!"

Eighteen

"*AND SO HERE I AM*," she is saying to him, "with nothing. I have a fancy new title, but no specific duties, and now no daughter. I've been abandoned by everybody. My phone hardly rings anymore, and I get hardly any office memos. I've turned over my old office to Eric, and Alix has decided to redecorate it, and they're painting it dark green. Miss Martino complains that she has nothing to do, and she's asked my permission to start looking for another job. The new broom must sweep clean — and sweep me under the carpet in the process, like yesterday's newspaper, out with the garbage. All alone, and helpless, and seventy-nine years old."

"Seventy-four," he corrects.

"It feels more like eighty-four when you're all alone and useless, after a lifetime of hard work. *Sixty Minutes* doesn't want me on the show. Nobody wants me. I'm yesterday's news. I'm obsolete. I'm utterly useless, Gabe."

"You kicked yourself upstairs voluntarily. You didn't have to, you know."

"I know. And I could kick myself for having done it. I only did it so Joanna wouldn't have the last word. But it's too late now, and I'm left with nothing at all."

"Well, if you expect me to sit here feeling sorry for you, you're wrong," he says. "You're one of the richest women in California. You can afford to do anything you want."

"Do? Do what?"

"Well, I can think of a number of things."

"Such as? Such as what?"

"Well, the Condors are playing Detroit on Saturday. They'll expect you to be up there in the stands, rooting for them."

"Oh, I will be. But that's not a job."

"What about another rehabilitation project, like the Odeon? There are still a lot of good old buildings in the south-of-Market area waiting to be restored and put to use."

"Oh, you're talking about do-goody stuff, Lady Bountiful stuff. That's not like a job, either. Don't forget, you're talking to a woman who's worked since she was ten years old."

"Thirteen," he corrects again.

"I'm tired of Lady Bountiful stuff. Rehabbing old buildings isn't something you do yourself, anyway. You farm the work out to contractors. It's not like running a company — your own company."

"Why not," he says half-seriously, "get your commercial pilot's license and start your own air freight service?"

But she takes him seriously. "Can't. I'm considered a handicapped person."

"I was only —"

"So you see? There's absolutely nothing for me — an old woman, at the end of her life, left with nothing to do but spend her last years twiddling her thumbs and waiting for death. All alone."

"Poor, poor Sari," he says. "Poor little rich girl. Your story is sadder than Barbara Hutton's."

"Money is nothing," she says. "I never wanted money. Without something to do, money is just dust in the mouth. Peter taught me that — the importance of keeping busy. Even if it was just cutting down trees.''

"Have you made your peace with Eric?" he asks.

"What do you mean, made my peace?"

"Well, there's been some pretty heavy weather between the two of you these past few weeks, a lot of rough things said. Have you and he buried the hatchet?"

"He's got the presidency of the company! What more does he want from me?"

"Maybe a kind word or two?"

"Actually," she says, "I was rather proud of Eric for taking me on the way he did. It showed he's a good fighter, and I like that. It showed that Eric's got gumption. Eric's not put together with wheat flour and water paste. He fought me, and he fought fair, and it was a good fight."

"It might be nice if you told him that."

"Well, I hadn't thought of it, but maybe I will. Of course it's no secret that Eric's always been my favorite of the twins. He's smart, and he's tough, and he works hard. He'll be a good president, wait and see. But Peeper — Peeper's just the opposite, all bubbly, bubbly charm on the surface, but is there anything solid underneath? Peeper's a follower, Eric's a leader. I guess I like Eric best because Eric is more like me. Peeper is more like Peter — the old Peter. Do you remember the old Peter, Gabe? Fun-loving, gay, charming, reckless, afraid of nothing. Of course, that was before . . .''

"Yes."

"Of course, Eric is going to need some supervision — and I'll see that he gets it, Gabe. But Peeper? I'm afraid I've really got some hard work ahead of me in Peeper's case. If Peeper's going to be a decent executive v.p., I'm really going to have to put the screws on him. Eric's almost ready to be given his head, but I'm going to have to keep a tight rein on Peeper for a while."

"You see? It's already beginning to sound as though you've got plenty of work cut out for yourself, Sari."

"Oh, I intend to keep my hand in things, don't worry about that. I don't intend to just sit on the sidelines and watch those two make a mess of three generations' worth of hard work. After all,

I'm still a majority stockholder, Gabe, and that gives me a certain amount of — ''

"Power."

"Right! They're not going to run roughshod over a majority stockholder — don't worry about that. They're still going to have to answer to me."

"You'll keep those boys on their toes, Sari."

"Right!"

"So — are you feeling a little better about the situation now?"

"Well, maybe. Maybe a little. Except — Melissa. I miss her so, Gabe. That big apartment downstairs — completely empty now. I wish there were some way to get her to come back."

"I'm sure she'll come back for visits."

"Do you think so? I don't know. Our last fight was — pretty bad. Do you know what she said to me? She said, 'We're not even related to each other.' But that's not true, is it? She's my step-daughter, and doesn't that make us related in a way? But of course, she doesn't know that. Which means —''

Suddenly, she swings her wheelchair in a half circle, facing away from him. To Gabe, this is a signal. It is a signal that Assaria LeBaron has just had some new idea. "Which means what?" he asks her.

"I know the secret of who her father was, which she'd dearly like to know. I know that secret, and I'm the only one who could ever tell it to her. That gives me a certain amount of — control over her, doesn't it? If I told her that I knew that secret, that might bring her back. Mightn't it? She'll come back — once she knows I know!"

"Are you sure you want to tell her, Sari? I'm the only other person you've ever told."

"I'm not sure. I'll decide that later. The point is that I *know.*" All at once she laughs. "It's like the secret of what's in Grandpa's old wine barrel, isn't it? We'll never know what's in there until someone pulls the bung out, and all we know is that *something's* in there, some living, breathing thing. And look how that old wine barrel has dominated our lives, the way it dominates the portrait gallery! Think about it, Gabe. I know the secret! We used to talk about Melissa being the loose cannon in the family. Now *I'm* the loose cannon, aren't I?''

He shakes his head in wonder at her. "Meanwhile," he says, "Archie McPherson is putting the finishing touches on the story about the failure of the Kern-McKittrick takeover bid. In it, you emerge as something of the heroine of the day. That should make you even happier."

"Ah, yes. Archie. Your little pet. Well, he can still be useful to us, I suppose."

"He's young. He has talent. But I should warn you, Sari. He still has this idea in his head about writing up the whole LeBaron family story."

"Don't let him do it, Gabe. I know he's bright, but I don't trust him. Anyone who'd do work for me while he's also working for you isn't to be trusted. Besides, he wouldn't do it right. He'd make Peter into the heavy, or something, and Peter wasn't the heavy. He was just an ordinary man who happened to be scarred by love. Love was like a snake that bit him once, and he never recovered from it, no matter how hard we all tried to help him. Gabe — I've just had a wonderful idea! Why don't *you* write our story? Yes, you're the one who should write it, Gabe. You're the one I want to write it. I'll help you. Oh, do it, Gabe. You're the only one who knows all the facts, who knows what really happened, and who knows all the family secrets, all the lies and deceptions and cover-ups. You know the truth, so write it warts and all. Make me the heavy if you like, because some people might say I was, but remember that I kept my promise to them, and never told anyone their secret. I made a deal and stuck to it. Write our story. You could put a little plug in for the Condors. They'll need every little boost they can get this season. And after the book is written, after we've told everything — then we'll decide whether to get it printed up, and whether to let Melissa read it. Because maybe, if Melissa could read the book, and learned the truth about all the sacrifices I've made for her, and all the suffering I've done for her, she'll forgive me, and come back! Don't smile, Gabe — I really think she might. Don't you think she might, if she reads how much I love her and how much I miss her? I think she *might,* Gabe. Because I do miss her. I even miss our fights, and we had some doozies. And how could I help but love her, having raised her from a tiny baby? Do you think you could write our story in such a way that it would bring Melissa back?"

Gabe has moved to the window, and is looking out on Washington Street. An afternoon fog is drifting in from the Golden Gate and, across the street at the Russian Consulate, the guards are changing.

"I think you're about to have a visitor," he says.

"Who?" She wheels herself to the window, and pulls aside the curtain. "Look!" she cries. "It's Eric — Eric coming to apologize to me for all the worry and heartache he caused me! Isn't this exciting? It's Eric, coming to apologize!" But then, as the figure on the entrance walk draws closer, and disappears under the porte cochere, she lets the corner of the curtain drop. "It isn't Eric," she says. "It's only Peeper. What do you suppose he wants from me?"

"Sari, Sari, you'll never change," he says.

"But quick — quick before Peeper gets here — promise me you'll write our story. Make it a love story, Gabe, because that was what it was — a love story about three women in love with the same man, each in her own way. Even the three women in the story loved each other, once upon a time. Please do it, Gabe. But promise to write it as a special kind of love story, and try to write it with love. Will you do it, Gabe?"

And we waited there in her big White Wedding-Cake House that afternoon, waiting for Peeper and whatever it was he wanted, and the house and all its possessions seemed to say, *You own us. But we also own you. We are your memories.*

"Write it about a kind and simple man who wanted to love us all as much as we loved him," she said. "But couldn't, and died of a broken heart. Put that in, too. Promise me."

And so that is what I promised her I'd try to do, because I loved her too in my own way, though I sometimes wonder if she ever really understood my way, and that is what I tried to do, and this is it.

Envoi

*F*ROM THE San Francisco Chronicle:

FATAL CRASH ON BAYSHORE FWY
APPARENTLY CAUSED BY PEDESTRIAN

A fatal crash on the Bayshore Freeway today, involving six passenger automobiles and a 24-wheel semi-trailer rig, was apparently caused by a pedestrian crossing the freeway.

The pedestrian, a white male, had stepped across the 3-foot-high median divider into the southbound lanes, about 300 yards from the foot of the exit ramp from the Bay Bridge, during the busy morning rush hour, according to Gary Costello, the driver of the rig. Costello, braking to avoid hitting the pedestrian, caused his truck to jackknife and overturn across all three southbound lanes. The automobile behind him, a 1980 Ford Pinto, crashed into the side of Costello's truck and immediately burst into flames. Its driver, an unidentified female, was burned beyond recognition. Five additional automobiles, skidding to avoid the flaming wreck, crashed into each other and into the median divider, one of these jumping the divider and landing in a northbound lane. Its driver, David Rust, 40, of Petaluma, was taken to Shriners' Hospital with multiple rib fractures and possible internal injuries. His condition was described by hospital officials as guarded. Others involved in the accident were treated for minor injuries and released.

Police immediately closed off a 3-mile section of the freeway between Exits 9 and 11, and southbound traffic was diverted through Daly City. Two northbound lanes remained open, but were impeded by curious motorists slowing to examine the fiery crash. In all, the 8½-hour traffic jam was the worst in San Francisco history.

Following the crash, the pedestrian, apparently unaware of the death and destruction that lay in his wake, continued walking southward along the freeway. Costello, who had been able to escape from the cab of his truck uninjured, stood weeping in the center of the highway, shaking his fist and shouting, "He's the one who should be lying dead!" at the retreating figure.

Police later apprehended the pedestrian about a mile from the scene of the accident, and brought him to the station house where he was detained, pending identification.

Police also declined to release the license number of the Pinto, pending identification of the female driver and notification of next of kin.

From the same newspaper, the following day:

IDENTITY OF PEDESTRIAN WHO
CAUSED FATAL BAYSHORE CRASH
IS REVEALED

The identity of the pedestrian who caused yesterday's fatal rush-hour crash on the Bayshore Freeway has been revealed. He is Maurice Littlefield, 23, who gave his address as the Airport Marriott Motor Inn. The Marriott's manager, Bill Oakley, confirmed that Littlefield had been a guest at the motel earlier this year, but had not been seen there since February 24, when he departed without paying his bill. Littlefield was unable to give a clear account of his whereabouts during the two months since that date.

Earlier this year, Littlefield, a rock guitarist who uses the stage name "Luscious Lucius," had performed with a group that called itself The Dildos at the refurbished Odeon Theatre on Market Street. It was Littlefield who horrified young concertgoers by beating to death, onstage, a live rock python which he had been using in his act. Littlefield's rock group has since disbanded, and it had not been realized that Littlefield himself had apparently remained in the city.

The identity of the young woman burned to death in the crash, which resulted from Littlefield's attempt to walk across the busy freeway, has also been established. She is Mrs. Martha Tennant, 34, mother of three, of San Mateo, a grade-school teacher in the San Mateo school system.

After being detained for questioning in the accident, Littlefield was fined $28, the maximum fine permitted for obstructing traffic on an Interstate highway. Among Littlefield's possessions, police noted, was a live baby alligator which he was carrying with him in a plastic bag. Littlefield explained that he often uses exotic animals in his act, such as the python he clubbed to death on the Odeon's stage after it had bitten him in the arm. The alligator will be part of his new act, Littlefield added.

Littlefield explained that he had been on Bayshore yesterday trying to hitch a ride across the Bay Bridge on his way to New York. Having no luck in obtaining a ride in that direction, he had decided to change his plans and crossed the freeway in hopes of hitching a ride to Los Angeles. . . .